D0436138

SURVIVORS

SURVIVORS

A NOVEL OF THE COMING COLLAPSE

JAMES WESLEY, RAWLES

ATRIA BOOKS

New York   London   Toronto   Sydney   New Delhi

ATRIA BOOKS

A Division of Simon & Schuster, Inc.
1230 Avenue of the Americas
New York, NY 10020

First Atria Books hardcover edition October 2011

ATRIA BOOKS and colophon are trademarks of Simon & Schuster, Inc.

For information about special discounts for bulk purchases,
please contact Simon & Schuster Special Sales at 1-866-506-1949 or
business@simonandschuster.com.

The Simon & Schuster Speakers Bureau can bring authors to
your live event. For more information or to book an event, contact the
Simon & Schuster Speakers Bureau at 1-866-248-3049 or
visit our website at www.simonspeakers.com.

Designed by Rhea Braunstein

Manufactured in the United States of America

10   9   8   7   6   5   4   3   2   1

Library of Congress Control Number: 2011012317

ISBN 978-1-4391-7280-3
ISBN 978-1-4391-7284-1 (ebook)

Disclaimers

This is a work of fiction. All of the events described are imaginary. Most of the characters in this novel are fictional. A few real life individuals gave permission for their names to be mentioned. Aside from these individuals, any resemblance to living people is purely coincidental.

The making and/or possession of some of the devices and mixtures described in this novel are possibly illegal in some jurisdictions. Even the mere possession of the uncombined components might be construed as criminal intent. Consult your state and local laws! If you make any of these devices and/or formulations, you accept sole responsibility for their possession and use. You are also responsible for your own stupidity and/or carelessness. This information is intended for educational purposes only, to add realism to a work of fiction.

This novel does not constitute legal advice. Consult a jural society or lawyer if you have legal questions. The medical details contained within this novel do not constitute medical advice. Consult a doctor or herbalist if you have medical questions. The purpose of this novel is to entertain and to educate. The author and Atria Books/Simon & Schuster shall have neither liability nor responsibility to any citizen, person, or entity with respect to any loss or damage caused, or alleged to be caused, directly or indirectly by the information contained in this novel.

Dramatis Personae

Diego Aguilar—cook, Wrangler and Hay boss

Nabil Jassim Ali—Afghan storekeeper

Jamie Alstoba—resident of Dewey, Arizona; ten years old at the onset of the Crunch

Arturo Araneta—father of Blanca Araneta-Doyle

Kurt Becker—bicycle store owner, Landstuhl, Germany

Major Alan Brennan—Ian Doyle's squadron leader

Chambers Clarke—Monsanto fertilizer and pesticide salesman

Hollan Combs—retired soil scientist and property manager, Bradfordsville, Kentucky

Clifford Conley—Prescott, Arizona, land developer

Consuelo Dalgon—schoolteacher and Spanish teacher

Pablo Dalgon—husband of Consuelo Dalgon

Alex Doyle—gun salesman, Prescott Arizona; brother of Ian Doyle, Prescott, Arizona

Blanca Araneta-Doyle—the Honduran-born wife of Ian Doyle

Major Ian Doyle—a U.S. Air Force F-16 pilot stationed at Luke AFB, Arizona; brother of Alex Doyle

Linda Doyle—daughter of Ian and Blanca Doyle

Larry Echanis—Stryker battalion S-1, FOB Wolverine, Afghanistan

Ben Fielding—an attorney in Muddy Pond, Tennessee

Rebecca Fielding—wife of Ben Fielding

Dan Fong—a college classmate of Ian Doyle

Ignacio Garcia—leader of a criminal gang called *La Fuerza*

Charley Gordon—member of the Phoenix Ultralight Flying Club

Todd Gray—a college classmate of Ian Doyle, owner of a ranch/
    retreat near Bovill, Idaho

Pedro Hierro—horse breeder near Orange Walk, Belize

Dustin Hodges—deputy sheriff in Marion County, Kentucky

Maynard Hutchings—member of the Hardin, Kentucky, board
    of supervisors

Peter Ivens—innkeeper in Blair Atholl, Belize

Dr. Robert Karvalich ("Doctor K.")—widower and retired
    pediatrician

Tom "T.K." Kennedy—Todd Gray's dormitory roommate

Captain Andrew "Andy" Laine—Ordnance Corps officer; ham
    radio call sign K5CLA

Grace Laine—daughter of Lars and Lisbeth Laine; six years old
    at the onset of the Crunch; nicknamed "Anelli"

Major Lars Laine—recently disabled U.S. Army veteran; ham
    radio call sign K5CLB

Lisbeth "Beth" Laine—wife of Lars Laine

Joseph Lejeune—captain of the fishing boat *Beau Temps*,
    harbored at Boulogne-sur-Mer, France

Ricardo Lopez—Cuban-born petrochemical process engineer at
    the Bloomfield refinery

Michael Lyon—police officer, Kent County Constabulary, England

L. Roy Martin—owner of Bloomfield refinery; Nicknamed "El
    Rey" by his Spanish-speaking employees

Phil McReady—Bloomfield refinery plant manager

Darci Mora—retired vocational nurse in Dangriga, Belize

Gabriel Mora—retired tropical wood logger and husband of
    Darci Mora

Ted Nielsen—a Prescott, Arizona, banker; formerly an electrical engineer

Colonel Ed Olds—Stryker battalion commander

Arsène Paquet—harbormaster of Calais, France

Matthew Phelps—orphan; sixteen years old at the onset of the Crunch

Reuben Phelps—orphan; sixteen years old at the onset of the Crunch

Shadrach "Shad" Phelps—orphan; seventeen years old at the onset of the Crunch

1st Lt. Bryson Pitcher—Air Force intelligence liaison officer, U.S. Embassy, Tegucigalpa, Honduras

Jerome Randall—tire store assistant manager

Sheila Randall—part-time accountant and wife of Jerome Randall

Tyree Randall—son of Jerome and Sheila Randall; ten years old at the onset of the Crunch

Kaylee Schmidt—Andy Laine's fiancée; ham radio nickname "KL"

Carston Simms—retired school administrator and owner of the yacht *Durobrabis*, harbored at Oare Creek, Kent, England

Donna Simms—wife of Carston Simms

Alan Taft—investment banker

Jules Taft—son of Alan and Simone Taft; fourteen years old at the onset of the Crunch

Simone Taft—housewife and part-time interior decorator

Yvette Taft—daughter of Alan and Simone Taft; eleven years old at the onset of the Crunch

Yvonne Taft—daughter of Alan and Simone Taft; eleven years old at the onset of the Crunch

Brian Tompkins—U.S. Army Armor Corps officer

Major General Clayton Uhlich—post commander and chief of armor at Fort Knox, Kentucky

Emily Voisin—grandmother ("Grandmère" or "Memère") of Sheila Randall and great-grandmother of Tyree Randall; seventy-six years old at the onset of the Crunch

Author's introductory note: Unlike most novel sequels, the story-line of *Survivors* is contemporaneous with the events described in my previously published novel, *Patriots*. Thus there is no need to read it first (or subsequently), but you'll likely find it entertaining.

Deo volente, another contemporaneous novel in this series will be published next year. Check my blog, www.SurvivalBlog.com, for updates.

1

Urgency and Exigency

"Weapons compound man's power to achieve; they amplify the capabilities of both the good man and the bad, and to exactly the same degree, having no will of their own. Thus we must regard them as servants, not masters—and good servants to good men. Without them, man is diminished, and his opportunities to fulfill his destiny are lessened. An unarmed man can only flee from evil, and evil is not overcome by fleeing from it."

—Col. Jeff Cooper

FOB Wolverine, Task Force Duke, Zabul Province, Afghanistan
October, the First Year

Andy was awoken by the sound of mortars. His many months in Afghanistan had taught him the difference in sound between outgoing and incoming mortars and various artillery. These were distant mortars, so he knew that it wasn't friendly fire. Andy already had Operation Enduring Freedom camouflage pattern (OCP) pants and interceptor body armor (IBA) on, and was snatching up his M4 carbine and helmet when the take-shelter warning siren sounded. He popped out the door of his containerized housing unit (CHU) and jumped down into the entrance of the heavily sandbagged shelter, just a few steps away. Moments later the two lieutenants from the CHU next door piled in behind him. One of them took the precaution of scanning with a flashlight the floor and walls of the shelter for scorpions. He found just one and stomped it without comment.

The mortar rounds started to come in, with a succession of sharp blasts that shook the ground. There were about twenty impacts, arriving in a span of ten seconds. They could see the flashes of the explosions reflected on the wall opposite the doorway. The closest round impacted about one hundred feet away—close enough that shock waves could be felt.

As the rounds came in, Andy Laine said a silent prayer. He knew that only a direct hit would endanger him, but it was still unnerving, since he had less than a month left in-country.

"That may be all she wrote, sir," said one of the lieutenants dryly.

Laine agreed. "You're probably right. Just another shoot-'n'-scoot deal."

At the far side of the forward operating base (FOB), they could hear the echoed commands from the Arty boys, and then the deep-throated crumps of outgoing mortars. They sounded like big 4.2-inch mortars, just three rounds. Andy marveled at how quickly the counter-battery radar team could pinpoint the insurgents' firing location and direct return fire. Less than a minute after the enemy rounds impacted, the reply was sent, no doubt with considerable precision. It was no wonder that the mortar duels with the *jihadis* had become less frequent in recent months.

As they waited for the all-clear horn, Andy leaned against the sandbag wall and stretched his calf muscles, more out of habit than because of any stiffness. At six feet two inches, with a runner's physique, he weighed just 180 pounds, and prided himself on his flexibility. When doing physical training (PT) with his units in garrison, he was always among the most limber.

The next morning, along with dozens of his fellow Fobbits, Laine did a bit of gawking at the damage done by the mortars. It actually wasn't much. One round had shredded the corner of a CHU and another perforated a tent with dozens of small holes—the largest about three inches across. All the rest of the mortar impacts had no effect, leaving only black marks on the ground and some scattered shrapnel. A couple of the newbies to the FOB posed for pictures in front of the damaged CHU. "So what? Big deal," Andy muttered to himself as he walked to the company headquarters.

At thirty-one years old, Andrew Laine was the typical lean and fit U.S. Army captain. He was on his second deployment to Afghanistan. His first had been to Iraq. On this new deployment, his assignment was "branch immaterial." Although he was branched Ordnance Corps, he was assigned as a staff officer in a Stryker battalion, an infantry unit equipped with sixteen-ton wheeled armored personnel carriers (APCs). With the heavy manpower requirements of ongoing deployments to Afghanistan, it was not unusual for officers to get assignments outside of their usual career path. "The needs of the Army" was the reason often cited when making these assignments.

Andy and his older brother Lars had grown up in the shadow of their late father, Robie Laine, a Finnish-born Army officer who retired as a full colonel. Their father earned his U.S. citizenship by joining the U.S. Army, and eventually retired to a small horse ranch near Bloomfield, New Mexico. Robie had been raised on a farm and was convinced that he should retire on a farm. Their late mother was an American of mostly Swedish ancestry. She had died of breast cancer when the boys were in high school.

Following the mortar barrage, Andy spent a frustrating ten-hour day of pushing paper for the battalion, which was greatly complicated by the process of the unit's upcoming redeployment to Germany. That afternoon, Andy chatted with Larry Echanis, the battalion S-1, the staff officer in charge of personnel. Echanis had been Laine's martial arts sparring partner for the past several months. He had taught Andy some Hwa Rang Do *kata*s, and Andy reciprocated, teaching Larry his mixed martial arts moves.

Their battalion (or "squadron," in Stryker parlance) was a forward deployed part of the 2nd Stryker Cavalry Regiment, headquartered in Vilseck, Germany. The incoming squadron was a sister unit in the same regiment, and also part of Task Force Duke. But Andy's squadron was headed back to Germany, in a regularly scheduled unit rotation.

Laine and Echanis had been discussing events back home. Lately, the war effort had been taking a backseat to tumultuous economic events emanating from New York City and the world's other financial centers. Larry Echanis seemed worried but was trying to be upbeat. He asked, "You think that this'll blow over, right?"

Laine put on a glum face. "At this point, there's no way. The whole system is breaking down. The global credit market is frozen, the sovereign debt problems have blown up past the GDP levels for most countries, and the derivatives have totally imploded. We're in a world of hurt. I think there'll be some major riots and looting soon."

Echanis bit his lip. "Well, that won't be a big deal for my family. Most of them live in eastern Oregon. Have you ever been through Ontario, Oregon? It's out in the middle of nowhere. The disruption will be in the big cities. Our town is three hundred miles from Portland, and more than three hundred and fifty from Seattle as the crow flies."

Laine shook his head. "I wish it was that simple. Sure, the riots will be in the big cities. The metro areas will be death traps. The suburbs will be only marginally safer. But you got to realize that these days even the small towns are dependent on long chains of supply. When the eighteen-wheelers stop rolling, *everyone* is gonna be hurting. It will definitely be safer out in the boonies. But you should tell your family to stock up on every scrap of food they can find. They need to get *out* of dollars and into canned goods right away."

"You really think it'll get that bad?"

Laine answered soberly, "I'm afraid it will. Does your family live in town or out on a ranch?"

"Used to be ranchers. All in town now, but we're Basques, so we still know how to live the old-fashioned way. My mom used to cook a lot of our meals in a dutch oven. I didn't even know how fast food tasted until I went off to college. There's no comparison to my mom's cooking."

"Well, with those skills, and living where they do, they'll probably ride the storm out pretty safely."

The conversation left Andy feeling uneasy about his plans for leaving active duty. Strapping on his MOLLE vest to leave his desk at the battalion headquarters, Andy turned to Echanis to say, "Well, when the going gets tough, the tough go *shopping*. I'm going to stop by my CHU and grab a duffel bag and then I'm off to the Haji-mart."

It was 90 degrees but felt even hotter, since Andy was wearing IBA and had the weight of an M4 carbine slung across his back, a PRC-148 radio, and numerous MOLLE magazine pouches. The only concession to being in a relatively safe area was that he was wearing a boonie hat instead of a MICH helmet.

As Captain Laine walked past the guards manning the HESCO barriers at the FOB's main gate, he read the signs on the Haji market windows just across the road. They proclaimed: "Very Best PriceS," "DVD," and "Custtom TailoreR." As he walked in the door, the smell of the market hit Andy like a hammer. It was an odd mix of Turkish tobacco smoke, incense, kerosene, sweat, and overcooked lamb. It certainly didn't smell like the exchange store back at the FOB. Aside from the hint of JP8 jet fuel, which was a presence everywhere in the FOB, the exchange smelled just like any retail store in America: hardly any smell at all—almost antiseptic. In contrast, Ali's store reeked. An aging Italian-made air conditioner was roaring above the door but not keeping up. It was perhaps 10 degrees cooler inside than outside.

Nabil Jassim Ali gave his usual "Salaam, salaam, Mr. Colonel" greeting. The portly and balding Pashtuni flashed his yellowed, crooked teeth. He called all the American soldiers "Colonel," even the privates. It still made Andy laugh every time he heard it.

Eyeing the empty duffel bag slung over Laine's shoulder, Ali chortled. "Perhaps you are wanting to buy plentiful numbers of thingings, Mr. Colonel?" Laine nodded. Ali waved him in and added, "The store I am closing in a few minutes, but for you, Colonel, I am willing to be late."

"You always have the best deals, Mr. Ali," Andy said with a smile.

"Do you have afghanis? The American dollar not so good, today. It is slipping off another five percent."

"Down five percent in one week?" Andy asked.

"In *one day,* Colonel," Ali replied seriously. "Soon, I think, I take no more American money."

"Don't worry, sir. I have plenty of afghanis." His front pocket indeed bulged with a huge wad of cash: a mix of afghanis, dollars, and a few euros. In the bottom of his pocket he also felt the weight of eighteen American Eagle one-ounce silver coins in plastic sleeves.

Ali's store had the usual "Haji-mart" merchandise. There were cigarettes, pirated CDs and DVDs, imitation designer sunglasses, magazines (mostly in Arabic), cheap Chinese knives and ersatz Leatherman tools, candy, sunflower seeds, sodas and sports drinks, jerky, chewing gum, and assorted trinkets.

There were three young Stryker troops already in the store when Captain Laine arrived. When he passed them in the dimly lit narrow aisles, they each acknowledged him with a hushed "High speed, sir!" That was the newly arrived battalion's unofficial motto. But Andy was accustomed to hearing it at a much higher volume inside the FOB.

Laine sorted through packets of jerky, settling mostly on the teriyaki flavor, piling up a large stack in the crook of his left arm. The three enlisted soldiers completed their purchases, buying the usual Fobbit food: energy bars, packets of salty chips, and Coca-Colas that came in cans with both English and Arabic markings.

After the three soldiers left the store, Laine stacked the packets of jerky on the counter. Then he walked back to the shelf to get a second armload. This, too, he stacked on the counter. Ali smiled. "Perhaps you are wanting to buy all of my jer-kee?" he asked. Laine chuckled, and replied, "Well, not all of it; just most of it."

Next he went to stock up on batteries. He ignored the Egyptian bargain brand—of dubious quality—and selected a dozen four-packs of Energizer AA batteries, being careful to pick the ones with the latest expiration dates. While Laine was sorting battery packages, Ali locked the front door and turned the "OPEN" sign around.

Laine stacked the batteries in a couple of piles next to the jerky on the counter, then his gaze shifted to Ali's permanent smile. After a pause, Laine asked, "I've heard that you sell some other, ah, unusual merchandise that you keep in back." He pointed to the doorway to the back room, which among other things served as a kitchen and bedroom.

"Sir, I have none alcohol. It is forbidden."

"No, no. That is not what I meant. I've heard that you have some more expensive merchandise, like watches, some good optics, and guns."

Ali's smile got bigger than usual and he nodded. "One moment, Mr. Colonel," he said, then disappeared into the back room.

Ali returned lugging a large suitcase, and Laine knew that he'd struck pay dirt. This was where the rumor mill at the FOB said the shopkeeper reputedly kept "the good stuff."

Ali gently slid the heavy suitcase onto the store counter, unfastened the latches, and spun it around. He opened it to display a large assortment of new and used wristwatches, digital cameras, film cameras, binoculars, assorted boxes of ammunition, and a few pistol holsters.

Laine and Ali spent the next five minutes haggling over the price of a pair of rubber-armored Nikon 7x30 compact binoculars. They finally settled on a figure that seemed high to Andy, but he assented, realizing the prices would surely be double that in less than a month, perhaps in just a few days.

Laine paid for the jerky, batteries, and binoculars, nearly depleting his wad of afghanis. Eyeing the boxes of ammo, he said: "I see you have some nine-millimeter ammunition here. Do you have any pistols in that caliber?"

Ali frowned. "Yes, Colonel, I do, but you are cannot be afford them. Prices are—what is it they say—'escalating.' For a pistol, a good one, we are conversing of $5,000, American."

"What if I paid you in silver, uhh, *lujain* coins? *Lujain?*"

"Ahhh! *Lujain!* This works for me. In Kabul, silver closed today at eighty-three American dollars for one ounce. In London it was eighty-one dollars." Andy nodded. The man certainly knew his markets.

Mr. Ali turned and again walked to the back room. Laine heard the sounds of boxes being shifted and restacked. Soon the store owner returned with another suitcase that looked even older than the first. He put it on the counter, flipped the latches, and swung it open. Captain Laine let out a slight gasp when he saw the contents. The suitcase was crammed full of pistols, revolvers, holsters, and magazines.

Andy sorted through the guns. He saw older Afghan Army–issue Tokarevs, a few ancient revolvers that looked either Belgian or German, and a couple of Egyptian Helwan pistols. One revolver immediately seemed suspect. It was a Pakistani copy of a Webley .38 revolver. Looking closely at the gun, he saw that it was peppered with fake proof mark stampings and was erroneously stamped "WELBEY." That made Andy laugh.

Seeing Andy's expression, the storekeeper noted: "The guns from Peshawar, they are not so good."

Andy replied, "Now, that's an understatement!" He didn't trust their metallurgy and mechanical tolerances any more than he did their spelling.

Putting the revolver down, Andy noticed that there were several plastic Glock Model 19 magazines but no Glock pistols.

"Do you have any Glocks?"

"Sorry, Mr. Colonel, but none of those I have. Those guns of Glock sell very quick, when I am getting one."

Then Andy spotted a pistol in a well-made holster that looked different from the others. Withdrawing it from the holster, Andy was pleased to see a SIG P228 9mm pistol in nearly new condition. It looked just like the U.S. Army–issue P228s that the CID agents carried, except that it wasn't stamped "U.S. PROPERTY."

"This is my most nice of my pistols. You are liking it?"

The moment that he saw the SIG, Andy knew that he was going to buy it. The moment felt portentous somehow. He nodded and said, "Yes, I do like it." He knew that it was against regulations to bring any weapon home from the OEF theater of operations.

Andy rummaged through the suitcase and found six spare SIG P226 series magazines, including two thirteen-rounders, three fifteen-rounders, and just one scarce magazine of twenty-round capacity. He took a few minutes to closely inspect both the gun and the magazines. The pistol had no rust pitting and just a bit of finish wear at the muzzle. Locking back the slide, he examined the bore, holding a slip of paper behind the barrel to act as a reflector. Cupping his hand over the rear sight and holding the back end of the pistol nearly to his face, he could see the faint glow of tritium dots. He muttered to himself, "Eleven-point-two-year half-life." The magazines were genuine SIG Sauer made—with the distinctive zigzag seam on the back—and they, too, looked nearly new.

Setting the holstered pistol and the four magazines next to his previous purchases, he said, "This will do."

"I will sell you this ZIG with just of only one magazine for thirty ounces of silver, and one ounce more for each magazine more."

Laine shook his head and answered: "No, no, no. That is too much. My offer is eight ounces, and I want you to include these magazines."

"This is an insult to my family. Shall my children starve and beg in the street? I am not a fool. But for you, as good and honorable officer, I will make a price of twenty ounces, with those extra magazines including."

"No, make it twelve."

Ali shook his head. "Eighteen ounces."

Andy countered, "Nope. Fifteen."

"Sixteen," Ali snapped back.

Andy replied firmly, "Done!" They shook hands. Andy counted out sixteen of the American eagles, all still packaged in two-coin "flip" plastic sleeves. Ali took the time to scrutinize the pairs of coins closely, removing several of them from their sleeves. He looked satisfied.

"You are needing of amma-unitions?"

"No, thanks, I've got plenty. Nine-mil is standard for the Army."

Andy spent a few more minutes rummaging through the suitcases, selecting a pair of magazine pouches that had obviously been made for different double-column pistol magazines but fit the standard SIG magazines—a tight fit, but they would do. Each pouch held a pair of magazines. The two pouches cost $220 in the increasingly worthless greenbacks.

Starting with the holstered pistol at the bottom, Andy filled the duffel bag with his purchases and again shook hands with Ali.

It was nearing sunset, and the temperature outside was down to 80 degrees. Ali unbarred the door, and they exchanged *"Salaamu alaikum"* (Go in peace) good-byes. Andy wondered how peaceful things would be in the near future. "Not very," he muttered to himself, as he shouldered the duffel bag.

2

Stocking Up

"What people did not realize was that war had started. By 1 p.m., a few minutes after Molotov's speech, queues, especially in the food stores, began to grow. The women shoppers in the gastronoms or grocery stores started to buy indiscriminately—canned goods (which Russians do not like very much), butter, sugar, lard, flour, groats, sausage, matches, salt. In twenty years of Soviet power Leningraders had learned by bitter experience what to expect in time of crisis. They rushed to the stores to buy what they could. They gave preference to foods which would keep. But they were not particular. One shopper bought five kilos of caviar, another ten.

"At the savings banks the people clutched worn and greasy passbooks in their hands. They were drawing out every ruble that stood to their accounts. Many headed straight for the commission shops. There they turned over fat packets of paper money for diamond rings, gold watches, emerald earrings, oriental rugs, brass samovars.

"The crowds outside the savings banks quickly became disorderly. No one wanted to wait. They demanded their money seichas immediately. Police detachments appeared. By 3 p.m. the banks had closed, having exhausted their supply of currency. They did not reopen again until Tuesday (Monday was their closed day). When they opened again, the government had imposed a limit on withdrawals of two hundred rubles per person per month."

—Harrison E. Salisbury, *The 900 Days: The Siege of Leningrad* (1969)

Farmington, New Mexico
October, the First Year

At that same time that Andy Laine was at the Haji-mart in Afghanistan, his brother Lars was 11,500 miles away, rolling a cart into a Sam's Club store in Farmington, New Mexico. It was 6:52 a.m. in New Mexico and 5:22 p.m. in Zabul province, Afghanistan. Both men had the same thing on their minds: stocking up, in quantity and immediately. The Laine brothers shared a sense of urgency, realizing that there would likely be very few opportunities to stock up on things before mass currency inflation destroyed the value of their savings. The news outlets made it clear that things were falling apart quickly—*very* quickly.

The Sam's Club store in Farmington, New Mexico, was about to open for the day. There was a large crowd of perhaps a hundred anxious shoppers, many waiting with their membership cards in hand, standing behind oversize shopping carts and flat cargo carts. Lars Laine eyed his wife, Lisbeth, who was seated on their cart, next to their six-year-old daughter Grace. Beth was thirty-four, with curly brown hair and hazel eyes. She was slightly overweight and had struggled all through their marriage to maintain her figure. As Grace was doodling in her coloring book, Beth was adding items to an already long shopping list. She stood up, leaned close to Lars, and spoke directly at the hearing aid in his good ear, "We'd better hit the canned-food section first, hon," she suggested. He nodded and answered, "Roger that." Beth smiled, gave him a peck on the cheek, and again sat on the cart to wait.

Lars glanced around, sizing up the crowd. The middle-aged woman standing next to him was staring at his left hand. Lars hated that. It was hurtful to him that people stared so much at the flesh-colored rubber prosthetic. They always seemed transfixed, as if the hand were some alien creature that had just landed on Earth. They stared at his left hand, or at the left side of his face, or alternated between them, staring at both, and it made him feel like a circus freak.

The reconstructive surgery on his left cheekbone—which had used a piece of one of his ribs—was less than perfect. Sometimes people he hadn't met before or who hadn't seen him in many years would approach him from the right side, smiling, and then he'd turn his head toward them and they'd suddenly look repulsed. "The Quasimodo effect" is what Lars called it.

One month earlier, on a street corner in Durango, Colorado—the nearest city with large department stores where Lars was shopping for a new refrigerator—a man who appeared to be in his seventies walked up to Lars, and asked simply, "Iraq?"

Lars answered, "Yes, sir."

"I was in that little Dominican thing, and then I did a tour in Vietnam. I came back without a scratch." The old man looked Lars in the eye and said firmly, "Thanks for your service, and for what it cost you. Welcome home." He shook his hand and strode away. Laine's eyes welled up a bit, but he didn't cry. That one encounter made up for a whole lot of previous Quasimodo moments.

Finally, the roll-up door opened, and the crowd rushed in. Lars and Beth headed for the canned-food section and started stacking full cases on the cart. That was just the first cartload. They stacked the cart high on three successive trips into the store that morning.

The television news anchors had recently started calling the intensifying economic crisis "the Crunch." The term soon stuck with the general public, becoming part of the general lexicon. Government spending was out of control. The credit market was in continuous turmoil. Meanwhile, bank runs and huge federal bailouts had become commonplace.

The debt and budget deficit had spiraled to stratospheric numbers. A Congressional Budget Office report stated that to pay *just the interest* on the national debt for the year, it would take 100 percent of the year's individual income tax revenue, 100 percent of corporate and excise taxes, and 41 percent of Social Security payroll taxes. As the Crunch began, interest on the national debt was consuming 96 percent of government revenue.

The official national debt was over $6 trillion. The unofficial debt—which included "out-year" unfunded obligations such as entitlements, long-term bonds, and military pensions—topped $53 trillion. The debt accumulated at the rate of $9 billion a day, or $15,000 per second. The official national debt had ballooned to 120 percent of the gross domestic product and was compounding at the rate of 18 percent per year. The federal government was borrowing 193 percent of revenue for the year.

The president was nearing the end of his term in office. The stagnant economy, rising interest rates, and creeping inflation troubled him. Publicly, he beamed about having "beat the deficit." Privately, he admitted that the low deficit figures came from moving increasingly large portions of federal funding "off budget." Behind the accounting smoke and mirrors game, the real deficit was growing. Government spending at all levels equated to 45 percent of the gross domestic product.

In July, the recently appointed chairman of the Federal Reserve Board had a private meeting with the president. The chairman pointed out the fact that even if Congress could balance the budget, the national debt would still grow inexorably due to compounding interest.

In Europe, international bankers began to vocally express their doubts that the U.S. government could continue to make its interest payments on the burgeoning debt. In mid-August, the chairman of the Deutsche Bundesbank made some off-the-record comments to a reporter from the *Economist* magazine. Within hours, his words flashed around the world via the Internet: "A full-scale default on U.S. Treasuries appears imminent." His choice of the word "imminent" in the same sentence with the word "default" caused the value of the dollar to plummet on the international currency exchanges the next day. T-bill sales crashed simultaneously. Starting with the Japanese, foreign central banks and international monetary authorities began to dump their trillions of dollars in U.S. Treasuries. None of them wanted the now-risky T-bills or U.S. bonds. Within days, long-term U.S. Treasury paper was selling at twenty cents on the dollar.

Foreign investors began liquidating their U.S. paper assets: stocks, bonds, T-bills—virtually anything denominated in U.S. dollars. After some weak attempts to prop up the dollar, most of the European Union nations and Japan announced that they would no longer employ the U.S. dollar as a reserve currency.

The Federal Reserve began monetizing larger and larger portions of the debt. The Fed already owned $682 billion in Treasury debt, which was considered an asset for the purposes of expanding the money supply. In just a few days, Federal Reserve holdings in Treasury debt more than doubled. The presses were running around the clock printing currency. Soon after, the domestic inflation rate jumped to 16 percent in the third week of August. To the dismay of the Fed, the economy refused to bounce back. The balance of trade figures grew steadily worse. Leading economic indicators declined to a standstill.

Legislators in Washington, D.C., belatedly wanted to slash federal spending but were frustrated that they couldn't touch most of it. The majority of the budget consisted of interest payments and various entitlement programs. Previous legislation had locked in these payments. Even worse, by law, many of these spending programs had automatic inflation escalators. So the federal budget continued to expand, primarily because of the interest burden on the federal debt. The interest payments grew tremendously as rates started to soar.

It soon took 85 percent interest rates to lure investors to six-month T-bills. The Treasury Department stopped auctioning longer-term paper entirely in late August. With inflation roaring, nobody wanted to lend Uncle Sam money for the long term. Jittery American investors increasingly distrusted the government, the stock market, and even the dollar itself. In September, new factory orders and new housing starts dropped off to levels that could not be properly measured. Corporations, large and small, began massive layoffs. The unemployment rate jumped from 12 percent to 20 percent in less than a month.

Then came the stock market crash in early October. The bull stock market had gone on years longer than expected, defying the traditional business cycle. Nearly everyone thought that they were riding an unstoppable wave. Just before the Crunch, the Dow Jones Industrial Average was selling at a phenomenal sixty-five times dividends—right back where it had been just before the dot-com bubble explosion. The market climbed to unrealistic heights, driven by unmitigated greed. Soon after the dollar's collapse, however, the stock market was driven by *fear*.

Unlike in the previous crashes, this time the U.S. markets slumped gradually. This was due to circuit-breaker regulations on program trading, implemented after the 1987 Wall Street slump. Instead of dropping precipitously in the course of one day as it had in '87, this time it took nineteen days to drop 7,550 points. This made the dot-com bubble burst in 2000 and the 2008 stock market meltdown both look insignificant.

The London and Tokyo markets were hit worse than the U.S. stock exchanges. The London market closed five days after the slump started. The Tokyo market, which was even more volatile, closed after only three days of record declines. Late in the second week of the stock market collapse, the domestic runs on U.S. banks began. The quiet international run on U.S. banks and the dollar had begun a month earlier. It took the citizenry in America that long to realize that the party was over.

The only investors who made profits in the Crunch were those who had invested in precious metals. Gold soared to $5,100 an ounce, with the other precious metals rising correspondingly. Even for these investors, their gains were only illusory paper profits. Anyone who was foolish enough to cash out of gold and into dollars after the run-up in prices would have soon lost everything. This was because the domestic value of the dollar collapsed completely just a few weeks later.

The dollar collapsed because of the long-standing promises of the FDIC. "All deposits insured to $100,000," they had pledged. When the domestic bank runs began, the government had to make good on its word. The only way that it could do this was to print money—lots and lots of it. Since 1964, the currency had no backing with precious metals. Rumors suggested, and then news stories confirmed, that the government mints were converting some of their intaglio printing presses. Presses that had originally been designed to print one-dollar bills were converted to print fifty-and one-hundred-dollar bills. This made the public suspicious.

With overseas dollars being redeemed in large numbers and with the printing presses running day and night turning out fiat currency, hyperinflation was inevitable. Inflation jumped from 16 percent to 35 percent in three days. From there on, it climbed in spurts during the next few days: 62 percent, 110 percent, 315 percent, and then to an incredible 2,100 percent. The currency collapse was reminiscent of what had happened in Zimbabwe.

The value of the dollar began to be pegged hourly. It was the main topic of conversation. As the dollar withered in the blistering heat of hyperinflation, people rushed out to put their money into cars, furniture, appliances, tools, rare coins—anything tangible. This superheated the economy, creating a situation not unlike that in Germany's Weimar Republic in the 1920s. More and more paper was chasing less and less product.

With a superheated economy, there was no way for the government to check the soaring inflation, aside from stopping the presses. This they could not do, however, because depositors were still flocking to the banks to withdraw all of their savings. The workers who still had jobs quickly caught on to the full implications of the mass inflation. They insisted on daily inflation indexing of their salaries, and in some cases even insisted on being paid daily.

Citizens on fixed incomes were wiped out financially by the hyperinflation within two weeks. These included pensioners, those on unemployment insurance, and welfare recipients. Few could afford to buy a can of beans when it cost $150. The riots started soon after inflation bolted past the 1,000 percent mark. Detroit, New York City, and Los Angeles were the first cities to see full-scale rioting and looting. Soon the riots engulfed most other large cities including Houston, San Antonio, Chicago, Phoenix, Philadelphia, San Jose, San Diego, Dallas, Indianapolis, and Memphis.

It was when the Dow Jones average had slumped its first 1,900 points that Lars Laine decided to stock up. But by then it was nearly too late. Gas cans had all been snapped up a week before. The shelves at the supermarkets were already being cleaned out. Unable to find extra batteries at department stores, Lars and Beth started looking elsewhere. They finally found some that had been overlooked at a Toys "R" Us store. They were able to find a few first-aid supplies, but those, too, were being rapidly depleted, along with everything else at the local CVS drugstore. The local gun shops had been completely cleaned out of inventory. There wasn't a single gun or box of ammunition left for sale.

At night, after the stores closed, Lars and Beth stayed up late, ordering things like batteries, lightbulbs, Celox wound coagulant, mason jar lids, and gun cleaning equipment from Internet vendors and from individual sellers on eBay. They placed multiple orders, realizing that in the scarcity of the new market paradigm, at least half of these orders would never arrive.

To their dismay, they found that the Internet ammunition vendors had completely run out of ammunition and extra magazines. After much searching, Lars did manage to order a spare firing pin, a spare extractor, and a few stripper clips for the pair of Finnish-made M39 Mosin-Nagant rifles that he and his brother had inherited from their father.

As the local stores began to run out, there were fewer and fewer things that Lars and Lisbeth could buy. Beth suggested buying extra blue jeans and tube socks, to trade, but they found that the clothing store shelves had already been decimated. Realizing that their money was rapidly becoming worthless, they resorted to buying motion-sensor yard floodlights, plumbing parts, sheets of plywood, and two-by-four studs at the local building store, just as something that they could later barter. A week later, even those were unavailable. It was like a huge nationwide fire sale in progress. Everyone wanted out of dollars and into tangibles. But it soon became abundantly clear that there were too many dollars and too few useful tangibles available. Prices could only go one way: up.

The local banks were overwhelmed with cash withdrawals and soon got into the pattern of having their cash supply wiped out each morning, and then renewed each night, as local merchants made their deposits. Their transaction volume soared, but their deposit accounts quickly dwindled to below regulation levels. The queue of customers outside the bank each morning soon became the inspiration for jokes and jeering. "They have to print fresh money each night" became the standard joke.

Lars was thankful that he had a three-hundred-gallon above-ground tank of gasoline at the ranch, and that it was nearly full when the economic crisis set in. He added a padlock to it, but he was worried that someone might try to steal the gas at gunpoint.

Both in Bloomfield and the much larger city of Farmington just a few miles west, many of the retail businesses that remained open were cleaned out, leaving the owners with piles of increasingly worthless greenbacks. Eventually, even the local gift store ran out of inventory. People had become so desperate to get rid of their dollars that they traded them for New Mexico logo T-shirts and coffee mugs made for the tourist trade.

3

The Crunch

"If the American people ever allow private banks to control the issue of their currency, first by inflation then by deflation, the banks and the corporations will grow up around them, will deprive the people of all property until their children wake up homeless on the continent their fathers conquered. The issuing power should be taken from the banks and restored to the people, to whom it properly belongs."

—Thomas Jefferson, from the debate on the recharter of the Bank Bill (1809)

An Najaf, Iraq
Two Years Before the Crunch

Pain. That was his most vivid memory of the past two years. It had started with a fairly routine convoy of five up-armored Humvees in the old quarter of An Najaf. His last memory of that drive was of sitting in the sweltering backseat of the Humvee, looking down at a map and gripping a SINCGARS radio handset. Captain Lars Laine had been in liaison with his Afghanistan National Army (ANA) counterpart, discussing the planned locations of a couple of random checkpoints for the next day. The .50 gunner standing above him yelled "Possible device, left!"—a warning that he had spotted a suspicious object that might be an improvised explosive device. Then he saw a flash and heard a loud explosion.

The next thing that Lars remembered was waking up in a field hospital, trying to focus his vision. And no sooner did he realize that he was in a hospital than he passed out again.

He awoke again twenty-eight hours later, more than three thousand miles away, at Landstuhl Regional Medical Center in Germany, with his head throbbing. He asked in an almost unintelligible voice, "Can you take the edge off this pain?" He vaguely remembered the face of the E-6 male nurse who stood by his bedside. The nurse obliged with a fresh dose of Demerol IV via his Luer-Lock intravenous fluid connector.

The nurse gave Lars some water on a sponge stick that looked like a lollipop. It was as Lars was getting these first dribbles of water that he realized that he had no vision in his left eye. Several hours later he further realized that the vestiges of his left eye had been removed from its orbit and replaced by a nitrile rubber and gauze packing, supplemented with a drainage tube.

Losing his eye put Lars into a brief depression. But then seeing much more badly wounded soldiers around him made him count his blessings. As he later told Beth: "At least I'm walking around on two good legs. Every day aboveground is a gift from God."

Lars gradually regained some awareness of his surroundings. A male nurse walked up to his bed and handed him a cup of water with a straw. The nurse held the cup while Lars took a couple of clumsy sips.

Lars nodded and said, "Thanks, that's better."

The nurse put the glass down within reach on Laine's bed table and said, "You were delirious. The first time I gave you water on a sponge stick, you tried to eat the sponge. Oh, and you kept repeating some phrases; I think they were Pashto or Arabic."

"Such as?"

"Two of them that I remember are 'Wayne riff attack' and 'Erf-e-dack.' What language was that?"

Lars thought for a moment and answered, "That was Arabic. Uhhh, well, *'Wayn rifakak'* means 'We are your friends' and *'Irfa'a eedak'* is an order—it means 'Put your hands up!'"

"Kinda strange that you'd be using both of those in the same conversation," the nurse said, looking bemused.

"No, not where I've spent the last couple of years, up in Injun Country. It happens all the time, believe me."

It was while at the Landstuhl hospital that Lars was told the extent of his injuries: Most of his left hand had been amputated. His left arm was broken in three places, and he had six broken ribs. His left eye, left cheekbone, and nine teeth were gone. There were multiple lacerations and second-degree burns to his face, neck, and arms. Days later he was told that he also had a "mild to moderate" traumatic brain injury (TBI). It was much later that he learned that he had lost all hearing in his left ear and had a 60 percent hearing loss in his right ear. This news made Laine doubt whether he'd ever return to regular duty, and pushed him into another bout of depression.

After four days at Landstuhl, Lars was flown on a C-5 to Andrews Air Force Base and transferred to Walter Reed Army Medical Center, in Washington, D.C. It was the most agonizing flight of his life. It seemed to last for days, and the pain was incredible. Lisbeth was there to meet him at Walter Reed. She and Grace stayed at the home of her cousin in Silver Spring, Maryland, for the next five months, visiting him almost every day. Lars spent four months at Walter Reed, where he got his reconstructive surgery and skin grafts. More pain. Then another month at a Walter Reed satellite hospital, getting his hearing aid and glass eye. It was there that he started doing more intense physical therapy.

It was also while he was at Walter Reed that Lars was awarded a Purple Heart, pinned on his pillow by the vice president, who was there for a photo op. Lars caused quite a stir when the vice president asked him what he planned to do when he got out of the Army and went home.

Lars responded, "Home? If I may speak freely, sir, I intend to return to the Big Sandbox and take command of a Civil Affairs Company. I'm not a quitter, unlike some people at the top of the chain of command. Your administration's Accelerated Draw-Down is premature: it's putting both American soldiers and the citizenry of Afghanistan in peril. Now, sir, please leave my room before I say something rude about your boss!" Just minutes after the vice president and his entourage left the hospital, Lars Laine was dressed down by the attending physician (an O-6), who very soon after placed a letter of reprimand in Laine's permanent 201 personnel file.

Finally, he was transferred to Fort Sam Houston Hospital, in Texas. That was where he got the rest of his dental work, his prosthetic hand, and an Army commendation (ARCOM) medal.

Lars jokingly called his spring-loaded prosthetic left hand "Mr. President," in homage to the movie *Dr. Strangelove*. He hated the hand. The hand had very few advantages. One was that it allowed him to do electrical work without fear of getting shocked. It also gave him the ability to pick up hot pots and pans from the kitchen stove without using a hot pad. But in almost all other respects, it was a hindrance and an annoyance.

Hampered by the letter of reprimand, Lars was never approved to return to active duty without limitations. Then came a frustrating year of branch immaterial duty, pushing quartermaster paperwork at Fort Hood, spending as much time with the MEDDAC oral surgeons and physical therapists as he did behind a desk. Lars held on for that last year to finish his dental work and to get his bump to major—the O-4 pay grade—providing him with a more substantial disability retirement. His branch manager at PERSCOM confided that it was only because of some politicking of the promotion board by two of Laine's former brigade commanders that he was not passed over for promotion to O-4. Once his promotion to major came through, Laine immediately resigned his commission.

When he was discharged, Lars was thirty years old, and an "O-4, over six"—a major with more than six years of service. He was also suffering from depression. His arm had healed well, and he was back to his normal exercise regimen of running two miles every two days, with two hundred sit-ups on the alternating days. Physically, aside from some nerve damage in his left arm, he was nearly as strong and limber as he had been before the ambush. But if it were not for his faith in God and the presence of his wife and his daughter, he had doubts that he would have ever recovered mentally.

4

Fujian Tulou

Turning and turning in the widening gyre
The falcon cannot hear the falconer;
Things fall apart; the centre cannot hold;
Mere anarchy is loosed upon the world,
The blood-dimmed tide is loosed, and everywhere
The ceremony of innocence is drowned;
The best lack all conviction, while the worst
Are full of passionate intensity.
Surely some revelation is at hand;
Surely the Second Coming is at hand.
The Second Coming! Hardly are those words out
When a vast image out of Spiritus Mundi
Troubles my sight: somewhere in sands of the desert
A shape with lion body and the head of a man,
A gaze blank and pitiless as the sun,
Is moving its slow thighs, while all about it
Reel shadows of the indignant desert birds.
The darkness drops again; but now I know
That twenty centuries of stony sleep
Were vexed to nightmare by a rocking cradle,
And what rough beast, its hour come round at last.
Slouches towards Bethlehem to be born?

—William Butler Yeats, "The Second Coming"

Bloomfield, New Mexico
May, the First Year

Moving to the ranch had been his wife Lisbeth's idea. Laine had inherited the ranch two miles east of Bloomfield, New Mexico, from his father, Robie Laine, a retired lieutenant colonel. The elder Laine had spent the last four years of his life as a widower. He had died unexpectedly of a heart attack when Lars was attending the Civil Affairs Officer's Basic Course and while Andy was still in high school. After Robie Laine's death, the ranch had been leased out for several years to Tim Rankin, a part-time horse trainer and a full-time alcoholic. Meanwhile, as the beneficiaries of Robie Laine's $600,000 life insurance policy, his two sons finished their educations and started their own Army careers.

The ranch was in the Four Corners region, where the state lines of Utah, Colorado, New Mexico, and Arizona meet. Beth thought that the activity of running the ranch would occupy Lars and lift his spirits. As it turned out, moving there was the best choice that they could have ever made.

The property was a twenty-acre ranchette that sat just above the south bank of the San Juan River, with a slightly run-down house that had been built in the 1960s. The place had a solid barn, a bunkhouse, a hay barn, a shop building that was built in the 1980s, and a couple of small outbuildings. It was on Road 4990, commonly called the Refinery Road, which paralleled the San Juan River east from Bloomfield. After passing by the refinery, the doglegged road traversed dozens of ranches and hay farms. Lars and Beth moved to the ranch just six months before the Crunch.

In the October following their move to Bloomfield, when he heard that the Dow Jones average had slumped its first 2,000 points, Lars shifted his attention away from fixing up the ranch, to stocking up for what was sure to be a cataclysmic Second Great Depression. Lars and Beth realized that they were, as he put it, way behind the power curve. They made multiple trips to the local Target store and Sam's Club.

To fund some of their storage food purchases, they asked Andy's fiancée, Kaylee Schmidt, to rent a room from them. She was self-employed, working at home, and doing substitute teacher scheduling for the San Antonio School District. Her manager was agreeable to the move, so long as she provided her own telephone. With a Voice over IP (VoIP) phone service, she had unlimited calling. Her work transition to Bloomfield went smoothly, but ironically, she was only there for three weeks before the phones went dead and the Internet disintegrated into a few isolated autonomous networks. Since she was firmly engaged to marry Andy, Lars and Beth made it clear that Kaylee was welcome to stay with them indefinitely, even if she couldn't find work.

Kaylee was of German extraction and grew up near New Braunfels, Texas. She spoke the local German dialect, called "Texas German," although not as fluently as her parents. She had strong features, dark hair, and a trim figure. Kaylee was twenty-five years old when the Crunch began. She had just recently graduated with a bachelor's degree in marketing from Texas A&M University. She met Andy during her senior year of college while attending a Christian concert at Victory Church in College Station, Texas. She had dated several members of the Corps of Cadets while at Texas A&M, but had never met a young Christian man who she considered marriage material until she met Andy. They immediately fell in love. But unfortunately Andy was just on a brief stint at Fort Hood, between overseas deployments. They were fated to a long-distance relationship.

One evening, as Lars, Beth, and Kaylee were reorganizing the pantry to make room for their new supplies, Lars mentioned, "My dad was pretty smart. He picked a town out in the middle of nowhere, but it's got agriculture, and its got huge natural-gas fields and some oil wells. He once told me that he picked Bloomfield because it would be a safe place to be, 'if and when the stuff hits the fan.' You remember all those right-wing economic newsletters and the Tea Party things he subscribed to—Ron Paul, and all that?"

Beth nodded and said, "Yeah, he always struck me as a bit batty. All of his 'I don't trust paper money' talk. But I gotta admit, it turned out he was right."

"Well, at least Dad converted Andy and me into goldbugs. If it weren't for that, we'd be in the same boat as most other folks, with 401(k)s that have turned into 'Point-01(k)s.'" Lars adjusted the Velcro strap on his prosthetic—something he often did out of habit more than because of discomfort—and went on:

"Anyway, I figure the best place to ride this out is here in the Four Corners. Not a lot of rain or snow, but at least if the main grids go down, there will probably still be power here—since there is local generation—and some agriculture. Most everywhere else in the country will be SOL, but around here we've got natural gas, and drip oil, so we can still pump water from the rivers and up out of the aquifer. My dad specially picked this ranch since it is flood-irrigated from the Hammond Irrigation District ditch. Dad even pulled a sneaky and put in a water line to the house up at the ditch head gate, just in case of a power failure. That provides just enough water pressure, although the shower is a bit weak."

He added, "There are a lot of orchards around, especially west of here, downriver. They grow apples, peaches, pears, plums, apricots, nectarines, and cherries. And they dry prunes and make cider. And everybody and his uncle around here cuts hay—"

Lars was interrupted by the phone ringing. He snatched it up, and answered automatically: "Laine." Out of habit, he felt like he should add, "This is an unsecure line. How can I help you?"

"Hey, it's me. How are things going?" Andy asked, his voice sounding remarkably crisp for someone practically on the back side of the globe.

Lars replied, "We're still not mission ready on logistics, but we're catching up as best we can. A lot of things are sold out. How about you?"

"Same-same. It sucks to be me. It sucks to be here. It sucks to not be with Kaylee. The only update is that I got hold of a bring-back, from a local."

"A good one?"

"Genuine Swiss. Do you remember the Swiss . . . uhh . . . watch that your college roommate had?"

"Yeah, of course. That one with the three tritium markings?"

"Right. Think of sorta the same model, only slightly smaller."

"Oooh, excellent—those are Hotel Sierra. I love their . . . 'watches.'" Lars winked at his wife, cupped his hand over the phone's mouthpiece, and whispered to her, "He bought a SIG pistol on the local economy!"

Just then Kaylee came into the room.

Lars continued, "Look, I'm sure you want to yak with Kaylee, so I'll keep this short, little brother: Get your ass-ets back here as soon as you possibly can. If need be, do something that will torpedo your next officer efficiency report, but just *get here*! Remember, if the phones go down, we'll still have our shortwave contact sked for Tuesdays."

Andy replied, "Roger that. We stick to the sked. The thirty-meter band rules, now that the sunspot numbers are back up."

"Okay, here she is." Lars handed the phone to Kaylee, who was anxiously waiting. The couple conversed animatedly for another twenty minutes, until Andy's phone card expired. When she hung up the phone, Kaylee was weeping. Beth gave her a hug and said, "You've gotta have faith that he'll make it here, sooner or later. Don't have doubts. We just 'trust and obey,' like it says in the old hymn."

5

Hornet's Nest

"The only purpose of a government is to protect a man's rights, which means: To protect him from physical violence. A proper government is only a policeman, an agent of man's self-defense, and, as such, may resort to force only against those who start the use of force. The only proper functions of a government are: The police, to protect you from criminals; the army, to protect you from foreign invaders; and the courts, to protect your property and contracts from breach or fraud from others, to settle disputes by rational rules, according to objective laws."

—**John Galt in Ayn Rand's *Atlas Shrugged* (1957)**

Houston, Texas
October, the First Year

Growing up on the streets of Houston had made Ignacio Garcia both wary and smart. He never used any drugs other than some occasional marijuana. And he never sold drugs. He realized that was sure to get him arrested eventually, because customers always talked. His only contacts with heavy drug users were some that he hired to work his burglaries. Garcia developed a reputation as a clever burglar who never got caught. His modus operandi was exacting: hit between ten a.m. and two p.m. on weekdays, when nobody was home. Avoid lower-class neighborhoods, where the pickings weren't worth bothering, and avoid the wealthy neighborhoods where they all had burglar alarms. Instead, he hit middle-class neighborhoods, where there were still things worth stealing, but where they didn't have their guard up.

Garcia started out by doing burglaries himself, but soon moved on to organizing and equipping teams to do the work for him. To approach middle-class houses surreptitiously, he outfitted his teams to look like plumbers, carpet cleaners, or gardeners. Their vehicles looked very convincing. Garcia then fenced his goods though a network of pawnshops, flea market dealers, and coin dealers who could keep their mouths shut. He had his teams concentrate on jewelry, guns, coin collections, cash, and high-end digital cameras. He made a point of never keeping any stolen merchandise at home. He paid several little old ladies to rent storage spaces for him. Eventually he had almost a dozen places to hide his stolen goods.

Garcia was never associated with any of the big gangs, although he did recruit a few members of MS-13. He kept his own gang—"the gang with no name"—as quiet as possible, and discouraged them from antagonizing any other gangs. Garcia often said, "Let them bicker and kill each other while we hang back and just make lots of money."

The stoners who worked for Garcia sometimes did stupid crackhead stuff. Even though he gave them explicit directions, they'd ignore him and bring back things like big-screen HD televisions, bottles of various prescription medicines, and kitchen appliances. One time one of his men brought back plastic bags of live koi carp that they had stolen from a pond. This pond was in the backyard of a house that they had trouble entering. Some of the items had to be discarded, or took weeks to fence.

Three years before the Crunch, Ignacio realized that some upper-middle-class people rarely let their guard down. For these targets Garcia started to train and equip his home invasion team. He selected his most ruthless yet most levelheaded men. He gave them some of his best guns and carefully selected targets, mostly ones that he'd previously had to pass up. He called this team La Fuerza—The Force. Most of their home invasions took place at midday, when there would likely be just one adult at home.

The home invasions went remarkably well. Because Garcia insisted on a strict six-minute time limit inside a target house, La Fuerza never met the police face-to-face. Eventually he split La Fuerza into two teams of six men each. Their take was so lucrative that he eventually stopped using his traditional burglary teams altogether. He gave control and ownership of that whole operation to his cousin Simon.

Garcia grew up in Houston's Second Ward, but after he built up capital from his burglaries, he bought a house in Greenspoint, on the north side. This was a nice suburban neighborhood that was roughly half Hispanic. He did his best to blend in. Ignacio told his neighbors that he was in the import/export business. In a way, he was right. He just exported things from people's houses and imported them into his own.

When the Crunch started, there were sixteen full members of Garcia's gang. As the economy cratered, Garcia realized that he had to switch gears quickly. Previously, his goal had been converting stolen goods into cash. But now cash was perishable and even undesirable. The goods themselves were more valuable. He also realized that once Houston became the target of rioting, the whole city would be locked down, and he'd be just as at risk from burglary or robbery as anyone else.

Garcia leased a large warehouse in Anahuac, a white-bread community on the east side of Trinity Bay, in Chambers County, east of Houston. He rented a nearby apartment and moved his wife and children there. The warehouse had thirty-five thousand square feet and a pair of large roll-up doors in the back. He set all of his men to work ferrying the best of his accumulated loot from his various storage spaces to the warehouse. Then he had them start stealing late-model cargo vans and pickup trucks with camper shells. He didn't ask them to stop until he had seventeen of them parked in the warehouse.

Using his gang members as agents, Garcia scrambled to convert as much of his cash as possible into practical tangibles. He had them buy ten jerry cans for each van and truck, and set each vehicle up with roof racks. They each also got water jugs, canned goods, camp stoves, sleeping bags, ammunition, tools, and freeze-dried foods. They bought or stole four spare tires mounted on rims for each vehicle, and strapped them down on the roof racks. After just three days at the warehouse, he asked his cousin Simon to join him, and to bring along his eight toughest men who were bachelors.

Garcia spent many hours talking what-ifs with Tony, his most trusted lieutenant. Tony had three years of artillery experience in the Army, with a tour in Iraq. That was before his Article 15s and dishonorable discharge. It was Tony who suggested putting CB radios in every vehicle. It was also Tony who recommended buying up as many cans of flat tan and flat brown spray paint as they could find. Tony was good at planning ahead.

They had everything almost ready at the warehouse by the time that the riots started in earnest. He ordered the men and their families to get used to sleeping hard—essentially camping—inside of their vehicles in the warehouse. There were some complaints at first, but then, once Houston started to burn, they thanked Ignacio for rescuing them from the chaos and for getting them ready.

The entire gang eventually adopted the name La Fuerza. Ignacio set them on a well-calculated campaign of nighttime robberies of sporting goods stores, department stores, and recreational equipment stores. They were cautious, though, so none of these stores were located in Chambers County.

Once the gang was equipped for traveling and living independently, La Fuerza started stealing armored vehicles. Their first targets were members of the Military Vehicle Preservation Association (MVPA), a group that Garcia's wife found with an Internet search. The MVPA members meticulously restored jeeps, trucks, and armored vehicles. Their roster—complete with the addresses of members—was there for the taking on the Internet. The gang's goal was acquiring wheeled armored personnel carriers.

Their vehicles of choice were the Cadillac Gage V-100 Commando (a four-wheeled APC) and the Alvis Saracen a (British six-wheeled APC). Garcia sent out four-man teams in stolen cars to as far away as Oklahoma and Louisiana to steal them.

His men would arrive after midnight, batter down house doors, and force people from their beds at gunpoint. They marched them to their garages to show the gang members how to start and operate their vehicles. To give them more time to get away before an alarm was raised, the gang members killed the homeowners and their families. Over the course of three nights, they drove back to Anahuac with three Saracens and two V-100s.

Garcia was disappointed to find that most of the MVPA members had only non-firing dummy weapons mounted on their vehicles. Only one of the vehicles had a live gun. This was a semiautomatic-only Browning Model 1919. So their next targets were belt-fed machine guns, taken in storefront or home invasion robberies of Class 3 licensed full-auto weapons dealers. These robberies netted six .30 caliber belt-feds, two Browning .50s, and 15 submachineguns of various types. They were surprised at the quantity of ammunition and extra magazines that the dealers had. In all, there were 232 cans of ammunition, much of it already on linked belts.

It was not until after they had the guns and Tony started reading their manuals that they realized they needed belt-linking machines to assemble belts of ammunition. They then brazenly went back to a store that they had robbed just two days before and took both .30 and .50 caliber hand-lever linking machines and several 20mm ammo cams containing thousands of used links.

6

Getting By

"Most people can't think, most of the remainder won't think, the small fraction who do think mostly can't do it very well. The extremely tiny fraction who think regularly, accurately, creatively, and without self-delusion—in the long run, these are the only people who count."

—Robert A. Heinlein

Radcliff, Kentucky
October, the First Year

Sheila Randall was fretting. Her husband, Jerome, had moved them from New Orleans to Radcliff, Kentucky, just a few weeks before the Crunch. After he was laid off in New Orleans, Jerome had been offered the steady job in Kentucky. But that meant leaving behind their extended families in Louisiana. They brought with them Tyree, their ten-year-old son, and Emily Voisin, Sheila's spry seventy-six-year-old grandmother. They settled into a three-bedroom rental house on Third Street in Radcliff. The town was just outside the south gate of Fort Knox, the home of the U.S. Army's Armor Center and School—the school for tanker troops.

Jerome got a job at a Big O tire shop, just as he had in New Orleans, but with a higher salary and the promise of bonuses. Jerome had also been promised inflation indexing for his pay. Sheila took a job in data entry for the local phone company's billing department, much like the one that she had held before for a power utility in Louisiana. It was boring, repetitive work, but it helped pay their bills, and she was able to work six hours per day, five days a week, which allowed her to pick her son up after school each day. Even working only thirty hours per week, the job offered full health and dental benefits. And this was a plus, since her husband's job didn't provide a dental plan.

Jerome had thought Radcliff was a good place to work because the Army payroll meant that a steady stream of cash customers came into town every week, mainly on the weekends. All the local stores did well. The soldiers mainly spent their money at the grocery stores, Wal-Mart, and the many bars and tattoo parlors. But the town had a slightly unsavory air to it, and that bothered Sheila. Most of all, she missed her large Creole family. Sheila had such fair skin that she could pass for white, but her husband had much darker skin.

Their house was nice, as rentals go, and had a big yard, but there was noisy traffic, since it was close to the Dixie Highway. The city park and the Big O tire store were both within walking distance. At least the backyard was fairly quiet, since it had an alleyway behind it, and it had a fence, so it was a safe place for Tyree to play. Their neighbors were a mix of whites, blacks, and Mexican-Americans. Most of the houses in the neighborhood, including theirs, had been built in the 1920s. The owner-occupied homes had been well maintained, but most of the rentals had shabby yards. Their next-door neighbor was Mrs. Hernandez, a divorced woman who worked as a shipping clerk at the U.S. Cavalry Store. It seemed that half the town currently worked for the Cav store or had worked there in the past. The company had started out in the early 1980s as a military uniform store that made machine-stitched uniform name tapes and sold tanker boots to soldiers from Fort Knox. It eventually grew into a multimillion-dollar enterprise, mainly selling by mail order.

When the inflation started, Grandmère Emily advised Sheila to buy up vegetable seeds. Jerome said he thought it was evidence of senility, but Sheila went along with the plan, since her grandmother was very wise and had lived through the Great Depression. So they spent three Saturdays in September driving to nearly every seed store in Hardin, Meade, and Breckinridge counties, buying up their late-summer seed closeouts. Also on Emily's advice, they bought dozens of pairs of gardening gloves in various sizes.

Without telling her husband, Sheila also spent some of her lunch hours at work mail-ordering seeds via the Internet. These were mostly the open-pollinated "heirloom" varieties that Emily had suggested were best because they bred true, as opposed to hybrid seeds. Sheila followed that advice and concentrated on the non-hybrid varieties. She bought nearly all vegetable and herb seeds. The only flower seeds that she bought were nasturtiums, which could be eaten as salad greens, and marigolds, which Emily said could be planted around the perimeter of a garden as a barrier to protect it from rabbits, moles, and even slugs.

As the dozens of seed mail orders arrived, Sheila had her grandmother hide them in her bedroom closet. Jerome had only begrudgingly gone along with the seed-buying plan, knowing that the money all came from Emily's retirement nest egg. But Sheila saw no need to tell Jerome about the mail orders of the heirloom seeds. If he found out about her *"petit secret"* with her mother, she knew that he'd go ballistic. But since Sheila handled paying all the family's bills, Jerome never caught on. Eventually, there were boxes containing thousands of seed packets stacked up in the back of Emily's walk-in closet.

Even with all of the economic chaos, the mail was still coming through, and the seed companies—mostly family-owned businesses—were good to their word: nearly all of the orders eventually arrived. While all of their neighbors were desperately scrambling to buy canned food, Sheila Randall was quietly buying enough vegetable seeds to plant hundreds of gardens.

Seeing what was happening, many small-business owners wisely went "on vacation" or "closed for inventory." This started with the local coin shop. Then the local jewelry store and the Cav store closed. The privately owned gas stations followed suit, but many people suspected that they had quit business while they still had fuel in their tanks. The big chain stations and truck stops soon had supply difficulties. Every time that word circulated that a tank truck delivery had been made, that station was swarmed with customers, who would line up their cars for blocks.

Short of gas cans, people resorted to filling unsafe containers such as two-liter bottles, ancient milk cans, and water barrels with gasoline and diesel fuel. This wasn't allowed at the gas stations, but that didn't stop customers from filling their fuel tanks at the station and then driving home to siphon the gas into small containers at home. It seemed that the main occupation of many people was either standing in line in front of the bank or sitting in their cars in long queues at gas stations.

Jerome spent many evenings after work driving up to thirty miles to buy staple foods. His dwindling supply of cash was spent primarily on canned foods, pasta, pasta sauce, and breakfast cereal.

Jerome's other contribution to the family's preparedness effort was to withdraw their savings from the bank to buy a shotgun from one of his coworkers. The only gun that he could find was a 20-gauge "Youth" version of the Remington Model 870, with a special short stock designed for small shooters. The gun was obviously well used and had a scratched stock, a dented barrel rib, and a few rust spots from previous improper storage, but it was serviceable. It cost Jerome $1,400 in the rapidly inflating dollars. As a teenager he had hunted ducks with his father's 12-gauge Model 870, so he was quite familiar with the gun's operation. With much searching and what he considered a huge outlay of cash, he was also eventually able to buy forty-five boxes of 20-gauge shotgun shells—an odd assortment of mostly birdshot of various sizes, #0 buckshot, and a few slugs. Some of the birdshot shells were so old that they had paper hulls, and Jerome wondered if they would still fire.

On their third weekend seed-buying trip, Jerome took his family to the Hoosier National Forest, just across the river, in Indiana, to try out the shotgun. He explained and demonstrated how to load and fire the gun, and the operating of its safety button: "This gun had a duck-hunting plug in it, so the magazine would only hold two shells. But I took that out, so now it holds five shells, plus one in the chamber. Now, let me show you something my daddy taught me. Right after you shoot one shell, after you pump the action, without taking the gun off your shoulder, you right quick shove another shell into the magazine from your bandoleer. You need to learn how to do that just by touch. That way you always keep the gun's magazine full. And then if you ever have to shoot multiple, uhhh, ducks, then you can keep pumping from a full magazine. Okay?"

"Okay, shoot one, load one, unless it's an emergency," Sheila echoed.

"That's right, *ma chère*."

They shot only the oldest shells, aiming at empty soda pop cans set up twenty feet away. This gave an impressive display of the gun's power, thoroughly shredding the cans with birdshot. Since he had only two pairs of earmuffs, one of them had to plug their ears with their fingertips. While the gun was small for Jerome, the stock was just the right length for Sheila, who was five feet two inches and weighed just 110 pounds. Sheila soon got used to shooting the gun, obviously enjoying it. Even Emily fired a few shells, and Tyree fired three shells while sitting between his father's knees. He was thrilled. As they walked back to his car, toting the shotgun and a paper bag full of ventilated aluminum cans, Jerome said, "Well, now we're all ready for World War Three."

Sheila snapped back, "More likely Civil War Two."

Luke Air Force Base, Arizona
October, the First Year

Two weeks earlier, in Arizona, Ian Doyle and his Honduran-born wife, Blanca, had been sitting in their living room, watching the ten o'clock news. Their daughter was already asleep in her bedroom. The news show was dominated by reports about the stock market crash on Wall Street.

Ian asked, "Remember what your dad told us, after his vacation trip to South Africa, about how they don't transport diamonds from the mines on the ground, only in helicopters?"

"Sure, I remember. He said the hijacking stopped after they switched to flying the diamonds."

"Well, that has me thinking: if the economy totally falls apart—and it might within a year—if the three of us ever *need* to travel, then the safest way will be by air. Since our Laron only seats two, we need to buy a second plane—something like ours that can burn regular automobile gasoline. With a second plane, we'll have a seat for Linda and can bug out of here with a marginal quantity of gear."

Blanca answered, "Not being able to drive, that sounds pretty extreme. But I suppose it could happen." After pondering for a moment she asked, "What about Charley, from the ultralight club? He has that tan-painted Star Streak. With that, we'd have common parts, in case we ever have to cannibalize."

"I'll give him a call."

Two days later, Ian met with Charley Gordon at his home in Old Stone Ranch, one of the nicest neighborhoods in Phoenix.

Gordon was overweight and balding. He wore a golf shirt and a flashy Patek Philippe wristwatch.

Ian spent twenty minutes talking with Charley about light experimental aircraft. Charley mentioned that he hadn't flown his much recently because of chronic lower back pain.

In one of the bays of his three-car garage sat an enclosed aircraft trailer, almost identical to Doyle's. Gordon explained that he had bought a Laron Shadow in kit form just before the turn of the century. Building it had been a two-year project. He later upgraded it to the larger four-stroke Hirth engine, effectively making it into a Star Streak. It only had eighty-three hours clocked on the new engine. Like Doyle's plane, Charley's Laron had the optional wing lockers for extra cargo space.

Ian asked Gordon if he'd sell his plane. He replied, "Yeah, maybe, but with inflation, I probably couldn't replace it for less than $25,000." He offered Ian a glass of lemonade. They settled into the living room with their drinks, and the conversation shifted to the recent stock market collapse. They agreed that it was the most dramatic economic event since 1929. Doyle then asked, "What do you plan to do if things get a *lot* worse, Charley?"

"You mean a Depression that lasts a decade or more? My house is paid for. I'm scheduled to retire in just six months—that is, *if* I still have a job and *if* the company stays afloat."

"No, I mean, what if there are riots, looting, that sort of thing. Would you move then?"

Gordon's arm swept around the perimeter of his well-appointed living room, and he said, "My wife's whole life is wrapped up in her antiques and her paintings. I don't think she'd ever budge an inch from this house. So if times get hard, we'll just hunker down right here. If it looks like the power might go out, my plan is to drain my pool and refill it with tap water." He added with a laugh, "Then I'll sell it to my neighbors, one gallon at a time."

"Do you have any guns?"

"I've got a snub-nosed .38 and old .22 pump action."

"That's not exactly an anti-riot arsenal." Doyle leaned forward and went on: "I don't have $25,000 in cash to buy your kite, so here's a trade proposal for you: you don't *need* your plane, but you may soon *need* a serious self-defense gun. Do you know what a Sten gun is?"

"Yeah, sure, I've seen 'em on the History Channel. The Brits used them back in World War II and Korea—oh, and in Malaya. The one where the magazine sticks out to the side."

"Right. Well, what would you say if I traded you my Sten gun, a sound suppressor for it, a dozen magazines, and a big pile of 9mm ball ammo . . . That in exchange for your Laron, any spare parts you have for it, and its trailer."

"A *real*, fully-automatic Sten submachinegun? Are you kidding?" he snorted. "But is that worth as much as my plane?"

"Charley, I'm not sure if you've shopped for guns and ammo recently, but the prices are sky-high, and you can't even *find* most ammo calibers on the shelf."

Gordon scratched his chin. He asked, "Is that Sten registered—I mean, the $200 tax stamp thing with the Feds?"

"No, and neither is the suppressor."

Gordon started to laugh. "Ian, you always did strike me as the kind of guy who thinks outside the box."

Ian added bladder fuel tanks to the second Laron, just like he had already done the previous year to his Star Streak. Originally, the Star Streaks only had a range of about 320 miles at 80 percent power. The main tank held fourteen and a half gallons. The bladders weren't connected directly to the primary fuel system. Ignoring FAA safety regulations, he installed two Black & Decker Jack Rabbit hand pumps, attaching them with Velcro cable ties alongside the front seats. Transferring fuel from the bladder to the main tank was time-consuming but fairly easy to do when flying straight and level. The bladder tanks extended the range of both planes to about 480 miles without landing to refuel.

Bloomfield, New Mexico
October, the First Year

Lars and Beth continued to stock up by ordering things on the Internet. There, prices were being bid up to the stratosphere. Lars had to pay $14 each for a handful of extra ammunition stripper clips for the M39 Mosin-Nagant rifle that he had inherited from his father. But they did find a few overlooked bargains that most people considered antiques and collectibles. These included two hand scythes and a hand-cranked bench grinder. Lars was also successful at bidding on nine filter cartridges for the ranch's whole-house water filter.

Laine also bought dozens of three-packs of obsolete Magic Cube flash camera cubes. He explained to Beth and Kaylee that with just a piece of monofilament fishing line and a paper clip, these could be used as an improvised intrusion alarm device. The flash would both startle any nighttime intruders and alert anyone awake in the house that there was a prowler in the yard. He explained that standard flash cubes were set off with a battery, but Magic Cubes were set off with a mechanical striker. An NCO who was a Desert Storm vet had showed him the trick.

Beth did a detailed inventory of the ranch house, barn, and outbuildings. The only serious shortcoming that they found was gas lamp mantles: they discovered that they had only two spares. So Lars e-mailed:

Andy:

The only mantles for dad's wall gas lamps that work without falling apart are made by Falks and Humphreys.

When you're in Germany, can you try to find at least 20 spares
for me?

Thx Bro,
    Psalm 37,
        —Lars

FOB Wolverine, Task Force Duke, Zabul Province, Afghanistan
October, the First Year

Andy was able to test-fire and zero the SIG pistol on a hot afternoon two days after he bought it. Because the unit rotation was
under way, and the incoming Stryker squadron's first range fire
wasn't scheduled for another three days, the FOB's shooting range
was deserted. Unlike range fire at U.S. installations in CONUS,
which was extremely controlled, things were much more casual in
Afghanistan. Andy simply walked to the range and raised its red
flag. There were no formalities, no inspections, no safety briefings,
and no bullhorned "Is there anyone downrange?" warnings. Andy
just stapled up three targets and started shooting.

Firing at first very deliberately to establish "zero" for the pistol,
Laine put 250 rounds downrange without a stutter. He made a
point of using each of the magazines to ensure that none of them
had feeding problems. Andy was very pleased. He knew that he
had a pistol that he could rely on.

Radcliff, Kentucky
October, the First Year

It was 9:10 p.m., just past Tyree's bedtime. Jerome had not yet
come back. Sheila and her grandmother were getting worried. For
the past three weeks, each workday he had carried a nearly empty
backpack with him when he walked to work. Then, on his lunch

breaks and after work, he went out bartering seeds and some extra hand tools in exchange for canned foods and staples like bags of breakfast cereal.

Now Sheila nervously pulled the shade aside and looked out the front window.

"He's never been this late."

"We need to pray," Emily said firmly.

The next morning, after checking at the tire shop and hearing that Jerome had left at 5:30 p.m. and hadn't been seen since, Sheila walked to the police department and asked to file a missing-person report. The harried front desk clerk replied, "Yeah, you and about five million other people." She told Sheila that an informal check would be made and to return at noon the next day to file a report.

Two days later Sheila went again to the police department. After she had waited twenty minutes in the police department lobby, a plainclothes detective came out. After he identified himself, he told her, "I'm sorry, but there's no sign of your husband. We checked all the usuals: the sheriff's department, the state police, at the hospital. That took some doing, with the phones out. No luck."

After a pause he added, "There was one John Doe, though. A black man in his thirties or forties, but they said that he had only eight fingers. Did—I mean, does—your husband have all of his fingers?"

"Yes, he does. He just lost one fingernail, working as a mechanic."

"Then that can't be him. Please be patient. With the phones down, he could be most anywhere and just unable to contact you. Maybe he caught a ride somewhere to make a trade and couldn't get a ride back. It takes a long time to cover thirty or forty miles on foot. Your report said that he was a faithful husband—"

"I'm *sure* of that!"

"Okay, well, if we hear of anything, we'll send an officer to your house."

The following morning the same detective knocked at the Randalls' door.

"Could we sit down and talk for a minute?" he asked.

Sheila felt a knot in her stomach when he mentioned sitting down.

After they were seated, the detective said, "Something was bothering me last night, so I double-checked with the county coroner this morning.

"It turns out that the body of the, uhh black male with no shoes, no shirt or pants, and no identification, who had been shot . . . it turns out that he had *just recently* lost two fingers, either just before or just after he died." Grasping together the two smallest fingers on his own left hand to illustrate, he added: "The coroner said that it looked like they had been cut off with an axe or a hatchet."

"His left hand?"

"Yes, it was his left."

Sheila turned pale, and she whispered, "His wedding ring always was a tight fit. He had to put butter or oil on his finger and pull it hard to get it off."

7

Paperwork

"A commander can delegate authority, but not responsibility."
—**American military axiom**

Bloomfield, New Mexico
March, the First Year

L. Roy Martin had purchased his Bloomfield, New Mexico, plant just eight months before the Crunch. His reputation as a maverick Texas oilman meant that the purchase of the troubled refinery for cash and stock didn't raise many eyebrows. The plant had been temporarily shut down by Western Refining in 2010, mostly because of insufficient feedstock in the vicinity of Bloomfield. Since then, under new ownership by a "green energy" consortium, it had been reopened, but was operating at less than half of its full capacity, with frequent layoffs and rumors of a permanent shutdown. Martin bought the moribund plant for pennies on the dollar. Most industry analysts surmised that he planned to bring it back to full operation with a couple of long-distance pipelines. The purchase announcement also made just passing mention that Martin Holdings planned to increase the refinery's co-generation capacity.

But the news that did start rumors in Bloomfield was that the Martin family had purchased a 120-acre cattle ranch and three 20-acre ranchettes, each with modest homes. All four of these properties were on the same road as the 285-acre refining plant. A 3,000-square-foot tan metal shop building was added to the 120-acre place, which by then had been nicknamed "Martin's Mystery Ranch" by the locals. It was a mystery why Martin would sell his 8,000-square-foot home in a fashionable Houston neighborhood and move his family to a 1,500-square-foot 1950s-era ranch house. One of the rumors was that the house had been quickly transformed to nearly 3,000 square feet after remodeling.

The ranch was better known for its natural gas output than its beef production. There were three low-production gas wellheads dotted across the place. From the S-Bar-L ranch house, the view of the San Juan Mountains far in the distance (across the state line, in Colorado) was overwhelmed by the view of the Bloomfield plant's cracking towers and holding tanks only a half mile away. At night, the sky glowed from the light of the excess fractions being burned off.

To explain his family's relocation, L. Roy said that he was winding down to retirement, that he wanted a slower pace of life, and that he wanted to personally oversee the operation of the Bloomfield plant, especially since this was his first refinery. (All of his previous experience had been in drilling and oil field development.) Despite these low-key public statements, there were rumors buzzing of L. Roy Martin opening up new oil fields in various parts of the Four Corners. Why else would a famed Texas oilman with a background in oil exploration move his family bag and baggage to the middle of nowhere? And why would he buy a dumpy old house out in the sagebrush when he could afford to build a mansion on the south bank of the San Juan River? It just didn't match the public's expectations of a Texas oilman who owned a Cessna Citation private jet, a pair of Hummer H1s, a Shelby Cobra, a restored 1963 Corvette, and a dozen motorcycles.

The Bloomfield plant was nearly thirty years old and fairly standard for a modern refinery, being set up for crude distillation, hydrotreating of naphtha and distillate, re-forming units for aviation and automobile high-octane gasoline, and fluid catalytic cracking units. The only unusual things about it were its close proximity to the San Juan River, and that it had polymerization units to convert liquefied petroleum gas into gasoline. Most of the plant's production was from local "Four Corners Sweet" crude oil, but some came from natural gas.

L. Roy (or "El Rey" as some of the locals soon called him) was sixty-two years old when the Crunch hit. He had seen it coming but still felt underprepared for its severity. Martin's younger brother, his brother-in-law, and his first cousin—all Martin Holdings employees—took up residence at the three contiguous twenty-acre ranches. They also embarked on rush-job additions and remodels, albeit less grandiose than the work at the S-Bar-L ranch house. Even though they were on local grid power supplied by the Farmington Electric Utility System (FEUS), all four ranches were soon equipped with identical pairs of Onan twelve-kilowatt generators with natural-gas-fueled engines. Several of Martin's petroleum engineers also got in on the purchase, buying additional backup generators for their own homes at a bargain group purchase price. Like the grounds of the refinery, Martin's ranch was dotted with sagebrush and rabbit brush.

Southwest of Farmington was the largest agricultural project in northwestern New Mexico. The Navajo tribe owned the Navajo Agricultural Products Industry (NAPI) farms. There, the tribe grew enormous quantities of alfalfa hay, corn, pinto beans, pumpkins, potatoes, grains, barley, and onions. Close to sixty thousand acres were under cultivation in circular-irrigated fields when the Crunch hit. The majority of the water for NAPI came from Navajo Dam, about thirty-five miles away. The reservoir pushed back twenty miles. The project that got the water to NAPI included a huge tunnel that was completed in the mid-1960s.

FOB Wolverine, Task Force Duke, Zabul Province, Afghanistan
October, the First Year

Andrew Laine knew that it was horribly bad timing to have been named head of the three-man "Rear Party" for the Battalion. But as the Property Book Officer (PBO), he was the logical choice. The additional duty of PBO has always been dreaded by Army officers. There are very few brownie points to be earned and umpteen ways to mess up as a PBO, just for failing to pay very close attention to detail.

It had become standard practice to rotate troops and small arms but not vehicles whenever a unit left the Operation Enduring Freedom (OEF) theater of operations. The logistics of moving vehicles with each unit rotation were monumental, so lateral transfers of vehicles and heavy weapons made sense. This process also made a tremendous amount of work for supply NCOs and PBOs. While the rest of the unit rotated back to Germany, Andy, the battalion's E-8 supply NCOIC, and a PLL clerk would stay behind to hand off both the containerized housing unit (CHU) billets and the many items designated for lateral transfer to the new battalion.

In the case of his unit, a Stryker battalion, a unit shuffle was a PBO's nightmare. By his unit's table of organization and equipment (TO&E), there were dozens of lateral transfers to accomplish, including the Stryker wheeled APCs, each with their complement of TOW missile launchers, 25mm chain guns, frequency-hopping VHF radios, thermal sights, and so forth. Each of these items had a unique serial number. There were also spare engines, generator trailers, tentage, camouflage nets, and the umpteen other "fiddly bits," as Master Sergeant Rezendes called them.

Word had come down from the incoming unit commander that he wanted every serial number double-checked. After all, who could blame him? It was the PBO's job, but it was the incoming commander's *responsibility*. A $196 million property book was nothing to be trifled with, especially when the loss of just one sensitive item would be deemed "non-career-enhancing." Ultimately, it would be the outgoing and incoming battalion commanders who would answer for any discrepancies. Everything had to be accounted for, right down to two radios that were currently off for depot-level repair.

Before the main party of the unit departed, Laine walked into his commander's office, carrying the Electronic Property Book (EPB). Colonel Ed Olds looked up from his desk with his characteristic squint. Olds asked, "So, how are those laterals going?" Andy spent the next few minutes giving him the details. Colonel Olds leaned backed in his chair and probed, "Any unresolved discrepancies?"

"None yet, sir, but if I find anything, you'll be the first to know. The good news is that if it is something minor, with all the IED incidents, we can easily write something off as a combat loss."

Olds laughed and said, "Let me tell you a little story from my ancient history, Andy. I remember back in the early days of the Desert Shield deployment—this was months before the actual Desert Storm invasion—there was a UH-60 helicopter that went down in a sand storm. The crew got out okay but the aircraft burned up. Six months later, when the IG followed up on the accident report paperwork, they discovered that there was supposedly more than two thousand pounds of miscellaneous equipment on board that aircraft: radios, starlight scopes, an MWR television and VCR, two gen-sets, you name it. Everything but the kitchen sink. According to all the paperwork—with all the *i*'s properly dotted and the *t*'s crossed, mind you—there was gear from every company in the brigade on board that bird. If what was on that manifest was actually on board, there was no way that Blackhawk could have got off the ground. And in fact it wouldn't have even fit in the available space."

Olds laughed. "Every 76 Yankee in the brigade used that crash to make up for years' worth of missing inventory items. Thankfully, the IG team kinda thought it was a bit of jest and gave it a wink and a nod. Fact is, there was a rather droll statement included in the after-action, somethin' like 'The aircraft's high takeoff weight may have contributed to this incident.'"

Laine and Olds both laughed this time. Andy took a breath and then asked: "Sir, given the deteriorating security situation in our AO, I'd like permission for the rear party to keep our issued weapons with us, using hand receipts. We'll be here at least a week and possibly a lot longer, depending on when we can find transport. We all know how irregular the MAC flights are getting."

Colonel Olds bit his lower lip and asked, "Can we do that by regulation?"

"Yes, sir. I just researched it today. Paragraph 9 of AR 190-11 allows detachments to travel armed at the local commander's discretion. And, of course, AR 190-14, chapters 2 and 4 apply."

Olds rubbed his chin.

Laine added, "With your permission, sir, I'll prepare hand receipts for each of us in the rear party."

"Just don't lose them, or it'll be nearly as bad as losing the weapons themselves. That would be a major goat rope."

"Understood. Tell you what, sir: just in case, I'll make a backup copy of each hand receipt, also for your signature, and I'll leave them in the TOC Crypto safe."

"That would be prudent, Andrew. *Make it so.*"

Andy rolled his eyes as he walked out of the office. Colonel Olds was famous for that phrase best known from *Star Trek*. Behind his back, some of the junior officers jokingly called him "Colonel Picard."

It was 90 degrees outside. As he walked back across the quadrangle, Andy wondered when the weather would change. The standing joke in his unit was that Afghanistan had 180 days of summer and 180 days of winter, leaving two days each year for fall and three days for spring.

Some things in the Army were still done the old-fashioned way, especially when units were deployed overseas. One time-honored tradition was preparing hand receipts on a 1980s-vintage ball-head Selectric typewriter that was still soldiering on. Just as he had been instructed, Andy typed two sets of DA Form 3749s for the three M4 carbines, carefully keying in the nomenclature and serial numbers. But he intentionally left off the standard ruler-drawn ballpoint pen line with "Nothing Follows," something that is always added as the last step before getting signatures.

Just before close of business for the day, Andy took the six forms to Colonel Olds. "Two sets, as you directed, sir." Olds nodded and signed them with hardly a glance or a word.

After the commander had left for the day, Laine returned to his desk and took just one of the pair of forms that was made out in his own name, put it in his typewriter, and added a line that read "Pistol, M11 Compact (SIG P228), 9mm" along with his newly purchased pistol's serial number. Finally, he added the slashed "Nothing Follows" lines to all six forms. The subterfuge was that simple. Now Laine could carry home the SIG pistol with "official" paperwork, yet have a second set of paperwork to also make the pistol disappear.

Back in his CHU, Andy realized that if the SIG was going to be his only self-defense tool for his travel back to New Mexico, then he needed to research its capabilities. So he brought his laptop to the MWR tent and logged on to the Internet. A quick Bing.com search led him to JBMBallistics.com. There he entered the values for standard M882 9mm ball ammunition with 112-grain bullets. Running the ballistic calculator, he ran the bullet drop values for 100, 200, 300, and 400 yards.

He was surprised to see that at 400 yards he would have to hold over—aiming at a point far above his target—a whopping

228 inches. He determined that was roughly three and a third man-heights. He was also disappointed to see that the energy of the bullets decreased from 451 foot/pounds at the muzzle to just 176 foot/pounds at 400 yards. Andy jotted down the yardage and bullet drop values.

Back at his CHU, he printed out a small drop table with a fine point Sharpie pen on an index card, trimmed it to fit on the top of one of his magazine pouch flaps, and taped it on. He knew that he'd be horribly outclassed in a long-range gun battle with anyone armed with a center-fire rifle, but at least he wouldn't be in the dark about how much to hold over.

Andy and Lars had been taught about long-range pistol shooting by their father, five years before the Crunch, Robie had attended a class by Cope Reynolds of Southwest Shooting Authority in Luna. Robie was enthusiastic about sharing his new skills. After completing the class, Robie could hit a man-size target at 250 yards with roughly 50 percent of his shots from his Lahti 9mm pistol. When Andy came home to visit their father on leave, Robie showed both of his sons the basics of what he'd learned in the course. Soon they were scoring fairly consistent hits on a twenty-four-inch steel disk at 200 yards.

Andy was officially released for his return to Germany, but he was in limbo. He was desperate to find transport—any transport—out of Afghanistan. The Military Airlift Command (MAC) flights had already become less frequent because of the ongoing troop drawdown, but more recently flights had been nearly suspended. The reason cited was the new Fuel Austerity Program (FAP) that was mandated by Congress. Cutting the military fuel budget by 80 percent left most naval ships idling at port and most transport planes grounded. The U.S. military's new catchphrase was "Billions for bailouts, but not a nickel for fuel."

After more than a week of begging on the phone and texting,

Andy was finally allotted a seat on a German Luftwaffe C-160 transport. To make this flight, Laine had to be at the military side of the Kabul airport in just five hours. This would be impossible by road travel, so Andy called in a favor with the FOB commander to prevail on a West Point classmate who was the commander of the nearby 3rd Armored Cavalry Regiment, which had organic air assets. Just forty minutes after his call, an AH-64 Apache attack helicopter flown with an empty gunner's seat touched down on the main pad at FOB Wolverine. The helicopter never shut down. It took a while to cram Laine's gear into a cargo compartment and into the gunner's seat, where Laine also sat. Unlike the older Cobra gunships, where the copilot/gunner sits in the rear, with the Apache, the copilot/gunner sits in the front seat. The pilot, a crusty CW4 named Halverson, gave Andy a nickel ride, winding up the main rotor and pulling pitch with gusto, making the tips of the main rotor come within five feet of the ground, and kicking up a substantial cloud of dust.

After getting his helmet on and figuring out the microphone switch, Andy exclaimed, "Thanks for the lift!"

"Not a prob, sir. I love making unscheduled flights like these. I just hope that someone's willing to do the same for me when I've got my date with the Freedom Bird. Just enjoy the scenery and, uh, needless to say, keep your nose-picker off the controls—aside from the 'Rambo mic switch'—and we'll be on the ground in about thirty-five minutes." That mention of the microphone switch referred to the red button atop most U.S. military helicopter control sticks. In a notorious movie gaffe that made military helicopter pilots groan, that was the button shown used for launching rockets.

"That sounds great! You are a gentleman and a scholar." Andy felt a huge rush of emotion. He was finally headed home. Watching the landscape below, he mainly thought about Kaylee. He snapped almost fifty digital pictures of Afghan villages, typical walled family farm compounds, the outlines of ancient ruins, and, finally, the hazy skyline of Kabul. He clicked the red microphone switch and commented: "I wish my fiancée could see this."

The warrant said, "No you don't! Because if she were seeing this, then she'd be deployed here in the Big Sandbox."

Laine laughed, "I suppose you're right."

Andy stood on the tarmac at Kabul International, watching the AH-64 fade to a speck in the distance. Even though it was now October, it still felt hot. He had a comfortable two hours before his Luftwaffe flight was scheduled to take off. He shouldered his pack and duffel and his M4 carbine, then walked over to the FLOPS shop—the new, dramatically scaled-down and consolidated U.S. Army Aviation Flight Operations Center, Kabul. There he quickly bummed a two-minute ride to the German hangars. Part of the route cut across an active taxiway, which was unnerving, but the specialist who was driving acted as if it was nothing out of the ordinary. Just another day in the land of Kipling.

Checking in for the Luftwaffe flight was a breeze, even though he didn't have a scrap of documentation for the flight itself, just his movement orders. All of the arrangements had been made by phone, and the German officers had gotten the word that he was expected. They handed him a complex itinerary marked *Luftfahrt-Bundesamt* with typical German date formats and dotted times. It had just his name and rank typed at the top, yet they repeatedly assured him that was all the documentation he needed for every leg of his journey: *"Ja, ja, Herr Major. Das ist alles."*

Thinking about the SIG 9mm pistol buried near the bottom of his duffel, he felt a bit of anxiety. Strangely, even the obvious presence of his M4 carbine was not questioned. Since nearly all of the Heer troops around him carried Heckler & Koch G36 rifles, it didn't look out of the ordinary. Some of these troops carried their rifles by their long top-carry handles, and this almost made Andy laugh. It looked like they were carrying attaché cases. None of his bags were inspected. Only his military ID card and the flight itinerary sheet were checked.

The series of cargo shuttle flights, by way of Azerbaijan, took a grueling thirty-seven hours. The planes were too noisy for a comfortable conversation, and most of his fellow passengers—a mix of Heer ground troops and Luftwaffe airmen—seemed tipsy from preflight drinks. At least they shared Andy's joy to be heading home.

8

Ankunft

After what seemed like an eternity, Andy's flight touched down at Rhein-Main air base. But the hurry-up-and-wait was far from over. He still had to travel to the Stryker Cavalry Regiment's headquarters in Bavaria for his last few days of outprocessing.

He spent the next night holed up at an Air Force Bachelor Officers' Quarters (BOQ), waiting for a flight to Ramstein Air Base—the base nearest to Vilseck with regularly scheduled flights.

The long-distance phone lines in the United States were "temporarily out of service," so Andy was not able to call Kaylee. But he was able to e-mail her and get her e-mails in reply. They each sent dozens of notes during the two days and nights that Laine was stuck at Rhein-Main. For some reason the Skype voice and video service wasn't working. He knew their headquarters were in

Luxembourg, but he wondered where the Skype server was, and if that was causing the problem. He surmised that the server was probably in a fire-gutted building in some riot-ravaged city in the eastern United States.

It was while he was at Rhein-Main that the European Aviation Safety Agency (EASA) announced that all commercial flights to the United States had been suspended. Kaylee's e-mails then took on a frantic tone. In one, she wrote:

> Andy:
>
> GET HOME, SOON, DARLING!!! Ship yourself in a big Fed-Ex box if you have to! I am SOOOOO worried about you. I can't sleep, thinking about this travel mess.
>
> XXOOXX
>   —Kaylee

Although he was just as concerned as Kaylee, Andy tried to make his replies as upbeat as possible. In one of his last e-mails before checking out of the BOQ, he wrote:

> Subject: Re:RE: [U] Outprocessing & Travel Home!
> From: Laine Andrew CPT 2SCR (FWD)
>
> Classification: UNCLASSIFIED
>
> My Darling Kaylee:
>
> I cannot wait to hold you in my arms. Please remain prayerful, and do not worry. All that worrying doesn't accomplish anything.
>
> Read Philippians 4:6–7 and Psalm 46 and write them on your heart.

The commercial flights may have stopped, but there are still a few MAC flights. I also talked with a gal at the Military Travel Office, and she said that there are still flights going back and forth between Madrid and Mexico City. I will take a bus home from Mexico, if need be!!! Or I'll get a flight to Havana and rent a row-boat. I mean it. I WILL get home. Trust in the LORD. I'll get home, *Deo Volente*, but remember that we are on God's timetable.

You are in my Constant Thoughts and Prayers,
With My Love,

Andy

Classification: UNCLASSIFIED
If this e-mail is marked FOR OFFICIAL USE ONLY it may be exempt from mandatory disclosure under FOIA. DoD 5400.7R, "DoD Freedom of Information Act Program," DoD Directive 5230.9, "Clearance of DoD Information for Public Release," and DoD Instruction 5230.29, "Security and Policy Review of DoD Information for Public Release" apply.

While waiting for his flight to Ramstein, Andy discovered that all of the ATMs on base were shut down. He also learned that the BX, commissary, and NAAFI store were all operating on a cash-only basis, with no checks, credit cards, EC Cards, or debit cards accepted. Only the Burger King was still taking credit cards, and because of this, it was deluged with customers.

The second evening that he was stranded, Andy stopped at the Burger King and ordered a Whopper Combo and a beer. The cashier said, "That will be ninety-six dollars, please." Pulling out his VISA card, Laine muttered "That's highway robbery." A faceless voice behind him said, "Get used to it. It will be closer to two hundred bucks tomorrow." He turned to see an Air Force major, dressed in an olive drab nomex flight suit, with his blue "p-cutter" cap tucked into one of his leg pockets. In a more distinct voice Laine replied, "Signs of the times, I suppose."

Rio Arriba Youth Center, Gallina, New Mexico
October, the First Year

Shadrach Phelps sat on his bunk in the Rio Arriba Youth Center dormitory, looking glum. He was seventeen, but the other two boys were both only sixteen, so that made him the leader. He summed up the situation to them succinctly, "Basically, we're screwed."

As the Crunch set in, the boys had been warned that their days at the center were numbered. The school was about to be shut down. The Rio Arriba Youth Center was originally established in the 1940s as The Phelps School for Orphan Boys. It was sixty miles north of Albuquerque, on the edge of the Santa Fe National Forest, just north of the town of Gallina. Donations from churches had dwindled, so both the staff and the number of boys had been pared down substantially since their peaks in the early 1970s. When the Crunch started, there were just nineteen boys and three resident staff members remaining at the sprawling 160-acre center.

The orphans were given a sound education and taught the value of hard work—plenty of hard work. The center included eighty acres of irrigated hay fields, which provided some cash income for the school. It had two dormitories (one of them shuttered in the late 1980s), a classroom and multipurpose building, three staff residence buildings (one of which was unoccupied), a stable, and two large hay barns.

Shadrach Phelps was lanky, and dark-skinned—undoubtedly with at least half African-American blood—but his facial features showed some other, unidentified heritage. Like the other infants that had come to the orphanage without a name, he had been given the surname Phelps in honor of the school's benefactor, a wealthy widow from Santa Fe. She had passed away in 1962. After her death, the school was supported by church donations from fifteen different churches in New Mexico and West Texas, and the annual sale of hay. The Rio Arriba County road department sporadically filled the school's walk-in freezer with roadkill deer. All of the boys grew up accustomed to eating venison and learned how to field dress and butcher deer as taught by Diego Aguilar, who served as cook, wrangler, haying boss, and jack of all trades for the center.

Following the announcement of a school budget crisis and the planned closing of the school, fifteen of the nineteen boys had been claimed by family members. As they packed up and left, the remaining boys without any known relatives began to despair. The departures left just Aaron Phelps, who was the headmaster's favorite student, and the trio of Shad, Reuben, and Matthew. The headmaster made it clear that he would be adopting Aaron, but his stony silence about the other boys was devastating. The evening after Aaron moved into the headmaster's house, Shad, Reuben, and Matthew gathered to pray and talk.

"The way I see it, everyone's going to be starving here, inside a few weeks. The deer hunting has gone straight to *la mierda* since the mountain lion population explosion. And even if they wanted to grow row crops here instead of hay, the irrigation water will go away if the power goes out. This country is going back to a big desert, especially in the lower elevations."

Reuben chimed in, "Diego says the grid will probably collapse in a few weeks."

A voice from the hallway startled the boys, "That's right, it's going be a cold and hungry winter." It was Diego Aguilar. Diego walked into the room and sat down on a wooden chair that faced the bunk beds where the boys sat. He folded his hands across his potbelly.

"You Phelps boys are, as they say, 'in an unenviable position.'

You've got no *familia*. You are maybe just old enough to do a man's job, but there are no jobs anyhow. You can maybe go beg for a place to stay, maybe with one of the churches that still send the support money. Or maybe you could ask for a job and bed and board on one of the reservations—"

Matthew interrupted. "That's easy for you to say. You've got a real last name. But we're Indians who don't even know what tribe we belong to! I was a baby that got left in a fruit box on the doorstep of the Lutheran church in Rio Rancho. All that they knew was my first name. 'Please take good care of Matthew.' That was all that the note said. Not even signed."

Aguilar eyed the boys. Reuben Phelps and Matthew were obviously both American Indians, with round, fairly indistinct facial features that did not give a hint of a tribal connection. Hopi? Navajo? Zia? Mescalero? Probably not Apache.

The old Mexican said, "I'm sorry, you're right. Forget the reservations. They're practically starving there already. They been taking government handouts for too long."

After a pause, Aguilar went on, "I talked with the headmaster. He says you are each welcome to take two good saddle-broke horses. Two apiece. I'll get you all tacked up—each with one *vaquero* saddle and one pack saddle. The sleeping bags we got here are all cheapies, so you'll each get two of them. That way you can put one inside the other so you can sleep warm."

The boys looked at each other nervously and then turned toward Aguilar.

"I've got to warn you boys: Don't go anywhere near Albuquerque or Santa Fe. There's nothing but trouble in the cities these days. That's where they'll be hunting each other to eat. I'm not kidding. And stay away from the border. *Hombres malos*, there. And since winter is coming, you gotta stay out of the high country."

The boys nodded.

Shad asked, "So which way do we go?"

"My mama told me, in lean times you head toward the bean pot. I think you should go right on through the Jicarilla Apache Res, and go up toward the northwest corner of the state. That's pretty good country, and there, many places they have gravity-fed water—you know, from an irrigation ditch. Not like our water here, where water has gotta be pumped. You could stop at churches along the way and ask about finding work."

Reuben offered, "Maybe we could get jobs as cowboys."

"You've never roped a cow in your life," Shad chided.

"I could learn."

Diego Aguilar added: "He's right. You could learn. So I'll also give you boys *las reatas*. I still have several good lassos that your classmates never managed to destroy." He stroked his chin. "But don't forget, your main value is that you got strong backs. I'll send you each with a pair of flat-forged hay hooks and a pair of heavy gloves. I know for sure you can move hay bales. I seen you do it. You boys all know how to shoot, too, so you'll each get one of the school's old .22 target rifles. They are single-shots and their barrels are heavier than an anvil. But at least you'll be able to shoot rabbits. And from a long distance, seeing them, nobody will know that they're just .22s, so hopefully they will leave you alone."

Diego stroked his chin, and went on, "My plan is to send you boys with as much good camping gear as your pack horses can carry. Anything extra you can trade for food. Same for the .22 shells that I'm giving you. I won't tell the headmaster how many bricks of .22 ammo you have until after you are long gone."

The three boys nodded, and Diego continued, "The way I see it, he is treating you mean and sending you packing, so I have to balance it out by sending you out heavy, to give you the best chance possible."

"We should be fine," Shad added hopefully.

"I hate to see the headmaster cut you boys loose like this. But at least you've got some practical skills, and you're hard workers, and you'll have good horses under you."

"Don't worry about us, Diego," Matthew assured him.

Shadrach stood up to shake Aguilar's hand. "Thank you, sir. I promise you that we'll look after each other. So, yeah, don't worry about us. We're Phelpses, and that means even though we aren't brothers by blood, we're still brothers in Christ."

They spent the rest of the evening with Aguilar, packing.

9

Twisted

"Inflation is a special concern over the next decade given the pending avalanche of government debt about to be unloaded on world financial markets. The need to finance very large fiscal deficits during the coming years could lead to political pressure on central banks to print money to buy much of the newly issued debt."

—Former Federal Reserve chairman Alan Greenspan,
the *Financial Times*, June 26, 2009

Luke Air Force Base, Arizona
October, the First Year

The weeklong Diversity, Sensitivity, and Sexual Harassment class had one-hour lunch breaks. Even though his wife had packed him a lunch, Major Ian Doyle decided to hop in his car and take a drive around the base on his lunch hour. It was October, but still pleasantly in the high seventies and low eighties. Luke Air Force Base, adjoining the city of Glendale, Arizona, benefited from the sunny desert weather. This was one of the key reasons why it had been developed by the U.S. Air Force in the 1950s as one of its main centers for pilot transitional training and operational fighter squadrons. The base boasted "360 flying days a year," and given the prevailing weather, most of those were VFR—visual flight rules—days.

The class that he was in gave Doyle the creeps. He couldn't

stand to stay in the building during the lunch hour. The greatest irony was that one of the lead civilian contract instructors, an acne-scarred woman in her thirties, was hitting on some of his classmates—both fellow pilots and some of the doctors from the 56th Medical Group—during breaks. She had even leered at Doyle and made some suggestive remarks, though he frequently made a show of twirling his wedding band. The chaplain was right: "Flee from sin!" The last thing he wanted to do was share his lunch hour with a liberal bed-hopper.

Under the Air Force's new twisted rules on sexual harassment, officers of either sex of equal rank could be propositioned, as well as civilians within four steps of equivalent pay grade, all regardless of their marital status. And those rules only applied to duty assignments *within* each command. For individuals not assigned within the same command, an airman first class could date a colonel, or his wife, or both, without any repercussions. As near as Doyle could figure out, under the administration's "New Century Military" guidelines, only children, pets, and livestock were verboten. But even those, he was told, were "now under study, as gray areas" and had just tentatively been given the same "Don't ask, don't tell" protection that had previously been afforded to homosexuals. The change of policy made Ian wonder why he was sticking it out in the Air Force, hoping to make lieutenant colonel before his retirement. In recent years, promotions above O-3 had slowed to a snail's pace as the Air Force contracted in size. Ian had already been passed over for promotion once, and he had his doubts about the next promotion board meeting.

On his drive, Doyle was amazed by what he saw. Luke Air Force Base was becoming a ghost town. His own wing, the 56th Fighter Wing, had just started a rotation to Saudi Arabia, but clearly all of the other "tenant" units at the air base were depopulating while still ostensibly "mission capable" and "in place." The parking lot at the 56th Maintenance Group (MXG) was nearly empty, as was the lot for the Mission Support Group (MSG). The Base Exchange (BX) lot was also barren, since the BX had sold out of all their grocery inventory the week before—mostly to "blue card" and "gray card" retirees who lived in the surrounding communities. There were just a few would-be patrons seated in their cars. Ian assumed that they waited there in hopes of seeing an approaching delivery truck.

The entire Taiwan and Singapore air force training contingents had quietly decamped two weeks earlier, on the pretense of mobilization orders. There were no ritualistic drunken farewell parties this time. They just quickly got on commercial flights and left a considerable quantity of household goods behind in their haste.

The parking area for the 56th Med was less than half full, mostly with cars belonging to dental patients waiting to get some work done while any dental services were still available. Finally, closer to the hangars and flight line, he drove by the operational group's buildings. He counted only five cars and SUVs there. "Sweet Jesus," Doyle muttered to himself. "Where did everyone go?" Doyle had heard that there were desertions, but since he was no longer in a flightline squadron, he hadn't realized the extent of the problem. He surmised that once the mess halls ran out of their limited food supplies and the MREs kept on hand for short-term contingencies were gone, airmen started deserting in droves. And from what he had heard, when they went, they took a lot of equipment, fuel, and nearly every scrap of food on base with them.

Doyle pulled his car off to the side of the road and pulled out a thermos of *café con leche* and his lunch, two leftover *baleadas*—Honduran-style burritos—and an apple. He started munching absently, hardly noticing the taste. He was playing the *Passion, Grace, & Fire* CD with John McLaughlin, Paco de Lucía, and Al Di Meola. But since he was so absorbed with worrying about his homeschooled daughter, Linda, he didn't pay much attention to the music. He turned on the car radio and punched the pre-set for

KNST 790 AM. The news announcer was repeating an FAA order that all commercial airline flights in the United States had just been temporarily suspended because there was unrest in so many American cities, and in several instances planes had been hit by gunfire as they made takeoffs and landings.

Ian shouted, "No!" and slammed his fist on the dashboard.

Linda was on her annual six-week-long Grandmom and Grandpop trip, staying with Ian's parents in Plymouth, Michigan, an upscale suburb of Detroit. Linda was eleven years old and this was the first year that she had made the trip alone, escorted on the flight by an airline stewardess. After making the trip for several years in a row, accompanying their daughter, Blanca decided to stay home and relax and do some oil painting and pastels. "She's old enough to fly up there herself," Blanca had told Ian. "There's no connecting flight. It's a direct shot from Phoenix Sky Harbor to Detroit."

When class was over, Ian drove home to Buckeye, a thirty-five-minute commute from the base. It was originally a farming town, but it had gradually become a commuter bedroom and retirement community. The housing developments were an odd mix of 1950s and 1960s one-story houses with composition roofs, interspersed with neo-southwestern developments of earth-tone stucco three-thousand-square-foot McMansions built in the 1990s and in the decade of the aughts, just after the turn of the century. Interspersed between these developments, there were still many fields, mostly cultivated with cotton and alfalfa. There were also a couple of large dairy farms that produced milk and cream for Glendale and Phoenix.

The rent in Buckeye was just half what it would have been in Glendale. They also had benefited from a lower crime rate and much less smog. Ian had picked their house because it had an extra deep garage that had room for his hobby airplane, a Laron Star Streak, which was normally kept in its trailer with the wings removed.

The night before, Ian had had a lengthy discussion with Blanca. They were horribly worried about their daughter.

"I think that on Saturday I should fly up to Detroit personally to get her."

"But, Ian, all of the flights are cancelled."

"No, I mean a cross-country, in a D-model Viper. They're two-seaters. I can zip up there to get her and be back all in a day—that is, if my dad drives her down to meet me at the airport."

Blanca frowned and shook her head, but Ian continued in rapid fire: "Wayne County Airport is too big and it's close to Toledo, so that's too risky. The Canton-Plymouth airport is only two miles out of town, but it's only a 2,500-foot strip. I'm sure you remember, an F-16 *officially* needs 8,000 feet, but it's actually under 4,000 in a pinch. I suppose that's a little hard on the brakes. Like my F-16 Transition instructor used to say: 'If it's a short strip, then pop the 'chute and *stand* on those brakes, boy!' So I checked on the Internet last night: the Detroit Lakes–Wething strip is 4,500 feet. I could do that easily in good weather."

"Are you crazy, Ian? You've got sixteen years in. Just four years to go until you qualify for retirement. You steal a plane—"

"*Borrow* a plane," Ian interrupted.

"—you'll get court-martialed."

"I'll just log it as a cross-country," Ian argued.

"You put a civilian passenger in a fighter, it's a court-martial offense. You file a false flight plan, its at least an Article 15, maybe a court-martial. You make an unauthorized landing on a civilian strip of insufficient length, also probably a court-martial. Some busybody writes down the tail number with an 'LF' prefix, and the finger is pointing right at you. No way! You cannot play 'You Bet Your Bars' when you've got sixteen years in. *Es imposible.*" After a pause she added, "That's *muy loco!*"

Doyle meekly dipped his head to his chest. He said, "Look, I also thought about flying the Star Streak up there, but that would take at least six hops each way: there's only two seats. It would be a six-day round trip for one of us. I can't get that much leave on short notice."

"I agree, the Star Streak is out. With that many hops, I don't know where for sure you'd get avgas. You could get stranded in the middle of nowhere with no fuel."

Blanca went on: "We just have to wait until the riots die down in Detroit, and wait until they start up the commercial flights again, or you take a couple of days leave, and one of us—or maybe both—drives up there and back."

Ian frowned. "Do you know how many cities we'd have to drive through to get to Plymouth? The rioting is too unpredictable. We'd have to zigzag up there. And how will we get gas to get that far and back?"

Blanca hugged him, and said, "Look, this is just a temporary thing. Your parents, they live in a very safe neighborhood. The riots and lootings, they are just in Detroit, not any further. We wait until things calm down. If need be, we dip into our savings and we pay a charter pilot from one of the General-A strips in Michigan to fly her down here. If things keep going like they're going, the money will be *nada* in another month, so we might as well spend it. Let's just wait a few days. You can't take any leave until after you are done with your *fruta* class, anyway."

"Okay. Tomorrow is Tuesday, and the stupid course ends on Friday. But here's another idea: How about we rent a Cessna 172 or maybe a Beech Bonanza from the Glendale airport? We fly out at oh-dark-early on Saturday, we take turns on the yoke, with the other one napping, and in about four hops we fly straight to the Canton-Plymouth airport. Then we do a four- or five-hour RON and we get back here either late Sunday or early Monday. After all, I still have my civilian ticket. Your ASEL just lapsed, but who'll be looking if we rent the plane in my name?"

Blanca smiled. "With *El Infierno*, renting a plane will be expensive, but hey, renting a General Aviation plane's the perfect solution. In the morning I'll call around and find a plane. I'll work out all the refueling stops at little country airports—you know, private FBOs—I can call ahead or do e-mails and make sure which ones still got avgas to sell. This can work, Ian! We'll get Linda back home."

Major Doyle's unit was one of the last operational units in the active component of the U.S. Air Force still equipped with F-16s. The 56th Fighter Wing had just begun a rotation to Saudi in its first overseas deployment since its TO&E began the transition from a tactical training wing to a tactical fighter wing two years before. This change was necessitated by the simultaneous downsizing of the Air Force overall, the ramping-down of the F-16 fleet, and the emergence of the pitifully few "re-scoped" F-22 squadrons. Three years earlier, for political reasons, F-22 transition training had been shifted from Luke AFB to Shaw AFB in South Carolina. As it was explained to Doyle, the chairman of the House Armed Services Committee was a third-term South Carolina Democrat. Some last-minute petitions before Congress saved the 56th from extinction. It would go back to being equipped with all F-16s, with nearly all of them in operational squadrons. But the Armed Services Committee chairman made it clear: "Once F-16s are obsolete, so will be the whole 56th and its support groups."

Doyle came on board just a few months into the shift from pilot training to an operational wing. In the first staff weenie position of his career, Doyle was assigned as the wing maintenance officer. In recent weeks his duties necessitated spending most of his time doing paperwork at either the 56th Operations Group (OG) or the MXG hangars. It all seemed rather pointless, since all but a few members of his own wing were in Saudi. He expended many hours writing maintenance training plans and standard operating procedures (SOPs) for notional units that would be needed for a theater-wide war contingency. He realized that his unit would never get the funding for F-22 Raptors and that they were indeed doomed to eventual deactivation. His work seemed absolutely pointless.

Doyle had orders to catch up with the wing in Saudi in late November, but he dreaded doing the rotation. It would take him away from Blanca and Linda. With the current economic meltdown, he worried about their safety in his absence. Several times Ian thought out loud, "What if things get even worse?"

On one of his class breaks, Doyle used his cell phone to call one of the civilian technicians at the 56th OG headquarters who always had his finger on the pulse of the organization. The news startled Doyle. "The chief of staff of the Air Force is working up contingency plans for the emergency redeployment of almost all of the close-air-support aircraft in the Air Force inventory back to the States. Some know-nothing at the White House must have dreamed this one up! Rumor has it that our whole Wing will deploy to Hurlburt Field."

"Florida? What for?"

"Get this: 'riot control and looting suppression.' They want to be able to use close-air-support planes."

Doyle was flabbergasted. "What kinda bad weed they been smokin' at the White House? Use C-A-S planes against rioters? The collateral damage would be hideous!"

Doyle paid little attention to what was presented in the class for the rest of the day. His mind was racing.

When he got home, he found Blanca in tears. She ran to Ian's arms, sobbing. "Commercial flights are all still grounded. I spent the whole day on the *expletivo* phone and the *expletivo* Internet. I tried and tried to find a rental plane. I called as far away as Chandler, Laveen, Sun City. No go. Nobody, and I mean *no*body, is doing any more rentals. They say too many planes are getting stolen on 'no-return' flights. One of the managers said to me that they're getting told, like, 'You can keep my security deposit, but you have to send somebody to pick the plane up, in Montana.'"

"How many planes are getting stolen?"

"Before they cut off the rentals, like 80 percent. Some charter pilots were also getting hijacked, so they also stopped doing any charters, too. So then I started calling FBOs and the general aviation airports up in Michigan. It's the same thing up there. I can't find a charter outfit to fly her down, not for any sum of money. What are we going to do?"

Ian thought for a moment, then said, "Don't worry. My dad has several guns. He can handle any rioters that come down their block."

On Friday, just after Ian got home from his class, they got a call from one of his parents' neighbors in Plymouth, Michigan. Though she lived just across the street from the house, she was calling from Iowa. Sobbing, she said to Doyle, "Your dad shot two of the gang that were trying to kick in my front door. He saved my life, Ian. I am so thankful." There was a long pause, and then she went on, "I don't know how to say this, Ian. After your dad started shooting, they got really mad, and they surrounded your dad's house and used those Molotov things, and they burned it down—right down to the basement. Nobody got out of the house." She sobbed again, and then said, "Your daughter was in there. I'm so, so sorry!"

The next few days were very difficult for the Doyles. Ian took two days of emergency leave. Though they were grieving deeply, they still had current events on their minds. Over the weekend, the television news showed more and more American cities descending into chaos.

10

Initiative

"If man is not governed by God, he will be ruled by tyrants."
—William Penn, founder and first governor of Pennsylvania

Radcliff, Kentucky
November, the First Year

As the frequency of gunfire and police car sirens in Radcliff increased, Sheila decided that it was time to relocate. With her husband dead, there was nothing to keep them there. Consulting with her grandmother, Sheila ruled out moving back to Louisiana, which was even more chaotic than Kentucky. Sheila mentioned Bradfordsville, Kentucky, a small town that they had seen just once. It was a one-hour-and-twenty-minute drive east of Radcliff. "Do you remember it? It was way off the interstates, and there was an old store building for lease there."

"We have enough gas to get there?" Emily asked.

"Yeah, but not enough to drive back here if it doesn't work out."

Emily said softly, "Then let's pray."

They bowed their heads and prayed for ten minutes. Then they looked up at each other and smiled.

"You feel a conviction?" Sheila asked.

"*Oui, tout à fait.* Indeed I do."

They called Tyree into the room and started packing the car immediately.

The drive to Bradfordsville was stressful. Tyree nervously held the shotgun all the way there.

They encountered two roadblocks, both manned by sheriff's deputies. At the first, just outside Hodgenville, a brief radio call was made to check their license plate number. Sheila heard the deputy mention, "It's just two women and a kid." After a few anxious minutes of waiting, they were waved through.

The second roadblock was just west of Bradfordsville. This was strategically placed on a low bridge west of High View Drive, on State Highway 337. It consisted of six large trucks and truck trailers in a staggered formation, intended to slow the traffic to a slow, serpentine crawl. It was manned by a uniformed sheriff's deputy and two private citizens who were wearing jeans and baseball caps. All three held identical rifles that Sheila didn't recognize, but from their protruding magazines she knew that they were automatic or semiautomatic.

The deputy who approached Sheila's car window asked suspiciously, "What is your business here?"

"I'm going to see the owner of a commercial building that I saw was up for lease."

"Which one?"

"There wasn't a sign. There was an old building next to it, as I recall, the Superior Food Market."

"Well, they're *both* vacant now," the deputy grumbled.

"I intend to open a store in that smaller building, Lord willing."

The deputy nodded and remarked, "Well, somebody oughtta get a store going again here or there'll be folk starving." After a beat he added, "It takes a lots of guts to open a business in times like these. You just keep yourself safe. You have any trouble, just ask for me, Deputy Dustin Hodges, okay?"

Sheila nodded and smiled.

Deputy Hodges gave a sweep of his hand and said, "God bless you, ma'am."

As they proceeded to slowly drive through the remainder of the roadblock's sharp S-turns, Emily quoted one of her favorite sayings, from the play *A Streetcar Named Desire*: " 'I have always depended on the kindness of strangers.' "

The old store building was on the main street running through Bradfordsville. It was sandwiched between the defunct Superior Foods and a gas station, also closed. At the gas station, a large hand-painted sign across the boarded front door proclaimed: "NO GAS."

Sheila got out and examined the building. It was of the old false-front style and looked to have been built in the 1920s or even earlier. Peering through the dusty windows, Sheila could see a small sales floor ringed by a semicircle of glass cabinets. Behind was a doorway leading to a back room. There appeared to be an apartment upstairs.

A small hand-penned sign taped inside the window read: "For Sale or Lease, Contact Hollan Combs," and gave an area code 270 phone number.

Sheila pulled out her notepad. On the inside of the front cover she saw something that her late mother had penned the year before she died of uterine cancer:

> "A prudent *man* foreseeth the evil, and hideth himself: but the simple pass on, and are punished."
>
> —PROVERBS 22:3

Sheila jotted down the name and phone number on a blank page.

She told Emily and Tyree to wait in the car. Then she strode toward the pay phone booth at the gas station.

Tyree protested: "Mom, the phones aren't workin'. Not even the cell phone."

"I know, I know."

Thankfully, the plastic phone book holder still held a local phone book. Listed under C she found: "Combs H, 200 S. 6th Street, Brdfsvl."

The house was just two blocks away. Again leaving her son and grandmother in the car, Sheila knocked on the door of a 1960s-style house. A weathered sign read: "Combs Soils Lab."

The man who answered the door was in his seventies, gaunt, with thick black plastic-framed glasses. He carried a stubby Dan Wesson .357 revolver in an inside-the-waistband holster. He asked, "Can I hep you?"

"My name is Sheila Randall. I would like to lease that store building and apartment above it—next to the gas station. You own it, right?"

Combs seemed hesitant, "Well, there *is* water working here in town—it's all gravity from a big spring up by the Taylor County line—but no power, and I don't even know what to charge in rent these days."

"I propose five dollars a month."

The old man laughed and slapped the side of his thigh. "You gotta be joking. Five dollars won't even buy you a piece of penny candy."

"I mean five dollars in *silver* coin."

Hollan Combs jerked his chin back and said, "Oh, well, that's different." After pondering for a moment, he said, "I'll need you to pay two months in advance, but you can lease it from month to month after that. I'll also need a signed statement from you that you're getting it as is, with no guarantee that the power will ever come back on. If and when it does, the power bill will be separate."

Just a few minutes later Combs unlocked the store's front door and ushered in Sheila, Tyree, and Emily.

"My last tenants here were brothers. They had a unique combination gun, cigar, and liquor store. They called it 'Alcohol, Tobacco, and Firearms' and they even answered the phone that way. That was good for a laugh. But the recession just went on and on—double-dip and then triple-dip, you know. They folded a year ago. I heard they moved back to Tennessee."

Sheila examined the glass display cases as Combs went on, "The roof was redone just three years ago. The apartment ain't much, but it's been repainted since the 'ATF' guys moved out. I had a man clean the chimney, and he put a new elbow on the back of the wood stove, since the old one had rusted out. The place *was* clean, but I'm afraid the mice have made a mess up there."

Sheila was pleased to see that the store building had plenty of windows that provided light to conduct business in the absence of grid power. Traces of the building's former use lingered. The back room was still cluttered with empty gun and whiskey boxes, and one of the glass display cabinets still had a distinct tobacco smell. There was an empty twenty-rifle rack on the north wall of the store, behind the counter. The only entrance to the apartment was via an inside staircase that led up from the store's small window-less back room. The stairs creaked as they walked up. The apartment had two bedrooms, a gas cooking range, a small Jøtul wood/coal stove, an electric refrigerator (propped open with a stick of firewood), and a small bathroom with a toilet and a tub-shower.

"Bring me the lease papers. I'll take it," Sheila said.

Less than an hour later they had unpacked the car and moved in. Sheila's packets of seeds filled two of the glass display cases, in neat rows. They put a few other items suitable for trading in another case.

"Not a lot to start with," Emily remarked.

"Trust in the Lord, Gran, we trust in the Lord."

Emily warned, "And you know the ten dollars in silver that you gave Mr. Combs was almost all the coins we had. I gots just three silver quarters and one dime left."

"Trust in the Lord, Gran, trust in the Lord."

Sheila dug out her tempera paints and soon started painting signs on the inside of the front windows. The signs read: "The Seed Lady," "Sundry Merchandise," "Buy—Sell—Trade," and "Open 8 to 8. Closed Sundays." She had her first customer walk in even before the paint had dried. He traded a box of 12-gauge shotgun shells for three packets of seeds. In the next few days a steady stream of customers began to arrive, all eager to trade. Eventually, some came from as far as the towns of Lebanon and Campbellsville. Sheila soon developed a reputation as a savvy yet fair storekeeper.

People brought Sheila all sort of things to trade for seeds, or at least to try to trade for them. Most of what they offered was junk, and Sheila got in the habit of saying politely yet forcefully, "Pass." But she did trade for hard items, like tools, cans of WD-40, batteries, rolls of duct tape, ammunition, and hardware like nails and nuts and bolts. She made it her habit to reject any appliance that required electricity, since the grid power was down, and batteries were in short supply.

Late on the afternoon of the sixth day after they arrived, a slightly drunk man brought in an old Pilot brand vacuum tube table radio that had a wooden case. It had both AM and short-wave bands, and according to the man it worked well, back when utility power was available. He also said that his grandfather put all new capacitors in it, to replace the older, paper-wrapped ones. Sheila was about to reject it when her mother asked: "Look in the back. Has it got a transformer? And how many tubes does it have?"

Puzzled, Sheila did as she was told, which was easy, since the radio's original back cover was missing: "It's got no transformer, and it has five tubes."

"Go ahead and trade for that."

"But, Gran, it takes AC power. We don't have a generator."

Emily insisted, "You go ahead and trade for that radio, and I'll explain later."

Sheila drove a hard bargain, trading just one packet of squash seeds for the old radio. After the man had left, Emily gave an explanation: "Sheila girl, that radio is what your late Grandpère— rest his soul—he call an 'All-American Five' radio. He used to fix them. With five tubes and no transformer, it can run on AC *or* on the DC power. Out on the bayou in the old days, where there was no co-op power line, our kin would hook up ten or eleven car batteries in a row. That makes you about 115 volts of DC power. That will run one of them radios for days and days! And what do you see all over the place these days? I tell you what: abandoned cars with no gasoline. But they each got a 12-volt battery, now don't they? You put out the word that you'll trade for car batteries that still have a strong charge. We're gonna listen to the shortwave, maybe even tonight!"

11

Provisional Beginnings

"There are two methods, or means, and only two, whereby man's needs and desires can be satisfied. One is the production and exchange of wealth; this is the economic means. The other is the uncompensated appropriation of wealth produced by others; this is the political means."

—Albert Jay Nock, *Our Enemy, The State* (1935)

Radcliff, Kentucky
Late October, the First Year

The situation in Radcliff was out of control. The sound of gunfire punctuated every night. There were an average of eight home invasion robberies per day, and most cases went unsolved. Many were never even investigated. The mayor had left town with no notice, towing a Ryder rental trailer, with no indication of his destination. The chief of police had been shot and killed, and more than half of the police officers were not showing up for work.

It was just after seven a.m. and Maynard Hutchings was sitting in his bathrobe in his den, drinking some of his last remaining jar of instant coffee, alternating between listening to his police scanner and his CB radio. The latest rumor was that Washington, D.C., had burned down—all of it. His wife came into the kitchen and asked expectantly, "Well?"

"Well, *what*, darlin'?"

"Well, what are you gonna *do*? Isn't it time you called a meeting or somethin'? Ain't you the *chairman*?"

He nodded. He was chairman of the Hardin County Board of Supervisors. In a city without a mayor or even an acting mayor, and with just an acting police chief, he had more right than anyone to try to sort things out. The utility power was off, but the local phones were still working. Maynard started making calls.

None of the other county board members would agree to meet. They thought that it would be unsafe and that their families would be in danger in their absence. Two of them gave Hutchings their resignations verbally.

Then he started calling some of his golfing friends to serve as stand-ins. He set a meeting time for two o'clock that afternoon at the county courthouse. Almost as an afterthought, he called to invite General Uhlich. Under the Army's new Streamlined Management system, Major General Clayton Uhlich wore two hats. He was both the post commander of Fort Knox and chief of Armor—the head of the U.S. Army's tanker school and armor development programs. All that Hutchings knew about Clay Uhlich was that he was a two-star general who drank Scotch before five p.m. and that he cheated at golf.

Rio Arriba Youth Center, Gallina, New Mexico
Late October, the First Year

The Phelps boys were on the trail leading west from the Rio Arriba Youth Center by eight the next morning. The headmaster, obviously embarrassed by the situation, didn't even come to the stable to say good-bye to the boys. Just as Aguilar had promised, he sent them out heavy with each saddle horse equipped with full-size saddlebags, and sleeping bags carried on the pillions, and smaller saddlebags at their fenders. The packhorses—all large, gentle, "bombproof" geldings—had full loads in bulging *alforjas* hanging from their packsaddle trees. Each packsaddle was equipped with a fairly new rubberized brown canvas cover secured by diamond hitches. Aguilar had thought through the packing lists very carefully. He even provided each boy separate bills of sale for each of their horses as proof that they were not stolen.

Aguilar closely watched the boys as they packed their loads, adjusted the girth straps, and dogged-down the diamond hitches. Matthew asked him for help, but Aguilar wagged his finger, admonishing, "No, no, no. You won't have my help out on the trail, so don't go askin' for it now. You gotta show me that you can tack this boy up, *tu solito*." After a couple of more tries, Matthew finally got the diamond knot centered and the ropes cinched tightly. He gave a big smile when he did. Slapping him on the back, Aguilar exclaimed, "You can be prouda that!"

After the three boys had mounted their horses and straightened out the leads for their packhorses, Diego Aguilar shook their hands. He advised Shadrach, "Ready or not, you're going out into a man's world, sink or swim, and I hate to say, it's a world of hurt in some places right about now. We're going to be praying for you. You take good care of yourselves and these horses. *¡Vaya con Dios!*" The boys said thank-yous and then raised their hats and waved them at the headmaster, who was standing outside of his office two hundred yards away. He raised his hand and waved in reply. All three boys tried to hide the fact that they were crying.

When the boys reached a level spot a mile up French Mesa Road, Shad called a halt. They looked back on the patchwork of fields in the valley below. Shad said, "Mr. Aguilar wanted me to wait until we were away from the center to get this out. He didn't want the headmaster to make a big fuss, since all that he told him about us getting was the .22s."

Handing his horse's reins to Reuben, Shad loosened his bedroll bag from behind his saddle and rolled it out, exposing the two halves of a well-worn Marlin Model 1893 takedown rifle. The front half was nestled in a scabbard. With a bit of fumbling, Shad assembled the rifle, just as Aguilar had showed him how to do, and loaded it with seven flat-tipped .30-30 cartridges. He emptied the remainder of the twenty-round box into his jacket pocket and snapped it shut. Then, after attaching the .30-30's scabbard to his saddle, he stowed his .22 rifle under the hitch ropes on his pack-horse. "Okay, now we got us a rifle that can knock down a deer or stop a predator."

"Yeah, the kind that come on two legs," Matthew added.

Luke Air Force Base, Arizona
Late October, the First Year

Ian Doyle's last two days at Luke Field were surreal. As he drove through the Lightning Gate at the corner of Litchfield Road at 0635, he could see that it was completely unmanned. Incongruously, a "Threat Level Orange" warning sign was posted next to the gate. He spent the morning driving around the post, looking for anyone still on duty and doing a visual inventory of the base's assets. At the NCO housing complex, he saw a group of gang members brazenly loading loot into the back of a pickup truck.

Doyle found that there were no aircraft remaining on the ramp. All of the military vehicles had also disappeared—either "requisitioned" or stolen. This included all of the fuel trucks. The C-21 Learjet used by the general staff and several F-16s were gone.

Ian then spent most of the afternoon searching for fuel containers. He couldn't find any gas cans. He eventually found dozens of empty two-liter soda pop bottles in the recycling Dumpsters near the BX. He took these to the POL terminal and found that some-one had left a small Honda generator there. They had rigged it to energize two of the fuel pumps. One of these pumps dispensed 100LL, a leaded high-octane aviation gasoline. That afternoon he returned to Buckeye with almost 140 gallons of 100LL in the cargo area of his Suburban with the rear seat folded down. A few of the containers had leaking caps, so he spent most of the drive with his head out the window, sucking fresh air. He prayed that he wouldn't be ambushed, since the slightest spark would surely cause a huge explosion.

Ian waited until after dark, then he and Blanca carried the fuel containers to the backyard and covered them with a tarp.

The next morning he was back on base at 0615. He spent the morning wandering through the largely abandoned 56th Operations Group (OG) and 56th Maintenance Group hangars and buildings. By 0930 he found only a few young pilots and a couple of E-5 NCOs. The rest were lower-rank enlisted airmen. After finding such a pitiful contingent still on base, Doyle was dejected. He went back to the 56th Maintenance Group hangar and office buildings and came upon a lieutenant who was rummaging through closets and wall lockers, vainly looking for something edible. "Lieutentant, spread the word. I want you to announce that there will be an all-hands formation, for all groups, in the main 56th OG hangar at 1100 hours," he ordered.

By 1100, only twenty-one ground crew and seven pilots had gathered. There was just one other captain. They quizzed each other and found that Doyle's date of rank was eighteen months earlier, giving Ian seniority. In the distance they could see smoke rising from fires all over Phoenix, and there was an almost constant crackle of gunfire. Some of it sounded nearby, in Glendale. Doyle ordered the assembled gaggle to fall in to a proper formation. He called: "Attention! Stand at . . . ease!"

He took a deep breath and began, "Gentlemen, this is a sad day for me and a sad day for the Air Force. As a captain, I am the ranking officer on base, so that makes me the de facto commander of all of the Luke facilities. As you know, the rotation to Saudi had our numbers greatly depleted even before the Crunch. And now there's no grid power, and the backup ATC generators have run out fuel. The water towers are now dry and of course there's no electricity to refill them. As I'm sure you've heard, there were a lot of emergency requisitions of aircraft, some under dubious pretenses. More recently, there have been several aircraft that were without a doubt *stolen*, with no flight plans filed and without benefit of tower clearance. Those were our last flightworthy aircraft. The local gangs are starting to strip outlying buildings, and there are no more security personnel to maintain any kind of perimeter. We have no unit integrity or any functioning chain of command. I have determined that our position is untenable, and we are incapable of carrying out any useful mission. At this point, even our personal safety is at risk."

Doyle let that sink in and then continued, "The last straw was this morning, when I was informed that there isn't so much as a can of beans left in the dining facilities. The bottom line is that we can't keep you if we can't *feed* you. Therefore, I'm hereby releasing all of the personnel on base. As of the end of this formation, your status will be on indefinite leave until either your ETS date or until you hear further orders from any commissioned Air Force officer from any command that is in a bona fide position of authority. Gentlemen, you are hereby released. You will be in my prayers. That is all. Dismissed!"

After the formation, Ian drove to the Air Force Security arms room. He found that the front door's latch mechanism was missing. It had been cut out with a cutting torch. Inside, he found that the building had been ransacked. The bodies of two dead men in civilian clothes but with short-cropped military haircuts were sprawled on the floor. Between them was an oxyacetylene torch cart. Both of the men had been shot. Their bodies were puffy and smelled putrid. The sight sickened Doyle, who had never seen a human corpse up close before. To Doyle, it was obvious that the men had used the cutting torch to get into the arms room. Nine rifle and pistol racks had been cut open and emptied. What had happened after that was anyone's guess. Perhaps there had been a double cross. All of the arms racks were empty, save one that was still locked. It held five M16A2 rifles. Doyle muttered to himself, "Well, I can't leave these unsecured."

He lit the torch and cut the lock off the remaining rack. Carrying out the five M16s to his Suburban took just one trip with the rifles slung over both shoulders. His search of the building revealed a box of twenty-three loaded M16 magazines that was underneath a duty roster binder in a file cabinet. He also found just one M16 cleaning kit.

Anahuac, Texas
Late October, the First Year

When the Texas power grid went down, Dallas, Houston, San Antonio, Dallas, Austin, and Fort Worth were soon overcome by riots and looting. Once the local radio station reported simultaneous rioting in all of those cities, Garcia declared it was time for La Fuerza to roll.

A total of fifty-three adults and twenty-three children wheeled out of the Anahuac warehouse in a parade of twenty-six vehicles, and they never came back. They poured out of the warehouse like hornets from a nest. Downtown Anahuac was first on their list.

12

Little Ricky

"A nation is the more prosperous today the less it has tried to put obstacles in the way of the spirit of free enterprise and private initiative. The people of the United States are more prosperous than the inhabitants of all other countries because their government embarked later than the governments in other parts of the world upon the policy of obstructing business."

—Ludwig von Mises, *The Anticapitalistic Mentality* (1972)

Elizabethtown, Hardin County, Kentucky
Late October, the First Year

"I hereby call this meeting to order. Sally is taking the minutes." Hutchings scanned the faces around the table. Most of them looked nervous and uncertain. Uhlich just looked slightly bemused. There were three attorneys, two bank managers, an IRS special agent, and Uhlich. Aside from the general, Hutchings had known most of the men since high school. Seated by the wall were the county sheriff, the acting chief of police, and two men wearing OCPs who had arrived with Uhlich: a command sergeant major and a young lieutenant, Uhlich's aide-de-camp. A court reporter sat to one side, silently tapping at a battery-powered stenotype machine. The County Office Building smelled musty with the power out.

Hutchings continued: "Given the, uh, unprecedented situation nationwide, it has become clear that action must be taken to restore order in Hardin County and beyond. I've asked General Uhlich to be part of this emergency council in an advisory capacity. I need y'all's agreement that we will take whatever means are necessary to get things set back in order."

There were nods of agreement, so Hutchings went on, "I'd like to make a motion that martial law be declared, amplifying the existing declaration from the state of Kentucky, and that henceforth looters will be shot on sight. Requisitioning of supplies and manpower will be made by force, if need be."

Bloomfield, New Mexico
May, the First Year

L. Roy Martin hired the Cuban just six months before the Crunch, snatching him away from a refinery in Oklahoma. Ricardo Lopez had a reputation as a very resourceful petroleum engineer. Growing up in Cuba in the 1970s and 1980s, he had learned to improvise everything. Under Lopez's leadership, the Bloomfield plant's Unit No. 2 was immediately diversified, adding the ability to isolate and decant a variety of fractions and compounds that previously had been dismissed as uneconomical for the plant. Heretofore, working with Four Corners Light Sweet Crude and natural gas was seen as economical for just light fuels.

Having been given carte blanche by Martin, Lopez soon developed a reputation as a space hog, filling up nearly all of the available warehouse space with plastic containers of various shapes and sizes and in large quantities.

He bought thousands of unmarked five-gallon oil cans (the type most typically used for commercial sale of hydraulic fluid), military-specification twenty-liter "Scepter" cans and spouts, and thirty thousand empty one-quart oil bottles. Lopez bought so many small containers that additional storage space had to be brought in: fourteen continental express (CONEX) forty-foot shipping containers were purchased, repainted white to match the Bloomfield storage tanks, and lined up in a phalanx next to the Bulk Lube building, near the front gate. These CONEXes were stuffed full of factory-new unlabeled bottles, jugs, cans, and small drums of all descriptions.

It was Lopez's large purchase of the Scepter cans that caused Phil McReady, the plant manager, to finally complain to Martin. McReady walked into L. Roy's office with a stern look on his face. He was carrying a copy of the Scepter purchase order. McReady slapped the PO down on Martin's desk and exclaimed, "Sir, have you seen this?"

Martin looked up from his oversize flat-screen monitor and pivoted his chair. He tilted his head down to look at the document with his bifocals. "Well, not this actual generated PO, but Rico and I did discuss it, and we did agree that eight thousand of the twenty-liter cans, and three thousand donkey-d . . . ah, 'spouts' was a good number. Our only debate was about how many of the spouts should be the small-diameter type, for unleaded gas."

"But, Ray, those cans and spouts are banned from civilian sale in the U.S. because they don't meet the CARB-compliance rules. Now, I mentioned that fact to Lopez yesterday, and he just said to me, 'I know they're banned, but we can still get them if we say they are for export.' Is he crazy? How will we ever recoup that investment? We aren't in the export market! We don't even have any sales representation in Mexico. I'm sure you know PEMEX has that market sewed up tight in a sweet little deal with the PRI party. It's a total monopoly down there. So, why buy all those cans if we have no market? This doesn't make any sense to me! And Lopez has this strange fixation with small containers. We're in the bulk business. We don't package itty-bitty retail containers. We don't have the distribution channels. This just doesn't compute."

Martin chuckled. "I think in less than a year you'll be *thanking* Dr. Lopez profusely for buying the gazillion containers, and maybe even wondering why we didn't buy more of them. The way the economy is headed, we're in for some deep trouble."

McReady gave Martin a puzzled look.

Martin explained, "The Schumer is about to hit the fan. Just suffice it to say that I believe that the marketplace and the legislative environment are about to shift substantially, so fuel-can legalities will be the least of our concerns. Just keep in mind that I don't have a board of directors to answer to. This plant is mine. I paid *cash* for it, and although some of the things here may seem unorthodox, I have my reasons. It's my baby."

Without giving time for the plant manager to respond, L. Roy went on, "So, henceforth, I expect you to mention Dr. Lopez's projects only if there is a safety issue that is not being properly resolved, or if you think that there is some malfeasance." Martin clasped his pudgy hands together and rested them on the desk. He put his chin down and eyeballed McReady.

McReady gave a quiet "Understood," and walked out.

Ricardo Lopez's shift in emphasis for the plant at first mystified and soon chafed old-timers like McReady. They considered him a bit of a mad scientist and thought that most of his projects would be unlikely to break even. Since Lopez was Cuban and only five feet three inches tall, he was soon nicknamed "Ingeniero Ricky Ricardo" or "Little Ricky." It was not until after the Crunch that they all realized that L. Roy and Lopez had repositioned the company to be able to continue to operate in the midst of a massive economic upheaval.

Immediately after the Crunch began, Martin ordered three of the plant's four units mothballed and closed out all the company's existing commercial contracts. "No paper money accepted. Silver only!" Martin decreed. Gasoline, diesel, and propane sold for twenty cents per gallon, payable in pre-1965 U.S. silver coins or equivalent weight in .999 fine silver trade dollars. Empty Scepter fuel cans were $4 each in silver coin, and their spouts were fifty cents. Martin began paying his employees in silver, and they had the opportunity to buy gas at a 10 percent discount. The average wage was $1.20 per day—all paid in pre-1965 U.S. silver coins. Their feedstock suppliers were happy to be paid in a mixture of silver and transferable vouchers for finished product. In many ways the business model for the refinery was similar to before the Crunch. It was only the scale that had changed. But the smaller scale of production made for a tight profit margin, since many of the overhead costs in running the plant were the same, whether they were running all four refinery units or just one.

At L. Roy's direction, seventeen refinery employees with recent combat experience in the Big Sandbox became full-time security guards for the Bloomfield plant, working round-the-clock shifts. Many of them were armed with "black guns" from Martin's extensive gun collection: AR-15s, M4s, M1As, AR-10s, L1A1s, and HKs.

13

Kasserne

"Inflation has now been institutionalized at a fairly constant 5% per year. This has been scientifically determined to be the optimum level for generating the most revenue without causing public alarm. A 5% devaluation applies, not only to the money earned this year, but to all that is left over from previous years. At the end of the first year, a dollar is worth 95 cents. At the end of the second year, the 95 cents is reduced again by 5%, leaving its worth at 90 cents, and so on. By the time a person has worked 20 years, the government will have confiscated 64% of every dollar he saved over those years. By the time he has worked 45 years, the hidden tax will be 90%. The government will take virtually everything a person saves over a lifetime."

—G. Edward Griffin

Laine's flight to Ramstein was on a C-17 with a mixed load of cargo and passengers. About thirty passengers lined one wall, on flip-down seats. It was an uneventful but noisy flight. He wore his earplugs. While on the flight, he composed draft e-mails to send to Kaylee and to his brother. Then he read some psalms.

After arriving at Ramstein, Andy got nervous when he saw a scene unfold in an adjoining hangar. A Texas National Guard unit that was on an emergency redeployment back from Bosnia was undergoing a "health and welfare" inspection overseen by officers and senior NCOs from the unit as well as some MPs. All of the troops had to completely unpack their duffel bags and backpacks. They even had dog handlers there, with German shepherds sniffing through the spread-out baggage. As an officer traveling alone and on a flight *inside* Germany, it was unlikely that Laine would ever be searched. And if he was, he wondered if his forged hand receipt would stand up to scrutiny. After all, it was fairly common knowledge that SIG P228s (called M11s by the U.S. Army) were not on the TO&Es of any but a few CID and MP units.

At Ramstein, there was more frustration: Because of fuel economy measures, he would have to wait until the next day to get transport to Grafenwöhr Training Center. From there he could easily catch a ride to Rose Barracks, his unit's home near Vilseck. So it was one more night in an Air Force BOQ.

There was no wireless Internet service at the "Q," so he was forced to "war walk" with his laptop to find an open wireless network. He finally found one in an NCO accompanied housing complex. After he had logged on, he sent out his draft e-mails and checked his in-box. There were three new "Hurry home" e-mails from Kaylee. Then he checked the AFN Germany weather page and the HQUSAEUR G3 Road Conditions Web page. Out of curiosity, he checked the spot price of gold at Kitco.com. He was startled to see gold at $5,453 per ounce. It had gained $312 per ounce in the past twenty-four hours. Since his laptop's battery was down to 32 percent, he turned it off and walked back to the BOQ. He was in a foul mood.

The next morning at breakfast, he discovered that the local Internet was up but that no connections to anywhere in the United States were working—for both e-mail and Web pages. The AFN television news soon reported the same Internet outage, with no known time or date for resumption of service. Andy shut down his laptop and prayed.

The bus to Graf at noon the next day was crowded. Most of the passengers carried six or more loaded shopping bags. They said that they had been forced to come to Ramstein because the shelves at the small commissary at U.S. Army Garrison Grafenwöhr were nearly stripped clean.

Simultaneously, the price of food on the civilian economy—in the town of Grafenwöhr—became astronomical, after the conversion from U.S. dollars to euros.

Andy overheard two military wives sitting in the seats ahead of him, discussing their mandatory next-of-kin evacuation orders (NEOs), NEO contingency suitcases, and the lack of transport to the United States. They were quite anxious and at a loss as to what they should do. While on the bus, Andy copied all of his personal files onto a flash-drive memory stick. He also copied the PDFs of several field manuals, including a joint service "Survival, Rescue, and Escape" manual, several out-of-copyright books on primitive skills like candlemaking, and a copy of the book *Where There Is No Doctor*. Then he took a deep breath and deleted all of his personal files from the laptop.

Once he had arrived at Graf, Laine borrowed a cell phone to call for a ride to Rose Barracks. But before he could finish, he was interrupted by a staff sergeant who had overheard him. He said, "Sir, if you don't mind riding in a War Pig, I'm headed to Rose in just a few minutes." Andy recognized him as a supply NCO from one of his unit's sister squadrons. Laine nodded and gave a thumbs-up to the NCO and then, turning back to the phone, said, "Strike that—I just got a lift. Out here!" He flipped the phone closed.

The sergeant helped Laine with his bags as they walked to the M1078A1 truck. The two-and-a-half-ton truck—the replacement for the venerable M35 deuce-and-a-half—was an ugly boxy truck with a long step up to the cab. This was the same up-armored variant that Andy had ridden in many times in Afghanistan. A corporal was standing guard behind the tailgate, holding an M4 with a magazine inserted. It seemed odd, seeing that level of security in Germany. To Andrew, it looked more like A-stan mode than what he was used to seeing in Germany.

As they loaded Laine's baggage, Andy could see a large pile of boxes and crates with "ORM-D" labels and large orange diamond-shaped "Class B Explosives" stickers.

"Ammo?" he asked incredulously. He cleared his throat and asked, "I thought that none of the squadrons were doing range fire until next April."

"Sir, I guess you've been out of the loop. At 2330 last night Regiment put everyone on an alert for civil disturbances."

"Whoa! Sounds serious."

Laine's first stop at Rose Barracks was the brigade orderly room. It was humming with activity. Before he even had a chance to put his bags down, Colonel Olds spotted him and shouted: "Andrew! Good to see you finally made it back here. Transportation problems?"

"Yes, sir, plenty. A major Charlie Foxtrot almost every step of the way." He set down his overseas bag and flight bag but held on to his duffel bag. They shook hands.

"Well, I'm glad to see you back. We could really use your help. I think for the time being, I'm going to lend you to the S3 shop up at Regiment."

"Sir, with all due respect, I've passed my active duty obligation date. That was seventeen days ago. I'm just back here to TI my gear, clear quarters, and outprocess."

"Oh, that's right. Hmmmm . . . and if I remember correctly, you have a fiancée waiting for you." After a pause, Olds said, "Well, at least *one* of my staff is going to make it back to CONUS this year." He sighed, clamped his hand on Andy's shoulder, and said in a quieter voice, "Good luck, son."

Laine's next stops were the arms room, where he turned in his

M4 carbine, and the NBC cage, where he turned in his M40 protective mask. After so many months of deployment, he felt naked without them. For the next two days he had brief moments of panic each time he stood up, realizing that his weapon was missing. But remembering that he still had the SIG P228 buried in the bottom of his duffel bag gave him some comfort.

By regulation, U.S. military service members always mustered out of active duty inside the United States. But a very recent emergency order from the Army Personnel Command (PERSCOM) stipulated that anyone of E4 pay grade or higher could now be released from active duty in situ anywhere except inside combat theaters at the discretion of a brigade S1 or higher. And a release for anyone E6 or higher could be made even inside a combat theater with a divisional commander's approval.

At just after 1600, Laine checked into the Rose Barracks BOQ and finagled a field-grade single room by mentioning that he was in his last few days of service and that he was exhausted from his long journey. After dropping off his bags in the room and getting a shower, he rushed over to the squadron S4 cage in a nearby warehouse. He wanted to get there before close of business for the day. There he checked out the key to the luggage cage, where he had two footlockers and a large cardboard box in storage. All three items were stenciled "1LT Andrew Laine—8277," the last four digits of his Social Security number. Luckily, his items were stacked together near the *top* of the eight-foot-high pile that lined one side of a sixty-foot-deep security cage. Using a large cart, he retrieved his items, signed a release form, and returned the cage key.

Although he was entitled to have these items shipped back to the United States as hold baggage, Laine realized that, given the circumstances, he would probably never see them again. It was better to sell or give away most of the gear as soon as possible. So he borrowed a two-wheel hand truck overnight and got a ride back to the BOQ.

Andy put a fresh set of batteries in his Kaito KA202L compact general coverage receiver radio and dialed in 1107 kHz AM for the local Armed Forces Network station, AFN Bavaria ("The Big Gun"). The transmitter was just outside of Vilseck, so it boomed in loud and clear. He caught the end of *The Afternoon Mix* show, then heard the familiar top-of-the hour announcement: "It's six o'clock in Central Europe, and AFN is on the air!" Andy listened to the news summary while he sorted gear. It was more bad news.

From the news reports, the rioting seemed to be the worst in India, Pakistan, Israel, Brazil, and the eastern United States. There were also some riots reported in French cities with large Muslim populations. But unlike in previous uprisings, the French police had the gloves off. They were shooting rioters on sight.

Andy Laine hadn't seen the contents of his footlockers and boxes for nineteen months. The first footlocker was completely filled with books. He emptied it onto the other bed in his room and then carried it to the BOQ foyer, where he left it standing on end with its lid swung open. Atop it he taped a sign: "MOVING SALE—TONIGHT ONLY—2.4 GHz Laptop, Books, CDs, DVDs, Clothes, and More! 1830 Hrs. TONIGHT ONLY—BOQ Room 106."

Andy changed into civilian clothes and popped the top of a can of Afri-Cola. He continued sorting. Just a few minutes later there was a knock at the door. He answered it to find a pair of black female second lieutenants from down the hall. One of them asked, "Are you Lieutenant Laine?"

"Captain, actually."

"Oh, sorry, sir. We, uh, we just saw your footlocker with the sign. Can you start your sale now?"

"Sorry, but I'm not ready yet. Give me until about 1820 to sort through all this and come back here with cash. I'd prefer euros."

"Will do, sir."

After they left, he started sorting books. Laine's collection included a lot of classics, biographies, Christian apologetics, reference books, and military field manuals.

After some deliberation, he settled on carrying just four books with him: his King James Bible, a compact copy of the *SAS Survival Guide* by John "Lofty" Wiseman, a small English-French/French-English dictionary and phrasebook, and a copy of *FM 5-34, Engineer Field Data.*

The books that it pained him the most to sell were his hardback set of *Matthew Henry's Commentaries* and his set of *The Rational Biblical Theology of Jonathan Edwards.* But he knew that he had to travel light.

He unlocked the second footlocker. It contained mostly clothes, about thirty audio CDs and a dozen DVDs. He already had MP3 backup copies of the CDs burned onto Kaylee's laptop in New Mexico, so there'd be no regrets in leaving those behind.

Laine cut the tape seal on the cardboard box and pulled out the modular sleep system (MSS) sleeping bag that he had bought at the post clothing sales store during his officer basic course. Also in the box was a civilian bivouac bag, a Millet brand "Cyrano." This was a top-of-the-line bivy bag made with an olive green Gore-Tex top and a heavy brown rubberized waterproof fabric bottom. This sleeping bag's cover could take the place of a tent and was so waterproof that he could practically sleep in a puddle and it wouldn't leak. The bottom of the box was filled with clothes, a rappelling Swiss seat, and a binder full of his college term papers.

Andy sorted and then resorted his civilian clothes, paring them down into two piles: "Keep" and "Sell." He sorted through the contents of his suitcase, duffel, and flight bags with the same ruthlessness. He placed everything that he planned to take on his trip home in the closet, so that it would be out of sight when buyers arrived. He took the time to check the condition of his compact Elecraft KX1 QRP shortwave transceiver. This low-power rig could be used to transmit Morse code in the 20-, 30-, 40-, and 80-meter ham radio bands.

Powered by six AA batteries, the ten-ounce radio was capable of transmitting around the world when ionospheric conditions were right. It put out just 1 to 2 watts of power (or up to 4 watts if using an external 12-volt battery). Using his 200-watt Kenwood HF rig in Texas, Lars had several successful two-way contacts with Andy in Afghanistan, even though his younger brother's transmitter put out only a few watts of effective radiated power. Andy carefully repacked the transceiver and accessories in two thicknesses of zipper-lock bags and then in a pair of Tupperware containers.

The two lieutenants returned at 1815. Right behind them were a TDY Marine Corps captain and a WO2 aviator. Then came a couple of majors: one was a field artillery officer and the other was a chaplain.

As they crowded into the room, Laine announced:

"Okay, here are the ground rules: I hold up each item, describe it, and name a price. The first one that says 'Dibs' gets it. The prices will be very reasonable but nonnegotiable. Keep in mind that I just had to pay $125 for a dinner at Burger King, so don't try to nickel-and-dime me. Each of you grab a notepad from the desk there and keep your own tally. We'll settle up at the end, in cash. Now, any part that you pay for in euros, you can divide by four—a four-to-one exchange ratio. *Klar?*"

The sale was over in less than a half hour. Most of the items sold for between $10 and $50 each. Laine was surprised to see some of the officers buy clothes in sizes that didn't fit. Then he realized that they were desperate to get *out of dollars* and into anything tangible that they could later barter or sell. He even sold the two empty footlockers for $100 each.

The one item that brought in the most cash was his laptop. It sold for $2,500, which was a pittance, considering the recent inflation. Andy was sad to see it go, but unless the Internet connections inside the United States started working again, it would just be a boat anchor. And if the connections *were* reestablished, Andy surmised that he could keep in touch using borrowed laptops or rented PCs at Internet cafés.

Laine took the small remaining stack of the books that hadn't sold and put them on the half-empty bookshelves of BOQ lounge. Most of what was already there were *Reader's Digest* condensed books, out-of-date travel books, and romance novels. After he had added his books, the collective IQ of the shelves rose dramatically.

Andy returned to his room and wrapped his remaining gold coins in duct tape. He similarly wrapped the wedding band mate to the engagement ring that he had presented to Kaylee just before his Afghanistan deployment. He then removed the screws to the Primus backpacking stove lid's sheet metal heat shield. He inserted the duct tape squares inside the lid and used even more tape to hold them in place. When the heat shield was reinstalled, the extra thickness was undetectable.

14

Clerks and Jerks

"This first stage of the inflationary process may last for many years. While it lasts, the prices of many goods and services are not yet adjusted to the altered money relation. There are still people in the country who have not yet become aware of the fact that they are confronted with a price revolution which will finally result in a considerable rise of all prices, although the extent of this rise will not be the same in the various commodities and services. These people still believe that prices one day will drop. Waiting for this day, they restrict their purchases and concomitantly increase their cash holdings. As long as such ideas are still held by public opinion, it is not yet too late for the government to abandon its inflationary policy.

"But then, finally, the masses wake up. They become suddenly aware of the fact that inflation is a deliberate policy and will go on endlessly. A breakdown occurs. The crack-up boom appears. Everybody is anxious to swap his money against 'real' goods, no matter whether he needs them or not, no matter how much money he has to pay for them. Within a very short time, within a few weeks or even days, the things which were used as money are no longer used as media of exchange. They become scrap paper. Nobody wants to give away anything against them.

"It was this that happened with the Continental currency in America in 1781, with the French mandats territoriaux in 1796, and with the German mark in 1923. It will happen again whenever the same conditions appear. If a thing has to be used as a medium of exchange, *public opinion must not believe that the quantity of this thing will increase beyond all bounds. Inflation is a policy that cannot last."*

—Ludwig von Mises, *The Anticapitalistic Mentality* (1972)

Rose Barracks, Vilseck, Germany
Early November, the First Year

Andy was ready to turn in his green active-duty ID card, but there was some confusion and a day's delay while some red Army Reserve card blanks were couriered down from the Garmisch Garrison. Technically, after leaving active duty, Andy still had a two-year obligation in the Individual Ready Reserve (IRR) control group, but he wouldn't be expected to be in a local Army Reserve unit.

A GS-12 civilian clerk—a jovial and rotund retired chief warrant officer—prepared his Form DD-214. Handing Laine a draft copy to check for errors, the clerk said, "Here are your walking papers, but I'm afraid they really are *walking* papers!" Andy groaned. The clerk added, "I guess you heard about the groundings."

"Yeah," Andy replied glumly. There had been two recent Islamic terrorist incidents in the three days since Laine had returned to Bavaria. The first was a bombing of a train station that adjoined the airport in Nürnberg, and the next day a 9/11-style hijacking in France had ended tragically in a fiery crash just short of the Parliament building in London, killing 242 people. These events had prompted a grounding of all civilian aircraft for at least a week. Most trains except for some local *U-Bahn*s and *Strassenbahn*s had also been stopped. Even long-distance bus lines had been halted.

With the drama of the economic news, riots, and the terrorist attacks, the newscasters had plenty to talk about. In Europe, the focus seemed to be on the terror attacks, while in the United States, the emphasis was on the galloping inflation and the riots.

The volume of news was so overwhelming that the day-to-day clerical bureaucracy at the post slowed to a crawl. Several times in the past two days, Andy had to nearly shout, "Hel-looo! Can you please get this outprocessing finished for me?" to get the various "clerks and jerks" to turn their attention away from their laptops, computer monitors, televisions, and text screens on their cell phones.

Andy and the clerk next turned their attention to his quarters clearing papers, making sure that he had all the proper clearance stamps. They were variously stamped in blue and black: "CIF," "Cleared Finance," "S2 Outbrief," "No Mess Charges," and "PMO."

"Where's your 'YOYO' stamp?" the clerk asked.

"YOYO?" Laine asked suspiciously.

"That stands for 'You're on Your Own,' pal."

"Very funny."

That afternoon Andy went off post to go to the local Raiffeisenbank branch. He got in a long queue in front of the counter with a sign above it that read: "Geldwechsel/Change/Cambio." After twenty minutes he came to the front of the line and began to pull out his remaining afghanis, U.S. dollars, his few remaining U.S.-dollar-denominated traveler's checks, and Iraqi dinars that were left over from his previous deployment. They made a fairly large pile on the counter. The teller seemed unfazed. Obviously, in recent weeks he had seen much larger piles of cash.

"Euros, *bitte*," Andy asked quietly.

As the teller began counting the stacks of afghanis, Laine countersigned all of his traveler's checks. He then pulled out his passport and his military ID card and set them on the counter, knowing that they'd be needed next.

The teller clucked a "Tsk, tsk" after he did the *Wechselkurs* calculation.

"The exchange of dollars rate, I am afraid, sir, is very poor."

"That's understandable," Laine replied.

After clearing the counter and handing Andy back his ID, the clerk said matter-of-factly, "Five hundred and eighty euros." Then he asked Andy, "Cash or EC card?"

"Cash—*Bargeld, bitte.*"

Andy already had another forty-five euros in his wallet. Together, those notes totaling 625 euros would barely cover the cost of a two-hundred-mile bus ride or a dinner at a decent restaurant. Such were the ravages of the recent inflation.

Next, Andy walked across the bank lobby to the indoor *Geldautomat* ATM machine. He tried both of his credit cards, with the same result: the message "Credit Card Transactions Suspended" flashed on the screen. "Oh, joy," Andy muttered.

Back at Rose Barracks, Andy Laine was told that there would be no scheduled military flights for at least a week, possibly longer. At the rate things were deteriorating, he dared not just wait and hope that flights would be resumed. Even if flights were resumed, active-duty personnel might have higher priority than someone traveling on an Army Reserve ID card. Or, worse yet, civil order could collapse in Germany, just as it had in the States, and flights might not resume for months or years. Andy wondered how he'd get back to the States and, once he did, how he'd be able to travel to New Mexico.

He had the vague idea of heading west through Germany to the coast of France to see if he could find a ship of any description heading to the U.S., or perhaps even to Mexico or Canada. Just before close of business at the post headquarters, he made arrangements to get a flight back to Ramstein. There, in the U.S. military's largest complex in Germany, he'd have the best chance of getting transport out of Europe.

Two more frustrating days of hurry-up-and-wait landed Andy at Ramstein. The BOQ there was full, so he was sent to the nearby

Sembach Annex. Seeing Laine's red Army Reserve ID card, the desk clerk asked him for a copy of his orders. "I don't have any orders," he said. "I've just been released from active duty and I'm trying to get home." Even after seeing Laine's DD-214, the clerk was belligerent. "No rooms without orders for reservists." It was only after threatening to call the clerk's manager that Andy was finally given a room.

Shepherding his rapidly dwindling cash, Andy bought food for dinner entirely from vending machines. Because the inflation was so rapid, the vending machine prices had not yet been raised to match the store counter prices. The news on television was all bad. Flights were all still grounded and most trains and buses were not running. Some runs on grocery stores had begun in Germany, Austria, and the Czech Republic. There were also some large street protests and riots building up in the larger cities throughout the European Union. Reserve police and military forces were being mobilized throughout the EU and in the UK. There had been a widespread power blackout in Greece caused by a labor union dispute. It was also reported that no long-distance calls were getting through to the United States except, oddly, to Hawaii.

Andy turned off the television and called a couple of acquaintances stationed in K-Town, begging favors. One of them phoned an hour later to say that they had found him a ride.

Early the next morning, Andy got on a five-ton supply truck that was headed to Landstuhl Regional Medical Center. Following the end of U.S. military presence in France, this was the westernmost Army installation in USAEUR, the U.S. Army's European command. Beyond there, he truly would be in YOYO territory.

The next morning was depressingly foggy. Laine did not feel his best, since he had slept so poorly the night before. The Specialist E-4 driving the truck to Landstuhl was envious that Laine had ended his service and was headed home. "Sir, I still got 112 days and a wake-up," he said forlornly. "I don't know what things'll be like by then. My family all lives in Atlanta. You've seen it on the TV, right? There's big dang riots there. They say half the city is on fire." Laine decided that it wouldn't be helpful to mention that this was the second time that Atlanta had burned, so he made no reply.

The truck, he learned, was mainly filled with MREs. It was just one of many truckloads of MREs from as far away as Wiesbaden that were being sent to the Army hospital, since local transport of food for patients and staff had become intermittently disrupted. Even more MREs were being sent to various Air Force bases and to U.S. embassies. The big MRE shuffle was part of a "contingency stock leveling" measure, just in case food supplies and grid power were to suffer more severe disruption. "It's like some kinda siege mentality, sir," the Specialist commented.

At just after ten a.m., Laine was dropped off at a *Strassenbahn* stop not far from the hospital complex, and the driver left with a wave.

Andy stood alone at the tram stop, feeling overwhelmed. The fog was beginning to lift, and he could begin to see hills of the Palatinate Forest in the distance, stretching to the south. After a few chilly minutes, a streetcar approached on Eisenbahnstrasse. Andy put on his duffel bag using both shoulder straps. Then he picked up his flight bag in his left hand and his overseas bag in his right hand. He waddled to the streetcar. The weight of the duffel bag pressed the holstered SIG uncomfortably into his lower back. When the door opened, he asked the driver, *"In Richtung Land-stuhler Stadtzentrum?"*

"Ja, klar, klar," the driver answered, gesturing him in.

Laine stepped up into the streetcar, which was nearly empty. He thumbed in his fare card and then awkwardly sat down, placing two of his bags in front of him and hunching out of his main duffel bag.

An elderly German woman was sitting across the aisle from

him with the seat beside her piled with string shopping bags. A long-haired Dachshund sat in her lap. The streetcar lurched and picked up speed.

The woman recognized Laine's bags and asked, "You are away going on leave?"

"No, I am going home to America permanently—*ständig*—if I can find a way."

"The *luft* flights are all aground *und die Züge fahren nicht*."

"Yes, I know about the trains." After a moment Laine added, "Are there any *Omnibusse* still running to Frankreich or to the Low Countries? *Das Benelux?*"

"*Nein. Alles eingestellt.*"

Andy shook his head. "These are crazy times."

"*Ja*, and the money, it is no good. This is like the Weimar time again, I think."

As they neared the center of Landstuhl, the *Strassenbahn* stops got closer together, and Laine began to eye the shop signs: "Apotheke," "Deli," "Bäckerei," "Optometrist," "Moden," "Eisenwaren," "Schallplatten," "Kaufhaus." The many buildings with whitewashed walls, exposed beams, and red-tiled roofs looked nineteenth-century vintage or earlier. Andy wondered if the city had been spared any damage in the Second World War. The old buildings looked remarkably intact.

"Is there a *Fahrrad* shop in Landstuhl?" he asked the old woman.

"*Ja*, at Adolph-Kolping-Platz. I tell you when you are getting off."

After another three stops, the woman said, "Here it is you are!" and pointed to a sign that read, "Gebrüder Becker, Fahrräder."

The bicycle shop was smaller than Laine had expected, but then he realized that this might be a good thing. One of the big stores wouldn't have the flexibility to make the deal that he had in mind.

Andy lugged his bags through the front door of the shop and

glanced at some price tags on the bicycles as he walked toward the store counter. He set all three of his bags down in a pile. He felt like he already had the aura of a vagabond.

Since it was not yet the noon hour, there were no other customers. The store was in an older, poorly lit building, but most of the selection looked new and state-of-the-art. There was a fairly large inventory, with a mix of children's bikes, mountain bikes, and high-end racing bikes. It was much like a bike shop that he had visited in Germany before his tour in Afghanistan. The difference was the inflated price tags. Two years ago, a *typisch* mountain bike was about 300 euros, but now they ranged from 800 to 3,000 euros.

Andy introduced himself, and the store owner did likewise. His name was Kurt Becker, a slim, muscular man in his forties who spoke good English. Judging by his physique, Andy concluded that he must be a daily cyclist. An older mustachioed man wearing a heavy leather apron sat at a bench in the back of the store. He was balancing a bicycle wheel, adjusting the spokes by hand.

Laine explained that he had just left the Army and was looking for a bicycle and trailer for a cross-country road trip.

The store owner sighed and said, "Yes, I have heard about the planes and the trains. Not even the buses are running on the long lines."

They spent the next fifteen minutes looking at Kurt's inventory of mountain and road bikes. Then they discussed panniers and trailers and how much cargo they could carry. Laine settled on a nearly new Giant brand mountain bike that already had a headlamp, a blinking LED taillight, and both a small tool kit and a tire pump clipped to the frame. Next he picked out some sturdy racks, a pair of Ortlieb waterproof black nylon panniers and matching handlebar bag, and a well-used trailer. The trailer had a scuffed frame and road-tar-stained yellow nylon sides, but it looked sturdy and serviceable. It had a clear plastic front, since it was originally designed for hauling toddlers.

During this time, another customer came in, but occupied the shop owner only for a few minutes to buy some optic yellow rain pants and a pair of trouser leg clips. After he had left, Laine picked out a similar pair of pants—except in forest green—and a matching jacket with hood. He bought the jacket slightly oversize, knowing that in cold weather he would want to wear a sweater beneath. He also didn't want the bulge of the holstered SIG printing through the jacket. So looser was better. Andy knew that he was in for a series of long, cold, wet rides.

Next he asked for two spare inner tubes and a bottle of Slime tire sealant, in case of punctures.

Gesturing to his pile of selected merchandise, Laine said: *"Die Rechnung, bitte."*

Kurt pulled out a notepad and started listing and totaling with a fat pencil. Finally he said, "With VAT, 3,315 euros—so let's just call it 3,300, okay?"

Andy let out deep breath.

"I don't have that in *Papiergeld*. But I have it in *geld* coin, *echte Geldstücke*—you know, *Goldmünzen*. Are you familiar with the *französische Goldmünzen* from early in the last century, the 'Rooster'—'*Der Hahn*'—*zwei Franc Goldmünzen?*"

Kurt's eyes brightened and he exclaimed *"Ja!"*

Andy pulled out his wallet and from an inner Velcro flap pocket he withdrew two French two-franc Rooster gold coins in a plastic flip. The coins were dated 1905 and 1907. Handing the coin sleeve to the shop owner, he declared, *"Diese ist nicht gefälscht*—the genuine article."

Kurt took the coins, closely examined them under a desk lamp, and said, "I am not an expert of coins, but I do want to accept these for you to pay. Can you please come with me while I go and ask a guarantee of a *Goldmünzenhändler*—a dealer of coins—to test their value? He has a shop just five doors away, and he is a friend."

Andy replied, *"Freilich! Kein Problem."*

"My father will watch the store and your baggages."

Before they left, Andy picked up his overseas bag, which held his most valuable possessions, including the SIG's extra ammo and accessories. He slung the bag's strap over his shoulder. "This *Gepäck* goes with me," he explained.

Kurt nodded and said softly *"Ich verstehe"* as he took off his oil-stained canvas apron and handed it to his father.

As they prepared to leave the shop, Becker became momentarily flustered. He did not know whether he should hand the coin back to Andy before they left the store or hold it himself. Andy pointed to Becker's front pants pocket. Kurt obliged.

They walked down the street to a smaller store with barred windows with a sign declaring: "H. Kurtz, Goldmünzenhändler." A neon sign that read "Silber/Geld Bullionhändler" shone in the window.

They had to first knock on the door and then be buzzed in after a clerk recognized Kurt's face. The small store was unusually crowded with both buyers and sellers. "We take a number, I guess," Kurt joked.

They had to wait nearly fifteen minutes while other transactions were completed. Once at the counter, Kurt and the coin dealer exchanged friendly greetings and then, as he handed over the coin flip, some rapid-fire German that Andy didn't catch much of. The only portions of the exchange that Andy understood were *"Ja, ja, alles klar"* and the word *"Schätzung,"* which Andy remembered meant "appraisal."

Laine watched as the coin dealer examined the coins with a loupe, weighed each of them on his scale, calipered them with a Fisch coin gauge, and finally brushed their edges against a touchstone, but not without first asking, *"Wie bitte."* He looked up with a smile and nodded, declaring: *"Ja, die sind echt."*

For Andy's benefit, the coin dealer switched to English: "These coins are, yes, genuine. They weigh, both by the book of coins and by my scale, point one eight six seven troy ounces of the fine gold. That is almost one-fifth of ounce troy for each." Pointing to some figures on a chalkboard behind him, he said: "Today, spot gold in London is 9,112 euros per ounce. That makes these coins worth both together 3,402 euros."

Kurt thanked the coin dealer and handed him a fifty-euro note for the appraisal.

As they walked back to the bike shop, Andy marveled at how the gold had held its buying power, while the U.S. dollar had become so worthless. Once back inside, Kurt declared to his father: "Three thousand four hundred euros!" Turning to Laine, he said, "I am still owing you one hundred euros difference, or the same in goods from my shop."

"But, Kurt, you had to pay for the *Schätzung*."

"I am not worried about that, *Herr Kapitän*, for tomorrow gold bullion it will be higher and the euro will be lower, just as sure as the rising of the sun."

Back at the store counter, Andy asked: *"Haben sie Landkarten?"*

"Ja."

Laine asked, *"Für Frankreich?"*

"Ja." The shop owner pulled out a Michelin large-scale road map of France that had a heavy cardboard cover. "These maps are now twenty euros." Becker also opened up a similar road map of Germany. Taking it over to the shop's photocopier, he said, "Also, you will need to have our little corner of Germany. No charge for this." He made two photocopies of the western end of the map and handed them to Andy, who slipped them inside the cover of the map for France.

Laine said, "Okay, that leaves me eighty euros credit. So I'd like to use that to pay for your time to help me attach the racks and trailer hitch."

Becker nodded.

"Then we have a deal, for the two gold *Hahnmünzen. Klar?*"

They shook hands.

Andy left the store an hour and a half later, after the bicycle modifications and packing had been completed. As he was packing, Becker gave Andy a box of heavy black plastic trash bags to use as waterproof liners for the panniers, handlebar bag, and the now half-empty overseas bag. The latter initially went into the almost-full trailer, for fear that Becker might spot the SIG ammo and accessories. Laine would have preferred that his sleeping bag and bivouac bag stuff sacks be strapped to the top of the cargo rack, but the gooseneck of the trailer was in the way. So they, too, went in the trailer.

Kurt and the old man both shook Laine's hand before he wheeled the bike and trailer out of the store.

The younger Becker waved and said, *"Viel Glück!"*

"Thanks, but I'll need more than luck," Andy replied. "I'll need God's Grace."

"Well, then . . . *Möge Gott mit Ihnen sein!*"

Andy took the Saarbrücker Strasse out of Landstuhl, heading west. Getting accustomed to the feel of the bike and trailer took some adjustment. After the first few uphill grades, he decided that he should carry less food and water. He kept three liters of water but poured out two other one-liter bottles. He decided to gradually reduce by half the amount of food in the packed trailer.

15

Der Pilger

"To my mind it is wholly irresponsible to go into the world incapable of preventing violence, injury, crime, and death. How feeble is the mind-set to accept defenselessness. How unnatural. How cheap. How cowardly. How pathetic."

—Ted Nugent

Bruchmühlbach-Miesau, Germany
Early November, the First Year

Andrew Laine kept on the secondary roads as he headed toward the French border. He stopped when he reached the first dense stand of timber, loaded the SIG, and put it in his holster.

The L395 expressway had surprisingly few passing cars and trucks. Laine passed through the town of Bruchmühlbach-Miesau late in the afternoon. Just after turning southwest on L119, the terrain again got hilly, and Andy was feeling exhausted. Paralleling a major railway line, the road was heavily treed on both sides. It was a long day of riding, and his muscles were unaccustomed to the new strain.

Andy started looking for a secluded place where he could camp for the night. He wanted to stop before he got to Homburg, which was a sizable city. Huffing and puffing his way up a grade, now in low gear at barely more than a walking pace, Andy was surprised to see three young men burst from behind the screen of trees. They came running at him to intercept, with their boots thudding on the pavement. Before Andy could either pick up his pace or turn, they were upon him.

All three of the men had shaved heads. Two of them wore black flight jackets, while the third was in an obsolete Flecktarn camouflage pattern Bundeswehr jacket. All three of them wore what looked like Doc Martens boots, or something similar. One of them grabbed the bike's handlebars while another shoved a one-inch diameter tree branch through the spokes of the front wheel. Laine wasn't going anywhere.

The one standing the closest taunted, *"Wo willst du denn hin, Pilger?"* His breath stank of beer.

Andy jumped off the bike and backed up five steps. He held his hands just out from his thighs, showing his palms to the men.

The tallest one made a show of flicking open a German parachutist's gravity knife. He held it up and cackled. Then he looked down at the bike's pannier and trailer and asked, *"Alles für mich?"* He set the bicycle's kickstand and then closed the knife and put it in his pocket. The third man loosened his grasp on the handlebars and began to walk around to Andy's side of the bike.

Laine took two more steps backward. Then, in one smooth motion, he pulled back his jacket, drew the SIG pistol, leveled it, and took up the slack on its trigger. He took yet another two steps backward.

He commanded them to leave: *"Haut ab! Verschwindet!"*

The skinhead in the Bundeswehr jacket shook his head and hissed, *"Nein, Pilgergeiger. Deine Pistole ist nicht echt!"* (No, Pilgrim fiddler, your pistol is not real.")

"Sorry, boys, but it's *echt*. Now, *verschwindet, macht schnell und zwar schnell!"*

The one that had used the tree branch pulled it from the spokes, raised it over his head, and shouted *"Lügner!"* He took a step forward.

Andy aimed carefully and squeezed the trigger twice. The second shot hit the tree branch, ripping it from the man's hand. He looked startled. The one in Flecktarn shouted, *"Lass uns gehen!"* All three of the skinheads ran off into the woods, shouting and cursing loudly.

After seeing them top a hillock seventy-five yards away, still running at full speed, Andy thumbed the SIG's de-cocking lever. He switched magazines with one of the full spares on his belt, and reholstered the gun. It was only then that he noticed that his hands were shaking and his ears were ringing.

Back astride the bike and again starting to pedal uphill, Andy's nerves calmed a bit and he started to chuckle. Pumping his legs in cadence, he repeated to himself, like a running Jodie, *"Schweizer Qualität.* Swiss quality. *Schweizer Qualität.* Swiss quality."

He spent the first night just over a mile farther down the road. It was getting dark, and he could see the lights of the village of Bruchhof in the distance. According to his map there would be at least five miles of urban area beyond that. So he turned left onto a farm road, and then again onto a smaller lane that ran into the woods. Now that it was almost full dark, he pulled his bicycle off the road and into the woods. There were just a few scattered lights from farmhouses. Unlike a typical American forest that was choked with fallen trees, this forest was of the orderly German model: it looked more like a park than a woodlot. He had no trouble wheeling his bike and trailer two hundred yards into the timber.

Finding a brushy patch, Andy disconnected the trailer and laid his bike down. Then he backed the trailer into a clump of brush. The ground here was fairly level. Fortunately, it wasn't raining. It took him just a couple of minutes to set up his camp. His sleeping bag was kept stowed inside his bivouac bag. All that he had to do was lay it out on top of his ground pad.

After rolling back a large rock and relieving himself, he returned to his bike trailer and washed his hands with a water bottle.

Andy sat and prayed. He had a lot to be thankful for. He pulled out an MRE at random. He was ravenous, and wolfed down nearly all of its contents in just a few minutes, not bothering with the niceties of the heating packet and the drink mixes. After eating the chicken and rice entrée, he gobbled down the entire packet of crackers, followed by several slugs of water. Then he tore off the corner of the peanut butter pouch and began squirting it directly into his mouth. Finally, he put all of the candies into his shirt pocket.

After zipping closed the clear plastic front of the bike trailer, Andy sat down and kicked off his sneakers. They were still wet from an earlier rain shower. He realized that he would have to alternate between his two sets of sneakers on this trip: this pair that would only rarely dry out, and the pair that he'd keep dry. The latter he would wear only on days when there was no threat of rain. He put the shoes into a plastic bag and tucked it into the foot end of his bivy bag. He draped his rain gear over the sides of the trailer to help camouflage it. He'd have to do something about the bright yellow color. Before crawling into his bag, he rolled up his coat inside out to use as a pillow, and tucked the SIG under it. He took off his damp socks and put them between his outer shirt and T-shirt to dry overnight.

It took Andy several hours to get to sleep. The stress of the incident with skinhead robbers still had him cranked up. His mind was racing with a thousand questions: What could he have done differently? Probably not much. Had they reported him to the local *Polizeistation*? Probably not. Had they wet their pants? Probably. Andy chuckled. He was worried about his prospects for getting back to the United States. He was worried about his fiancée. He was even worried about the chain and derailleur on his bicycle.

Unable to sleep, he nibbled on the leftover candy and listened to the breeze and the sound of the raindrops dripping off of the tree branches. He whispered to himself: "Dang, I forgot to brush my teeth. Oh, well, starting *tomorrow*." As he finally drifted off to sleep, Andy worked on a mental checklist for the next day: "I need to get more calories. I need to keep fully hydrated. I need to watch my gear settings well in advance for hills. I need to reorganize the trailer so that the gear that I need most frequently will be closest at hand. I need to check my six more often. I need to find a way to keep my socks dry. I need to take smaller snacks rather than just three large meals. I need to reposition the magazine pouch so that it won't dig into my side. . . ."

He awoke just before dawn the next morning, feeling sore in his buttocks, thighs, and lower back. Obviously, bicycling used different muscles than he had been using with his regular PT regimen. There would be some inevitable adjustments to this mode of travel.

After the eastern horizon started to lighten, he shook the water droplets off his bivy bag and rolled it up. In the distance, a cow was mooing for its calf. He could hear but not see just one car or light truck drive by on the nearby road.

He took ten minutes to clean and oil the pistol and to top off the magazine that had two rounds expended. Between the boxes and what was already loaded in the magazines, he still had almost 450 rounds of 9mm ball ammunition available—about nine pounds of ammunition and magazines. He was willing to shed weight from his load in water and food, but *not* ammunition. That was a priority.

His breakfast was a small can of peaches, a half-crushed breakfast roll that was left over from the previous morning at the BOQ *Frühstück* room, and a bit of jerky.

Out of habit, he buried his empty food wrappers and the dirty pistol cleaning patches. That was what he had always told his troops was good litter discipline for the field.

Andy stowed his gear and, in the process, shifted a few items between his various bags and compartments to put things within closer reach. He checked the pressure of the bike's tires, then hooked up the trailer. Looking around his campsite, he was satisfied to see that the only signs of his presence would be some crushed grass.

He quietly walked the bike back down to the road. It was starting to rain again.

Andy pressed on, westward. The weather was rainy in the morning, soon soaking his shoes and socks. At times the spray from passing trucks was brutal. There was no good way to avoid riding through the city of Homburg without taking a huge detour. The traffic in the city was surprisingly light. Obviously, *Benzin* was becoming more precious with each passing day. Other than some long queues at gas stations, the activity in Homburg appeared relatively normal.

Even though the terrain was more mountainous, Laine decided to take the smaller road through Friedrichsthal and Heusweiler, rather than get near Autobahn 6—the major route west that went through Saarbrücken.

The weather started to clear and warm up in the afternoon, and Andy made good time. He stopped at an *Eisenwaren* store in Heusweiler and bought a can of flat brown spray paint as well as the Falks gas lamp mantles that Lars had requested. He bought the store's entire inventory: sixty-two mantles. Even if these were more than Lars needed, they'd be a very lightweight and compact yet valuable barter item.

Exhausted after a long day of riding, Andy made camp in some dense woods north of Saarwellingen just before dark. Other than a candy bar, he had skipped lunch, so he was again ravenous. He ate a can of sausages, a packet of crackers, and a package of ramen soaked in cold water.

Laine detached and unpacked the trailer. He then used the full contents of the can of spray paint, covering up the "untactical" bright yellow trailer. He even sprayed the clear plastic front of the trailer, since there was no need to have visibility in or out of it. The trailer now blended in with the forest for his bivouacs.

He was anxious to set up his radios, since it was a Tuesday—one of his scheduled shortwave contact nights. He set up his pocket-size Kaito receiver on a large stump and rolled out its long-wire antenna, hanging the far end up on a tree limb. He placed his overseas bag in front of the stump to use for a low chair. Then he put on his headphones and dialed in 10.000 megahertz. The WWV time signal in Colorado had a faintly audible signal, even though there was daylight between him and the United States. "So far, so good," he whispered to himself.

Andy confirmed that the radio's clock was set to GMT. In Germany, it was GMT plus one hour, but in New Mexico it was GMT minus seven hours—still not yet noon. Next he programmed the radio's alarm function to wake him at 0325 GMT—4:25 a.m. local time. Andy heard it announced that it was seventeen minutes after the hour, so he continued listening to WWV for the geophysical data report that always came on eighteen minutes after each hour. They reported a solar activity of K2/K3 ("weak to unsettled"), which was marginal for long-range propagation in the shortwave bands. Andy's face sank into a frown.

Next, Andy erected the dipole antenna for his transceiver. He lined it up so that the antenna's broadside would face to the northwest—the "Great Circle" direction from him to Lars in New Mexico. Fortunately, he didn't need to worry about grounding the radio, since he was using a dipole antenna.

Lars had helped Andy build and test the QRP transceiver four years earlier. It was one of a pair of kits that they ordered from Elecraft, in California. Andy justified the price to Kaylee by telling her that this radio had slightly more output power than a traditional "flea-power" rig (ham slang for a transmitter with less than one watt) but the extra bit of power would really make a difference for DX (long-distance) communications. Shortly before his departure for Afghanistan, Kaylee had decorated the exterior of the transceiver's Tupperware box with some of her artistry: Andy's call sign, "K5CLA," and a humorous stylized cartoon of a flea wearing headphones, with yellow lightning bolts emanating from its hind end. Kaylee had laughingly reminded Andy to pack his "Mighty Flea" as he was preparing to deploy.

Inside the waterproof storage box, the transceiver was so small that there was enough room left over for a small spiral-bound notebook, an external power cord with both car battery clips and a cigarette lighter plug, and several small spools of wire for spare antenna or ground leads. He inserted six batteries into the battery tray and used the radio's battery voltage monitor to verify that they were good. Andy flipped open his notepad and turned it to a page of notes from when he was explaining radio procedure to Kaylee. He paused to read it again, because Kaylee had annotated it with questions, comments, and her ever-present cartoon doodles. He missed her so much that it hurt. The page read:

Some Common Abbreviations Used in CW (Morse) Transmissions

These are sent as if they were a single character:

AR—End of message. Typically sent on your last transmission, before you send the call signs the final time.

BT—Paragraph break, or just a break in our thoughts.

Kaylee wrote: "How do you say 'Period'? We rarely use periods (too slow and awkward to send compared to BT) unless we're relaying literal text where they matter."

SK—If sent after sending the call signs the final time, it means we are shutting off the radio and not accepting any more calls.

Common abbreviations, sent as words using normal characters:

ABT—About

BK—Break. This means back to you; no need to use call signs.

CPY—Copy

CU—See you (later)

DE—From. This is used between call signs.

ES—And

FB—Fine business. Basically means "That's great" or "That's wonderful."

FER—For. Beneath this, Kaylee wrote: "That is goofy. Why not FOR???" Andy penned: "Laziness. It's just quicker in Morse to send FER than FOR:

$$..\text{-} ... \text{-}. \text{ (FER)}$$
versus
$$..\text{-}. \text{- - -} .\text{-}. \text{ (FOR)}$$"

HI—Laugh

HR—Here

HW—How

K—Go ahead

KN—Go ahead ONLY the station I am calling or talking to

MNI—Many

NM—Name

OM—Old man. All men are OMs in the ham world. Beside this line Kaylee drew a caricature of an old bearded man tripping on his beard.

PSE—Please

R—I heard everything you said and don't need you to repeat anything. Kaylee wrote: "So R is the first thing we'll reply with on each 'Over' (or not if we need a repeat), right? RIGHT!"

TNX—Thanks

TU—Thank you

UR—Your or You're (depending on context)

VY—Very

YL—Young lady. All females are YLs in the ham world. Kaylee annotated
    this line with a caricature of an old witch wearing headphones, the
    cable from the headphones was dipped in a cauldron.

73—Best regards. Always used singularly. (Only CB-ers and ex-CB-ers
    use the plural "73s.")

88—Hugs and kisses

?—Sent by itself, it means "I'm going to repeat what I just said."
    Beneath that, Kaylee had written, in larger block letters: "KL: HI 88
    PSE COME HOME SOON FER 88 UR YL 73 AR."

Common Q-signals sent as words:

QRM—Interference from another station

QRN—Static

QRP—Low-power (less than 5-watt) transmitters

QRZ?—Who is calling me? Or at the end of the contact, sent instead
    of SK, it means "I'm listening for more calls and would like to
    receive some."

QSB—Fading

QSO—A contact (conversation)

QSY—Change frequency

QTH—Location

NOTE: Call signs are always sent in this order: {OtherGuy'sCallSign}
    DE {YourCallSign}. And below that, Kaylee had drawn a cartoon of
    an outhouse with an enormous antenna mast on top, captioned:
    "QTH #1—OM QSO WITH TP"

Andy laughed and closed the notebook. He plugged in the antenna and his headphones. Andy didn't need to plug in or even
carry an old-style hand key, as the KX1 had an internal electronic
keyer and a set of keyer paddles that plugged directly into its case
for the ultimate in portability and operating ease. The paddles

were manipulated via slight movements of the thumb and forefinger (squeezing the paddles), enabling him to send Morse much
faster and smoother than he could with a traditional telegrapher's
hand key. The paddles also had the advantage of being virtually
silent, versus the familiar clackety-clack of a hand key.

For convenience and to allow him to keep one hand free, he attached the radio to his thigh using a Velcro strap. Andy switched
it on and set it to 10.106 MHz—the international 30-meter band
QRP calling frequency.

Andy put on the headphones, gave a brief silent prayer, and
then whispered, "Okay, Mighty Flea, do yo' stuff!" Squeezing the
KX1's keyer paddles, Andy remembered to add "DL/" in front of
his call sign to indicate that he was transmitting in Germany, and
keyed: "CQ CQ CQ DE DL/K5CLA DL/K5CLA K"

He was surprised to hear an immediate answering call, only
slightly off frequency, "DL/K5CLA DE PA3ADG PA3ADG K"

As he listened, he quickly adjusted the radio's incremental tun-
ing for a comfortable medium-pitched tone and wrote PA3ADG
on his notepad.

Excitedly, Andy replied: "PA3ADG DE DL/K5CLA FB UR 589
589 NM IS ANDY BT"

Then he quickly added: "I AM EX US ARMY OFFICER BIK-
ING THROUGH DK ES F TRYING TO GET TO THE COAST
TO FIND A SHIP HOME TO USA BK"

"BK R FB ANDY UR 449 BT
NM IS WIM ? WIM BT
QTH AMSTERDAM BT
BIKE OR MOTORCYCLE? BK"

"BK R FB WIM BT
PEDAL BIKE AM CAMPING BT
RIG KX1 QRP ABT 2W BK"

"BK R SOUNDS LIKE TOUGH WAY TO GO IN WINTER
HI BK"

"BK R YES TOUGH HI BT
WIM PSE DO U KNOW OF ANY SHIPS FROM FRANCE
OR BELG OR NETH SAILING TO THE US? BK"
"BK R WILL CHECK ES CALL U THIS FREQ AT 1845Z BT
CU ES 73 DL/K5CLB DE PA3ADG SK"
"BK R VY FB WIM MNI TNX BT
73 73 AR PA3ADG DE DL/K5CLB QRZ?"

Andy let out a sigh. He listened to the radio for a few minutes, but no other hams jumped in. He turned off the transceiver, reset the Kaito radio's alarm to 18:42, and said a prayer. He covered both radios with a trash bag held down by his coat. While he was waiting for the follow-up from Holland, he set up his bivy bag and ground pad, and ate a can of applesauce.

It was almost dark. Andy could hear what sounded like a dove or pigeon cooing in the trees above. He felt chilled after sitting still while sweaty, so he peeled off his Windbreaker and rain pants and wrung out his socks. Then he crawled into his sleeping bag to wait.

He half-dozed for the next hour. The Kaito's alarm went off, and Andy crawled out of the bag. He picked his way toward the dim outline of the stump in the dark, and switched off the alarm. It was getting colder, so he put his coat on. Again seated on the overseas bag, he fumbled to put on his headphones and turned on the KX1 transceiver.

Right on the dot at 18:45, Andy heard Wim's crisp Morse code:
"DL/K5CLA DL/K5CLA DE PA3ADG KN"
Laine replied: "PA3ADG DE DL/K5CLA FB WIM UR 589 BK"
Wim answered:
"BK R BAD NEWS ANDY BT
NO SHIPS SAIL TO US OR CANADA BT
INSURANCE COMPANYS SAY ITS TOO DANGEROUS BT
SRI BT
PLANES STILL AGROUND INDEFINITELY BK"

Andy sent back: "BK R OK WIM TNX MUCH FER CHECK-ING BK"

Wim added:

"BK R I THINK UR BEST HOPE TO FIND SHIP TO UNITED STATES IN HAMBURG OR LE HAVRE OR MAR-SEILLES BT

BONNE CHANCE TO U ANDY BK"

After exchanging a few pleasantries, Andy signed off. He reset the Kaito's alarm to 0325 and again covered the radios to protect them from the weather.

He slept uneasily, waking several times to glance at the tritium markings on his watch dial. When the alarm went off again at 0325 GMT, he was better prepared, with his red lens subdued LED flashlight close at hand.

Blinking, he said to himself, "I need a cuppa java."

Andy switched the transceiver to 10.128. This was prearranged as the primary contact frequency for the Laine brothers. His note-pad included a list of alternate frequencies, to use in descending order, in case of interference.

At 0330 GMT (9:30 p.m. in New Mexico), Andy heard a weak Morse code signal: "K5CLB DE K5CLA, K5CLB DE K5CLA" The transceiver's signal strength indicator barely lit up. That did not bode well, since Lars had a 200 watt transmitter.

Andy reached for the paddles and replied, "K5CLA DE K5CLB KN"

Lars repeated his "K5CLB DE K5CLA, K5CLB DE K5CLA" transmission.

Again Andy replied, but it was apparent that his transmission was not propagating with enough strength to be heard above the static noise floor. After ten minutes of this frustration, Andy heard:

K5CLA DE K5CLB BT

IN CASE U CAN HEAR ME BT

ALL IS WELL WITH US AND KAYLEE BT

LOCAL POWER IS UP BUT US GRIDS DOWN BT
SITUATION LOOKING VERY MAD MAX ALL OVER
THE US BT
KL SAYS LUV ES 88 ES HURRY HOME BT
PSALM 91 TO U AR DE K5CLB SK

After three more attempts to make contact, Lars repeated the same brief report and then signed off.

Disgusted at his lack of success at two-way communication, Andy packed up his transceiver in the zipper bags. Realizing that he probably wouldn't be able to get back to sleep, he moved his ground pad and bivy bag closer to the stump and, being careful not to snag the antenna lead, he crawled in, cradling the shortwave receiver in his left arm.

Andy tuned through several bands, searching for English broadcasts. He caught a brief news summary on BBC at 0430 and a more lengthy news show on Radio Netherlands at 0500.

None of the news was good. The disruption in civilian air traffic in Europe was expected to continue for at least several weeks. Yesterday there had been a simultaneous pair of bombings by al Qaeda in Bonn and Frankfurt. Hundreds of Arab immigrants were rioting over the currency inflation. In Paris and several other large cities in France, they were back to their old tricks: torching dozens of parked cars. Meanwhile, New York City, Baltimore, Chicago, Dallas, and "Loss Angie-Lees" were in flames.

16

Grid Down

"Whole nations depend on technology. Stop the wheels for two days and you'd have riots. No place is more than two meals from a revolution. Think of Los Angeles or New York with no electricity. Or a longer view, fertilizer plants stop. Or a longer view yet, no new technology for ten years. What happens to our standard of living? Yet the damned fools won't pay ten minutes' attention a day to science and technology. How many people know what they're doing? Where do these carpets come from? The clothes you're wearing? What do carburetors do? Where do sesame seeds come from? Do you know? Does one voter out of thirty? They won't spend ten minutes a day thinking about the technology that keeps them alive."

—Larry Niven and Jerry Pournelle, *Lucifer's Hammer* (1977)

Bloomfield, New Mexico
November, the First Year

The collapse of the power grids was a turning point in the Crunch. Before the grid went down, life in the U.S. went on with just the stress of mass inflation. But after grid power disappeared, life changed radically. The Texas grid was the last one to go, just a few days after the eastern and western grids failed in rapid succession.

The cities of Farmington and Bloomfield had power supplied by the Farmington Electric Utility System (FEUS), a local power co-op that had its own production capacity from three natural-gas-fired plants, as well as a hydroelectric plant at the Navajo Dam, on the San Juan River. These provided nearly all of the power needs for their 1,700-square-mile service area. The remainder of their power was purchased from the western grid at wholesale rates. When the western grid collapsed, the FEUS was able to get local power—detached from the main grid—back online within a minute. If it were not for this local production capacity, the cities of the Four Corners region, as well as many farmers and ranchers, would have run out of water. Meanwhile, most other cities in the nation only had a three-day supply of water in the gravity tanks that provided pressure to the municipal lines. When the grid went down, the municipal water systems in those cities failed.

Robie Laine had carefully researched and chosen Bloomfield for relocation, primarily because of its local power generation capacity and agriculture. The communities' growth in the 1980s and 1990s eventually outstripped the local power production capacity of FEUS. However, by removing daytime service to some industrial customers and begging the local community to take extreme conservation measures—by asking customers to refrain from using electric heaters and to not use electric kitchen ranges during daylight hours—the utility was able to meet local needs. The local public relations ad campaign emphasized: "Save power, so we'll have water, and save water, so we'll have power." That message was heeded by most customers and power consumption dropped by 20 percent.

The other reason that Robie Laine had picked the Bloomfield area was that the region was served by a number of irrigation ditches that ran year-round. These were entirely gravity-fed as diversions from the San Juan River, far upstream to the east. The ditches north of the river were administered by the Bloomfield Irrigation District (BID) and ditches south of the river by the Hammond Ditch Association. The maze of ditches included the Porter Ditch, Citizen's Ditch, Jacquez Ditch, and the Pumpa De La Sequia. Thanks to fairly reliable rains that kept the Navajo Dam full, and seasonal releases from the dam, the irrigation ditches never went dry.

Throughout the United States, EPA water quality standards instituted in the 1980s and 1990s forced even cities with gravity-fed water systems to install electric pumps for water filtration. Older gravity filters were replaced with new filters that met the 0.3 nephelometer turbidity unit (NTU) standard filters. In most cases, this meant that new filters that were pressurized with electric pumps had to be installed. When the grids went down, many city water utility engineers were reluctant to bypass the pressurized water filtration systems for fear of being fined by the EPA. So people who otherwise would have gravity-fed drinking water available were no better off than those who lived where electrically pumped water from aquifers was the norm. This needlessly turned millions of additional people into refugees.

The San Juan Generating Station, on Navajo tribal land fifteen miles west of Farmington, near the town of Fruitland, was a coal-fired plant with four operating units that together could produce 2,000 megawatts of power, making it one of the biggest coal-fired generating stations in North America. After the western grid failed, the plant's managers took the plant offline. For the grid to function, nearly all of its production units had to be online: it was essentially an "all or nothing" grid, and the catastrophic grid failure of the Crunch was something that had never been fully anticipated.

In normal operation, the San Juan Generating Station consumed 15,000 tons of coal per day. The plant was the first of several western "mine-mouth" co-located power plants that drew from contiguous deposits of sub-bituminous coal. Much of the coal came directly to the plant by way of a 2,800-yard-long conveyor belt system.

By itself, San Juan could not serve the entire western grid.

Efforts to reconstitute the grid were almost comical. Only the hydroelectric plants of the Pacific Northwest and a couple of mine-mouth plants like San Juan stayed online during the reconstitution attempts. All of the smaller plants were off-line, mostly due to lack of workers, many of whom were striking in an attempt to get inflation indexing of their salaries. The nuclear plants all went off-line. Frustratingly, the Nuclear Regulatory Commission refused to recertify the plants for operation unless a three-day checklist restart procedure with umpteen inspections was strictly followed.

Wholesale payments to the San Juan Generating Station from the power utilities—averaging 2.5 cents per kilowatt/hour—had already become a joke, so the grid collapse was actually a relief to the plant management. With inflation raging, the break-even point for the plant would have been somewhere north of fifty cents per kilowatt/hour in the inflated dollars.

The adjoining coal mine, wholly owned by the Navajo Nation, stayed in operation for just two days after the San Juan Generating Station went offline. This production filled their staging area to capacity: 178,000 tons in open-air piles. It was decided that this coal would be designated a "tribal asset" and that it would be made freely available to "any registered Navajo Nation member, or anyone else who spoke fluent Navajo." All others had to pay cash. The rate was eventually settled at twenty cents in silver for a pickup load or one dollar in silver for a fifteen-yard dump truck load. Although the coal was inferior to hard anthracite, it sufficed for home heating.

Despite the collapse of the larger power grids, the lights stayed on almost continuously in the Farmington-Bloomfield region because the FEUS had its own generating capacity.

When Lars, Liz, and Kaylee gathered for breakfast one morning in November, they decided to put their preparation in high gear. On three legal pads, they created three priority lists, titled "Urgent," "Important," and "Tertiary."

The "Urgent" list had just four items:

Alps Prosthetic Skin Lotion (or maybe a safe oilfield goop silicone
     equivalent that will work with chafing for prosthetic arm?)
Detailed topo maps—preferably 7½-minute or 15-minute scale;
     need our local map sheet and the eight contiguous sheets
Gas lamp mantles—need 20+
Contact lens saline solution and spare glasses for Kaylee

The "Important" list included:

More batteries—especially need NiMH rechargeable; prefer later low
     self-discharge (LSD) type
Extra chains and spark plug for chainsaw
Distilled water for battery bank (Can make a solar still, if need be.)

The "Tertiary" list included:

Tampons
A LOT MORE salt for preserving meat and attracting deer
Playing cards
Books
More spices
More kerosene—any extra would be great for barter or charity
.22 LR ammo for bartering
Elk hunting calls

The Laines and Kaylee Schmidt were only able to work their
way through part of these lists before they ran out of cash. After
that, they successfully bartered for a few items, using ammunition
and pre-1965 silver coins.

17

Buckaroos

"You've got to understand that we had a big ranch but we only got money once or twice a year out of it. The money wasn't very free. All the money you got was in gold coin. I remember I was nearly fifteen or sixteen years old before I saw much paper money. It was all gold and silver. They didn't have any greenbacks that I remember. My dad would take the wool and mutton to sell, and he'd come back with some tobacco sacks full of twenty-dollar gold pieces. He used to drive three or four hundred head of sheep down to Cloverdale. They only brought about $2 a head. A big four horse [wagon-]load of wool taken over to Ukiah would pay for the groceries and clothes for the next winter. That was the big trip of the year, when I was a boy. That was when the money came in. That was the way that we used to get paid for things. Gold and silver coins. As kids, they used to let us play with the gold coins now and again. That was quite a celebration."

—Ernest E. Rawles (1897–1985)

Their trip to Berea Baptist Church on Sunday was memorable. Kaylee, who attended church only infrequently because of doctrinal differences, stayed at home to guard the roost. Lars, Beth, and Grace drove to church in Beth's Saturn Vue, since it got better mileage than Lars's Dodge Durango. They expected a light turnout. From what they had heard, the gasoline shortage had spooked many people into extreme conservation mode. Others were afraid to leave their homes unattended for fear of burglary.

As they pulled off of Blanco Road into the church parking lot, Lars chuckled and pointed to the overflow parking lot behind the church, which now had fifteen horses hitched up to a newly erected rail. Saddles were draped over a row of fifty-five-gallon drums resting on their sides, lined up in a phalanx. After they parked their car, they stepped over to the fence to look at the horses and saddles. Grace exclaimed, "Oooh, Daddy! Are we gonna get a horse?"

"Probably very soon, Anelli," Lars replied, using her pet name, which was Finnish for "Grace."

Beth pointed and said, "Notice that three of those are pack-saddles?"

Lars replied, "That's odd." He made a mental note to donate some more drums, since if the trend in transportation in this new era of insanely expensive gasoline continued, the church would soon need room for more saddles. He could spare the drums, since he had a dozen that had been painted white for use in horseback barrel racing back in the 1970s, but they were now useless for storing fluid, since their bottoms were badly rusted.

After walking through the sanctuary to the building's multipurpose room for their usual pre-church cup of coffee, they saw that the room was newly lined with two rows of pallet boxes on both sides, for donations. These were marked "Canned Food," "Perishables," "Women's Clothing," "Boys' Clothing," "Girls' Shoes," and so forth. As they walked by them, Beth said, "Let's sort through some extra clothes and shoes that Grace has outgrown, to donate." Lars nodded in agreement.

Ray, the leader of their adult Sunday school class, was there as usual, but he looked a bit self-conscious, carrying a SIG P250 in a hip holster, with four spare magazines in open-top pouches on the opposite hip. Lars said reassuringly, "I'm glad to see you're packing. Thanks for making everyone feel safer. Even though the police department is right across the road, we can't be too careful." As they sat down at one of the classroom tables, Beth asked quietly, "Is there any way we can still buy handguns?"

Lars shook his head. "No way, hon. You'd have to trade a couple of new cars to get a decent pistol these days."

During the "Prayer and Praise" time before the class began, when prayer requests were made, a black teenager who the Laines didn't recognize stood up, and announced: "You folks don't know me—or us. My name is Shadrach Phelps. My friends and I would appreciate your prayers. The three of us come from an orphanage over in Rio Arriba County that was closing down. We don't have anyplace to go, and we're looking for work around here, even for just room and board and hay for our horses. We're all hard workers; we each got our own horses and tack. We can buck hay all day long, split wood, butcher deer, and we know which end of the shovel goes in the ground. Oh, and a-course we're Christians. We're trusting in God's providence. Thing is, we all want to get hired on somewhere together; we're tight, so we don't wanna split up. Anyway, again, we'd appreciate your prayers." Phelps gave an embarrassed grin as he sat down. As he did, there were murmurs throughout the classroom.

After the Sunday school class, the Laines approached the Phelps boys. They were talking with a widow that Lars recognized as the owner of a ranch near Bloomfield. Shad Phelps was gesturing, pointing to his friends. "I'm sorry, but if you can't take all three of us, then I'll have to say no, but thank you." The woman nodded and turned away. Lars approached Shadrach Phelps and shook his hand. He looked Shad in the eye and pronounced, "My father always used to say, 'If you want to go fast, go alone. If you want to go far, then go together.' I'd like you young men to come work for me and my wife, at our ranch. I think that we'll go far, together."

Hiring the boys was a straightforward arrangement, but feeding their six horses was a bit more complicated. When Lars and Beth first took over the ranch, they found that Tim Rankin had not done a very good job of maintenance. The little brush and roller painting that he had done had left copious spatters, and the spray-painting had left obvious overspray. The elder Laines' saddles were still there, but Rankin had "borrowed" and never returned their girth straps as well as several horse pads and blankets. At least Rankin had been vigilant about poisoning the mice and pack rats, and he had done a decent job of weed control in the pastures.

Lars and Andy were both away on active duty when Tim Rankin moved into the house. When they asked about their father's guns, Rankin said that he hadn't found any in the house. This made Lars and Andy suspicious, because they knew that their father owned several guns. Since these guns had mostly sentimental value, they didn't push the issue with Rankin, who pled, "Well, if they were in the house, they musta been burglarized before I ever got there. There were a lot of strangers in the house after your dad passed on: the paramedics, the cops, the coroner, and probably more. Any one of them could have lifted your dad's guns."

When Tim Rankin left, there were still two tons of year-old alfalfa hay in the hay barn and about three tons of baled straw in the stable loft. As soon as his job offers to the Phelps boys were accepted, Lars started to make inquiries about hay, grain, and firewood. After much searching and dickering, he bartered a mint-condition U.S. $5 gold piece in exchange for nine tons of alfalfa, five cords of Pinyon Pine firewood, seven salt blocks, and two hundred pounds of molasses-sweetened COB—a mix of cracked corn, rolled oats, and barley. Lars felt that he got the worst end of the deal, because gold was then selling for $8,460 per ounce. Since not even counting its numismatic value, the $5 gold piece contained almost a quarter ounce of gold, Lars felt cheated.

The ranch's pair of fifteen-acre irrigated pastures were in decent shape, but to be useful to their full capacity once again, they needed to be reseeded. The local feed store still had some sacks of orchard grass pasture blend seed on hand. It took some dickering, but Laine was able to get fifty pounds of the seed blend in exchange for three silver quarters and a box of fifty .22 Long Rifle cartridges.

Laine soon put the Phelps boys to work, broadcasting half of the sack of seed with a hand-cranked broadcaster, primarily in the pastures' many bare spots. But the more difficult work came in the next two weeks, when they laboriously raked the seed into the soil. They also had to be vigilant in scaring off any passing birds until after the seed had sprouted. Like so many other things that had previously been taken for granted, grass seed had become a precious commodity.

It was after the orphans arrived that Lars also discovered that Tim Rankin had pilfered most of the horse-care tools and veterinary supplies for his father's horses. There was little left other than a couple of half-empty jars of Swat fly repellent. Luckily, the boys had brought with them a pair of hoof nippers, a hoof rasp, a brush, and two horse combs. Diego Aguilar had also providently sent along a sixteen-ounce bulk can of horse wormer. Instead of using a mouth syringe like the one Lars had previously used, the boys heavily coated a mouth bit with the paste and attached the bit, just as they would do for riding. Giving a horse a double-handful of sweet feed then ensured that the medicine went down. While the "Diego method" of dosing was less accurate, Laine presumed that it was effective.

18

Rock 'n' Roll

"Note that Finland's five million people own four million personal firearms. Just wait till Congressman Schumer finds out about that!"
—Jeff Cooper, *Jeff Cooper's Commentaries*, Vol. 3, No. 2,
January 1995

Stowing the boys' tack and moving into the bunkhouse didn't take long, as they hadn't carried much gear. The bunkhouse was utilitarian but well insulated. The interior walls were covered with unpainted plywood. It had two narrow rooms that sat side by side, each with its own door, off the foyer. One of them had a window at one end with some gauzy curtains, and two sets of bunk beds that were positioned end to end. The other room didn't contain much except for about thirty boxes, most of which contained *National Geographic* magazines that had belonged to Laine's maternal grandmother. Some of these dated back to the 1930s. Both of the rooms were heated by a barrel woodstove on a low flagstone pedestal in the foyer.

Soon after moving in, and starting their monthly rotating "OP" duty shifts, the boys realized that one of them would have to sleep during the day, but the daylight would make it difficult for that individual to sleep. So Shad asked Lars if they could move the bunk beds to the other room, which could be kept completely dark. Lars gave his consent. But just ten minutes later Shad returned to the house, looking confused.

"Mr. Laine, there's something wrong with that other room in the bunk house."

"What do you mean, 'wrong'?"

"When the bunk beds were in the south room, they fit fine, but now, when we moved them into the other room, they don't fit. That's weird, because the rooms are supposed to be the same length. Can you come and take a look?"

Lars pulled a twenty-five-foot tape measure from his desk drawer and followed Shad to the bunkhouse. With the tape measure, they found that the windowless room was six inches shorter than the other. Lars chuckled. Pulling the bunk back from the far wall, he began rapping with his knuckles in various places on the plywood, listening for differences in sounds.

Lars half sang, "Methinks my dad did some creative carpentry here."

"So it's like a *fake* wall?" Rueben asked.

"Yes, I suspect that it is. Give me just a minute."

Leaving the boys, Laine walked briskly to the shop and soon returned with his Makita cordless screw gun. Starting at the middle of the wall at chest level, Lars began backing-out the Sheetrock screws that held the plywood in place at sixteen-inch intervals. He was surprised when the first screw dropped to the floor after just a few turns. Looking down at the screw, he saw that it was just a stub.

"That's odd. Must have broken off."

The same thing happened with the next screw.

"What the . . . ?" Lars exclaimed.

Reaching down, he picked up the two fallen screws. They were both just three-eighths of an inch long. Examining them closely, he observed, "These didn't break. These were sawed off, with a hacksaw."

Lars resumed removing the screws from the plywood sheet in front of him. He found that most of the screws had been shortened and installed just to give the appearance of functional fasteners. But only six of them—four in the corners, and two that were at the midpoint of the plywood sheet—were a full two inches in length and went through to the studs behind.

"Oh, Dad! You clever Finn. Take a look at this, guys: this panel is designed to be removed, with only six screws to take out."

"Here, help me with this," said Lars as he backed the last screw out of the upper left corner.

Laine and the boys bounced the three-quarter-inch-thick sheet of plywood loose and pulled it away, revealing a cavity behind that was crammed full of stacked ammo cans—mostly U.S. Army surplus cans originally made to hold .30 caliber ammunition—and several odd-shaped items wrapped in heavy black plastic trash bags, sealed with Priority Mail packing tape. Starting with the third row of ammo cans, all of the items were either held in place with hardware wire attached to screw eyes or hung from closet hooks. It was now obvious that his father had added a framework of two-by-sixes at the far end of the room, and covered it to look like the original wall. Given the dimensions of the rooms, the difference in their depths was almost imperceptible.

Lars began laughing as he starting pulling the contents from the wall cache. "You boys may have heard that us Finns are the quiet, stoical type. Well, my dad—his first name was Robie—fit that description to a T. My mom said that my dad would go for days at a time without much more than grunts and a 'Good morning' and a 'Good night.' He never told me about this wall, and my mom and my brother never mentioned it, either, so I suppose that he kept it all to himself." After a pause he added, "And since he died suddenly of a heart attack after my mom died, he never got the chance."

It took the better part of the afternoon for him to inventory the gear. Meanwhile, Shad and Reuben used the Makita to remove other sheets of plywood throughout the bunkhouse, checking for more hidden compartments. They found none.

Starting first with the plastic-wrapped guns, Laine found four Finnish M39 bolt-action rifles, almost identical to his own rifle, except that one of them was built on an early hexagonal receiver, and they had barrels from different makers: One was a Tikka, two were made by Valmet (marked "VKT") and the other was made by Sako. Always thorough and safety-conscious, Robie Laine had attached tags to the trigger guard of each gun that read "Grease in bore and chamber. Remove before firing!"

Inside one of the plastic bags was a zippered green canvas case that, when unzipped, revealed an M1 Carbine equipped with M2 conversion parts. Lars exclaimed, "Son of a . . . This thing is rock-'n'-roll."

Shad asked, "You mean it's a full auto?"

"Well, technically the term is 'selective fire,' 'cause it will shoot either semiauto or full auto." After checking the gun's chamber to ensure that it was unloaded, Laine thumbed the carbine's selector lever on the left side of the receiver, explaining, "The rear position here is semiauto, but when it's flipped forward, it's full auto. A lot of guys converted M1 Carbines into M2s back in the 1960s, '70s, and '80s, since the conversion parts were pretty widely available, and it doesn't require any modification to the receiver."

Shad grinned, and said, "Oh, yeah, I read about M2 Carbines once, in a gun magazine. But that's a major bust if you get caught with it."

Lars went on, "Yes, legally it's a contraband gun, but given the present circumstances, I think that's about to become a nonissue, if it isn't one already. But just the same, I don't think that I'll go around advertising that I have an unregistered Class 3 gun. I'd appreciate it if you'd also keep your lips zipped."

Shad said, "Yes, sir!" The other boys gave exaggerated nods.

In another canvas case, this one reinforced with green leather at the ends, was a Valmet M62, the Finnish equivalent of the Russian AK-47, with a tubular stock. Laine let out a whistle when he saw the gun. He knew that the Valmet was considered the Cadillac of the AK family, and very valuable.

One ammo can held eleven spare magazines for the M2 Carbine, and another had seven green plastic "waffle" magazines for the Valmet M62.

There were also various slings and pouches for magazines, and an odd-looking bayonet for the Valmet M62, in a green leather sheath. It was marked "FISKARS." To Lars, it looked more like a filleting knife than a bayonet.

Later, after the boys went into the house to help get dinner ready, Lars was examining the Valmet M62 and realized that it, too, was selective fire. Looking closely, he saw that instead of just two positions, the safety/selector had three positions, with one in the middle for full-auto fire. He concluded that it was an original Finnish Defense Force M62, rather than a converted civilian-production Valmet. Later he told Beth that the gun had probably been smuggled into the U.S. by his uncle Aki, who for many years was an engineering officer on a Finnish merchant marine ship.

The last of the guns was a Lahti 9mm semiauto pistol with five spare magazines wrapped in brown waxed paper, along with an original Finnish military holster. The pistol had a single-column magazine and looked vaguely like a Luger. It had plastic grips marked "VKT." Lars chortled when he saw that, and put on a deep radio announcer's voice: "Yet another fine product from the industrious workers at Valmet." He explained to Lisbeth that since the end of World War II, Valmet had expanded into a conglomerate, branching out to make everything from log harvesters to military aircraft. Lars had read about Lahti pistols, but he'd never handled one.

Finally, Laine began to inventory the ammunition in detail. In all, there were 1,100 rounds of 7.62x54r for the bolt actions, al-most 1,500 rounds of .30 Carbine, 1,280 rounds of 7.52x39 for the Valmet M62, and 650 rounds of 9mm for the Lahti. He was thrilled to find that one of the .30 caliber ammo cans was filled not with ammo but with rolls of pre-1965 silver quarters.

It was not until the next day that Lars had the opportunity to examine the can holding the rolls of silver quarters. When he emp-tied it out to count the rolls, he found a sealed envelope tucked in alongside the rolls. It was marked "Lars and Andrew" in his father's handwriting. He opened it and found a typewritten letter. It read:

My Dear Sons:

It was my intention to give you these coins when you'd both graduated from high school, but back then I had my doubts about your maturity, so I decided to hold on to them until after you earned your commissions.

I want you to appreciate these silver quarters for what they really are--not just an investment, and not just a "family heirloom." They represent REAL money. Pardon the lecture, but you need to judge their value four ways--in terms of wages, manufactured goods, services and real property.

First, let's look at wages. Back in "the old days"--say, before World War I--the average wage for a working man was around one silver dollar a day. One day's wage right now for someone that works at a minimum wage job (at $7.25 per hour) is $58 for an eight-hour work day. A more typical wage for a workman with experience is around $11 per hour ($88 per day.) One dollar (face value) in 90% silver pre-1965 coinage contains 22.5 grams of silver, or 0.7234 troy ounces per dollar face value. Today's spot price of silver is $17.55 per troy ounce. So that makes a pre-inflation dollar (a true DOLLAR in silver coin) worth $12.79. (Or just think of it as roughly 13 times $1 in face value--"13 times face," whether it is silver dimes, quarters, or half dollars.) So, to put things in perspective, it takes $6.76 in pre-'65 silver coinage to equal one typical day's wages ($88 in the current fiat paper money). Thus, in terms of wages silver SHOULD have a spot value about five or six times its current value. By this measure, silver is now grossly undervalued.

Next, manufactured goods. In 1964 (the last year that silver coins were in general circulation in the U.S.), a basic blued-steel Colt Model 1911 .45 automatic pistol cost around $65 retail. Today, a comparable Colt M1911 (a Series 80) costs around $775 retail. So if you were to sell $65 face value of this cache of silver coinage at your local coin shop, and they offered you 12 times "face"--that would net you $780 in the current funny money. You could then easily go buy a .45 at your local gun shop with the proceeds. The bottom line: it is not pistols that have gone UP in price. Rather, it is paper dollars that have gone DOWN in purchasing power.

How about services? In 1964, a haircut cost around 75 cents, or perhaps $1 in the big city. My last haircut cost $14. I suspect that other services are comparable, whether it is your local dentist or your local brothel. (I trust and pray that neither of you will ever use the latter service.)

Now let's look at the relative values of silver coinage and real property. In 1964, the median house price in the U.S. was around $18,000. Today, it is around $170,000. (A 9.4x increase.) If you had set aside $18,000 face value in silver coins in 1964 (18 bags of $1,000 face value each), and held them until the present day, they'd net you around $216,000 if you sold them to a bullion coin dealer. That is enough for an ABOVE AVERAGE house. So obviously silver coins have held their value far better than paper dollars. Anyone who sits on PAPER dollars for very long--at least dollars that aren't earning much interest--is a fool.

I hope and pray that you keep investing in silver. You should acquire much more than this little nestegg.

In my opinion, you can trust tangibles (like silver and guns), but you shouldn't put much trust in paper currency in the long term. To safeguard your net worth in the inflationary days to come, always remember: Don't leave your earnings in paper money for long. As quickly as possible, convert it into tangibles, to protect your savings from the ravages of inflation. Consumer price inflation is mild now, but that probably won't be the case in the near future. So adjust your way of thinking and doing business, accordingly.

Never forget: Inflation is a hidden form of taxation!

Divide these coins equally between you. Spend them wisely, and up until the day that the balloon goes up, spend them only as a last resort. And never forget their REAL worth.

Love,
  Dad

As Andy tucked the letter back into the envelope, he said resolutely, "Yeah, Dad, you were right."

Each of the Phelps boys was given one of the M39 bolt-action rifles in lieu of their first two months' wages. The next day a few precious rounds of the hard-kicking 7.62x54R were used to sight in each of their rifles. Because that ammo was corrosively primed, Laine showed the boys how to carefully clean the rifles' bores and bolt faces, making sure that they cleaned their barrels for several successive days, to be sure that all traces of corrosive priming salts had been removed.

The bunkhouse was soon decorated with a Monument Valley poster and maps from *National Geographic* magazines. The boys settled into a routine of guard shifts, caring for their horses, some house chores, and reading—lots of reading.

Having the Phelps Boys at the ranch was a great relief to Lars,

Beth, and Kaylee, who up until then were starting to feel the strain of guarding the ranch by themselves.

Lars's morning routine was to first pray at dawn silently and then cuddle with his wife. Then he would sit up and put on his eye patch and his prosthetic hand. As needed, he'd put some silicone cream on the stump first. Lars had learned that the size of his residual limb changed during each day. Fluid pooled in the limb at night when the prosthesis was off, and was pushed back out when "Mr. President" was strapped on. Thus, the fit was slightly tighter in the morning than in the afternoon or evening.

Still in his pajamas, Lars did twenty rapid push-ups and forty sit-ups. Then he'd shower and get dressed. Before the Crunch, he would also read his e-mail and have a cup of coffee with breakfast. But both of those diversions soon became just memories. In recent days he would eat at the kitchen table with Matthew Phelps, who was the early riser of the Phelps trio.

19

Gainful

"As every individual, therefore, endeavors as much as he can both to employ his capital in the support of domestic industry, and so to direct that industry that its produce may be of the greatest value; every individual necessarily labours to render the annual revenue of the society as great as he can. He generally, indeed, neither intends to promote the public interest, nor knows how much he is promoting it. By preferring the support of domestic to that of foreign industry, he intends only his own security; and by directing that industry in such a manner as its produce may be of the greatest value, he intends only his own gain, and he is in this, as in many other cases, led by an invisible hand to promote an end which was no part of his intention. Nor is it always the worse for the society that it was no part of it. By pursuing his own interest he frequently promotes that of the society more effectually than when he really intends to promote it."

—**Adam Smith**, *Inquiry into the Nature and Causes of the Wealth of Nations* (1776)

Lars and Beth Laine were cuddled in bed, by the light of a single candle. For the first time in many days, they rested comfortably, knowing that one of the boys would be on guard duty all night long, listening and watching for intruders. Beth asked, "How are we going to make do? Your disability retirement checks are still coming, but they're a joke. The check for one month might buy a couple of days' worth of groceries, if we're lucky. And at the rate things are going, in another couple of weeks a check might just buy one can of beans."

Lars sighed. "Well, we aren't going to make a living on twenty acres in this country, especially with seven or eight mouths to feed. If we just barter for food and fuel, our stash of precious metals will eventually get depleted. It's pretty clear that I need to look for work, putting my military training to use."

"What? As a mercenary?"

"Not exactly. There are a lot of businesses in town that are doing a pitiful job of securing what they have. Whether it's a burglary or a robbery at gunpoint, they know that sometime within a few months somebody is going to come and clean them out. It's only the refinery that seems to have their act together so far, in terms of security. So I think I ought to go hire myself out as a security consultant. I could set them up some rudimentary physical security—maybe I could team up with one of the welding shops on that—and also train their employees on shooting and small-team tactics." Stroking his wife's back, he added, "Now that we discovered my dad's guns and that silver, I also have some leverage in bartering situations. I'd like your blessing to poke around town and see what happens."

Beth sighed, "That sounds good to me. You just be careful, and proceed with prayer."

Upgrading the security at the Laines' ranch went quickly, with the help of the boys. The main task was constructing an observation post (OP) with railroad ties. Lars carefully positioned it on a gentle rise fifty-two yards from the southwest corner of the house. From there, there was a good view of the house, barn, and bunkhouse. The OP measured just six feet square and five feet high. By heaping split pinyon pine rounds over it, they made it look like a nondescript pile of firewood.

After building the OP, they moved on to upgrading the house itself, for defense against looters. Lars was fond of saying, "When it comes to stopping bullets, there's nothing like mass, and sandbags are cheap mass." It was clear that they'd need sandbags—a lot of sandbags. There were sixteen empty feed sacks in the barn. These had been made to hold fifty pounds of grain, so they were oversize for their needs. If filled with sand, they would have weighed more than one hundred pounds. So Lars cut each sack in half and restitched the cut off ends to form additional sacks using a large curved upholstery needle. This task was just like the sailcloth stitching that his uncle Aki had taught Lars when he was twelve years old. But this yielded just thirty-two sandbags—not nearly enough for their needs.

They made inquiries all over Farmington and Bloomfield, but found that all of the available feed sacks had already been bought up by others with the same idea. After a few days of searching, they heard that feed sacks were still available from Southwest Seed, sixty miles away, in Dolores, Colorado. Unlike a typical retail feed store, this was a seed-packing and grain elevator operation set up to handle wholesale quantities.

When he arrived, Lars was not surprised to see several armed men guarding the feed and seed complex. They were, after all, guarding something quite valuable.

The sales manager walked Lars around. He pointed out their inventory, which included many pallets of brand-new bundled feed sacks. Most of them were white, but about one-third of the twenty-pound size were tan. It was those that Laine wanted, since they were the right size for sandbags and they'd blend in well in desert country.

Negotiating the sack purchase took a while. This reminded Lars of transactions he'd witnessed several years before, at the bazaar in Basra, Iraq. It started with pleasantries, followed by a few outrageous offers and counteroffers and finally some serious dickering for more realistic prices.

They eventually agreed on $4.50 face value in pre-1965 quarters and two hundred rounds of .22 Long Rifle rimfire cartridges in exchange for six hundred empty tan sacks. While he was there, Lars also bought forty more pounds of pasture blend for $1.20 face value in silver dimes. It was more than Laine needed, but he anticipated that it would be good to keep on hand for barter.

Life at the Laines' ranch was comfortable, at least by post-Crunch standards. Everyone had enough to eat, and the rotating security shifts were just four hours per day from Monday through Saturday, and six hours on Sundays. They soon instituted "L.&L.'s Standing Rules." These rules were penned on a large piece of card stock by Lisbeth and posted inside the door of the bunkhouse:

1. If in doubt, sound the alarm.
2. Keep all doors locked 24/7.
3. Never leave the house unarmed.
4. Never leave the house without a walkie-talkie.
5. Always carry at least 40 rounds of ammunition with each bolt-action rifle, and at least three magazines for semi-autos.
6. Treat every approaching stranger as a potential enemy.
7. Keep your friends close and your enemies at 9x distance.
8. No guard quits their post unless properly relieved.
9. Severe punishment for anyone who falls asleep while on watch.
10. Horse grooming and hoof work daily, without fail.
11. No lights visible from outside after dark.
12. Good stewardship in all things. No wasteful behavior!
13. Keep proper sanitation and cleanliness.
14. Leave every gate the way you found it, unless told otherwise.
15. Maintain everything to last a lifetime—it may have to!

16. Rust is an enemy. Oil and grease are allies.

17. Maintain the "need to know" rule. No loose lips!

18. Courteous behavior and Christian attitudes, always.

19. No foul or blasphemous language.

20. Respect everyone's privacy.

21. 100% effort. No slacking on chores.

22. Health and safety are top priorities.

23. Watch for signs of dehydration and hypothermia—self and others.

24. Be honest and forthright in all business dealings.

25. Recognize the head of the house as final authority on all decisions.

26. Count your blessings.

27. Be charitable and tithe consistently.

28. Smile! God loves you. You are in His covenant.

Below that, Lisbeth added a quote from her favorite Psalm:

> "The LORD knoweth the days of the upright: and their inheritance shall be for ever. They shall not be ashamed in the evil time: and in the days of famine they shall be satisfied."
>
> —PSALM 37:18–19

20

Tentacles

*"The government turns every contingency into an excuse for en-
hancing power in itself."*

—John Adams

Fort Knox, Kentucky
November, the First Year

Maynard Hutchings and his council that headed the Provisional
Government soon consolidated their power in Kentucky and much
of Tennessee, declaring themselves "The Sole and Legitimate Provisional Government of the United States of America and Possessions," with Hutchings himself voted by his council as "president
pro tempore."

The Provisional Government spread its sphere of influence
rapidly. Any towns that resisted were quickly crushed. The mere
sight of dozens of tanks and APCs was enough to make most
townspeople cower in fear. Anything that the ProvGov couldn't
accomplish through intimidation, it accomplished with bribes. A
new currency was spread around lavishly among the Hutchings
cronies. Covertly, some criminal gangs were hired as security contractors and used as enforcers of the administration's nationalization schemes. Some of these gangs were given military vehicles
and weapons and promised booty derived from eliminating other
gangs that were not as cooperative. Hit squads were formed to

stifle any dissent. These did so through abductions, arson, and murder. Nobody was ever able to prove a link, but an inordinately large number of conservative members of Congress from the old government disappeared or were reported killed by bandits.

Some foreign troops were clothed in U.S. ACU digital or OCP camouflage. But most foreign troops stayed in their own uniforms and were used as shock troops, to eliminate any pockets of resistance. Disaffection with the new government smoldered everywhere that they went to pacify.

Within the first three months of launching the new government, Hutchings was in contact via satellite with the UN's new headquarters in Brussels to request peacekeeping assistance. (The old UN building in New York had been burned, and the entire New York metropolitan region was nine-tenths depopulated and controlled by hostile gangs.) Hutchings had at first naively assumed that the UN's assistance would be altruistic, with no strings attached. It was only after the first UN troops started to arrive in large numbers that it became clear that UN officers would control the operation. Eventually, Hutchings became little more than a figurehead. The *real* power in the country was held by the UN administrators. They had their own chain of command that bypassed the Hutchings administration, and they had direct control over the military.

One closely guarded secret was that Maynard Hutchings signed an agreement that promised payment of thirty metric tons of gold from the Fort Knox depository to defray the costs of transporting and maintaining a mixed contingent of UN peacekeepers, mostly from Germany, Holland, and Belgium. The gold was shuttled out of the country in half-ton increments in flights from Fort Campbell, Kentucky. There had also been the offer of Chinese peacekeeping troops, but Hutchings insisted that no Asian or African troops be used on American soil, saying, "I want it to be all white fellas that'll blend in."

In early December, Lars Laine made an appointment to meet with L. Roy Martin at his office. Although Laine's daily "uniform" around the ranch was a pair of khaki pants and a digital ACU shirt—his best bet to blend in, given the predominant local sagebrush over sandy soil—he decided to brush his tan leather combat boots and wear his full ACU uniform. He even "de-sterilized" it, slapping on a Velcro flag on the shoulder, a subdued oak leaf on the center of his chest, and a "LAINE" nametape. Beth suggested that he wear his tan eye patch, saying, "It's better you look rugged, rather than him spending the whole time eyeballing your glass eye." Only Beth could say something like that to Lars without him feeling the least offended. She always knew what to wear to a party.

As Lars drove back from shopping, he passed a group of men who were constructing a reinforced fighting position beside the road on a low hill, about halfway between Farmington and Bloomfield. It was obviously part of the sheriff's posse work on Bloomfield roadblocks that he had heard about. They observed his passing vehicle suspiciously, and two of them stepped toward their rifles until they saw the license plate prefix.

Lars drove up to the refinery's gates and was not surprised to see that they were closed and manned by a pair of guards armed with both M1A rifles and holstered pistols. One of them had a clipboard. Lars rolled down his window and announced, "Major Lars Laine. I have an appointment with Mr. Martin."

Lars was asked for his ID, and the guard took twenty seconds to closely examine it, comparing it with the notes on his clipboard. This obviously was not just a perfunctory "Wave them through" sort of stop. As the guard was looking at Laine's driver's license and military ID card, Lars sized up the guard: He was in his early thirties and had a buzz cut. He had the bearing of an Army or Marine Corps veteran. He wore unmarked ACUs, desert boots, IBA, and slightly scratched Oakley sunglasses and a tan baseball cap, for the full-on Special Forces "operator" look. And just as he was being handed back his ID cards, Lars noticed a woven texture on the back of the well-worn clipboard. It was one of the "executive protection" Kevlar clipboards that he had seen in Iraq. Clearly, these guys were not your everyday rent-a-cops.

The guard whispered a code phrase on a handie-talkie, and ten seconds later the electric gate opened. Lars drove up to the plant's administrative office, a nondescript windowless concrete slab tilt-up building that looked recently constructed. He stepped out of the cab and slung his Valmet across his back.

To Lars, the building looked normal except that he could see a parapet of sandbags at one corner of the roof. And then as he approached the building he noticed the front door, which had probably originally been glass, had been replaced with what appeared to be plywood, painted dark gray to match the building.

A neatly printed sign with an arrow read, "Press buzzer and identify yourself. Door is heavy: Pull hard!" Lars pressed the button and looked up at a CCTV camera. "Major Lars Laine." A moment later a buzzer sounded and Laine pulled the door open. It was indeed very heavy. As he swung it open, he could see that the plywood was just a veneer, covering an unpainted sheet of half-inch-thick plate steel. After he stepped through, the spring-loaded door automatically closed behind him with a click. Laine turned to see that there was a green indicator light shining above the door and that there were heavy metal brackets installed to manually bar the door. He turned forward again to see that he was in a narrow passageway just over three feet wide and nine feet long, with a cinder-block wall on one side, the building's slab outer wall on the other side, and tongue-and-groove eight-inch planks sheeted above. At the end of the hallway was another door, also steel, this one unpainted, and he was again under the lens of a CCTV camera. He heard the inner door being unbarred. After a pause, a woman's voice on the intercom announced, "You may proceed."

Pushing open the inner door, which seemed even heavier—it looked like three-quarter-inch plate steel—Lars came into an entry foyer. A trim woman in her thirties with a stubby "breaching" riot shotgun slung at her side greeted him, "Good morning, sir, Mr. Martin is ready to see you. Follow me." She walked him past mainly empty desks to the far end of the building. Lisbeth would have been happy to see that Lars was giving attention to the secretary's Remington riot gun and not her rear end.

As Laine was ushered into Martin's office, he was taken aback to see that instead of a paneled executive office, it appeared to be a converted storage room, with no decorations. Martin had a round face and a middle-age paunch. He wore suit pants, a polo shirt, and small Giorgio Armani wire-framed eyeglasses. Martin had what Lars called a desk jockey physique.

Martin was seated behind an odd square desk that was constructed a bit like a church pulpit, with slab sides that went all the way to the floor. A Kenwood multiband transceiver and a police scanner sat stacked on one corner of the desk. Their antenna co-ax cables went straight up to the ceiling, adding to the utilitarian look of the office.

"Take a seat," Martin said, with a wave.

As he did, resting the Valmet across his thighs, Laine realized that the desk where Martin sat was probably constructed out of plate steel and just covered with wood for show.

Martin began, "I've heard some good things about you."

"Likewise. And I'm impressed with your security around here."

"You were in the Army?"

"Yeah, I was branched Civil Affairs. I got out as an O-4."

Martin responded, "I heard that was becoming its own branch just as I was leaving the Army. Times change."

"Yeah, Iraq and Afghanistan changed a lot of things for the Army. 'Low Intensity Conflict,' 'Nation Building,' all that."

Recognizing the distinctive "cheese grater" black fore end on Laine's rifle, Martin intoned, "That's a Valmet, isn't it?"

"You sure know your guns. Yes, it's a Valmet. It belonged to my father. Before he passed away, he collected guns from Finland, since he was Finnish."

"But I thought your family name was English?"

"Lane, without the *i* is English, but Laine with the *i* is fairly common for folks of Finnish descent."

"Oh, I see." After an awkward pause, L. Roy asked, "Can you sum up your military experience?"

"I did three tours: one in Afghanistan, and two in Iraq. I spent a lot of time outside the wire. Civil Affairs officers mainly do host country liaison. That got dicey at times. I was an IPI liaison. That stands for 'indigenous populations and institutions.' I picked up a bit of Pashto and a conversational level of Arabic. I was nearly done with my third tour when I got this present, courtesy of some *jihadi othek* who was given some electronics goodies by the Iranians." Laine raised his prosthetic hand and rotated it at the wrist. "So I hear that you want to set up roadblocks, like the ones they're building around Farmington."

"That's right. But I'm getting some resistance from the Bloomfield City Council. They think I'm an alarmist."

"They ought to go visit Phoenix or Denver. That would give them a whole new attitude, right quick."

Both men nodded.

Laine asked, "Say, before we talk too much grand strategy, can you tell me how you're keeping the refinery operational?"

"With a bit of Yankee ingenuity," L. Roy laughed. "The staff here is excellent. You've got to understand that most modern refineries run a 'closed-loop' twenty-four-hour-a-day continuous operation. The alternative to continuous ops is 'batch' operations.

Batch ops are usually confined to a specific grade of product, like diesel, and any operation waste is tanked. In the old days they simply pumped this waste in a nearby ditch or, if they were really 'green,' they put it in a clay-lined open holding pond.

"To run a continuous op, you of course need continuous feedstock that can meet the minimum 'throughput' and tankage for product storage for final distribution. The tricky thing is that all aspects have to be balanced to avoid stopping any of the process, whether that is feedstock delivery, throughput, or product distribution. Any bottleneck can upset the process. On the other hand, a batch op depends on a set volume of material for a set amount of yield for specific production runs and is not a reliable candidate for cogeneration due to its 'up-and-down' nature. You need to have around 150 pounds of steam pressure.

"So we opted to run continuously, by mothballing three of our four units. The one unit that we are running has a co-gen plant, just in case the local utility power has a hiccup. And that power can even back-feed, just in case their power plant goes down and it needs to be restarted." After taking a noisy breath, Martin went on, "It's a bit of a scramble, keeping enough feedstock coming in, but we're working the kinks out."

Laine nodded.

Martin folded his hands across his chest, and said: "I suppose you're interested in my background too. Here's the essentials: I spent twelve years in the Army, Signal Corps, mainly doing strategic long-haul communications systems, plus some tactical systems. In my time overseas, I saw a lot of Third World countries that were failed states. What I saw in Kosovo and in the '-stans' colored my perspective on the current Crunch. Here it is in a nutshell: I think people here in the Four Corners are vastly underestimating the impact that the big cities to the south and north of us are going to have on us. Our neighbors think that we're in a safe, isolated area, but we're really not."

Laine nodded in agreement, and L. Roy went on: "We're incredibly lucky here to still have electricity. Most of the country is in the dark, and because of it, they're rapidly descending into anarchy. Food is the other key resource, and here in the Southwest, water is scarce to grow crops. Most non-farming communities are at risk because they simply don't have enough calories stored to get them through any kind of crisis. But storage is no more than limited capital to allow people the time to grow more food. Food production requires land, water, and the requisite experience. On a large scale, it also takes fuel. The carrying capacity of the U.S. using traditional non-petroleum farming techniques will be just a fraction of what most people think it would be. Also, most areas of the U.S., especially the cities, don't have anywhere near enough farmable land to go back to some kind of agrarian pattern. Without public infrastructure and modern transportation, we're going to experience a huge die-off caused mostly by starvation."

Laine added: "I agree. And for those left, I think it'll come down to the 'haves' versus the 'have-nots.' The psychologists call that the 'we/they paradigm.'"

"Right! In a total collapse without immediate restoration of the power grid and the economic web, basically everyone who lives in a city is doomed unless they can take over some kind of farmland. Those that live in areas without enough farmland will be have-nots. Period. I don't care how much food that survivalists have stored in their basements. It will run out someday. In the long term, it's grow food and raise livestock—or die."

L. Roy continued, "But here's my point: those teeming millions will not just starve and go away. I believe that any family who thinks they can defend a working farm against raiders just by themselves is delusional. Humans are dangerous. The fact is, they are the most dangerous animals on earth. We must never lose sight of that. We're now surrounded by starving predators that are much more dangerous than tigers. It won't be like that earthquake in Haiti, where the bad guys had machetes. Here in the U.S. of A., the vast majority will be armed with firearms. The ones currently without firearms will obtain them by any means necessary, including looting government armories. These are thinking and highly motivated enemies. They know how to read maps. Some of them have a grasp of hydrology and can appreciate the difference between solely gravity-fed water systems and those that need grid power. They can put two and two together. Secondly, consider that raiders—the 'outlaw looting groups' that they call them now in the newspapers—may be a threat for a very short period, but I really don't see permanent groups of more than a dozen ever forming. They will be quickly replaced by much larger groups of 'citizens' doing essentially the same things, but much better armed and organized."

Laine interjected, "It may just be a matter of semantics—just what they call themselves, or the flag they fly. But they'll still be looters by any other name."

Martin gave Lars a thumbs-up and continued: "One of my overseas stints in stratcom was in, of all places, Albania in 1998. Talk about being in the wrong place at the wrong time! A few hours after Albania's political crisis started—which was caused by a huge national lottery pyramid scam—almost every adult male in the country procured an AKM from government stocks. Armories were the first targets looted. As the crisis started, I flew from Brussels back into Tirana packing a pistol and a sack of money, naively thinking I would be able to move around the country and defend myself, getting our in-place assets out of 'jams.' What a laugh. Everyone had me outgunned, and the vast majority of these yahoos had military training of some sort. I never got out of the capital city. Every road seemed to have roadblocks every few miles, blocked by armed local citizens."

Martin carried on: "Without central authority, people don't just starve and go away. They form their own polities—their own governments. These polities are often organized around town or city government or local churches. They may call it a city council or a committee or a senate. The bottom line is, 'We the People' will do whatever 'we' have to do to survive. That's your 'we/they paradigm' in its essence, all the way to the point of xenophobia. And that specifically includes taking away NAPI's grain or even just stored food that was prudently set aside by the more forward-thinking individual families. When things started to unravel, I realized that when—not if—a polity formed, I'd better be part of that process. If not, my refinery and my employees would be looked upon as 'resources' instead of part of—members of—the community."

Laine jumped in: "You've nailed it at its essence. The local polity will pass a resolution—or 'emergency order' or whatever—and 'legally' confiscate anyone's goods if they're deemed to be 'they' instead of 'we.' If you resist, you'll be crushed. They will have the resources of a whole community to draw upon including weapons, vehicles, manpower, electronics, tear gas, the whole works. Every scrap of government-owned equipment and weaponry will likely be used—by *someone*. Anyone who plans to hold out against that kind of threat is kidding themselves."

L. Roy again gave a thumbs-up and continued. "That is why I pushed as hard as I could to get the county sheriff to set up roadblocks. I planted the seed and laid out the details, and now he thinks it was all his idea. Hey, whatever works! My fear is that the local polity that is now coalescing is almost certainly going to make mistakes. Some of these could be lethal blunders. I frankly don't think the locals, except for a few of us, have given a lot of serious thought to facing long-term survival. They'll squander resources and they'll delay implementing necessary actions—like planting more food, or converting irrigation water systems into also handling domestic water, or working together to defend a harvest. Even worse, they may even decide to take in thousands of refugees from the big cities. That will almost ensure longer-term starvation."

Laine chimed in: "A much better approach is to be an integral part of the community and use the combined resources of the community to defend all of our resources together. This would be much easier if a high percentage of the community were like-minded folks who are committed to sharing and cooperating while still adhering to the free market—nothing communistic or command-driven: you know, 'top-down.' I agree that any communities like ours with ag production are going to have to somehow survive while facing even larger polities, like the cities, counties, or even state governments—or people that call themselves by those names, to give themselves an air of authority and legitimacy."

L. Roy said, "I can see that we are on the same sheet of music! I think we've both read some Ayn Rand."

Laine gave a nod and grinned in reply.

Martin continued. "I saw this happen in microcosm in Albania. So I don't expect to face a horde of lightly armed, starving individuals that will come at us on foot. No, sir! I expect to face a fairly professional, determined army formed by a government of some kind. Again, as you mentioned, the color of the flag they fly is meaningless. Small farming communities can support a few outsiders, but not very many. The community will need to both politically and, if need be, militarily deal with outside polities or we'll face a war that we can't win. In any case, the twin communities of Farmington and Bloomfield need to have a plan, and some resolve. I just hope we can muster it."

"God willing, we'll be able to shape that plan as community leaders instead of 'resources,'" Lars added. After a moment Laine went on, "Well, my roadblock proposal is going up for a vote next week. Hopefully common sense and the new realities will prevail. Now, assuming that it does, I want to proceed immediately with blocking positions around Farmington that will at least be able to sound the alarm about approaching forces. I'm afraid we're going to be on a shoestring budget."

"So . . . ?"

"So we're going to need fuel. The locations for the roadblocks will be chosen based on holding commanding terrain, not just plopping down barricades that are in walking distance, right at the city limits. That is stupidity. So some of our 'Committee of Public Safety' men may have to drive several miles—perhaps up to fifteen miles—to man their duty shifts."

Martin jumped in: "If we set up 24/7 security around Bloomfield, that means that they'll need one less roadblock to defend Farmington: they watch the west for us, we watch the east for them. I'm all for that! That will cut manpower requirements by twenty-five percent. Sure, I'll provide you the fuel."

Lars exclaimed, "Outstanding! Thank you, sir!" Lars pulled out a notepad and pen and went on, scribbling notes, "Let's do the math. Okay, not counting our in-town quick-reaction force—which will be set up on the Minuteman or volunteer fire department model—we'll have four Joes manning each roadblock 24/7. Three eight-hour shifts per day, that's twelve men per roadblock, and manning three separate roadblocks equals thirty-six trigger-pullers that need to get from Point A to Point B, every day. Each will need an average of one gallon of gas per day; I'm sure that they'll carpool, but the leftover gas will be a perk of the job. So 36 gallons of gas per day times 365, gives us . . . uh . . . 13,140 gallons."

"Fair enough, Lars. But you'll need a bit more fuel to get the vehicles and materials in place to construct your blocking points, and some for your QRF's vehicles. So . . . I'll issue vouchers for 15,000 gallons of gas annually, out of my own pocket. We only have a rudimentary printing facility, and I worry a lot about forgery, so I'll just open a standing account for each Bloomfield COPS man: 30 gallons monthly. Each time they get gas here at the plant, it will be deducted. It's the same sorta thing that I've done for the staff at my ranch and for the refinery employees. It's pretty simple accounting."

"And darned generous of you."

"Hey, I wouldn't be doing this unless it was in my own best interest. It's not just the '24/7, 365' that I worry about. Its the '24/7, 360.' As in: 360 degrees. I want my flanks covered. So far as I know, I own the only operational light products refinery this side of Texas. That's bound to be a tempting target."

"It's a humongous target."

"Just promise me that if you go work for the folks in Farmington, you won't go poaching for manpower in Bloomfield. We need to keep all our men with military training *here*," L. Roy said.

"You have my word, Mr. Martin."

"Did you have any other questions?"

"I'm curious. I've seen the ten-liter Scepter fuel cans that you've been selling, and I've heard that you bought thousands of them. That was quite prescient of you. But why do you have them priced at eight bucks in silver apiece? That's more than a week's pay these days. You bought them months ago, before the inflation went crazy, so they must have cost a tenth of your retail price for them in the equivalent—back in the paper dollars."

L. Roy leaned back in his chair and gazed upward. After a lull he replied: "Three reasons: Reason one, I don't have an unlimited supply, and we had no way of knowing when the grid might go back down locally, and if and when the big grids will go back up online. So I need to make them last. This way, when I pay my employees partly in gasoline, they'll be sure to have containers. Reason two, I need to have fuel that is packaged for barter over long distances. The way I see it, in a couple of years here in a fuel-producing region, it will be tires that will be in short supply, and I need to be able to trade for those. Reason three is that I need more than just fuel to barter for vehicles and heavy weapons. We need to amass some more armored vehicles. So if we go out far afield, trading with people that are 'fuel poor and vehicle rich,' then again I need to have the requisite containers."

"That makes sense. But, ah, what do you mean 'more' armored vehicles?"

"A slip of the tongue, Lars. Please don't mention it to anyone, but I have an old M8 Greyhound—that's a wheeled APC from World War II that's being restored and modified up at the shop at my ranch. After that's finished, I plan to keep it garaged here at the plant, sort of a 'hidden stinger.' But if things continue to deteriorate the way I imagine, we're going to need a lot more armor to be able to put up a creditable defense." After a pause he added: "Okay, then. We have an agreement!"

They shook hands.

As Laine stood up, he glanced over his left shoulder, and noticed a caged ladderway, leading to a trap door to the roof. Pointing with the muzzle of his rifle, he asked, "Does that ladder lead to your command post?"

"Yep. That's my CP. You're a very observant individual."

"Well, I admire a man that puts an emphasis on substance over style. I can see why you picked this room for your office. I would have done the same thing."

21

Up the Creek

"There is a certain relief in change, even though it be from bad to worse; as I have found in traveling in a stage-coach, that it is often a comfort to shift one's position and be bruised in a new place."

—Washington Irving

Eastern France
Late November and Early December, the First Year

Andy's cold and wet bicycle ride to the coast of France through the northern Départements was grueling, and took him two weeks of hard riding. Many of the nights were miserable, with few opportunities to dry his clothes. The roads were only lightly traveled, and he had no offers of rides, except for one elderly man who was driving a tiny two-seat Renault R5. There would be no room for Andy's bike or trailer, so he declined.

He camped in the woods most nights. As his stock of food dwindled, his trailer got lighter, and he was able to travel faster. He was only able to find a few bits of food that were still affordable. This included three retort-packaged "bricks" of vegetable soup and a couple of half-kilo plastic packets of instant oatmeal. Eating these cold was unappetizing but nourishing. Buying them expended most of Laine's remaining euros.

As he passed from Picardie into Nord-Pas-de-Calais, the population density increased. This made Andy nervous about his personal safety. His opportunities to camp unobserved in woodlands got further and further apart. His greatest fear was being attacked while sleeping. He prayed often and as usual kept his pistol handy inside his sleeping bag. While he was near the town of Douai, a large dog came sniffing around his camp at night. Laine half shouted: *"Chien! Vas-y! Vas-y! Va-t'en!"* That worked, but he had great difficulty getting back to sleep after the dog had left.

Laine was surprised to find the Port of Calais guarded by both police and soldiers. He was able to pass though the outer perimeter without being questioned, but at the inner *cordon*, he was stopped and asked by a French Army sergeant for his papers and told that the port was closed to civilian traffic. Andy pulled out his Army Reserve ID card and asked to speak with the harbormaster. This turned into a convoluted series of short meetings and interrogations, first with the lieutenant in charge of the *cordon*, then the harbor security officer, then with the harbormaster's office, and finally with the harbormaster himself. The harbormaster, Arsène Paquet, seemed distracted by the radio traffic, but he was amiable and sounded sincerely concerned about Laine's desire to get home to the United States.

Paquet immediately made three phone calls and punched in two SMS messages on his text phone. The resulting word was that there were no French ships that had filed sailing plans to the United States or Mexico. Paquet offered in a conciliatory voice, "I am sorry, *monsieur*, only *from* America, not *to*, for at least months in the future. The insurance companies will not allow it. To be precise, I should say that *if* they sail, it will be with the knowledge that their insurance is not in effect. Few would take that risk. This insurance situation is uniform for all ships that are European Common Market–flagged, or *étranger*-flagged but owned by EC-headquartered companies. But I think the situation may be different in England."

"How so?"

Paquet explained, "They have different insurance laws and procedures. Everything here in the EC has been so normalized. England is not a member of the European Common Market."

"So you're saying that to find a ship, I need to get to England."

"Yes, there is definitely a better chance. You can *try* to go to England, but with this terror thing the planes are grounded, the ferries are stuck in port, and even the Chunnel trains are not running. Did you see the news about the insulin?"

"No, what was that?"

"The transport is bottled up so tight they are worried that diabetes patients in England and Scotland may run out of insulin."

"So, any suggestions on how I can get to England? I am desperate to get there, to find a ship. I can pay in gold coin. Genuine *or*."

The harbormaster cocked his head.

"Gold coins? Really?"

"Yes, really. I have an old twenty-franc gold Rooster coin—*le coq gaulois*—that's about one-fifth of an ounce in gold. I'll trade that coin to anyone who can get me into England with no fuss."

"Hmmm. . . . My wife has a cousin, Joseph, who is the captain of a fishing boat near Boulogne-sur-Mer. Give me a moment and I will make another inquiry."

Twenty hours later, Andy and his bicycle had been deposited at the fishing docks of Boulogne-sur-Mer. His trip there, expedited by Paquet, was in a truck that smelled of fish. The road traffic was very light.

En route, the truck had made several stops to drop off and pick up cargo. One odd sight was when they made an intermediate stop at the Gare de Boulogne-sur-Mer to drop off some cargo. A *Train à Grande Vitesse* (TGV) high-speed train was sitting on a siding. Normally seen at speeds of up to two hundred kilometers per hour or at just very brief stops, the idle train looked odd.

Andy arrived at the Quai Gambetta with his bike and trailer in the late afternoon. The dock had mainly fishing boats and yachts tied up, but nested among them was a small two-masted sailing ship called *La Recouvrance*. Andy wondered if it was an historic ship or just a replica.

Joseph Lejeune didn't speak much English. His fishing boat, named *Beau Temps*, was smaller than Laine had expected. The captain was also younger than Laine had expected, perhaps in his early thirties. The boat had a crew of just three.

Lejeune met him on the dock. They exchanged names and shook hands. "I seek, *passage* . . . uh . . . *en Angleterre?*"

"Yes, I am taking you now. You have with you the gold?"

Andy obligingly showed him the coin.

Lejeune smiled. *"Bon, bon! Allons-y!"*

There was no delay. As the sun was setting, Andy's bike and trailer were carried on board and covered with a tarpaulin and lashed down. The mooring lines were cast off and *Beau Temps* pulled away from the dock with a roar. They quickly motored between the Jetée Nord-est and Jetée Sud-ouest and out to sea. A small lighthouse marked the end of the north jetty. The wind was chilly, but the skies were nearly clear.

Andy soon joined Lejeune in the wheelhouse. As a transistor radio blared French rap music, Joseph Lejeune offered him a cup of strong black coffee in an extra-thick mug. As Laine sipped the coffee, Lejeune said haltingly: "We sail for the village of Rye. The tide is good, and our draft, it is shallow. This Rye is a small town of fishes. No questions will be asked. You are in safety in Angleterre in just a few hours."

Ahead of them, the sky was darkening over fairly calm waters. The boat had a faint smell of diesel fuel and fish. Andy reckoned that that they would arrive after midnight.

He sat in the back of the wheelhouse, feeling the vibration of the engine and the gentle chop striking the boat's bow. Lejeune regularly checked the GPS receiver. The radio played on, with

one rap song after another, interrupted by annoying commer-
cials. The station ID declared that it was "Delta FM 100.7" from
Boulogne. The two crewmen popped in for cups of coffee and
to rip huge hunks of bread from baguettes. They hardly spoke
a word. One of them spent most of his time below, tending the
engine.

As they approached the British coastline, Andy was surprised
to see one long stretch to the south of them that was completely
blacked out. He pointed this out to the captain. "Wow! It's just
dark. It must be another power failure."

Lejeune wagged his chin in disgust and muttered, *"La fin du
monde tel que nous le connaissons."*

Laine cocked his head and queried: *"Excusez-moi.* My French
is very poor. What was that you said? Something about 'the end
of the land'?"

"My meaning, Monsieur Andy, was: 'the end of the world as
we've known it.'"

Andy retorted, "Oh. Yes, it does seem to be the end."

The fishing boat quietly pulled up the slough into Rye harbor.
It was nearly two a.m. when they pulled up to the dock. Since the
water was almost dead calm, the captain didn't bother to tie up
the boat. The tide was high, so Andy was able to simply step off it
right onto the dock. The two crewmen handed his bike and then
the trailer down to Andy.

Andy handed Joseph Lejeune the twenty-franc coin and said,
"Merci beaucoup."

Pocketing the coin and nodding, he replied, *"Que dieu soit
avec vous,"* and gave Andy a wave.

The throaty growl of the engine increased in tempo as the boat
reversed far enough to make a safe turn and head back out to the
English Channel.

Laine pedaled down the deserted dock under the yellowish
light of sodium vapor lamps. Turning onto Rye's main street gave

him a huge sense of relief. From here on, it was unlikely that he would be stopped and asked for identification.

Getting used to riding on the left side of the road was a quick transition, but it would have seemed more natural if there had been traffic on the road. Other than hearing some trucks in the distance, there was no evidence of vehicles moving. Andy didn't have a map, and the night was overcast, so he couldn't tell the direction he was heading. He just had the vague idea of turning right and heading up the coast. After leaving the town of Rye on Folkestone Road, Andy stopped and consulted his compass. He noted that he was headed northeast. That seemed correct and he knew that Folkestone was up the coast from Rye, so that seemed affirmative. He pressed on. The roadway was very quiet. Only two bakery trucks passed him in the first two hours of riding.

A half hour after dawn, Andy passed through the village of Brenzett, and he saw an elderly man with a walking stick who was walking his terrier on a leash. Andy stopped his bike and asked, "I'm sorry, but I'm without a map. Will this road take me up to the White Cliffs of Dover?"

The dog started yapping, and the man hissed, "Hush, you!" Then he looked up and answered Laine, "Yes, indeed it will, but you have to make a few turns to get to Dover. Come with me and I'll fetch you a map." Turning on his heel, the man said, "That's me house, just three down." Andy dismounted and walked his bike across the street. He walked alongside the man and the dog, talking as they walked. Andy said, "I appreciate your help, sir."

"Don't you mention it," the old man answered. He noticed the man had a bit of a wheeze to his breathing as he walked.

The man turned in a gate, and said over his shoulder: "Wait here, young Yank!" He emerged a minute later carrying a Kent Coastal Cities Ordnance Survey map. "This will show all the smallish roads you'll need to get to Dover on a bike. You can keep that map—I have a newer one. Safe home!" Andy thanked him and the old man soon popped back in his door. Setting the kick-stand, Andy spent a few minutes consulting the map, picking out the roads that would get him to a succession of harbors as he made his way up the coast.

That afternoon, he passed through Folkestone. As the terminus city for the Chunnel, Folkestone had some rough characters, who eyed his bike and trailer with hungry eyes. Andy gave them stern looks in response. To one ruffian who started walking toward him, he shouted "Back off!"

Once he got away from the city on the New Dover Road, Andy felt the most at ease since he had left Vilseck. The economy was a wreck, and there were very few cars and trucks on the road. But at least here he found more shops open than in France, and some friendly faces.

Bicycling through England in the winter wasn't much different than on the Continent. The weather was just as bad, but at least language wasn't a barrier, and he encountered more hospitality. His first night in England was outside the town of Church Hougham. Just as he was looking for a secluded copse of woods, he was flagged down by a middle-aged man carrying an umbrella. As soon as the man heard Andy's accent and learned that he was a stranded American, he often offered him a place to stay for the night. Sleeping in the man's barn was much preferable to sleeping in the woods in his bivy bag.

One downside was that Andy felt even more self-conscious carrying a pistol in England than he had in France. He decided that he would draw it only in the most dire circumstances. If he was ever arrested, he would undoubtedly be searched. His SIG pistol would land him in a world of hurt. The last place he wanted to end up was in Wormwood Scrubs Prison just as the world was falling apart.

As he was bicycling toward the city of Dover, Laine stopped to repair a flat tire. Just as he was finishing pumping up the tire with the replacement inner tube, a policeman pulled over to observe him. Andy nodded and waved. The policeman, dressed in a black raincoat that was half covered with optic yellow safety patches, strolled over to Laine. Andy clipped the pump back onto the bike's frame and reattached the trailer. "What do you have in that trailer?" the policeman asked.

It was again Andy's American accent that quickly changed the situation from a suspicious encounter into a friendly chat. The policeman, who appeared to be in his early thirties, had an acne-scarred face and was tall enough to look Andy eye to eye. Laine introduced himself and gave a one-minute summary of his trip from Germany. His only omission in the story was of the French fishing boat. By that omission and his mention of "arriving in Folkestone," the policeman assumed that Laine had come by train through the Chunnel. "So you're all on your lonesome, and you want to pedal up the coast, looking for a ship?"

"That's right."

"Well, sir, that's a very dangerous thing to do at the present time. It's a good thing that you didn't get merked right there in Folkestone. There's a bad lot down there. Yobs, they are. And there's more of the same in parts of Dover as well. Mind you: Don't go near the Dover docks. You'll find no yachtsmen there, just Barney—nothing but trouble."

"Yeah, I've seen their kind before. I had to stare down a couple of them." After a beat he added, "You know, just coming off active duty, I feel a bit naked, traveling by myself, unarmed."

"Can't blame you." The policemen hesitated and then said, "My name is Michael Lyon. I think you need my help."

Lyon's palm brushed the top of his baton, and he gazed at it. He continued in a matter-of-fact voice, "Let me explain the legalities, Captain Laine: You carry one of these, it's an offense. You carry a knife, it's an offense. You carry a cricket bat, it's an offense. You carry pepper spray, it's an offense . . ."

"So what am I supposed to stop the bad guys with? Harsh language?"

Lyon laughed. "Well, it's fortunate that you're a bicyclist and not just afoot. That gives you a bit of leeway. You see, here in the U.K., on a bike you can legally carry 'safety equipment,' and that includes flashlights . . . and the law doesn't specify what *size* flashlight."

Andy smiled and asked, "What do you recommend?"

Lyon glanced around nervously and said: "Hang on a sec, Yank. I've got something in the boot." He stepped over to his police car and opened its trunk. Unzipping a duffel bag, he pulled out a six-cell Maglite flashlight. It looked like the other turned-aluminum police flashlights Andy had seen before, but slimmer. Then he realized that it held C-cells instead of D-cell-size batteries.

In an even lower voice, Lyon said, "Now, this can be used just like a baton, but you can legally carry it on your bicycle. Not in your *hand*, mind you, and not on your person when you are walking down the street. But attached to your bicycle or in your pack when bicycling, it's a fully allowable exception."

"Is that one for sale, by chance?"

"Huh! I can't be peddling wares on the street whilst on duty, now, can I? That would be unseemly. But there is nothing that says that I can't *give it* to you."

"Are you kidding?"

Lyon shook his head. "No, sir, just consider it an act of Christian kindness."

"That is very kind of you! Tell you what: If you are ever in the state of New Mexico, my home will always be open to you and your family." Laine pulled out his notepad and a pen. He continued as he was writing, "Here's my address. When the Big Trolley gets back on its tracks, I fully expect to see you on a holiday. Plan on spending a week or two at my home. I'll take you to see Monument Valley and some of the Indian cliff dwellings. Ever heard of a place called Mesa Verde? From where I live, it's just across the state line, in Colorado."

Michael Lyon shook his head from side to side, and Andy continued: "Those are some amazing ruins. Now, again: I fully expect to see you and your family on my doorstep someday. In fact, I'll be disappointed if I don't."

Andy stuffed the flashlight into the loops on the back of his handlebar bag. He and the policeman shook hands and wished each other well. Lyon waved as Andy pulled out from the curb into the drizzle. As he pedaled away, Andy realized that the Mesa Verde ruins had belonged to a culture that had been erased from existence. In the late 1200s, Mesa Verde was abandoned, and the society was never rebuilt. He wondered about the hopes for his own civilization in the long term.

Heeding the policeman's warning, Andy avoided central Dover. Instead he skirted around the city. He kept on the Dover Road, which roughly paralleled the A258 highway. Eventually he got to Pegwell Harbor. There, Andy learned that there were no boats headed to the U.S., since the East Coast and Gulf Coast were reportedly in utter chaos. The few yachts and commercial vessels there that might be sailing were all headed to New Zealand. One of the motor yachtsmen kindly spent an hour on his VHF radio on Andy's behalf, calling yachtsmen and commercial vessels to ask of any boats with planned sailings to the U.S. or Canada that winter. There were none. This was discouraging news. But also hearing that all flights were still grounded, he had no choice but to press on up the coast.

As he was cycling up the Hereson Road, just north of Ramsgate, Andy was confronted by two young toughs on Kawasaki motorcycles. They zoomed up behind him, and one of them turned sharply and braked to a halt right in front of Laine. He was forced to apply his own brakes to avoid hitting the motorcycle. The thug quickly dismounted and shoved a length of hoe handle through the spokes of Laine's front wheel. It was déjà vu of the incident near Homberg. Andy jumped off his bike, simultaneously pulling his newly acquired flashlight from its retaining loops. Taking a high swing, he brought it down hard on the young man's forearm. The biker screamed and shouted, "My arm!"

Andy immediately turned and delivered a rapid series of baton strikes to the chest and arms of the other motorcyclist, who was slow in dismounting. Overwhelmed, he gunned his engine and sped off. Seeing Andy's furious show of force, the first biker jumped back aboard his Kawasaki and sped away unsteadily, shouting curses. As he picked up his fallen bicycle and inspected both it and the trailer hitch for damage, Laine muttered to himself, "There must be some international college of thuggery that teaches the bike-spokes technique."

22

A Semblance of Normalcy

"During the hyperinflation in post WWI Germany, what used to be a comfortable nest egg was suddenly the value of a postage stamp. If one held just a portion of their savings in precious metals, the crisis was greatly softened. Gold will never be worth nothing, even if the exact price fluctuates. There is a famous photograph, however, of a German woman during this time period burning piles of tightly bound banknotes to keep warm."

—Congressman Ron Paul

In better weather, another day of cycling the minor roads north from Dover brought Andy to the quintessentially Kentish town of Boughton, just short of the town of Faversham. He spent the night in the woods, just off the road from Boughton to Hernhill, uneventfully. After breakfast and a shave the next morning, he cycled back to the main road. Andy felt like he was deep in the heart of the land of thatched roofs and tweed jackets. At Faversham he turned down to the yacht harbor at Oare Creek. Laine was surprised to see such a large number of private sailboats and motor vessels in the harbor.

Although he was first met with suspicion at the harbormaster's office, he was eventually given a safe place to leave his bicycle and trailer, while he scoured the docks to make inquiries.

He arrived at low tide, with the water so low that most of the boats were resting on their keels in the mud, looking forlorn. The harbormaster explained that it was an unusual "minus tide."

In a series of conversations, Laine was told that there were three boat sailings expected within the next week: one bound for New Zealand, one for Tasmania, and one for Belize. There were no vessels of any description that they had heard of bound for the United States this winter. Andy sat down on a seagull-splattered bench and prayed. After ten minutes of fervent prayer, he returned to the motor-cruiser where they seemed the best-informed about the upcoming sailings. Asking about the boat headed for Belize, he was told: "Second or third slip from the end on the last dock. Look for a big Tayana: she's called the *Durobrabis*." Andy only had a vague recollection that Belize was formerly called British Honduras and that it was close to Mexico. He couldn't remember if there was another country in between. To Andy, the Central American countries, other than Panama, were just a jumble on the map.

Laine went to the dock as instructed and found a middle-aged man and woman transferring supplies from a cart onto the sailboat. It was a forty-eight-footer, and looked well cared for. Most of the other sailboats in the harbor were in trim form for intermittent casual recreational use, but in contrast, *Durobrabis* had some bulky items lashed to its foredeck, covered with brown tarps. Andy recognized the distinct blue color of water cooler bottles beneath one of these tarps. The slightly overweight gray-haired man was wearing a T-shirt emblazoned "Hollowshore Cruising Club" under an open windbreaker. As Andy approached the boat, the man stepped away from the cart, pulled a long kitchen knife from under his jacket and held it at his side, and ordered: "Stop right there!" Andy immediately halted twenty-five feet away and showed his palms.

The man's wife stood speechless, still holding two sacks of groceries. She looked terrified.

"We've been blagged before, and we *won't be* again," the man declared intensely.

"Sir, I can assure you, I'm no robber. My name's Andrew Laine. I'm an American Army officer, looking to buy passage to Belize. I heard you were headed there."

"That's right, but we're full up. Your money's no good here, Yank."

Andy said imploringly, "But I can pay you in *gold*."

The yacht skipper blinked, but then said, "Sorry, but what good is gold to me? The family that's going with us, they stocked up piles of food and fuel months ago, so they're supplying us with nearly all the provisions—enough for the whole journey. Right now, that's worth a lot more to me than gold. We can't *eat* gold."

"Well, then, what about lead?"

"What?" the man replied, sounding confused.

"I deal in lead, friend."

The boat captain laughed nervously and cocked his head.

Laine continued, "I'm willing to wager that you don't have much more than that knife to protect yourself and all onboard. So I'd like to make you an offer: to provide you with some more substantial security for your voyage as a *working* crew member."

"Have you ever crewed a yacht?"

"No, but I'm willing to learn, and I'm very good with a gun."

"That's all well and good, but you won't find a gun to be had in all of England, at any price."

"I'm willing to offer you *mine*, and a steady, well-trained hand behind it." He patted the jacket at the small of his back.

The man still looked hesitant.

Speaking slowly, Laine added: "Look, I really am an Army officer with six years of experience. I've done tours in both Iraq and Afghanistan. I'm a good Christian man. And importantly for you, I know how to make cutthroats of all descriptions either drop dead in their tracks or turn and run, crying like babies. I've been in some very tight spots, so I know exactly how to get out of them. Trust me."

The old man looked toward his wife and they nodded to each other. Turning back toward Andy, he said, "Come aboard and we'll parlay."

Carston Simms, the skipper of *Durobrabis*, filled Andy in about both the yacht and his background. Simms had served in the Royal Navy as an enlisted seaman for six years, back in the late 1970s. Soon after, he got a degree in psychology and worked as a school counselor and later as a private school administrator. He used the yacht on his long summer vacations. They had two sons, who had both emigrated to Australia twenty years before. Laine got the impression that Simms had strained relations with his sons, since he bluntly described them as "layabout alcoholics." Simms had lost his job in the recession that began in 2008, which caused private-school enrollments to plummet.

Simms spent a while expressing his concerns about the deteriorating conditions in England. He predicted a massive die-off because the island nation was so dependent on food and fuel from overseas. He put on a grim face and said: "They'll be eating each other in London and Colchester in just a few weeks. We've got to get someplace with a better climate and less population."

They sat in the boat's saloon area. The surroundings were heavy on teak and stainless steel, which was unfamiliar to Andy but pleasant. Carston Simms and his wife, Angie, seemed nervous and chatty. Before agreeing to take Laine on as crew, they spent a half hour quizzing Andy about his background, education, and experience. Here, Andy's DD-214 discharge papers came in handy. Finally, Simms wanted to see the SIG pistol. Pointing it upward, Andy deftly unloaded it. He then field-stripped and reassembled it on the saloon table. This particularly impressed Angie.

Then Carston began to open up about the situation on the boat and their plans to sail for Belize. Andy was nearly right about the Carstons' kitchen knife. Other than a few small knives and an Olin flare pistol, they were unarmed. The skipper habitually called the single-shot 12-gauge flare gun his "Very" pistol, which Andy thought sounded quaintly First World War. Simms conceded that they'd be easy pickings for pirates without Andy and a real gun.

Angie told Laine about the family that planned to travel with them: Alan and Simone Taft were in their late thirties. They had a fourteen-year-old son named Jules and twin eleven-year-old daughters, Yvonne and Yvette. Alan Taft was an investment banker with no boating experience. The Tafts were just casual acquaintances of the Simms before the Crunch, but their large stockpile of food and Taft's fluency in Spanish made him a logical choice to make the Belize trip.

Simms told Andy that he had sailed to the Caribbean once before and that he had a few "yachtie" acquaintances there. He admitted that none of these were close friends, but Simms considered the voyage worth the gamble. Carston summed up his rationale for the voyage tersely: "It obviously beats waiting here to see if we get eaten." They planned to sail on a predawn high tide in three days. In the meantime Andy would stay on the boat almost continuously to provide security.

Accommodations would be tight. Although *Durobrabis* had berths for seven, one of these was already stacked high with boxes of provisions and secured with heavy twine to both the wall behind and the overhead rail. To make up for this lost berth, the Tafts planned to have staggered sleeping shifts or have their daughters share a berth. *Durobrabis* was a forty-eight-foot Tayana built in Taiwan. It was a 1997 model but still well-maintained. It was a fiberglass monohull measuring fourteen and a half feet across the beam.

As a true blue-water yacht rather than a coastal sailboat, *Durobrabis* had watertight hatches and a 230-gallon freshwater tank.

The sails and sail covers had been replaced just two years before. The boat's 100-horsepower auxiliary diesel engine was mostly used for getting in and out of harbors. To fuel it, the boat had an internal 120-gallon diesel tank, and Simms had supplemented this with an additional 60 liters for the voyage, held in six plastic fuel cans.

The only available space for Andy to sleep was the forward sail locker. Simms explained why he didn't empty the seventh berth for Andy: "I'll still need to get sheets in and out of the sail locker on short notice. And it will be much quicker to get *you* in and out of there than it will be a pile of grocery boxes. In a storm I won't want much weight in the bow anyhow, and we'll run with just a little spitfire jib and a storm trysail. So at those times we'll need most of that locker's capacity for the big sheets. You and Jules, perhaps, can take turns in a bunk in foul weather." Andy agreed to the arrangement without complaint.

The yacht was well equipped for long voyages, with a reverse-osmosis water maker, an inflatable dinghy, and an impressive array of radios and navigation gear.

Andy was disappointed to hear that there would be no room for his bicycle and trailer. He was able to trade them to another yachtsman at the marina for eighteen cans of corned beef, five 12-gauge red meteor flares that could be used in Carston's flare gun, and a three-year-old Garmin GPS receiver.

Andy's only other transaction before their departure came after he spotted a teenager at the marina who was wearing a camouflage jacket that had some bright paint stains on it. Andy recognized these as paintball stains. Striking up a conversation with the young man, Laine learned that he was an aficionado of both paintball tactical training and shooting Airsoft pellet guns. The latter shot low-velocity rubber BBs. Laine persuaded him to trade a few of his Airsoft guns, since he had eleven of them.

In exchange for two Airsoft submachinegun replicas—an Uzi

and an H&K MP-5—Laine traded a full set of OCP fatigues with matching boonie hat and *shemagh* scarf, an older but working iPod, and a Chinese multipurpose tool—a knockoff of an American Leatherman tool. Both of the toy SMGs looked and even felt surprisingly realistic, aside from their bright red plastic muzzle caps that identified them as replicas. A few quick blasts from a can of black spray paint soon remedied that.

23

Roll Out

"A retreat is a place you go to live, not to die. Setting up a retreat is, for the most part, practicing the art of the possible. It's a matter of wisely and shrewdly identifying what you have and turning it into something usable . . . Fight if you must, but try your utmost to orchestrate events so that confrontation is absolutely the remedy of last resort."

—Ragnar Benson, *The Survival Retreat*

Buckeye, Arizona
December, the First Year

Once the looting in Phoenix started spreading out into the suburbs, Ian and Blanca agreed that it would be very dangerous to stay in Buckeye much longer.

The next morning they wheeled the Larons out of their trailers. Working in the driveway and on the front lawn, they bolted on the wings. Assembly and preflight testing only took fifteen minutes per plane. But then it took nearly an hour to efficiently stow their gear, with the heavier items as close as possible to the planes' center of gravity. As all this went on, a number of curious neighbors congregated to stare at the strange sight. Soon a few of them pitched in to help with the fueling process.

Ian handed his next-door neighbor the keys and the "pink slip" titles to his vehicles, and the keys to the house. He told him, "We won't be back, so you can have anything you'd like inside the house. I don't know what you should do with the trailers for the planes. I guess you can give these pink slips to my landlord, if you ever see him. He can apply that to our rent and keep the difference."

Just before they started their engines, Ian asked for volunteers to halt any approaching cars on the adjoining avenue. After starting up and doing another radio check, Ian and Blanca taxied off the lawn and down the driveway. They then continued out the court and turned on to Hastings Avenue, with Ian in the lead. Their neighbors gathered to gawk. There was about two thousand feet of the broad avenue available, which was plenty of runway for the Larons, even in their overloaded condition. Blanca keyed her radio and said, "Be careful—light poles on the left." Several neighbors stood at the ends of the avenue to watch for approaching cars and, if need be, to block traffic.

The planes staggered off the ground and climbed out eastward very slowly, into the smoky haze that hung over the entire Phoenix region. Ian did a 90-degree turn and slid in to form up alongside Blanca's Laron. She gave him a thumbs-up.

They turned due north, still climbing. Gazing to the east, Blanca could see house fires burning out of control in Phoenix, Glendale, and even as close as Goodyear. She radioed Ian, "*Ay, ay, ay,* look at all those fires . . . over."

"Yeah, it looks like we got out of Dodge just in time. After Goodyear, the looters are gonna hit Buckeye sure as anything. Climbing to 7,500, out."

Ian again looked toward Phoenix. He remembered Charley Gordon and wondered aloud, without pressing the mic switch, "So, what'll last longer: Charley or the thousand rounds of nine-milly?"

Their eighty-seven-mile flight to Prescott consumed just over seven gallons of avgas for each plane. At the midpoint of their flight, they practiced using Jackrabbit hand pumps in anticipation of longer flights. Refueling their fuel tanks in flight from their fuel bladders took only seven minutes.

After passing over some dramatic yellowish rocky hills on the east shore of Willow Lake, they landed their planes at Love Field, Prescott's airport. Once on the ground, they taxied to the general aviation area. The fueling area had a large sign spray-painted on a four-by-eight-foot sheet of oriented strand board with a frown face and "No Fuel." The phones were out, so Ian thought it was best to go directly to Alex's house.

Ian wangled a ride from the airport—in exchange for twenty-five rounds of 9mm hollowpoints—while Blanca stayed behind to guard the planes. Alex was impressed with the country. Granite Mountain loomed large in the distance. There was obviously more water here than down in the Phoenix area, but this was still Arizona. There were lots of trees here—a scarcity in southern Arizona. The elevation of the town was about 5,500 feet. This gave it a much cooler climate than Buckeye.

There was no answer when Ian knocked on the door of Alex's rental house on Oak Terrace Drive. Ian discovered that the door was unlocked, and inside there were signs that Alex had left hurriedly. Most of the furniture in the house was still there, but nearly all of Alex's other personal possessions were missing. The kitchen smelled of sour milk. There was a knock on the door. It was Alex's next-door neighbor, carrying a baseball bat.

After explaining who he was, Ian learned that Alex had just been hired on as a "full-time security consultant" for four families with adjoining properties in Conley Ranches, a fairly new gated community two miles north of town. Contacting Alex was a snap, once he knew how to do it: CB Channel 12. "They monitor it around the clock." The neighbor, a former trucker, had a CB radio in his SUV. Alex responded immediately to Ian's transmission and said that he'd be at his old house in less than half an hour to pick him up.

Alex pulled into the driveway in his Ford Excursion. Ian was carrying no baggage, so he just hopped into the passenger seat and Alex immediately backed out of the driveway. There was a long-barreled Dan Wesson .44 Magnum revolver resting in the center console.

After a palm-slapping high five, Alex asked simply, "Airport?"

"Yep."

As he drove, Alex explained rapidly, "I got hired as a security guy for a group of four families on contiguous one-acre lots, in a square, on the end of a block. Two of them are retired bankers from Tucson. Strictly a 'room-and-board' arrangement. There's four hundred lots in the development, but less than half of them have houses built: it's kind of a patchwork, with clusters of houses surrounded by empty lots. Its a bunch of half-million-dollar to million-plus houses there. A lot of retired executives with more money than brains. They watched it all go down on TV, and now they're scared spitless and playing catch-up."

Without allowing Ian time to comment, Alex went on: "I think we've got food and water covered, but they're pretty darn light on fuel, and pitiful on security. Some of the families in Conley Ranches don't even *own* a gun. And some of their 'committees' that meet at the clubhouse are a bit of a joke. But at least the most important one, Vegetable Gardening, is getting its act together. The plan is to haul in truckloads of manure and good topsoil to some of the empty lots with the least rocky soil. The water, thank God, is all gravity flow, from up in the mountains. The 'private gated community' aspect doesn't mean jack now: since the power is out, they have to leave the gates wired wide open. I'm trying to organize things to get that situation changed, pronto."

Ian nodded, and Alex went on: "The house where I bunk is 3,800 square feet, and it had just a couple living in it. They have room for at least two more full-timers, and believe you me, I *need* the help. We gotta get continuous 24/7 shifts going right away."

Alex pulled into the general aviation gate at Love Field. After the formalities of getting through the inner gate, he was able to drive up to where the pair of Larons were tied down.

They all exchanged hugs and shared some tears about the death of Linda. But then they were all busy with their first concern: getting the planes unloaded. All of Ian and Blanca's gear fit with ease in the back of the Excursion with its third-row seat folded down. Alex mentioned that he was impressed with how much Ian had been able to shoehorn into the planes. Ian explained almost apologetically: "I ran the weight and balance numbers, but they were marginal. Balance was decent, but gross weight was really pushing the envelope. Sometimes you just gotta do what you gotta do and pray for the best."

As Alex shut the back doors on the Ford, he said, "Judging from the guns that you brought, they will *not* say no to hiring you." His prediction proved right. That evening, after some brief objections about extra mouths to feed, Ian and Blanca were hired by the four homeowners. Like Alex, Ian and Blanca would receive no pay but would be provided meals and a comfortable bedroom. Their room was in the 2,750-square-foot home that sat behind the one Alex was in. It belonged to Dr. Robert Karvalich, a widower who was a retired pediatrician. Everyone called him Doctor K. Many years before, he had served a stint as a Navy medical officer, but only in an office setting, never at sea or in combat. He carried a World War II–vintage Remington Rand Model 1911 in a full flap holster daily. The gun, he explained, had belonged to his father, who was also a Navy doctor, during the Korean War.

Unlike the other homeowners, who took several weeks to get accustomed to constantly carrying guns, Doctor K. took to it immediately. The difference was that he had been robbed at gunpoint once before. As he told it, six years before the Crunch, Doctor K. answered his door to find a drug addict with a pistol in his hand. The man was after narcotics. Fearing for his life, Doctor K. reluctantly complied, giving the robber his small supply of Tylenol with codeine, Vicodin, and an oral solution of morphine sulfate. The robber fled in a car with California license plates and was never caught by the local authorities. When Ian Doyle asked everyone in the compound to be armed at all times, Robert Karvalich was one of the first to do so.

Transporting the planes to Doctor K.'s house the next day at first seemed like it would be difficult, requiring borrowed trucks, but then it proved easy: they just flew them there. The street in front of the four-house "compound," as Alex called it, was curving and on a slight slope, but there was a long, wide street a quarter mile away that was straight and nearly level. This street was in the new "Phase 2" portion of the Conley Ranches development, where the streets had been paved, but only a few lots had been sold and no houses had yet been built. In Phase 2, the streetlight poles had not yet been installed. The street made a very practical runway for the Larons. They were able to land there and then just taxi the planes to the street where Alex lived. The sight of this made quite a stir in the community.

Soon after they stopped the planes in the driveway, one of the neighbors from down the street came to threaten to file a complaint about the planes landing as "a safety nightmare," and about the very presence of the planes. She shouted that the planes were "flagrantly against the association rules." As she stood wagging her finger in Alex's face, Blanca and Ian were already at work disassembling them. Once the wings were removed and the planes disappeared into one of the bays in Doctor K.'s capacious four-car garage alongside his RV, the neighbor quieted down. Alex talked some sense into her by emphasizing that she'd be the indirect beneficiary of the additional armed security at no cost. "Well, I suppose that's okay," she said quietly, and walked off.

The Doyles—Ian, Blanca, and Alex—agreed to each stand a daily eight-and-a-half-hour guard watch, thirteen days out of each two weeks. The intense guard duty schedule left them very little time for recreation—and hardly even enough time to hand-wash their laundry—but at least all of their meals were provided by the four families on a rotating schedule.

Blanca began to carry one of the M16s that Ian had taken in for safekeeping from Luke Air Force Base. Alex provided her some 5.56mm ammo, both for target practice and to keep in loaded magazines. She disliked the M16, mostly because of the odd twang sound that the buffer made in the buttstock when it was fired. She also considered the gun ugly but would not elaborate beyond saying, "I know a good-looking gun when I see one, and this one ain't it. I like a gun with at least *some* wood. This thing is like a plastic toy."

The Doyles wanted to construct a sandbagged fighting position inside each ground-floor exterior window, but they ran into a problem: a shortage of sandbags. There were no nearby Army or Marine Corps installations, so the local surplus store had no sandbags available. And because Prescott was not in a flood-prone area, the county had just a small supply of sandbags for use if a water main broke. The local feed store had had its supply of empty feed sacks wiped out by just a couple of customers long before the Doyles inquired.

It was Blanca who came up with the answer: sewing their own, using rolls of black polyester mesh road construction underlayment material. This material came in ten-foot-wide rolls. They were able to trade a local road contractor a box of .30-06 ammunition for two rolls of the material.

Because the power was out, electric sewing machines were not available, but Doctor K. put his late wife's Singer treadle sewing machine table back into operation. The table's sewing machine had been discarded years before, when the table became a decorator item. But Doctor K. was able to install a much later model Singer machine into the treadle table. This one sewing machine eventually served the families in all four homes in the compound, for everything from patching blue jeans to making ammunition bandoleers. It proved capable of sewing the sandbags as well.

They cut the material to yield completed sandbags of the same fourteen-by-twenty-six-inch dimensions that had been standard-ized for U.S. military sandbags for nearly a century. Each sack weighed about forty pounds when filled.

Once filled and stacked, to the casual observer, the stacked black sacks looked like dark shadows inside the windows. The sandbag-making-and-filling project went on for three weeks. Clean sand was available from a large pile at the development's uncompleted golf course. When asked permission to use some of the sand, Cliff Conley replied, "You take what you need. I expect it'll be a long time before that golf course ever gets finished. Just don't ask me to help you fill 'em. I did my share of sandbag filling in Vietnam. I've now reached the 'supervisory' stage of life."

By SOP, all wireless connections were turned off, for fear that they might be detected by passing looters.

Ian and Blanca settled into an upstairs bedroom that sat above the living room, which was heated by a woodstove. A floor vent gave their bedroom sufficient heat. More important, the bedroom had a sliding glass door to a story deck with a commanding view of much of the compound and the neighborhood. A hot tub sat on the corner of the deck, already drained for winter. It was soon lined with sandbags, turning it into a soft-top pillbox. The hot tub's plywood lid was covered with Naugahyde and had flaps that hung down six inches. Ian and Blanca constructed a C-shaped framework with five two-by-four legs to support the lid. This positioned the lid seven inches higher than normal, providing a 360-degree horizontal vision slit. To anyone walking by on the street below, the hot tub-cum-pillbox didn't look like anything out of the ordinary, just a covered hot tub. Ian also cut five blocks from a length of four-by-four. These blocks allowed them to raise the lid an additional three and a half inches to provide better vision and hearing at night.

Because his master bedroom in the north wing of the house was too cold after the grid power went down, Doctor K. moved a single bed to what had formerly been his den. The den was just off the living room, and thus it was well heated. He and the Doyles then closed off the hallways to nearly half of the house by nailing up blankets with batten boards, to confine the heat to just the kitchen, living room, and den.

The Four Families staged a coup at the Conley Ranches homeowners association (HOA) meeting just a few days after Ian and Blanca arrived. By prearrangement with their sympathizers, they ousted two "Pollyanna" members of the HOA board. Both of them had wanted to maintain the status quo in the development, because they were hoping for an economic recovery in the near future. They were replaced with down-to-earth pragmatists.

In a series of voice votes that began almost immediately after the change in HOA leadership, all of the Conley Ranches restrictions on landscaping, gardening, pets, livestock, fences, antennas, solar panels, fuel storage, and vehicles were eliminated. Once it became apparent that they were badly outnumbered and that they were getting no traction at the meeting, the two Pollyannas and their handful of supporters stormed out in protest.

Under the new HOA rules for Conley Ranches, large-scale gardening on any unsold lots was encouraged. A 5 percent share of the crops grown on unsold lots was assigned to Cliff Conley, the original landowner and developer of the community. Conley later said that he was more than satisfied with that arrangement. A new HOA security committee was formed. This committee was later jokingly called the "Neighborhood Watch on Steroids."

After the Doyles arrived, security improvements for the Four

Families compound accelerated. With some hired labor to help, they built stockade-style fences connecting the perimeter of the four houses.

Ted Nielsen, one of the compound's bankers, had a degree in engineering and had worked for a telephone company on his summer vacations during college. He constructed a simple phone hot loop of four traditional rotary-dial telephones for the houses. It was powered by seven car batteries wired in series. This battery bank was connected to a solar panel trickle charger. The dials on the phones were inoperative. They were connected in a traditional party-line arrangement. Each phone had a momentary contact switch added. When any of these buttons were depressed, it put a ringing voltage through the circuit, and all four phones rang. Nielsen's simple phone system provided the means to coordinate a defense of the compound from intruders.

The interior fences in the four-house compound were removed, leaving a large inner courtyard. Most of this area was converted into four vegetable gardens. Clearing rocks took several days of hard work. Then soil, compost, and manure were hauled in, to be ready for gardening when warm weather returned.

At Sea, Coast of France
December, the First Year

The first week at sea was miserable. It was common to see Yvonne and Yvette vomiting over the stern rail in stereo. After the week of seasickness, everyone aboard *Durobrabis* got into a regular daily routine. There was plenty of hard work, including countless hours of pulling the handle on the Katadyn Survivor 35 desalinator, a reverse-osmosis unit that turned salt water into drinking water. Carston Simms ran a tight ship and insisted on keeping the fresh-water tanks full.

Until Andy and the Tafts got accustomed to navigating and

handling the rigging, the sailing was mostly handled by Carston and Angie, who each put in grueling ten-hour watches. Angie piloted from 0500 to 1500, and Carston from 1500 to 0100. As the days passed, everyone else on the boat took on more and more responsibility in handling the rigging and, eventually, piloting. At the end of his watch, Carston Simms would either set the Simrad autopilot (in calm seas) or drop sail and set the sea anchor (in rougher seas). Andy's topside security duty was nightly from 2100 to 0800.

Every morning after being relieved by Simone Taft (their day watch, eyeballs-only security), Andy would carefully oil the SIG and its magazines. He was very conscious of the depredations of damp, salty air on gunmetal. Then he'd do his best to sleep in the darkness of the sail locker.

One of Laine's top priorities was familiarizing the adults on the yacht with safe gun handling. He did this in one-on-one classes held late in the afternoons. He taught them how to load, fire, and reload the pistol. Jules got an abbreviated version of the same instruction. The Tafts' eleven-year-old twins weren't taught gun handling out of fear that one of them might accidentally drop the precious gun overboard. But they *were* taught how to refill magazines, which they practiced regularly.

Most of the training consisted of dry practice with an unloaded gun, and with all of the gun's ammunition safely in another compartment. But after a week of that, Andy gave Jules and all the adults the chance to actually shoot the SIG. Their targets were sealed empty bottles that were thrown off the bow. In all, they shot just twenty-eight cartridges.

After every lesson, Andy said, "If I go down, then you pick this gun up and you *continue the fight* until the threat is vanquished. You *do not* quit. Do you understand?"

After the first phase of firearms training, Andy moved on to hand-to-hand combatives and knife fighting, using his own amalgam of tae kwon do, pistol handling, and Krav Maga, which Laine dubbed "SIG kwon do." Adding to the standard katas, Andy taught how to use a pistol that had been shot dry as a club and as a pressure-point tool. For the latter, he used the barrel protruding from the pistol with its slide locked to the rear. The small surface area of the muzzle, he showed, could deliver tremendous force in strikes to the solar plexus, groin, kidneys, or neck of an opponent.

Each morning from ten to noon, Alan Taft taught everyone Spanish. Sailing instruction—also for everyone—took up most of each afternoon. Nearly every night after the dinner dishes were washed, there were endless games of cards, mostly cribbage.

Andy was having trouble getting to sleep. They were 250 miles west of Portugal. It was a Tuesday, and his contact was scheduled for that night, so he felt anxious. He was hoping for good propagation.

Andy set his radio's alarm for 0315. As he set up the dipole antenna along the rail, he was surprised to see Carston standing in the open hatchway. In a soft voice Andy explained what he was doing. Simms nodded. Andy sat down and completed hooking up the transceiver. Then he said, "Well, five minutes, and then I'll know if we've got good propagation."

Carston offered, "That can be tricky on shortwave."

Andy replied, "Yeah."

The silence was overwhelming. Andy watched Carston Simms still standing in the doorway. Still in a whisper, he asked, "Tell me, how did this boat get the name *Durobrabis*?"

Carston sighed and explained: "She's named after some old Celt ruins somewhere. You see, before I bought her, this boat belonged to an archaeology professor from the western end of Kent. He only rarely sailed her." After a pause he added, "I didn't particularly like the name, but being an old salt, I consider it bad luck to change a boat's name."

At 0329, at Andy's request, Simms tacked to put *Durobrabis* on a southwesterly heading. This left the dipole antenna roughly facing the Great Circle line of bearing to the western United States. Precisely at 0330 GMT, Andy heard a strong cadence in Morse, with Lars's distinctive stuttering "fist" on his preferred traditional Morse key:

"K5CLA DE K5CLB BT

"K5CLA DE K5CLB BT"

Andy replied: "K5CLB DE K5CLA BT"

Lars hammered back, "HOT DANG, GOT YOU AT S3. R-U AT SEA?"

"YES, MAKING GOOD TIME, FB, NOW IN DEEP OCEAN. NO WORRIES. HOW IS KL?"

"SHES FINE, LEARNING M-MORSE N WANTS 2 CHAT"

"PLZ PUT KL ON THE KEY"

Then, in a ponderously slow Morse rate of six words per minute, Andy heard: "I LOVE YOUU DRLING, 88, 88, 88. DYING TO SEE YOU. ANY ETA? BR"

How could he even begin to explain to her that it might be many months before he got home?

24

Down in Hondo

"We are steadily asked about the age at which to teach young people to shoot. The answer to this obviously depends upon the particular individual; not only his physical maturity but his desire. Apart from these considerations, however, I think it important to understand that it is the duty of the father to teach the son to shoot. Before the young man leaves home, there are certain things he should know and certain skills he should acquire, apart from any state-sponsored activity. Certainly the youngster should be taught to swim, strongly and safely, at distance. And young people of either sex should be taught to drive a motor vehicle, and if at all possible, how to fly a light airplane. I believe a youngster should be taught the rudiments of hand-to-hand combat, unarmed, together with basic survival skills. The list is long, but it is a parent's duty to make sure that the child does not go forth into the world helpless in the face of its perils. Shooting, of course, is our business, and shooting should not be left up to the state."

—Colonel Jeff Cooper

Tegucigalpa, Honduras
May, Twenty Years Before the Crunch

More than two decades before the Crunch, Ian Doyle had a temporary duty (TDY) assignment to Honduras that changed his life.

The leader of the Hondo Expedition was Major Alan Brennan, a quiet man who was the son of a retired Air Force colonel. Brennan's leadership was competent but very laid-back. He made it clear that he expected his squadron members to be punctual for all meetings, and completely sober before each scheduled mission. He summed up his guidance by stating simply, "We've got excellent maintenance NCOs, and the civilian techs know the gear inside and out. Stand back and let them do their jobs. Just be at the briefings and be on flight line on time. 'Kick the tire, light the fire,' and come home safe."

Brennan, who had recently been married, was fascinated by pre-Columbian history and spent a lot of his time off in a rented jeep wandering around ancient ruins, taking pictures. Other than on his mission days, Doyle rarely saw him.

The Air Force terminated its tactical reconnaissance program for F-16s in 1993, with plans to shift most of those missions to UAVs. But as a follow-on, there was an interim program using the U.S. Navy–developed Tactical Aerial Reconnaissance Pod System (TARPS) mounted on F-16s. Doyle's squadron was one of the two fighter squadrons that got tapped for this strap-on recon test program, which only lasted eighteen months. While technically a success, from an operational and logistics standpoint, the results were mixed. And since UAV technology was meanwhile maturing rapidly, the decision was made to mothball the TARPS pods and support gear. It was during the TARPS test program that Ian Doyle was part of the Hondo Expedition.

By the time that the USAF got involved, the TARPS pods were a well-matured technology. Most of the technical support was supplied by civilian contractors from Grumman, the company that had originally developed the system. The seventeen-foot, 1,850-pound pods were essentially a strap-on system, adaptable to many types of aircraft. They could be mounted on standard hard points. First developed for Navy F-14s and Marine Corps F/A-18s, the

TARPS pods were, as one of the Grumman camera technicians put it, "foolproof and pilotproof, but then, I repeat myself."

The expedition included four F-16s—two for missions and two for spares and side trips—four mission pilots, and a C-130 to shuttle the support crew and umpteen spare parts—both for the planes and for the TARPS pods. The TDY rotation was five months, making it just short of the six-month threshold for a PCS. This made the personnel paperwork easier and reduced the overall cost of the program.

All of the pilots were housed at the "White House" (La Casa Blanca), the guest quarters in Tegucigalpa that were run by the American embassy, in Colonia Loma Linda Norte district, on La Avenida FAO. The White House was a gathering place of myth and legend. It served as the catchall for visiting company-grade military officers, CIA types on temporary assignment, and assorted contractors on government business. The atmosphere was jovial and there were even some fraternity-style bashes on weekends. The CIA officers called it a safe house, but its presence was hardly clandestine. Even the local newspaper mentioned it from time to time, often by its nicknames, Rick's Café Américain or Rick's Place, in honor of the Humphrey Bogart movie *Casablanca*.

Junior officers at La Casa Blanca were expected to share rooms. Ian Doyle's roommate was Bryson Pitcher, an Air Force intelligence first lieutenant, who was permanent party with the intel cell at the American embassy.

Shortly after meeting Pitcher, Ian Doyle summed up the Expedition to him: "It's an intense assignment, but a good one. I'll fly three, maybe four missions a week, all in daylight hours, and they are just six hours each. Other than some intel briefing dog and pony shows once every ten or twelve days either here or down at Soto Cano, I get all the rest of my days off to hike, swim, and see the sights. My only regret is that this is only a five-month TDY. I wish it were a couple of years, to really soak up the local culture."

Bryson's curiosity was piqued. "Well, what are you doing, exactly? This is the first time I've seen F-16s in Hondo. We haven't heard squat about it, even in the intel shop."

"I could tell you, but then I'd have to shoot you."

Bryson snorted.

Ian grinned and said, "Just kidding. What's your clearance?"

"TS-SBI, with a bunch of funny little letters after that, for SCI compartments that I can't tell you about."

"Well, what *do* you do here, Bryson, in a nutshell?"

"I task and receive reports from a bunch of overeducated NCOs, and we analyze them for liaison with the Honduran government and for an unspecified strategic mission."

"Stuff from aircraft?" Doyle asked.

"Nope. Stuff from, ah . . . non-air-breathing platforms."

"Ahhh, gotcha." Hearing the euphemism for spy satellites made it clear to Doyle that he could ask no further questions.

"Okay, well, then, I guess I can certainly talk about the basics, even though you're in the strategic world, while my bailiwick is mostly tactical. A little crossover, I suppose. You'll probably get briefed in a week or two, anyway."

Bryson nodded.

Ian looked up at the slowly rotating ceiling fan and asked, "Are you familiar with a system called TARPS?"

"Sure, it's the Navy's pod-mounted photo recon system. It's pretty idiotproof, as long as they remember to hook up the external power and use a squirt of Windex before they take off."

"That's the one. Were going to be using F-16s with TARPS pods flying recon over Colombia, keeping track of the, ahem, 'opposition's' troop movements. Meanwhile there are some Army intelligence guys, using a system called Guardrail, out of Panama, to monitor the FARC's radio transmissions. You piece all that intel together, along with what you guys up in 'Echelons Above Reality' provide, and that gives a pretty complete picture for the theater command, most of which—after it's properly sanitized—can get shared with the host country."

Doyle sat up and turned to look at Pitcher, and continued: "It's pretty straightforward stick-and-rudder stuff. I just follow the pre-programmed flight profiles: Fly to these coordinates, spiral down to this altitude and assume this heading and fly straight and level for x minutes until you're at these coordinates, then turn to this heading and fly x minutes, then climb out, suck some gas at a tanker, and return to base."

Pitcher chided, "Ha! One of the new UAVs could probably handle that—from a lot closer in than Hondo."

"No kidding. I've been told that it was more political than anything else, to show support for the Colombian and Honduran governments—you know, show the flag. So they didn't want just a 'man in the loop' but an actual 'man on the stick.' For reasons of physical security on the ground, they couldn't base our planes in-country in Colombia, so they decided to base us at Tegucigalpa."

"Wouldn't it be safer for the planes to be at Soto Cano?"

"Yes, but *El Presidente* likes F-16s, so he insisted, since this is just a five-month gig, that we be here in the capital, rather than at Soto Cano. I think he's hoping to get a 'dollar ride' in a D-model."

"Do you have any two-seaters down here?"

"No, but I wouldn't be surprised to see that magically get added to the scope of the mission."

"So basing at Colombia was out, and the political fix was in for Tegucigalpa. Better for you, anyway. At Soto Cano, you'd be living in some corrugated steel hooch with no running water," Bryson summarized.

"Yeah, it would be *muy jodido* to have some FARC dude blow up a couple of F-16s on the ramp. As I recall, Vipers were nineteen million dollars per copy, back when the last ones rolled off the assembly line. Now that production has shut down, the airframes are basically irreplaceable. It would be very bad PR if we lost one."

"So you poor baby! You have three or four days a week on your hands for the next five months to chase skirts and to sip Port Royal beer. Don't worry, I'll tell you all the best places to go, and I have friends with cars that can take you there."

"I'm not much of a skirt chaser. You see, I believe in *courting* ladies, not dating them. But I have been known to enjoy a good beer."

"In moderation, no doubt."

Doyle echoed, "Yes, exactly: in moderation."

Bryson punched his shoulder. "I think you're gonna have a blast here."

Doyle's plans for the next five months changed radically the next day when he heard what he later called the voice of an angel, as he came in for a landing approach after a forty-minute operational test flight with the newly fitted TARPS pod. The voice on the radio from the control tower sounded enchanting, obviously that of a young woman. Soon after hitting the tarmac, he asked the liaison crew chief about the voice. The master sergeant replied, "Oh, that's Blanca Araneta. But I've gotta warn you: She's single, maybe twenty-one or twenty-two, and she's an absolute doll. But she's made of pure unobtanium. Many before you have tried and failed, young Jedi."

Doyle immediately took that as a challenge. He got his first glimpse of the young woman as he loitered outside the control tower during the evening shift change. He spotted her just as she stepped into her car, a battered old Mercedes station wagon. Ian was surprised to see that, having heard she was from a wealthy family. She drove away before he had the chance to approach her and introduce himself. She was indeed a beautiful woman, with large, expressive eyes, a perfectly symmetrical face, and full lips. Her shoulder-length black hair was pulled back in a ponytail. Ian Doyle was smitten.

He immediately started gathering intelligence and planning a strategy. He first learned that Blanca was indeed from a wealthy family that lived about an hour's drive north of the air base. After much prying with other members of the control tower staff, Doyle found out that Blanca Araneta was a recent graduate of Universidad Nacional Autónoma de Honduras and was a licensed private pilot. To Ian this meant bonus points: finding a woman with whom he could talk aviation and not have her eyes glaze over. She still lived in an apartment near the university.

Further inquiries garnered the married name of her college roommate: Consuelo Dalgon, a linguistics major who now taught public school and lived near the airport. Blanca still had a close friendship with Dalgon. After buying a few more beers, he was given Dalgon's phone number. That same evening, Ian phoned her, explaining that he was TDY and was looking for a Spanish tutor. Dalgon immediately answered affirmatively, explaining that she had married another recent graduate who was just getting started as a management trainee, so she could use the extra money.

Ian's lessons began the next Saturday at the Dalgons' apartment. Not only did he get a thorough immersion course in Spanish, but he also began to pick up tidbits about the mysterious Señorita Blanca Araneta.

He learned that Blanca's father, Arturo Araneta y Vasquez, was a semiretired mining engineer and investor. He was also a former member of the Honduran Olympic tennis team.

Consuelo confided to Ian that Blanca had told her that she hated tennis. This was because she had been forced to take tennis lessons from an early age. Doyle learned that Blanca loved swimming and aerobatic flying. He was also told that Blanca read and wrote English much better than she spoke it.

At his next Spanish tutoring session, he found out that Blanca loved Almond Roca candy. She also liked modern flamenco music—what she called "that folky jazz sound." She especially liked the Gipsy Kings, Armik, Paco de Lucía, and Ottmar Liebert.

Curious, Doyle bought several CDs at the local record store and was instantly hooked. As he listened to this music, he often day-dreamed about Blanca, picturing her dancing in a traditional fla-menco dress.

Ian met Blanca for the first time at the Plaza San Martin Hotel in Tegucigalpa. Consuela and Blanca often went to the hotel to swim. They had started going while they were in college. Though the pool was ostensibly reserved for hotel guests, the hotel man-ager quietly let it be known that pretty college girls of good moral character were welcome to come swim at the pool as often as they liked, just to provide some eye candy for the visiting businessmen. To the girls, it was a perfect arrangement. The hotel provided a safe place to park and a safe place to swim. The only downside was that they often got to practice how to politely brush off the occasional lovelorn or just plain lusty business travelers. Only the Japanese ones took pictures.

During his third evening lesson with Consuelo, she and her husband, Pablo, invited Ian to come with them for a swim fol-lowing the next Saturday lesson. Not wishing to be obvious, Ian didn't ask if Blanca might be meeting them there, but he thought the chances were good.

At the Tegucigalpa Multiplaza, Ian picked out a new swim-suit—opting for the long "surfer suit" look—a dark beach towel, a lightweight Windbreaker, and a pair of the best-quality leather *huarache* sandals that they sold.

A half hour after their swim session began, Ian emerged from the pool after a set of laps. He was thrilled to see Blanca Araneta had arrived and was sitting on a lounge chair, chatting with Consuelo.

Toweling himself dry, he walked toward them, doing his best to look nonchalant. Consuelo introduced him to Blanca in Span-ish. Señora Dalgon was, after all, a strict believer in true immer-sion Spanish.

Ignoring Consuelo's cue, Blanca switched to English.

"A pleasure to be meeting you, Ian."

Hearing the cute way she pronounced his name—more like "Eon" than "Ian"—was delightful to Doyle.

Avoiding the open chair next to Blanca, he sat down on the lounge that was beyond Consuelo's and Pablo's: he thought it best to talk to Blanca at first from a longer distance, rather than seem overly anxious or intrusive of her space.

Speaking to Blanca, over the top of Consuelo's back, Ian said, "Señorita Araneta, I have heard your voice before, from the control tower. I usually fly 'Viper 1-2-4,' and you've probably heard my call sign, 'Subgunner.'"

"Oh, yes, I know your call sign."

Doyle replied, "Yes, that's me. I always wanted to put a face to your name. I must say, you have a pretty voice, and a very pretty face to go with it."

Blanca just smiled and laughed politely.

Again trying to seem nonchalant, Ian added, "Well, enjoy your swim," and he reclined on an unoccupied lounge chair and put on his sunglasses. Lying there, he wondered if he had botched the introduction. His mind was racing. He felt very self-conscious, and oh, so pale-skinned among so many people with olive complexions. He dared not speak. Silently, he recited to himself Proverbs 17:28: "Even a fool is counted wise, when he holds his peace. When he shuts his lips he is considered perceptive."

Out of the corner of his eye, he saw Blanca stand up and whip off the ankle-length swimming skirt-wrap that she had been wearing. She tossed it on top of her flight bag. He noticed that she carried that bag everywhere. Beneath, she was wearing what by modern standards was a very conservative one-piece swimsuit with an integral skirt, but it couldn't hide her traffic-stopping figure. Ian Doyle gulped and whispered to himself, "Ay, ay, ay."

Blanca spent almost fifteen minutes in the pool, swimming lap after lap. After she got out and returned to her chair, Ian rose, smiled, and took his own turn in the pool, swimming in a medley of strokes for about ten minutes. He thought that at this stage it was best to seem slightly standoffish and more interested in swimming than in chatting her up.

After he climbed up the pool's ladder, he could see that Consuelo and Blanca had turned on their chairs and were applying sunscreen to each other's noses. Ian again toweled but just slightly, returned to his chaise, and put on his sunglasses.

Consuelo asked, *"¿Bloqueador solar, Ian?"*

He answered, *"Sí, muchas gracias por su amabilidad, señora,"* and raised his hands as if ready to catch the bottle.

But instead of tossing the bottle, Consuelo pivoted to hand him the bottle directly. Leaning forward, she whispered, "She has been very curious about you."

As Ian slathered the waterproof sunblock on, he explained, "With my skin, I don't tan, I just burn. I'm feeling a little too white to fit in here. I'm just another ugly ghost-pale *gringo.*"

As Ian handed the bottle back to her, Consuelo said matter-of-factly, "You know, here in our country, many people would be jealous of your fair skin. The more fair, the more aristocratic."

Doyle realized that he had lot to learn about Honduras.

Blanca eyed Doyle for a minute and, speaking over Consuelo's back, asked, "Has Consuelo been talking about me to you?"

"A little."

"So, what did she say?"

"Something about your father, *tu papá*, that he was *un experto de jugar al tenis.*"

"Not actually a champion. He was a bronze medaler—I mean medalist—in doubles of tennis."

She cocked her head and asked with a hopeful lilt to her voice, "Do you like tennis?"

"I've played the game, but you know, I never really liked it. *No me gusta el tenis.* It is just a whole lot of sweating just to hit a ball back and forth, back and forth. And it's kind of an aggravating game. I found it a little too competitive: even if you practice a lot and hit the ball just right, there is always someone who can hit it just a little bit better, or who is just a little bit faster, and they can ace you out. So, no offense, but it's not for me. If I want to practice my hand-to-eye coordination, I'd rather be in a flight simulator or, better yet, up in the air, formation flying or doing aerobatics."

Blanca smiled. "Aerobatics?"

"Oh, yeah. The F16 is built for it—well, with a big turning radius, that is. Lots of power, great handling. The controls are a dream. Incredibly responsive."

"*Ay,* that sounds wonderful."

Consuelo jumped in: "Ian, you should show Blanca those videos you shot from the backseat that you showed me and Pablo."

"*Sí, señora, me encantaría* . . . uh . . ." At a loss for the right words in Spanish, he finished: ". . . to do so." After a moment he added, "That video may make you dizzy to watch, and there is not much narration, just me and the pilot grunting, you know, tightening our abdominal muscles, doing our best to pull the g's."

"No, it won't make *me* dizzy!" Blanca said. She then just smiled, nodded dismissively, and lay back down, putting on sunglasses, and pulling her sun hat over her head. But Doyle noticed that she was looking in his direction.

With her large dark sunglasses, he couldn't be sure if she was sleeping, or staring at him. He was having trouble reading her. Was she genuinely interested, or just being polite and properly social? He decided that it was best to just give her more of the "silence and sunbathing" treatment. He reached down and pulled out his Sony Discman portable CD player and put the headphones on. He closed his eyes and got lost in the music for a few minutes. Then he noticed something had shaded his face. He opened his eyes to see Blanca standing over him.

"Oh, *hola,* Señorita Araneta," he said casually.

Gesturing to his CD player, she asked, "What are you playing on that thing?"

"Oh, this? Here, take a listen." Blanca perched on the edge of Consuelo's lounge chair and Ian handed her the Discman. He leaned forward to put the headphones on her head. It was the first time that he had ever touched Blanca. It gave him a tingle.

Blanca put on a huge grin the instant she heard the music.

"You like Ottmar Liebert? No way! This is his first album, *Nouveau Flamenco.* You really like it?"

"Yeah, I sure do. I'm a recent convert to that music. I've really gotten hooked on flamenco guitar since I came down here."

She nodded. "Well, Ian, what is currently your favorite band?"

"I'd have to say the Gipsy Kings. It's almost hypnotic. From the first time I heard them sing '*Bamboleo,*' I just couldn't get it out of my head."

Blanca shook her head in disbelief, then smiled and said softly, "Wow, I really like them too."

The next time that Ian met Blanca was at a weeknight dinner party, just three days later, hosted by Consuelo and Pablo. The evening before, in halting Spanish, Doyle asked Consuelo, "How should I dress for this?"

For the first time at one of his immersion class sessions, Consuelo lapsed into English: "Well, it is a dinner, you should wear a coat and a tie."

"I'm just TDY down here and I don't have a suit with me. The only thing I have with a tie is my service dress uniform."

"That will be fine. Wear that."

Ian arrived early carrying a clear plastic grocery bag with a bottle of Chilean white wine and a can of Almond Roca. In the crook of his other arm were two large bouquets of white orchids.

Inviting him in, Pablo Dalgon said, "You can relax, Ian. We're speaking all English tonight. This is not a class night. Purely social."

Ian was taken aback to see that Blanca was already there. Doyle handed the flowers to Consuelo, and said, "I brought a bunch for each of you." Pablo exclaimed, jokingly, "Oh, how nice of you. Flowers for both of us."

Consuelo gave Pablo a sharp look and elbowed him in the ribs, chiding, "He means flowers for both of the ladies."

Pablo laughed and said, "I know. Just kidding."

As Blanca and Consuelo each took their bouquets, Blanca glanced down to see what was in the bag. She recognized the pink can. Her jaw dropped a bit and she gave Doyle a quizzical look.

In rapid damage-control mode, Doyle explained, "I heard from Consuelo that you liked Almond Roca, so I bought a can. You know, to serve with dessert."

As Consuelo began serving dinner, Blanca's eyes locked onto the can of candy sitting on the sideboard. Then she stared at Ian.

Blanca started laughing. She pointed a scolding finger at Doyle and said, "Ian, I think you are trying to manipulate me."

"Yes, I am, *señorita*. I freely admit that. But I'm doing so in a kind of nice, gentlemanly way."

Through the rest of the dinner, the talk was mainly about aviation and differences between American and Honduran customs. It was a very pleasant evening. Pablo was quiet, as was his nature. Ian and Blanca made plenty of eye contact. Consuelo, clearly looking like a victorious matchmaker, steered the conversation. She often returned to topics in which she gave Ian and Blanca opportunities to ask each other questions and talk about their accomplishments.

After dinner, Consuelo served flan with a piece of Almond

Roca topping each piece of the gelatinous dessert. She was quite the diplomatic hostess.

Pablo and Consuelo stepped out to clear the dishes. In phrasing that he had practiced several times with Consuelo's coaching, Ian asked Blanca in Spanish: "Señorita Araneta, I wish to ask your permission to court you in the coming days, with completely honorable intentions, if you would be so kind as to have me in your presence."

Her answer was immediate, "You may call me Blanca, and yes, you may court me, with your promise to be a gentleman."

Their next meeting was a lunch the following day at the air base canteen. But just as their conversation was starting, it was cut short: one of Blanca's coworkers rushed to their table and exclaimed that the tower boss had fallen ill with a flu and Blanca was needed back at the control tower. Then he turned and stepped away just as quickly as he had arrived.

Blanca stood, and said, "I'm now in a hurry here, so this as you say is the *Reader's Digest* version: I like you a lot, Ian. I think you are fascinating. So now it is the time I should take you up to the *estancia*, so *mi papá* can give you the, uh, 'third degree.' You are seeming just way, way too good to be true . . . and my father, he is an expert at digging out the flaws of character in suitors. We'll see if he can scare you off." She raised her index finger and added, "He has scared off all the others, you know. I'll schedule a dinner for next Saturday."

Before he could answer, Blanca smiled, gave a little wave, and dashed away.

Ian sat dumbfounded at what he had just heard. Then he said a long, silent prayer and ate his lunch.

To meet Blanca's father, Ian decided to wear a suit, instead of his service dress uniform. But borrowing a suit that would fit him well took some scrambling, as did finding cuff links and dress shoes. This turned into an evening-long scavenger hunt for many of the junior officers and GS-9s who lived on his floor of Rick's Place. Knocking on doors up and down the hall, Bryson Pitcher led Doyle and a parade of suit beggars. This turned into a movable party, with plenty of alcohol served. Doyle heard repeatedly, "This deserves a toast!" The lovely Blanca Araneta was a legendarily unreachable enigma for anyone who worked in flight operations, so the reactions were a mix of envy and awe. The envy came mostly from the officers who were there on PCS assignments. They were miffed that a newly arrived TDY O-2 could break the ice with Blanca, and so quickly.

Blanca drove over from her apartment and picked Ian up at just after three p.m., for the hour-long drive to her family's ninety-hectare *estancia*, which was about three miles outside of Talanga. Blanca wore a simple black dress with a very modest neckline and hemmed below the knee. She wore very little makeup. Her hair was combed out and worn loosely. This was the first time that Ian had seen it in anything but a simple ponytail. The only adornment she wore was a single large teardrop-shaped pearl on a gold chain. Ian thought she looked gorgeous. She definitely had the Grace Kelly vibe going. Understated, but stunning.

The drive north from Tegucigalpa was fairly quiet and revealed the nervousness they both felt. There were just a few comments on the scenery and a bit of travelogue from Blanca on the local history and age of certain buildings. Ian felt a new level of anxiety as she turned the car into the *estancia*'s long driveway. Even from a distance, Doyle could see that the house was huge and that it had stables off to one side.

Just before they stepped out of the Mercedes, Ian straightened his borrowed silk tie. Blanca whispered, "Bring your video camera. My papa will want to see pictures." After the maid ushered them in, they met Blanca's father on the screened patio.

As was customary, Blanca began the introductions: *"Papá, éste es mi amigo, Ian."*

Ian carried on haltingly, *"Mucho gusto, Señor Araneta, su hija habla de usted con mucha admiración, es un honor y un placer de conocer a usted."* ("I'm pleased to meet you sir, your daughter speaks with great admiration about you, it is an honor and a pleasure to meet you.") Ian did this fairly well, since he had practiced it with Consuelo, but he was obviously nervous.

After shaking hands, Arturo Araneta asked, "So, Lieutenant Doyle, my daughter tells me you are a pilot of F-16 fighting planes."

"That's right, sir." Pointing to the rucksack on his shoulder, he said, "I brought my camcorder with some movies of myself and some of my squadron mates flying F-16s, if you are interested."

"Of, course, of course. Let's go to the library."

Arturo Araneta asked as they walked, "You have this movie in your video camera?"

"Yes, sir."

"Then let's watch it on my big screen. It is the latest from Japan."

The dimly lit library was quite a contrast to the brightness of the patio. It took a while for Doyle's eyes to adjust to the lighting.

As they were getting the camera's cable hooked up to the television input jack, Arturo Araneta asked Ian, "So, where did you go to college?"

Without looking up, Ian said, "The University of Chicago."

Arturo pointed to the jacks on the front of the television and said, "You may attach the cables here. And what did you study?"

"Engineering."

Arturo looked at him and said, "There are many types of engineers."

"I did a double major, in aeronautical engineering and industrial engineering. I also got minor degrees in English literature and military history."

The elder gentleman looked impressed. "Engineering, engineering. Excellent! I am surprised that so many other young people waste their time in other trifling fields." He again looked at Ian intently and asked, "That much work must have been difficult. How were your grades?"

Ian smiled. "It was a lot of work, but I enjoyed the material. I graduated cum laude."

Arturo stood up, smiled slightly while nodding his head, and said, "Very good. Very, very good." With a wave of his hand, the maid brought iced tea and they sipped it as they watched Ian's videotape.

Doyle introduced it by just saying, "These clips you'll see were all shot by me from the backseat of a D-model F-16—that's the version with two seats."

The first clip showed some tight-formation flying. The second showed takeoffs, landings, and touch-and-goes.

Just before the third segment, Ian voiced the caveat, "Now, this part coming up, it wasn't me at the controls, and I had no warning that my friend was going to do this. I was just along for the ride and to preserve the events for posterity." The video then showed the plane doing slow rolls high over San Francisco, passing through patchy clouds, and then diving to line up west of the city. It then flew under the Golden Gate Bridge and then under the San Francisco Bay Bridge with the pilot twice exclaiming "Yeee-haaaaaaw!"

Both of the Aranetas gasped and laughed. Ian then commented: "I found out later that Fred had the crew chief disable the plane's transponder so there'd be no comebacks."

Arturo chuckled and said, "Very clever. And I'm glad this was not you flying so illegally."

The last segment of the video was several minutes of aerobatics shot over the pilot's shoulder. In one corner of the screen, the plane's altimeter could be seen winding down from thirty thousand feet, at an alarming rate. The significance of some of the maneuvers was lost on her father, but Blanca was clearly impressed. She kept saying "Wow" and "Double wow!"

As Ian disconnected his camcorder, Arturo exclaimed, "That was fantastic. Simply fantastic."

Next the subject of tennis came up, as Blanca had warned it always did with her father. He started by saying, "You know, seeing San Francisco in that videotape reminds me . . ." He spent the next half hour in an animated description of how he had toured the United States playing tennis tournaments in the 1980s and how he had learned to disco dance. He ended by mentioning: "You know, when I was there, I became so fascinated with your basketball. Other than tennis, that is now the sport I watch the most, on the satellite television."

"Really?" Ian asked. "What is your favorite American team?"

The Honduran replied, "Oh, the Detroit Pistons. Most definitely."

Ian laughed. "Did Blanca mention that I was raised near Detroit?"

Arturo Araneta put on a huge grin.

Ian put in hesitantly, "Although I've gotta say, I'm just as much a Lakers fan as I am a fan of the Pistons."

"The Lakers, they are a fine team, too, but sometimes, with all their physicality, they lack the, ah, finesse and control of the Pistons."

Just when Doyle thought that he could not have hit it off more perfectly, Arturo asked: "So, what does a fighter jockey like you do, for hobbies?"

"I like to run, swim, and I do a lot of target shooting."

Araneta chortled. "You are a shooter? Come with me, my boy, and I will show you my modest gun collection!"

As the three of them walked together toward the other wing of the house, Blanca laughed and whispered, "The lost-long son returns!"

As they walked, Ian glanced over his shoulder and noticed the maid following five paces back, dutifully carrying a tray with their drinks. He realized that this sort of life would take some getting used to.

They spent the next half hour chitchatting and admiring guns pulled out of a climate-controlled walk-in vault. Araneta had a huge collection of perhaps two hundred guns and fifty swords and sabers. Sitting on a large wooden stand in the center of the vault room was an exquisitely ornamented saddle with a saber and a pair of holstered horse pistols. The saddle was clearly the centerpiece of his collection. Arturo explained, "This saddle belonged to a lieutenant of Simón Bolívar. I bought it by private treaty from a collector before it could go to auction."

Doyle noted that Arturo's collection was eclectic, ranging from a sixteenth-century Chinese hand cannon to one of the latest Colt Anaconda revolvers. But the collection mostly emphasized muzzle loaders and horse pistols, representing four hundred years of development for the latter. In deference to the humid climate in Honduras, they all wore white cotton gloves as they handled the guns.

As they were examining his modern guns, Araneta asked, "What do you think of Blanca's Glock 19?"

"You have a Glock?" Ian asked Blanca, surprised.

Blanca answered with a slight tone of condescension, "Yes, of course, the one I carry *every day*, in my flight bag. It's got night sights on it. I'm a very good shot."

"I had no idea that you packed."

Blanca laughed and said, "You *yanquis* have no idea how many Hondurans carry guns every day of the week. We just make no big deal about it.

"Daddy bought me the Glock and also the Mercedes. The car is intentionally old and ugly on the outside, but it has a brand-new engine and transmission. Actually, the rust spots on the door panels are not really rust: they are just painted on. It's the *perfecto* anti-kidnapping car. Not like anything anyone would expect me to drive. Even so, it is built like a tank and could knock most other cars off of the road!"

Ian stroked his chin and said, "The more I learn about you, *señorita*, the more there is to like about you. You're the complete package: 'She flies, she swims, she shoots, she dresses tastefully, she drives a stealth tank, she likes flamenco guitar . . . '"

"You left out that I'm a great cook and an excellent dancer."

All three of them laughed.

Finally, they sat down to a four-course dinner that was served by the cook and dutifully attended by the maid. The conversation over dinner ranged from flying, to shooting, to duck hunting, to Arturo's recollections of what Blanca was like as a little girl, and, of course, to tennis.

Ian got to try out some of his new Spanish phrases. His fractured grammar and conjugational foul-ups earned him a lot of good-spirited laughter. Arturo was gracious, saying only: "You are learning quickly, my boy. And I'm glad to hear you use a good Castilian accent. So many Americans I meet, even scientists and engineers, are educated only in the gutter Spanish."

After a long pause, Arturo glanced over the top of his glasses and asked gravely, "Are you Catholic?"

"Yes, sir. Born and raised, Irish-Catholic. I still attend Mass faithfully." Realizing that he was taking a huge risk of offending his host, he added: "But additionally, I have come to more of a personal faith in Jesus Christ. Between him and me, I feel no need of a mediator. The pope and the priests are fine for ceremony, but I truly feel that I'm saved personally: by Jesus, by faith in him alone, by his grace, and with my sins paid for by his sacrifice on the cross. I love Jesus with all *mi corazón*."

Arturo brightened and clasped his hand on Ian's shoulder. "I feel the same way also. It is refreshing to hear that from a fellow member of the church."

Everything continued to go well until it was time for cigars and brandy. Arturo was slightly miffed when Ian accepted a snifter but refused a cigar, saying, "*Lo siento mucho, señor,* but I don't smoke. *No fumo.*"

As he trimmed and lit his cigar, Arturo tut-tutted and then said resignedly, "Oh, well, you pilots are such health nuts. You don't know what you're missing. Honduran cigars are just as good as *los Cubanos.* But I can say I now smoke only about one of these a month."

Blanca joked, "You know, Daddy, I gave up cigars years ago, when I decided to follow in the steps of Amelia Earhart."

As Blanca gave Ian a ride back to the base, she went on and on about how well Ian had gotten along with her father, mentioning how unprecedented that was. After a couple of minutes of driving on in silence, she said simply, "I think he really likes you, Ian."

"I like him too." Then he asked: "Where'd you get that pearl necklace?"

"Before they were married, my father and mother went on a trip to the Islas de la Bahía. Those are our Bay Islands on the east coast. They were snorkeling and Daddy dove to bring up an oyster. Inside of this oyster was this pearl. Later on that same day my father asked my mother to marry him. The pearl, it was too big and fragile for a ring, so it was placed on this necklace. Ever since then, my father nicknamed my mother *conchita,* which means 'little oyster.' And now he sometimes calls me that."

After a long pause, she added, "My mother gave me this when she was dying of the cancer."

"*Lo siento mucho, Blanca.*"

"It's okay. That was a long time ago."

"May I call you *conchita*?"

Blanca giggled, "Yes, Ian, you may, but *not* in public! You see, among the lower classes—especially in Argentina—*conchita* has a different, a very crude meaning; so please don't you call me that around other people—or at least around anyone from Argentina."

"*Si, mi conchita.*"

She drove on in silence, obviously deep in thought.

After passing through the formalities with the air base's gate guards, Blanca turned to face Ian and said, "You know, Mr. Lieutenant Doyle, you were very clever, finding out all those things about me from Consuelo."

"Yes, I must admit I do overplan things."

"So, why did you do all that—the orchids and the Almond Roca? I think also the flamenco music." Her voice grew sharp. "Why?"

Doyle coughed nervously. "Because I fell in love with your voice on the radio from the tower, even before I ever laid eyes on you. And when someone like me loves someone as much as I love you . . . well. I'm the kind of guy that will nearly warp space and time, just to make everything fall into place. I am absolutely head over heels, crazy in love with you, Blanca."

Just then her car reached the driving circle in front of the White House.

"Perhaps I will see you again, Ian," she said, ushering him out with a wave and a smile. He blew her a kiss. As her eyes lingered on him for a moment, he added, half shouting: "*Encantado, Señorita!*"

As he approached the front steps of the White House, Ian Doyle stopped in his tracks. He realized why Blanca had worn the pearl necklace. That pearl had been a key part of her father's marriage proposal to her mother. Wearing it had been her way of telling her father: *This man is bona fide marriage material.*

The next few weeks were a blur. The squadron's operational tempo increased, and Ian was flying a lot. Most of his contact with

Blanca was by correspondence. Their love letters began cordially but became more familiar and gained a note of passion as time went on. Partly because two of the Hondo Expedition pilots had fallen ill with traveler's tummy, Ian was flying as much as six days a week, a grueling pace.

Most of Ian's missions were uneventful. The only real excitement came on a couple of flights when his plane's radar warning receiver went off over hostile territory. These were mainly Gun Dish radars, part of Russian-built ZSU 23-4s—four-barrel 23mm antiaircraft cannons. The plane's radar warning receiver (RWR) going off caused a bit of angst and prompted some lively discussion at the postflight debriefings.

On a Sunday forty days into his Honduras rotation, Blanca took Ian flying. Above his objection to split the cost, she treated him to a two-hour rental in her favorite plane, an Italian-built Pioneer P200. It was a very small, sleek, low-wing plane that had unusual dual sticks in a side-by-side cockpit.

As they approached the plane for their preflight, Doyle said, "I was expecting you to rent some zippy biplane with seats fore and aft."

She grinned. "I think a side-by-side configuration like this is much more, ah, *romántica*, no?" Quickly changing subjects, she said, "The dry weight of this bird is only 260 kilos—light as a feather!"

"Oh, man, that *is* light! Did you know that an F-16 weighs about twelve thousand kilos fully fueled?"

Blanca was wearing a very attractive white flight suit with zippers everywhere. As they walked around the plane, checking the fuel tanks, wiggling the wings, and checking the flaps and rudder, Doyle's eyes kept drifting back to Blanca. The flight suit certainly accentuated her trim figure.

They pulled the chocks and climbed aboard. Sitting in the

plane's left seat, he admired Blanca's finesse as she worked the radio and rolled out to the taxi strip, craning her head to do repeated 360 eyeballs of both the plane's control surfaces and her surroundings. She didn't miss a beat. After getting takeoff clearance, she punched in the throttle and took off after a surprisingly short roll. Climbing out at seven hundred feet per minute, she took the plane up to ten thousand feet and headed west as they chatted about the plane's characteristics.

"What's this bird stressed for?" Ian asked.

"Four g's pos, and two g's negative."

Doyle nodded approvingly.

Blanca continued, "It's been upgraded to a 110-horsepower plant. She'll do 145 miles per hour, at altitude. Redline is 5,600 rpms. Oh, and watch your sink rate if you pull more than a 60-degree bank. I think you'll like flying it. It takes very light control forces. I love this plane because you don't have to muscle the stick."

Glancing at the GPS, she declared, "Okay, *hombre*, now we are outside of the TCA, and we can plaaay." Banking sharply left and right to get a view under the plane's wings and swiveling her head, she said, "I see empty skies."

Doyle echoed, "Ditto, I confirm I see no traffic. Let's play!"

Blanca snugged the straps on her X-harness and, with no cue needed, Doyle did likewise. Blanca then immediately launched into a series of aerobatics that would have made most other passengers puke. Doyle was whooping and laughing. She burned through seven thousand feet in less than a minute, doing rolls, loops, and spins. At one point Blanca's flight bag levitated to the ceiling as they pulled negative g's. Doyle snatched it and tucked it under his arm.

After climbing back up to ten thousand feet, Blanca put on a devilish grin. She launched into another series of maneuvers, even more violent. At one point Ian's vision narrowed from the effect of pulling three g's. Doyle never once felt tempted to take the controls, even when she intentionally put the plane into a flat spin. She deftly recovered and they both laughed. She climbed once again and put the plane through a pair of Immelmann turns and then a neat four-point roll.

"Now *you* show *me* something!" she said, making a show of throwing her hands up, off the stick.

Quickly drying his palms on his pant legs, Doyle grasped the other stick. He then took a couple of tentative turns, getting a feel for the aircraft. He throttled the engine up slightly and then adjusted the trim wheel to counteract the propeller's torque. This took a couple of tries to get just right, since he was unfamiliar with the gradation of the wheel.

"*Está bien!* You just showed me a very nice four-point roll. Now, this is an eight-pointer!" After completing the roll, he continued: "And this is a *sixteen*-pointer."

After completing the second roll, he said, "Sorry, that was a little sloppy. I'm not used to a plane where I'm fighting prop torque like this. Flying jets spoils a man." After a beat, he shouted, "Hands on stick!"

She obliged.

He then declared, "It's your aircraft!" and dropped his hands.

She was quizzical. "What? That's all you show me?"

As she resumed control, he explained, "Look, Blanca, I didn't come up here to show off my fighter-jock stuff. I came to see *you* do *your* thing."

"And what do you think?"

"I think you're beautiful, and I think that your flying is just as beautiful. *Muy bella.*"

Blanca beamed and deftly banked to dive toward Lake Yojoa, visible in the distance. In the dive, their ground speed got above 160.

He truly was impressed by her flying ability. He recognized

that she was a natural for stick and rudder as well as situational awareness. The thing that impressed him the most was her gracefulness in both right- and left-hand turns. Most pilots were good at only one or the other, depending on their handedness. He commented to her on this, and she explained, "*Mi papá*, he's the tennis guy. Since I was a little girl, he insist that I learn everything ambidextrous—no, ambidextrously—even with the holding of a fork."

"*La tenedor*," Doyle reminded himself aloud, from a recent lesson.

"*El tenedor*," she corrected.

"Sorry, I always get my masculines and feminines mixed up."

She turned to give him another smile, "I think you are *very* masculine, Ian."

With the aerobatic maneuvering over, they both loosened their harnesses. Back in level flight and approaching the *lago*, Blanca again pushed the stick forward to swoop down low over the water. The plane scared up a huge flock of ducks. Marveling at the size of the flock of multicolored brown and black birds, Ian asked: "What are those?"

"Here, we call them *suirirí piquirrojo*. In English they are called, I think, the black-bellied whistling duck."

They flew well above the flock, safe from any bird strikes. Blanca repeatedly banked the plane to get a better view; then, after circling back, she pulled the throttle out, transitioning to slow flight to orbit the enormous flock. It looked like a veritable cloud of ducks. Ian snapped pictures with his camera. She then advanced the throttle to its mid-range and flew away from the lake, back toward Tegucigalpa.

Ian felt ecstatic. "Wow! That was an incredible sight, Blanca!"

Ian reached over to place his hand on Blanca's shoulder. He realized that it was the second time he had ever touched her. He asked, "Will you marry me?"

She punched the throttle to the firewall and the acceleration threw Ian back against his seat. She looked straight ahead and then glanced down at the instruments. At first Ian thought that he had angered her. Then she turned and smiled. "Of course I will marry you, Ian. But I gotta land this plane first."

25

A Tight Spot

"Anyone who clings to the historically untrue—and thoroughly immoral—doctrine that 'violence never solves anything' I would advise to conjure up the ghosts of Napoleon Bonaparte and of the Duke of Wellington and let them debate it. The ghost of Hitler could referee, and the jury might well be the Dodo, the Great Auk, and the Passenger Pigeon. Violence, naked force, has settled more issues in history than has any other factor, and the contrary opinion is wishful thinking at its worst. Breeds that forget this basic truth have always paid for it with their lives and freedoms."

—**Robert A. Heinlein,** *Starship Troopers*

In the first week of July, several of the men from the compound, including Alex, Ian, and Doctor K., were part of a firewood-cutting expedition to the nearby Prescott National Forest. Traveling in a four-pickup convoy, they went beyond the ponderosa pines at the lower elevations to cut Douglas firs, mostly along the road that led to the Mingus Mountain campground. Three exhausting daylong trips each took twelve hours at three-day intervals.

On the third day of the woodcutting enterprise, Blanca was on guard duty. She was startled to hear the sound of breaking glass downstairs.

She left the ringer engaged for thirty seconds continuously, followed by three short rings. This signal told everyone that the compound was being attacked by infiltrators.

Blanca thought that it would be safest to get back in the hottub pillbox. She poked the muzzle of her M16 out of the hot tub, rotated the gun's safety to "SEMI," and held still. She sighted the gun on the bedroom door, looking through the screen door that divided the bedroom from the deck.

The man who walked into the bedroom was armed with a carbine that looked a lot like Alex's Mini-14, except that it was shiny—perhaps stainless steel or chrome plated—and it had a folding stock.

The bullet hit him square in the chest. He went down, screaming and spurting blood. He didn't stop screaming and gasping for nearly a minute, and twitched for nearly another full minute after that. Blanca was horrified by what she had done. She had never imagined so much blood could come out of someone. And since she had never hunted, she was unprepared to see the man thrashing. Despite the fact that she had pushed her rifle's muzzle out beyond the lip of the hot tub, her ears were ringing.

Just as she was wondering what to do next, she heard several shots coming from the far side of the compound, and some indistinct shouts. Then there were two more shots. They sounded different. She surmised that these were pistol shots.

An hour later Blanca heard the full story. A group of five men and one woman, all armed, had attempted to sneak into the compound in broad daylight, assuming that they'd find the four families with their guard down. The end result was that the compound had more compost for their garden and more guns for their arsenal. Blanca inherited the Mini-14 from the man whom she'd shot from the deck. Alex was impressed with the gun, explaining that it was a scarce GB model, like those sold to police departments and prison systems. Unlike a standard Mini-14, this gun had a factory flash hider and a factory side-folding stock. It was also made of stainless steel, rendering it less vulnerable to the elements. Alex declared it a keeper. He gave Blanca six original factory magazines for the gun and a pair of M16 triple magazine pouches to carry them in.

26

A Fair Share

"A pistol defends your property and your person from unanticipated and barely anticipated threats from thieves and robbers. With it, you can control your immediate environment. A rifle defends your freedom from oppressors and tyrants. With it, you can enforce your will."

—Gabe Suarez

Hankamer, Texas
December, the First Year

After La Fuerza had cleaned out everything of use from the stores in Anahuac, they moved north. Their next target was the small town of Hankamer. It was so small that they were able to clean it out house-to-house. Once that process started, many of the town's five hundred residents fled, most of them on foot.

It was in Hankamer that Garcia found Rodrigo Cruz. Garcia was about ready to order him killed, along with the others, when Cruz shouted, "Wait! You *need* me, man!"

"Why do I need you, *pendejo*?" Garcia questioned.

Pointing to the big M2 machinegun on a pintle mount atop a V-100, he said, "I seen your guys fiddling with that Browning .50. They could only get it to fire single-shot. The timing is screwed-up. I can fix that. I was an armorer in the Marines. I know how to set headspace and timing, all that stuff. I got a whole set of machine-gun manuals and some tools in my house."

Ignacio snorted. "Show me and maybe I'll let you live."

After Hankamer, La Fuerza continued brazenly hitting small towns in east Texas. They first swung in a large arc north and then westward. They skipped Dayton but then hit Hardin and Moss Hill. In Moss Hill, Garcia found a full-length mink coat for his wife, who had chronically complained of being cold. That immediately became a status symbol for all the wives and girlfriends of the gang members. They all wanted a full-length fur coat, and eventually they got them—mostly mink, but some raccoon and fox skin. They wore them so often that the coats became a trademark of La Fuerza.

After losing one of their pickups in a spectacular fire, Garcia ordered that they replace their fleet of unarmored vehicles with diesel-engine equivalents as quickly as they could find them. They eventually standardized with pickups and vans with Ford Power Stroke 6.0-liter diesel engines. They systematically stole every one that they came across, gradually re-equipping their small army.

Their raiding methodology was simple: send one pickup ahead with a husband, wife, and two or three kids to scout, acting like innocent refugees. They would use a CB to relay the situation. Then the entire convoy would be timed to arrive at dawn. Any resistance was crushed. They took what they wanted: fuel, vehicles, tires, food, batteries, cutting torches, guns, ammunition, liquor, drugs, gold, and jewelry. Then they left.

In some of the smallest towns where they met any shooting opposition, they killed everyone that they could find. They stayed in those towns longer and stripped them to the bone. But typically they would just barge into a town, loot, and scoot. They very soon learned that it wasn't safe to stay in a large town overnight after looting, so they spent most of their nights camped at parks, airports, and wildlife refuges—wherever they could find plentiful water. Their modus operandi was to hit a town, spend the day looting, and then travel at least twenty-five miles before dark to camp.

It was after losing two more vehicles in a gun battle in Livingston that Garcia acquired his first two civilian armored trucks. One of his scouts found these parked in a lot on the east side of College Station, Texas. They had been owned by an armored car company that specialized in servicing ATM machines. Getting the keys only took a few minutes of torture. Eventually they gathered more and more armored trucks and vans as they went, mainly from the Rochester and Garda armored car agencies. Garcia and his family soon traveled exclusively in one of the armored car company trucks. It was a two-and-a-half-ton, built on a 1998 Ford F-800 chassis, with a 5.9 Cummins diesel engine. Because of its boxlike shape, Ignacio jokingly called it his bread truck.

La Fuerza accumulated a large collection of young armed men in its wake. Wherever he went, Garcia recruited those he met who were smart, skilled, and ruthless. As it turned out, most of them were paroled convicts, recently escaped convicts, and members of the MS-13 gang, which had been a natural gathering place for hardened criminals. Ignacio wanted to build up La Fuerza rapidly so that he could have at least one hundred vehicles rolling into a town, all at once. Very few would defy that show of force, at least not for long.

Their casualties when raiding small towns were fairly light. They made a point of never hitting any town with a population more than two thousand. To Garcia's surprise, most of their losses came when they were camped at night. Typically, in the dead of the night a shot or two would ring out, and one of their sentries would go down, often shot in the back from outside their perimeter. Then the camp would be in an uproar, and patrols would be sent out with night-vision goggles, but they'd usually find nothing. Sometimes they'd find just an accidentally dropped magazine or a piece of fired brass. Tony would say matter-of-factly, "Militia bastards."

They had so many tires shot out—usually when they'd first arrive in a town—that they eventually settled on carrying six spares, mounted on rims, on the roof of every vehicle. Eventually it was the loss of tires that forced them to abandon the Saracen APCs one after the other as they went along. The Saracens used special "run-flat" tires with a hard rubber inner rim. This size tire was not one stocked by American truck tire dealers. According to files that his wife had saved on her laptop, there was a dealer on the East Coast that catered to MVPA members who had a pile of tires and wheels for Saracens, but to Garcia those might just as well be on the moon. Once the outer tire was punctured by gunfire, it shredded and came off within two hundred miles. Then the APCs' top speed dropped to under twenty-five miles per hour, and they became more difficult to steer. La Fuerza's convoys needed to travel at least forty miles an hour.

In contrast, they were able to keep the Caddy Gage V-100s on the road because they used fairly standard tires that were found on some front-end loaders. One of the V-100s did have its rear transaxle fail, but they were able to replace it with one salvaged from a ubiquitous M-35 "deuce-and-a-half" Army transport truck.

Some of La Fuerza's favorite targets were firehouses, for two reasons: First, their kitchens often had well-stocked pantries with large containers of staple foods like pasta, rice, and beans. Second, and more important, they almost always had their selection of tools intact. These included Halligan pry bars, large traditional crowbars, fire axes, and gas-engine-powered, automated, prying Jaws of Life (or, as Ignacio called them, Jaws of Loot). All of these tools proved invaluable to the gang when they needed to break into a building or a home gun vault. The Halligans were particularly useful in prying doors away from their door frames. They found that once door frames were separated, the doors could be easily kicked open.

In West Texas, La Fuerza crossed paths with a gang that was affiliated with MS-13. Calling themselves Los Lobos ("The Wolves"), the gang was headed by Adolfo Cantares. This gang numbered

120 and, like La Fuerza, they had been skipping from town to town. They were less sophisticated than La Fuerza, but they were just as ruthless. Rather than fighting them or competing with them, Ignacio decided to assimilate Los Lobos. He called for a meeting with their leader and proposed that they work together to loot Floydada, Texas. This was agreeable, since the town was too large for either gang to take independently.

After they had taken Floydada, Ignacio called for a celebratory feast and rape party. The gangs met at the Floydada Inn for the party. Ignacio made arrangements in advance to have one of his men poison the drinks of Cantares, his girlfriend, and his second in command. He did this late in the evening, after everyone was well liquored and high on various drugs. The next morning Garcia blamed the three deaths on drug overdoses. He then declared, "We are heading to New Mexico. Anyone from Los Lobos is welcome to join us, but you will be under my command." Everyone joined.

Garcia's now greatly enlarged gang cut a swath through southern New Mexico and southern Arizona. As the gang continued to grow, they could hit towns as large as twenty thousand people with relative impunity.

Twenty Miles off the Coast of Guinea-Bissau
December, the First Year

The *Durobrabis* was making steady progress down the coast of Guinea-Bissau. The plan was to work their way far enough south, following the Canary Current on the old Clipper route, with the goal of catching the northeast trade winds, to sail west across the Atlantic. Carston Simms warned: "We must stay out of the South Atlantic High. We musn't get out in the Doldrums. On paper our planned course looks like a longer route, but in actuality, it is the fastest and safest route to Central America. The alternative is sailing the North Atlantic, but we daren't do that in winter."

During Taft's afternoon watch, Andy was awoken by a shout: "Could be trouble! Speedboat, coming up from behind."

Andy rolled out of the sail locker and trotted down the length of the cabin, blinking in the sudden transition to daylight. He could see that Taft's family and Donna Simms were seated at the saloon table, wide-eyed. The twins were both still holding hands of playing cards. Andy popped out the hatch to the aft deck and was handed a pair of binoculars by Taft. He focused on the boat, which was four hundred yards astern and gaining quickly. The *Durobrabis* was under full sail, one-quarter into the wind. Laine reckoned that even if they turned for full wind, they'd still be outrun by the speedboat.

"Break out the Airsofts!" Andy ordered.

Simms complied, pulling the two fake submachine guns from a locker beneath one of the forward cabin V-berths. The seat cushions were hastily tossed aside and the locker lid was swung open.

No one was on the low forward deck of the speedboat, but there were a couple of heads that could be seen through the windshield. Laine set down the binoculars and unholstered his pistol.

Donna took the wheel while Carston, Andy, and Alan positioned themselves kneeling on the deck with their elbows on the aft bench and their guns held below the stern rail, making a show of force, just as they had practiced. Carston shouted to his wife: "Hold that course!"

When the speedboat was within sixty yards, two men with AKMs popped up from prone positions on the foredeck seats and pointed their guns toward the *Durobrabis*. But before they could shoot, Andy took three well-aimed shots. A bullet struck one of the gunmen in the chest and he collapsed, dropping out of sight. Simultaneously, the other gunman let loose a wild burst of full-auto fire, aimed much too high to be effective. Andy fired four more times, with one bullet hitting the man in the neck. He, too, dropped out of sight.

Now just fifteen yards astern, the speedboat veered off sharply, and Andy rapidly emptied his pistol into the exposed side of the boat, concentrating his fire on the cockpit and just forward of it. Laine did a quick reload, tossed his empty twenty-round magazine through the hatch, and shouted, "Refill that, Jules!"

The speedboat made a run for the coast, with no sign of turning back toward them. Alan Taft looked pale. He stuttered, "Di-di-did you see the, the blood spraying up from those men—the men on the front deck?"

Laine nodded gravely, but then he turned and said calmly to Angie, "You can go back to your card game now."

After that incident, Simms changed their course to take them farther offshore. They found seven bullet holes in the canvas near the top of the mainsail. Patching the holes took less than an hour.

The trip across the Atlantic was surprisingly uneventful. With favorable winds and currents, they averaged 140 miles per day for most the journey. The cramped quarters on the *Durobrabis* led to a few arguments, but overall everyone got along fairly well. Simone Taft never had much harmony with Andy. She had been born in Paris but raised in London. She had a universally condescending attitude, even toward her husband. One day, in the midst of a disagreement about where and when hand-washed clothes should be hung up to dry, Simone got belligerent with Laine. She chided, "I don't like you, Andrew, and I don't like guns. If it weren't for your, your *pistol*, you'd still be in England."

"Correction: If it weren't for my pistol, we'd all be *shark food* right now. Ma'am, you need to get used to how the real world operates."

She shut up after that.

27

Hunkered Down

"Every action is seen to fall into one of three main categories, guarding, hitting, or moving. Here, then, are the elements of combat, whether in war or pugilism."

—B. H. Liddell Hart, *Strategy* (1929)

Bloomfield, New Mexico
January, the Second Year

The economy of the Four Corners was in shambles. With the power miraculously still on but the value of the dollar destroyed, the few merchants left in business soon reverted to simple barter or taking pre-1965-mint-date silver coinage for payment. The most commonly accepted currencies were silver dimes, silver quarters, .22 long rifle rimfire cartridges, cigarettes, and boxes of new mason jar lids.

All of the local banks and credit unions soon closed, but one community bank eventually reopened as a warehouse bank, primarily for the use of its vault space, by local merchants who needed a safe place to store their silver coinage. Eventually they bought another disused bank building as a second branch, just for the use of its vault space.

Word quickly spread that there was still gasoline available for sale and the power was still on in Bloomfield and Farmington. Customers drove from as far away as Moab, Utah; Durango,

Colorado; Tuba City, Arizona; and Window Rock, New Mexico. Many of them drove "pea cups" that were crammed full with enough gas cans to give a fire marshal a heart attack. The byword was: "Come with silver coin, or don't come at all."

The Bloomfield refinery started to do a land office retail business, but L. Roy wanted to work out wholesale deals with gas stations as soon as possible. The steady flow of retail customers coming through the gate represented a security risk. Soon after working the deal with Alan Archer, Martin set up a similar gas-on-credit arrangement with Antonio Jacquez, the owner of a gas station in Bloomfield. Jacquez, who came from one of the early pioneer families in the region, reopened his gas station. He did a brisk business and gradually built quite a pile of silver coins.

Muddy Pond, Tennessee
November, the First Year

It was a great place to ride out the Crunch. Ben Fielding believed that he had landed in Muddy Pond, Tennessee, providentially.

Ten years before the economy fell apart, Ben was an associate attorney in a Nashville law firm. He had been hired to defend a Mennonite man who had been charged in a wrongful-death lawsuit filed by the family of a tourist killed in a fall from a hay wagon. When he traveled to Overton County to see the scene of the accident and interview the defendant, Ben fell in love with the area. There he met two other Messianic Jewish families like his own, and he developed an affinity for the dozens of Mennonites who would become his neighbors. Although he had differences with them on some points of Christian doctrine and their hyper-pacifism, he admired their hard work and clean living.

When he returned home, he described the village to his wife, Rebecca, and they committed the issue to prayer. As Jewish believers in Jesus, they had an active prayer life and believed in heeding God's guidance in how, when, and where they should live.

Shortly after first seeing Overton County, and after much prayer, Ben felt led to shift to a body of law that would enable him to work from home. He transitioned to wills, trusts, and estates law. A year later he was able to quit the firm and go into practice for himself, working from home. His law practice was ideal for this. His clientele grew by word of mouth, and eventually he had clients from all over the nation. Eight years before the Crunch, he bought a forty-acre farm near Muddy Pond and soon moved Rebecca and their five children there.

Muddy Pond was a ninety-mile drive east of Nashville and an eighty-mile drive west of Knoxville. The town, located on the Upper Cumberland Plateau, was several turns off of any major road, so only local traffic passed through. Aside from a few bed-and-breakfast yuppie tourists who sought out "plain people" quaintness, few Tennesseans had ever heard of Muddy Pond. The village had a general store and just one summer tourist attraction: a horse-powered sorghum press.

Without planning it or, as Ben said, "By Ha-shem's providence," the Fieldings were in the right place at the right time when the Crunch occurred. His 1960s Mennonite-built farmhouse had a good well that produced twenty-two gallons per minute. A water tower above it was kept filled by a very reliable Dempster windmill. The house lights were propane, and he heated the house with wood and coal. Their only modern conveniences, necessitated by Ben's law practice, were two phone lines and a wind-powered alternative energy system, with a 2.4-kilowatt Skystream windmill and six Sharp Solar photovoltaic panels.

The Fielding family did most of their cooking with a propane range. There was also a propane engine backup generator for the battery bank, but they only rarely had to run it. Right after they'd purchased the farm, Ben was shocked with an estimate of $18,500 to have the Cookeville Electric Department extend the power lines to his farm. After doing some pricing, he concluded that it would be less expensive to simply make his own power. He hired Lightwave Solar Electric in Nashville to install the PV panels, and Ready Made Resources in Tellico Plains, Tennessee, to install the Skystream wind generator.

As the Crunch set in, Ben assessed his situation. He concluded that his family's greatest need would be more propane storage, so he replaced their existing 250-gallon leased tank with an 1,800-gallon tank that he purchased. He also ordered an extra two tons of coal. This exceeded the capacity of their basement coal bin, so they stored the rest in the pallet boxes in the barn. There was still a bit of gasoline available (for $18.99 per gallon) but no cans for sale. Ben filled the tanks on all of his vehicles, including his ATV, and his four five-gallon gas cans, but that still left him feeling woefully short of gasoline for an extended emergency. By the time that Rebecca suggested filling some steel milk cans with gasoline, all of the gas stations had closed.

Ben did his best to stock up on ammunition for his rifle and pistol, but he found very little available. Altogether, he had less than seven hundred rounds. But by scouring the Internet, he did manage to find some exorbitantly priced spare magazines for his pistol, an HK USP Compact .45, and his rifle, a Galil ARM .308.

After hearing the news about the riots spreading all over America's cities, Ben gathered his family for an evening of devotional study. His wife and children gathered on the two living room couches. That night he had selected Proverbs 1:24–33 for their reading. He thought it was particularly fitting, given the news headlines.

He read aloud, "Because I have called, and ye refused; I have stretched out my hand, and no man regarded; But ye have set at nought all my counsel, and would none of my reproof: I also will laugh at your calamity; I will mock when your fear cometh; When your fear cometh as desolation, and your destruction cometh as a whirlwind; when distress and anguish cometh upon you. Then shall they call upon me, but I will not answer; they shall seek me early, but they shall not find me: For that they hated knowledge, and did not choose the fear of the LORD: They would none of my counsel: they despised all my reproof. Therefore shall they eat of the fruit of their own way, and be filled with their own devices. For the turning away of the simple shall slay them, and the prosperity of fools shall destroy them. But whoso hearkeneth unto me shall dwell safely, and shall be quiet from fear of evil."

28

Terminal Ballistics

"There exists a law, not written down anywhere, but inborn in our hearts, a law which comes to us not by training or custom or reading, a law which has come to us not from theory but from practice, not by instruction but by natural intuition. I refer to the law which lays down that, if our lives are endangered by plots or violence or armed robbers or enemies, any and every method of protecting ourselves is morally right."

—Marcus Tullius Cicero (106–43 BC)

South of Farmington, New Mexico
April, the Second Year

In the April of the year after the Crunch began, Lars was summoned to the NAPI headquarters, seven miles south of Farmington, for some consulting work.

He was told that an isolated NAPI grain elevator had been taken over by an armed gang. One of the employees had been shot during the takeover and had died a day later.

Lars drove to meet the NAPI president at the company headquarters. He was a Navajo in his sixties. With him in the conference room were nine younger men, all tribal members.

Lars queried, "How many men were there?"

One of the employees raised his hand. "Hey. There was a bunch, maybe ten of 'em. They're Mexicans. The drove up in three pea cups and a minivan. There was just three of us there, and only two of us had guns. They shot Alvin first thing, so we ran. We had to carry Alvin part of the way to our pea cups."

One of the men asked Laine anxiously, "So, what do we do? Are we going to rush them?"

Lars shook his head. "No, no, no. Why risk taking any more casualties? Tell me, is there any really pressing need for any of that grain in the next few weeks?"

The NAPI president answered, "No, not really. We also got a tribal storehouse in town. Its got enough, I s'pose, even for the rest of the winter."

"So we wait them out and engage them on our own terms. What is the water situation at the elevator?"

"A cistern, above ground. I think it's five hundred gallons. We have to haul in the water for that. There's a flush toilet in the building that we don't use much, 'cuz it wastes water. Instead, we use a drop toilet about seventy-five yards out back, behind some Gambel oaks. But we don't dare tell the health department about it: no permit, and it sure don't meet no code."

"Is the cistern a metal tank or masonry brick?"

"Neither. It's one of the new blue poly ones."

"No other source of water there?"

"Nope. Not for miles."

Laine laughed and asked, "Who here is a good shot with a deer rifle?" Several men raised their hands. Lars said, "I've got a silver dollar for whoever can punch a hole in the side of that tank within three inches of the bottom."

The men laughed uproariously, realizing that they could simply force the bandits out by depriving them of water.

Lars laid out the plan: "We'll set up two-man teams with scoped rifles in shallow foxhole positions, 350 yards out. We'll use three teams, with full coverage of the elevator buildings. We'll make sure that they each have night-vision scopes or monoculars."

One of the men protested, "Three hundred and fifty yards? That's an awful long way to shoot."

Lars asked the entire assembled group, "Have any of you heard of Simo Häyhä?"

They gave him blank looks.

Laine continued, "He was a sniper from Finland in the Second World War. He was the world's most successful sniper. I read that he had more than five hundred confirmed kills. My dad said that Simo Häyhä was quoted as saying, 'When you are shooting at wild game, never shoot from two hundred meters when you can shoot from twenty meters. But when you are in combat, never shoot from one hundred meters when you can shoot from three hundred meters. You'll live longer.'"

Bradfordsville, Kentucky
February, the Second Year

Each day that the Seed Lady store was open, Tyree stood guard in the back room with the shotgun leaning against the wall. He spent most of his days there, absorbed in reading by lantern light. The partition between the two rooms was just a single thickness of horizontal one-by-eight tongue-and-groove knotty pine boards supported by twenty-four studs. The many small knotholes in the pine boards provided ample opportunity for Tyree to peer through the wall. Under Grandmère Emily's instruction, Tyree gently tapped out three large knots at shoulder level to give him the chance to shoot through the wall if need be. Each of these knots was replaced loosely and labeled with a piece of phosphorescent tape. These knot plugs could be easily popped out from behind the wall with just a forward thrust of the shotgun's muzzle.

Whenever Tyree heard the bell at the store's front door ring, he would spy through a knothole to observe the newcoming customer. By prearranged signal, if his mother rested her hands on the counter, that indicated all was well, and he could go back to his studies. But if she stood with arms akimbo or folded across her chest, then that meant that Tyree was to be vigilant and keep the shotgun in hand. And if Tyree ever heard his mother shout: "My husband is watching over me!" then that was the cue for Tyree to rack a shell into the chamber of the Remington. The first year that they were open for business, he had to do that only twice. Both times, that distinctive sound cleared everyone out of the store very rapidly.

Four months after they opened the store, Sheila bartered for two pieces of three-eighths-inch-thick plate steel. They both measured twenty-eight inches wide by four feet tall. To create some armored protection for Tyree, these two plates were stacked together and positioned below one of the pop-out knotholes. The heavy plates were held in place with two lengths of perforated plumber's steel strapping tape nailed to the studs.

Most of Sheila Randall's business was in bartering items of like value or for pre-1965 silver coins. She eagerly sought heirloom seeds for all vegetables. But when she traded her precious commercially packaged seeds for "saved" seed from family gardens, she did so at a one-to-five ratio, explaining, "I *know* my seeds are all fresh, and they are guaranteed to sprout, but I can't say that about yours, so my trading ratio is firm and nonnegotiable." She later resold the homegrown seeds at a substantial discount compared to what she charged for her commercially packed heirloom seeds. A large whiteboard on the wall behind the south display cases listed "Current Wants," "Specials," and "Freebies." A corkboard was put up next to the whiteboard for customers to post their "For Sale" and "Wanted" items on three-by-five-inch cards.

It took hundreds of trades, but Sheila gradually built up a substantial inventory. Some overstock went in the back room. Eventually, a larger sign on a slab board above the front overhang dwarfed her original window signs. It read: "Bradfordsville General Store,

S. Randall, Propr." As her inventory grew, Sheila started trading for items of greater value.

One of her first major purchases was a .41 Colt Army double-action revolver. It was an ancient gun, with hardly any bluing left on it, and one of its grips was badly chipped at the bottom. But at least it was mechanically sound. It came with a holster and just thirty-four rounds of ammunition. The merchandise that she traded for it was worth the equivalent of three months' wages for most folks.

Sheila had been warned that the revolver was chambered in an obsolete caliber, but it was the only handgun that she could afford. She carried the revolver on her hip every day, and oiled it frequently. The first year that she owned the gun, she fired just twelve cartridges practicing shooting it. By necessity, most of her practice with the gun was dry practice with the unloaded revolver in the upstairs apartment. She practiced drawing and dry firing the gun three nights a week. It was not until their second year in Bradfordsville that her frequent inquiries paid off, and she successfully bartered for two full boxes of .41 Long Colt ammunition. Those cost her $5.50 in silver coin each.

South of Farmington, New Mexico
April, the Second Year

Two nights after the water cistern had been pierced by a bullet, the bandits tried to pack up their vehicles. Then the NAPI men started shooting. Lars coordinated their fire by GMRS radio. He had positioned himself with the team that had the best vantage point to observe the main road to the grain elevator. The first night they dropped four of the bandits. The next morning they shot out most of the tires on the bandits' vehicles. In all, it took two days, but it was like shooting fish in a barrel. The final score was NAPI 9, Bandits 1. Lars was paid for his services in the form of a credit voucher for five hundred pounds of oats.

Other than the grain elevator episode, for many months Lars and Lisbeth led a quiet, mundane life. With the help of Kaylee and the Phelps boys, they raised chickens and took up large scale gardening, with mixed results. Some crops did well, while others failed completely. They were able to trade their excess produce, eggs, and pullets to fill in some of the shortfalls. Still, what they got from the poultry pen and the garden was not enough to feed the six of them. Thanks to the silver coins that Lars had inherited from his father, they ate fairly well. It was that silver that made up for the garden's shortcomings.

Prescott, Arizona
February, the Second Year

Life in the Four Families compound continued in a fairly uniform routine. There were a couple of burglaries at some of the outlying houses in the neighborhood, but otherwise things were quiet. They could occasionally hear gunfire in downtown Prescott. This was later explained as having come from small roving gangs who crossed the line when they attempted armed robbery. Later they heard that the problem was disagreements on what to do with the cars, trucks, and guns that had belonged to the deceased robbers. Their corpses ended up in the potter's field at Citizen's Cemetery on East Sheldon Street, interspersed with the numbered graves of indigents and criminals dating back to the 1890s.

29

La Casa de la Mañana Grande

"Belize was founded by British pirates ... Legend relates that the city was built in a swamp on a foundation of gin pots and mahogany chips. If this is so, it would have been better if the city's fathers had thrown in a few more pots and chips, for Belize is only a few inches above sea level."

—*Time* magazine, September 21, 1931

The GPS receiver showed the *Durobrabis* was forty miles east of the Belize Cays chain just before sunset on March 26. Four months after first setting sail, they were anxious to come ashore. The depth finder showed they were in three hundred feet of water, but fearing that they would approach reefs and shallows, Carston dropped all the canvas and set both sea anchors in order to wait overnight. He had nautical charts for Belize, but they were several years old. Knowing that profiles of sandbars could change in just one year, Simms decided to proceed with great caution. He said wisely, "I wouldn't want to make it this far only to end up aground on some sandbar."

They spent the evening excitedly listing to Wamalali Radio, an AM station in Punta Gorda. The city was most often mentioned by its nickname "PG." There were also a number of FM stations broadcasting, but they were mostly playing music.

Proceeding cautiously, Simms piloted his boat though the Cays late the next afternoon. Not knowing what sort of passport controls might have been enacted under the current state of emergency, they thought it best to wait at anchor on the far side of Lark Cay until after dark. They could see lights dotted up and down the coastline. Then, as the next high tide approached, they motored quietly to the nearby point, past the Creole fishing towns of Placentia on the point and Big Creek opposite, on the mainland side. As they entered the twelve-mile-long Placentia lagoon, Simms was pleased to note that the local electricity was still on. "A good sign, that," he told Angie.

The skipper ran the diesel engine at low revolutions for a quiet three knots as they progressed up the lagoon. Carston kept Angie constantly watching the depth finder. They passed by an odd mix of well-lit luxury homes—mostly at Seine Bight—and completely dark tin-roofed Creole and Garifuna shanties. They set anchor again just before dawn at the north end of the lagoon, near the village of Blair Atholl.

This end of the lagoon was very quiet. Just two other yachts were anchored nearby, with their sails covered and bright blue canvases snugged down over their stern piloting areas. From their stern markings, they could see that one was from Dunedin, Florida, and the other from Freeport, Texas. They soon learned that both of these yachts were under the protection of a paid "watchie man" from Blair Atholl. The black man, armed with a single-barrel shotgun, motored up in an ancient skiff with a round-topped outboard engine that looked like something from the 1950s. It used a hand-wound spin starting rope rather than a recoil starter. The man's shotgun had a well-worn stock and had all of its metal parts covered with thick white grease that looked almost like wax. Andy surmised that it was for protection from salt water.

The watchie man, who spoke in a curious Belizean singsong voice, told them that the recently arrived owners of the boats had moved into houses nearby, one on South Stann Creek and one in the village of Georgetown. Neither of the owners, he said, had any plans to sail back to the United States. He also had been told to relay that neither boat was available for sale or rent.

Simms continued talking with the man, making barter arrangements to refill his yacht's freshwater tanks, which were nearly depleted. Meanwhile, Andy went below and started gathering his gear. He explained to Angie: "I want to beat feet before anyone comes here with plans to do a customs inspection."

Angie answered, "I think that's wise, Andy. Of course, we won't mention that you arrived with us. It's best that you slip into the country the soft way." After clearing her throat, she added: "Andrew, I'll certainly miss the peace of mind that we've had with you on board. I think that buying a gun will be one of Carston's first priorities here."

Inflating the dinghy took less than fifteen minutes, and in the dead calm water of the lagoon, loading Andy's gear was easy. The most time-consuming part was first mounting the dinghy's engine and getting the fuel primed properly to feed the engine. As they packed the dinghy, Andy made his good-byes. Yvonne and Yvette were crying. Andy shook hands or hugged everyone but Simone, who just gave Andy a small wave from the doorway to the saloon.

Prescott, Arizona
March, the Second Year

Life at the Four Families compound in Prescott continued in a routine to the point of monotony. Without electricity, just hand-washing the laundry was a huge chore. And there was plenty of other hard work, mainly involving gardening and firewood. Their evenings were short and fairly quiet. Tuesday and Thursday nights were "old radio show nights" at Doctor K.'s house. Dr. Karvalich had more than a thousand old radio shows on a set of twenty-six

CD-ROMs in MP3 format. He had bought the collection through eBay several years before the Crunch for less than thirty dollars. These were played on his laptop. The most popular shows were comedies like *Fibber McGee & Mollie* and old science fiction and drama shows like *Dimension X* and *Suspense*.

Saturday nights were movie nights, with movies on DVDs played on Alex's seventeen-inch screen MacBook laptop.

Blair Atholl, Belize
April, the Second Year

Motoring over to the Cay took only a few minutes. The village of Blair Atholl looked small. There was one fancy estate development to the south, at Bella Maya, and a collection of modest tin-roofed houses to the north, in the town of Blair Atholl itself. In between was a sign that said "Blair Holiday Cottages." Since that sounded vaguely English, Carston steered toward it. They pulled up to the dock and were greeted by a rotund, aging English ex-pat named Peter Ivens. Ten minutes of quizzing Ivens made it clear that customs officials rarely checked this end of the lagoon, that the only reported troubles in Belize were near the Guatemalan border, and that he would be willing to store Laine's baggage for a nominal fee.

After depositing Andy's panniers and duffels on the dock, Simms shook Andy's hand firmly and said, "Well . . . safe home, Andrew."

"The Lord be with you, Skipper."

He spent the next half hour talking with Peter Ivens, getting up to speed about the situation in Belize and Guatemala. He concluded that Belize was fairly stable but that Guatemala was in a state of crisis. Several key government officials in Guatemala, Ivens said, had fled the country—rumor had it for Honduras—and had hence left a power vacuum. Criminal gangs and Communist rebels had commenced wholesale violence. Thousands of Guate-malan refugees and bandits were crossing into Belize, Mexico, and Honduras.

Andy summarized his situation for Ivens. He mentioned that he had "seen the bright lights of Placentia" and said that he had "made entry into the country," so the man assumed that Laine had cleared customs. Andy asked if there were any ships likely bound for the Gulf coast of the U.S. "Not a chance," the man said bluntly. "From all reports, Belize is strictly a 'to' destination, since everything in all directions is substantially more risky. You're sitting in the safe haven. You should think about staying here until things sort themselves out."

Then Laine asked about buses heading to the Yucatán. Those, he was told, had all been suspended because of the Honduran and Guatemalan refugee situation.

"Is there somewhere I could rent a car?" Andy asked. The man chuckled in reply and said, "My boy, getting a hired car was difficult in most parts of Belize even *before* this crisis. Even if you got to Orange Walk or Belize City, I have terrible doubts that you'd even be able to hire a moped, much less a car. The news on the radio is that they've been having problems with midnight flits. Same with boat rentals. People are petrified of renting out boats or anything on wheels because, sure enough, they'll end up in Mexico or Honduras, never to be seen again. Cars and lorries are getting stolen left and right these days, so you can't blame the firms for refusing to hire them out."

"Could I hire you to drive me up to the Mexican border?"

"Sorry, no. Fuel is nigh on irreplaceable at present. I can't spare any. I've drained all the petrol from my utility and hidden the cans back in the jungle. If they steal my vehicle, they won't get more than a quarter of a mile down the road."

Laine pondered that for a moment and then asked, "Do you know anyone who might have a bicycle or a horse that's for sale?"

"No, but you might go and make inquiries with some of the landholders at Stann Creek. They've lots of horses there."

"Okay." Laine gestured to his baggage and said, "Give me a few minutes to organize this gear." Ivens nodded and sauntered off to his office. Andy sat near the end of the dock and sorted his baggage. The dock sat below a set of stairs from the walkway and office above, so he felt safely out of sight.

He decided to travel light. He pulled out a one-ounce American Eagle gold coin and most of his remaining silver coins. He left the rest of his gold hidden in the stove. He briefly debated taking the SIG pistol but decided that on this trip the risks would outweigh the rewards. He tucked the SIG and all of its accessories in the bottom of the duffel bag with the stove. Then he restuffed the bag full and padlocked it shut. The key went on the chain around his neck that held his dog tags and his P-38 can opener.

It took two trips to lug the rest of his baggage up the stairs and into the office.

The luggage room was just an eight-foot-by-six-foot closet with deep, widely spaced shelves. But Laine was happy to see that it was equipped with a solid-core door and a dead-bolt lock.

In his rucksack he packed two cans of stew, a can of corned beef, a bag of raisins, a change of socks, his foul-weather jacket, a water bottle, and a small squeeze bottle of insect repellent.

Later, sitting at his kitchen table, Peter Ivens showed Andy a well-worn map of the district and pointed out the road route to Stann Creek. Andy copied his route onto a strip map on a clean sheet of typing paper. On the same page he jotted down the names of several ranchers whom Ivens had mentioned.

It took Andy a while to get his land legs back. When he first arrived on the dock, he had felt normal, but after he began the walk toward South Stann Creek, his legs felt rubbery beneath him, and he had the false sensation of the land rocking.

There was no traffic on the Riversdale road. Andy concluded that Ivens was right about the locals hoarding their fuel. As he walked, he passed by several citrus and cacao plantations and one banana plantation. The birdcalls were unfamiliar and the humid air had an odd smell that Andy could not place. The day was warming up rapidly, and Laine felt sweat gathering on his forehead and beneath his backpack. He started moving into more hilly terrain.

Suddenly, a group of five young men—four armed with machetes and one with a rusty FAL rifle—emerged from the dense jungle on his left. All of the men had shaved heads and three of them had bizarre facial tattoos.

The leader, holding the rifle at waist level, shouted, *"¡Alto!"*

Andy made a split-second decision: he ran. Knowing that he'd probably be shot in the back if he ran down the open road, he instead headed for the wall of jungle that began just a few yards to his right and plunged in.

He raced through the jungle as quickly as he could. He expected to hear gunshots but there were none. He could hear the men pursuing him, crashing through the brush of the jungle understory. They stayed just ten to fifteen yards behind him, never gaining or losing much ground. The underbrush was clumpy. He hardly noticed the thorns and branches that slashed his arms and cheeks as he ran.

Laine knew that if he tripped and fell, the bandits would be on top of him in just moments. His path started out level at first, but after three hundred yards the terrain began to drop off, descending toward a creek. Andy started picking up speed. He heard a shouted curse as one of his pursuers fell, but the others pressed on, losing only just a bit of ground. Andy found it hard to believe that they would follow him so far. He hoped to get ahead of them and hide in thick undergrowth. He could dimly make out some rocks along the creek, just sixty yards below. He was still running headlong when the ground dropped off unexpectedly, and Andy took a leap.

He fell fifteen feet, landing unevenly on one foot. He heard a loud snap and felt a sharp pain. He fell into a heap. Laine tried to get up to run again, but the pain in his right leg was incredible. It was a bad break, low in his femur. The pain was agonizing. He gasped for breath and looked up to see himself surrounded. He exclaimed between his gulping breaths, "Hoover Dam!"

His pursuers, also out of breath, were speaking rapidly in heavily accented Spanish. He didn't catch much of the bandits' conversation. He did hear *"en Petén"* twice and *"por Guatemala"* once, so he assumed that they were Guatemalan bandits.

He looked up to see the buttstock of the battered FAL rifle just two feet away from his face. "CHAVO" was carved in the side of the rifle's blue-painted stock, and farther up the stock were carved the letters "FSLN." In an oddly detached way, Andy wondered about the history of the rifle. Perhaps it came from the Nicaraguan Sandinistas three decades earlier. It seemed surreal, looking at the stock of the rifle with the rusty top cover and then at the tattooed faces of the bandits.

They quickly stripped him of his wallet, pocketknife, wristwatch, belt, and rucksack.

One of them started to take off Andy's boots, but his screams of agony stopped the man.

The Guatemalans started to argue among themselves. Laine was petrified when he heard one of them use the word *"Mátale,"* which he knew meant "Kill him."

The leader of the group, who wore jeans and a white tank top, ended the argument by grunting, *"Santo Dios. ¡Vámonos!"* He jabbed his forefinger toward Laine's face and ordered his silence with a stern *"¡Cállate!"* before turning to follow the others.

The five men quietly disappeared into the jungle, walking back up the hill toward the road.

Andy thought through his situation. He had no water, food, or shelter. His only tool was a tiny folding can opener. Getting back toward the road, he realized, was his only chance to get help. He also realized that he had to wait at least a half hour, to give the *bandidos* the opportunity to get away. If he called for help any sooner, they might come back and silence him permanently.

After a couple of minutes he caught his breath and became more conscious of his broken leg. He had never felt pain so intense in his life. Sweat poured off his forehead and dripped off the end of his nose as he did his best to straighten leg the out.

"Bastards!" Andy muttered to himself. Then, looking skyward, he said, "Give me the will to forgive them, Lord." He waited for what he estimated was thirty minutes, praying aloud. His throat felt dry.

Laine started to crawl up the hill, pushing himself with his one good leg. There wasn't much blood from around the protruding compound fracture. Each time that he dragged his right leg forward, the pain made him scream. The screaming set off a nearby troop of black howler monkeys. There seemed to be about eight monkeys in the troop. One of the monkeys, a large male, came to investigate. Peering down from a tree limb twenty feet above him, the monkey let out a grunt. Then it scampered off.

Laine shouted, "Yeah, some help you are, pal!"

30

The Samaritan's Purse

"One of the common failings among honorable people is a failure to appreciate how thoroughly dishonorable some other people can be, and how dangerous it is to trust them."

—Thomas Sowell

It took four agonizing hours for Laine to crawl up the hill. His elbows and forearms were soon raw. Once he got near level ground, he realized that he still had several hundred yards to go. He doubted that his voice would carry through the dense jungle, so he didn't bother to shout for help.

He remembered that he had been traveling due east when he was ambushed. And since he had headed south from the road, he needed to go back north to get back to it. The sun was heading toward the horizon. Andy found a loose branch and laid it down as a pointer, to indicate where he estimated that the sun would set. Now on level ground, he tried to stand again, but the pain was too much. He passed out.

Laine awoke sometime during the night to find mosquitos had been feasting on him. The pain in his leg had subsided slightly to an intense throbbing.

The buzzing of insects and the many strange noises of the jungle assaulted his ears. Gradually, he fell asleep.

He awoke to full daylight. His broken leg had started to swell.

He spotted his sunset pointer stick and compared that to the current position of the sun, which filtered through the double canopy of the jungle. He adjusted his direction of travel accordingly and pressed on, crawling.

After an hour Laine could hear a truck pass by on the road. He shouted for help but realized that he was probably still too far away to be heard. But at least the sound of the truck confirmed that he was heading in the right direction. He picked out a distinctive-looking tree with a splayed top that was along his desired path and began crawling toward it. He had worked out the most comfortable crawling motion, so that he screamed in pain only occasionally.

As the day wore on, the sky clouded up, and Andrew was treated to an afternoon thunderstorm. The rain fell heavily for a few minutes. He reached up and dribbled water from the wet leaves into his mouth. He did this over and over throughout the rain shower until he estimated that he had drunk a liter. He thanked God and pressed on with his crawl over ground that was now muddy.

Late in the afternoon, he finally reached the road. He was sweaty and filthy. His upper leg had swollen to ten inches in diameter. He propped himself up with his back against a stump just ten feet from the road. He prayed that someone would pass by. Just before sunset, a Good Samaritan did.

Andy regained consciousness only briefly, as a doctor was setting his broken bone. But then he was unconscious for another three days. He awoke in a bed in Dangriga Hospital, bathed in sweat. An IV bag was hanging over his head.

The swelling of his leg had decreased noticeably, and it hurt only when he moved. After a few minutes a nurse came in. She was middle-aged and matronly.

"Ah, the sleeper awakens!" she said pleasantly.

"What day is it?"

"It's Friday. You has been out for three days."

Andy ask weakly, "Could I have some water, please?"

Two police officers from the "Dangriga Formation" arrived that afternoon. Laine described the ambush, robbery, and his crawl back to the road. He thought that it would be best if he didn't mention his baggage at the cottages. The elder policeman described Belize as "overrun with Guatemalan refugees and robber gangs"—as well as some illegal border crossings from Mexico.

The words "I'm an American" and "They took my passport" were enough to assuage the police. They said that they'd have someone from the American consulate contact him. They didn't seem too concerned with getting detailed descriptions of the bandits.

That afternoon, a young Belizean doctor gave Laine a morphine injection. He returned fifteen minutes later and set the broken bone. This was an odd experience for Andy. Because of the pain medication, he could observe the procedure with an almost detached clinical attitude. His main concern was that the bones were set correctly. Later, an older doctor with a Spanish surname but who spoke excellent British-accented English examined Laine. He declared, "Now that the swelling is down, we'll need to double-check the position of the bone with an X-ray and then place a cast on your leg. We'll then follow up with another X-ray, just to make sure we didn't misalign the bones whilst casting."

Andy slept very peacefully that night. As he was eating his breakfast, a hospital administrator came to visit. Andy mistakenly thought that he was a doctor at first but then realized that he was the hospital accountant. "There is one convalescent hospital nearby, but they are having trouble staying in operation with the recent currency fluctuations. I'll see what can be done," the administrator told him.

The next day he returned to Andy's room and announced, "Your medical bill is being settled by the U.S. State Department under a reciprocal agreement. One of our vocational nurses just retired a few months ago. She and her husband have agreed to take you as a boarder, if you can either find a way to pay for that yourself or make some sort of additional payment arrangement through the American consulate."

Andy improved rapidly and was released from the hospital after five days. He was taken by ambulance to the home of Darci Mora, a retired vocational nurse. Darci's husband, Gabriel, was a semi-retired logger and commercial hunter who had also worked as a hunting guide. Their flat-roofed cinder-block house was just outside Sarawiwa, six miles west of Dangriga. There, Andy occupied the second bedroom of the house. This bedroom had until recently been used by the Moras' daughter, who had just married and moved to Nim Li Punit, a town in the southern end of Belize.

Darci was in her mid-fifties and overweight. Gabe was in his early sixties, and was lean and leathery, with a balding head. His skin was dark, but not just from his outdoor vocation. He had some Garifunan ancestry. The Moras were pleasant hosts. Darci was a great cook, and Gabe constantly cracked jokes and puns.

Andy missed his next Tuesday night ham radio contact night with Lars and Kaylee, but he had the strength for the next one. On that Tuesday afternoon, Gabe Mora helped Andy set up the radio. Following Andy's directions, Gabe strung the antenna up to a tree outside the bedroom window. A cold-water pipe provided a good ground. The propagation was good, so Lars and Kaylee had no difficulty hearing Andy's Morse tones. Lars, with a much more powerful transmitter, came in "Lima Charlie"—loud and clear. As Andy tapped out his messages, Gabe sat on the bedside chair wiping the sweat from his balding head with a handkerchief and sipping lime water. He was amazed that such a small radio could be used for two-way communication over such a long distance.

Andy was reassured to hear that Kaylee was safe and well, but he felt distressed, realizing that his broken leg would delay him by several months. He spent ten minutes summarizing what had happened since his last contact in stream-of-consciousness Morse code. Kaylee's reply sounded as if she was overwhelmed. She keyed:

"BK RU AS SAD AS ME? WOE IS ME. WOE IS ME. I MISS YOU TONS ANDY. I WANT TO B THERE TO SIGN UR CAST. XOXOXOXOXOX. BT"

After three months of hobbling around on crutches, Andy finally had his cast cut off. He was horrified to see how the muscles in his right leg had wasted away. Clearly, it would take several more months to fully replenish the muscle mass of the atrophied leg.

He began walking more and more on the pair of crutches, then just one crutch, and eventually just a cane. He walked farther and farther each day, pushing himself to the point of exhaustion. His days started with dozens of sit-ups and push-ups. Eventually the length of the sets and the daily aggregate number of repetitions increased. He also started doing pull-ups, using the horizontal bar that held one end of the Moras' clothesline in their side yard. Andy's exercise time started to stretch into the evenings. Watching him do his pull-ups, Darci commented: "You're a *driven* man, Andrew."

Bradfordsville, Kentucky
July, the Second Year

As the first summer that Sheila ran the store began, there were increasing requests for soda pop, mainly from the men who manned the towns' three roadblocks. Sheila began offering more and more in trade for the dwindling supply of bartered soda in cans and bottles, simply because the men were progressively willing to pay more—even as much as ten cents in silver per can of Coca-Cola or root beer.

As this strange price inflation developed, Grandmère Emily wisely began collecting used beer bottles. She also traded a considerable quantity of ammunition for a bottle-capping tool with a magnetic head and a ten-gross box of fresh bottle crown caps. These came from a maker of home-brewed beer who lived near Ellsburg. By June, she created her first batch of homemade root beer. She used spring water and locally grown birch bark, sarsaparilla root, ginger, burdock root, dandelion root, hops, wintergreen, and molasses, in her secret recipe.

Emily Voisin's first batch of root beer was uncarbonated and attracted a good number of customers. But her second and subsequent batches were carbonated using a large cylinder of CO_2 and a special seltzering apparatus. Hollan Combs had built this for Emily by scaling up the design from an old SodaStream machine and using some hardware from his moribund soil analysis laboratory. These later batches of root beer were a huge success—so much so that Emily eventually had to hire seasonal help to wash bottles and help her brew root beer in the erstwhile butcher room of the Superior Market building. "Grandma Emily's Ol' Timey Root Beer" attracted customers from as far away as Springfield and Munfordsville. She offered a discount to anyone who would return their bottles or sell her other brown glass bottles or who could provide fresh crown caps.

Sheila Randall could not believe the first descriptions of the Provisional Government when she heard them. At first she thought that they were wild exaggerations. Hollan Combs warned her: "Whenever you hear of a government agency that declares itself "Legitimate" in its own name, you gotta wonder about its legitimacy. Know what I mean? That gang of fools is about as legitimate as some Hollywood bimbo's baby."

More and more customers patronizing her store reported seeing and hearing the same things about the Fort Knox government.

In April of the second year, the first of series of "peacekeeping" convoys passed through Bradfordsville. Most of these convoys stopped in town for less than a half hour. The soldiers were all Americans, as were their weapons and most of their vehicles. But something struck Sheila as odd when she overheard a radio conversation between the convoy's commander and his battalion commander. The latter had a distinctly German accent. Later, there were reports of entire battalion-size foreign units deployed inside the ProvGov's area of operations.

Other than their control of key industries, the Provisional Government's authority seemed relatively benign in the first year. Then a new currency was issued. The small lime-green watermarked bills soon reached general circulation and by law had to be accepted for all transactions. But the full weight of the Provisional Government and the "guest" UN peacekeepers wasn't felt until the third year after the crash, when firearms restrictions were enacted.

Sheila Randall's first word of the new gun laws came when Brian Tompkins, an Armor Corps lieutenant, visited her store. One of the first things he said to her was "You gotta make that gun disappear or it'll get confiscated as contraband."

"Contraband?"

Tompkins answered, "Yeah, haven't you heard? It sucks, but handguns have been banned for civilians, though you can still own some rifles and shotguns. It'll all be explained in the poster that we'll put up at your sheriff's office and in some flyers the Civil Affairs guys will be handing out in town today."

The next day Sheila saw two posters nailed up side by side on the wall in the main hall of the Marion County Sheriff's Department. A table beneath held a pile of flyers that duplicated the posters in a smaller format, printed on their front and back sides. As she stood reading the posters, Deputy Hodges walked up behind her and said softly, "Hi, Sheila."

The poster on the left was a brief summary of the formation of the Provisional Government, a declaration of martial law, activation of the UN peacekeeping force, and nationalization of mass transportation and critical industries. The poster on the right read:

B-A-N-N-E-D

Effective Upon Posting in a prominent place in each County or Parish, and in effect until further notice, the following items are hereby banned from private possession by the recently enacted Amplified United Nations Small Arms and Light Weapons (SALW) Normalization Accord:

1. All fully automatic or short-barreled rifles and shotguns (regardless of prior registration under the National Firearms Act of 1934).
2. Any rifle over thirty (.30) caliber, any shotgun or weapon of any description over twelve (12) gauge in diameter.
3. All semiautomatic rifles and shotguns; all rifles and shotguns capable of accepting a detachable magazine.
4. Any detachable magazines, regardless of capacity.
5. Any weapon with a fixed magazine that has a capacity of more than four (4) cartridges (or shells).
6. All grenades and grenade launchers; all explosives, detonating cord, and blasting caps (regardless of prior registration under the Gun Control Act of 1968 or state or local blasting permits).
7. All explosives precursor chemicals.
8. All firearms, regardless of type, that are chambered for military cartridges (including but not limited to 7.62mm NATO, 5.56 mm NATO, .45 ACP, and 9mm parabellum).
9. All silencers (regardless of prior registration under the National Firearms Act of 1934).
10. All night vision equipment including but not limited to infrared, light amplification, or thermal, all telescopic sights, and all laser aiming devices.

11. All handguns—regardless of type or caliber.
12. Other distinctly military equipment, including, but not limited to, armored vehicles, bayonets, gas masks, helmets and bulletproof vests.
13. Encryption software or devices.
14. All radio transmitters (other than baby monitors, cordless phones, or cell phones).
15. Full metal jacket, tracer, incendiary, and armor-piercing ammunition.
16. All ammunition in military calibers.
17. Irritant or lethal (toxin) chemical agents including but not limited to CS and CN tear gas, and OC "pepper spray."
18. All military-type pyrotechnics and flare launchers.

> Exceptions only for properly trained and sworn police and the military forces of the UN and The Sole and Legitimate Provisional Government of the United States of America and Possessions.

> Any firearm or other item not meeting the new criteria and all other contraband listed herein must be turned in within the ten (10) day amnesty period after the UN Regional Administrator or sub-administrator, or their delegates arrive on site. Alternatively, if Federal or UN troops arrive within any state to pacify it, a thirty (30) day amnesty period will begin the day the first forces cross the state boundary. **All other post-1898 production firearms of any description, air rifles, archery equipment, and edged weapons over six inches long must be registered during the same period.**

> Anyone found with an unregistered weapon, or any weapon, accessory, or ammunition that has been de-

clared contraband after the amnesty period ends will be summarily executed.

As ordered under my hand, Maynard Hutchings, President (pro tem) of The Sole and Legitimate Provisional Government of the United States of America and Possessions.

Sheila asked, "So what does that leave us?"

Deputy Hodges answered, "Not very much. I 'spose .22s, and antiques, and maybe thirty-thirty lever actions. But even those have gotta get registered. You know, that list won't do diddly in stopping crime, since of course criminals never obey *any* laws. But it's worded just right for squelching resistance. Notice how radio transmitters, military calibers, and night-vision scopes are banned? Maynard's list would make Hitler or Stalin proud. This whole thing stinks." Gesturing to the SIG 556 rifle on his shoulder, he pressed on, "Now, why is it legal for *me* to have this as a deputy but not *you*? That's just plain unconstitutional. If and when they come into Marion County and try to enforce that load of hogwallop, they'd better be ready for one mighty big gunfight."

That evening Sheila hid her revolver, ammo, and holster inside the bin of a hand-crank seed broadcaster. She hung it up on the wall near the ceiling, amidst the profusion of overstock items in the store's back room. She explained to Tyree, "Sometimes its best to just hide things in plain sight. I want to be able to get to that in a hurry too."

31

A Bulwark Never Failing

"Political power grows out of the barrel of a gun."

—Mao Tse-tung

Fort Knox, Kentucky
August, the Second Year

Maynard Hutchings and his cronies laid out their goals like a military campaign. Military bases, food distribution warehouses, power plants, oil fields, and refineries topped their list of sites to be controlled. Kentucky, Tennessee, Alabama, and Mississippi were the first states to be pacified.

Chambers Clarke was the undersecretary of information for the Hutchings government. He accompanied many of the first convoys that contacted military installations and served as liaison for the ProvGov. Before the Crunch, Clarke had been a fertilizer and pesticide salesman for Monsanto Company. In many ways Clarke was just a bagman for the administration. He literally handed out millions of dollars in the new currency to the owners of mines that were being nationalized. It was Hutchings's wife who had first suggested the carrot-and-stick approach to nationalizing the industries. Mr. Clarke was the carrot, while General Uhlich provided the stick. Later, it was the UN peacekeepers that provided the whippings, with fewer compunctions than American troops.

One of the Council's first goals was controlling oil refineries. Hutchings initially dispatched an APC convoy to a small refinery in Pulaski County, Kentucky, near the town of Somerset. It was a very small refinery by twenty-first-century standards, producing just 5,500 barrels per day. But it was online, so Hutchings had a source of fuel to expand his area of influence. They next visited and served papers on the much larger refineries in Calletsburg and Perry, Kentucky, but both were off-line because the power grid was down, and they lacked sufficient cogeneration capacity.

The pacification, reunification, and nationalization campaign's first large prize was the ConocoPhillips refinery in Ponca City, Oklahoma. It was the largest refinery in the state of Oklahoma and it was still partially online. After Ponca City, the army advanced on the Oklahoma refineries in Ardmore, Tulsa, Wynnewood, and Thomas. Of these, only the Ventura refinery at Thomas was in operation.

In Ohio, all of the refineries that the Fort Knox government "visited" were found to be off-line. The regular pinging of bullets bouncing off their APCs as they advanced served as a reminder that Ohio was still unpacified country. A combination of harsh winter weather and the ravenous gangs had reduced the population by 87 percent. The only people left in Ohio were the gang members and a handful of farmers who had become accustomed to paying the gangs' so-called fair share crop taxes.

Meanwhile, other convoys were dispatched to electric power plants. These—coal, natural gas, and hydroelectric—were another high priority for the ProvGov. The hydroelectric plants were the easiest to get back online, and in fact a few of them were already operating on isolated mini-grids that had been reestablished soon after the Crunch took down the big power grids.

Because it takes a source of power to start up a gas turbine engine, and because most power plants in the U.S. built after the 1960s didn't have auxiliary power units for self-starting, the "black start" restarting process took several months to gradually work up the capacity to get the biggest power plants in Kentucky back online. These included the Big Sandy, Ghent, Mill Creek, and Paradise power plants.

Reconstituting the eastern power grid step by step, starting with the smallest power plants, was time-consuming and required a lot of manpower. Some of the manpower had to be procured with a combination of Fort Knox greenbacks and coercion. At first, coal miners refused to accept pay in the new currency. It finally took the promise of relatively high pay and the threat of involuntary servitude to get them back to work.

The ProvGov's first experience with nuclear power plants came when they nationalized the Watts Bar nuclear plant in Rhea County, Tennessee. The plant had been operating, uninterrupted, since before the Crunch. As with some of the hydro plants, a mini power grid was already in service there, and it merely needed to be expanded and tied back to the new grid. The reconstituted grid was often jokingly called "Maynard's Bubble Gum and Baling Wire Power Grid."

The cobbled-together Fort Knox grid was plagued by frequent blackouts and brownouts. Severe conservation measures were the norm. Storm damage often took months to repair. The level of expectation for reliability of service soon was on a par with Third World countries. Meanwhile, the residential rate charged was an average of twenty-five cents per kilowatt hour in the new dollars, which kept consumption low.

Local power distribution co-ops were allowed to be independent and privately owned, but it was mandated that they pay their employees in the new currency.

Dissent from the new administration was rapidly quashed, often with brute-force tactics. Newspapers that printed editorials opposing the nationalization schemes often had their offices burned to the ground. Radio stations that voiced antigovernment views had their transmitters destroyed or their transmitter towers dynamited. Antigovernment banners were torn down. In some cases, activists disappeared, never to be seen again.

The Oconee Nuclear Station in South Carolina was a difficult challenge. There, they found that the employees were standing guard with an odd assortment of weapons that included homemade flamethrowers. Talking them into opening the gate was difficult, because they had heard rumors that the Provisional Government was engaging in terrorism and had sabotaged another nuclear power plant. It was only through a mixture of threats and bribes that they were able to enter the plant. As with the other nuclear power plants that they had "liberated," the Provisional Government found that the plant was still capable of going back online but the local power infrastructure was in disarray. There were downed power poles, trees down on power lines, and miles of copper wire that had been stolen.

The military bases fell either very easily, or with great difficulty. In some cases, all that the Provisional Government had to do was wait until their convoys arrived and announce that the base commander either was being given new orders or was being relieved. This worked well at their first destination, Fort Campbell, Kentucky. They found Little Rock Air Force Base and Tinker Air Force Base were both semi-abandoned. The commander at Arnold Air Force Base in Oklahoma simply rolled over and played dead.

Offut Air Force base near Omaha, Nebraska, proved to be one of the toughest nuts to crack. The base commander would not recognize Hutchings's Provisional Government. Rather than fighting the small Air Force security contingent toe to toe, General Uhlich decided to simply back off and starve them out. They did the same with Camp Gruber, Oklahoma. The Army National Guard general there told Chambers Clarke that in the absence of orders from FORSCOM or the Pentagon, he would take orders only from the

Governor of Oklahoma. Surrounding and starving out Offut and Camp Gruber took just six months and resulted in only a few casualties.

There was brief resistance at Fort Riley, Kansas, but the fort's commander eventually acceded to a combination of threats and a substantial bribe in gold. By the time that Fort Rucker, Alabama, came under the Hutchings government, the latter controlled the majority of the remaining airworthy helicopters in the U.S. Army inventory. Fort Leonard Wood, Missouri, yielded a huge number of trained troops that were integrated into the Provisional Government's army. The army soon earned the moniker "the Federals."

Fort Sill, Oklahoma, the home of the U.S. Army's artillery school, was semi-chaotic when the Federals arrived, but its huge store of ammunition was still secure and intact. Fort Gordon, Georgia, was controlled by a corrupt and unstable general who was mistrusted by his own troops. The arrival of the Federals came as a relief to the troops there—mostly signal corps—but they were soon disillusioned to find that the Provisional Government leadership was even *more* corrupt than that of their former commander.

When the army reached the coast and "pacified" Charleston, South Carolina, the Hutchings government immediately made satcom contact with U.S. Navy logistics ships worldwide, ordering them to return to the U.S. Their remaining cargos, they were told, were needed to resupply the army. The ports of Wilmington and Savannah were opened soon after. And once the army had reached the Gulf Coast, another satcom call went out to the UN, letting them know that several ports were available for ships carrying peacekeeping troops and vehicles. This accelerated the arrival of UN troops, which previously had been just a trickle on aircraft landing at McConnell, Tinker, Charleston, and Pope Air Force bases. The reopening of the seaports allowed huge numbers of UN troops to enter the United States.

Sarawiwa, Belize
September, The Second Year

Five months after he came to convalesce at the Moras' house, and just as he was starting to feel that he was fully regaining his strength, Andy became ill after dinner. He had a high fever, sweats, and a stomachache. He had all the signs of a bad flu. But then a rash formed on his chest and his legs. Skin eruptions broke out in his armpits. His wrists started to ache. Andy had never felt so sick in his life. Darci Mora recognized it immediately: "It's the break bone."

Andy turned his head to look at Darci and asked, "What? How could a broken bone cause this?"

"No, no, no. Not your broken leg. Nothing to do with that. This is a fever, breakbone fever, the dengue fever. The people call it breakbone fever because it gives you such pain in the joints."

Andy was very ill. His feverish periods would last for ten hours or more, and he became delirious. The pain in his muscles and joints became intense. Tylenol kept the pain just barely manageable. A few times he was given Tylenol with codeine. He had three days of diarrhea and vomiting.

During one of his lucid periods, Mora explained that dengue fever was caused by a virus transmitted from person to person by the *aedes* mosquito, and that there was no specific treatment.

Andy asked Darci, "Should I go back to the hospital?"

"No. Unless you get much worse and need an IV, the treatment would be the same there: fluids and rest. I'll just keep checking your vitals. There is something called dengue shock syndrome. That's the real killer, but it is not very common. You just have to let your immune system fight this."

After ten days, the worst of the illness had passed, but Andy still felt miserable. Following Darci's advice, he drank lots of water. He complained of an odd taste in his mouth, almost as if he were sucking on a zinc lozenge.

His recovery from dengue fever was slow. He spent many hours in bed, feeling weak. He read his Bible a lot. Whenever he felt depressed, he read the book of Job, just to put his own minor troubles in perspective. To improve his limited command of Spanish, Andy would often do parallel readings, verse by verse, from his King James Bible and Mora's "Santa Biblia" Spanish edition.

Andy would often read his favorite verses aloud, such as a portion of Psalm 119: "Thou *art* my hiding place and my shield: I hope in thy word. Depart from me, ye evildoers: for I will keep the commandments of my God. Uphold me according unto thy word, that I may live: and let me not be ashamed of my hope. Hold thou me up, and I shall be safe: and I will have respect unto thy statutes continually. Thou hast trodden down all them that err from thy statutes: for their deceit is falsehood. Thou puttest away all the wicked of the earth *like* dross: therefore I love thy testimonies."

The Moras' pet green parrot, named Payasito, kept Andy entertained as he recovered. Andy asked for the bird to be brought to his room so frequently that Gabe eventually moved his cage to Andy's bedside, saying simply, "You two can keep each other company from now on."

Laine joked that Payasito was teaching him his Spanish vocabulary: "When I go to restaurants, people will wonder why I always order peanuts." He added in an imitation of a parrot voice, "*Cacahuetes, por favor.*"

Eventually, Andy was able to return to his exercise regimen, and began helping Gabe with his work. Gabe still hunted frequently, both to supply his own household with meat and for extra meat to barter. Andy became his skinning and butchering assistant.

Mora mostly hunted the native *gibnut*, a large guinea-pig-like rodent, more commonly called a paca or *tepezcuintle*, or more properly the lowland paca. He also hunted peccaries, deer, armadillos, iguanas, and tapirs. Gabriel liked *gibnut* hunting best.

They were good eating and always plentiful. He jokingly called them "the Queen's Rats," referring to when Queen Elizabeth famously ate *gibnut* when she visited Belize. That dinner prompted a British newspaper to run the headline: "Queen Eats Rat." Mora told Andy that these fast-breeding rodents could be found in large numbers throughout the country. Gabe prided himself on always shooting them in the head, so that he didn't waste any meat. He rarely missed his mark.

Mora owned two .22 rimfire rifles, a Taurus .22 revolver, a .303 Lee-Enfield rifle that had been "sporterized," and two shotguns. His better .22 rifle was a scoped Marlin. All of this gun's metal parts and its scope had been spray-painted green to help protect it from rust in the unrelenting humidity. The paint often flaked and it showed signs of being touched up. This was Mora's gibnut gun. When Andy asked if his guns were registered, Gabe chortled, and said, "No. No way! I think only about half the guns in the country are in the registry. That registry is a big joke, especially out in the bush. Some of those guys have full-on AKs and old submachineguns from the Second World War that aren't registered."

Andy began going on hunts with Mora. On these hikes Gabe tried to teach him the names of the local tree species, but they soon became a confusing blur. The old logger mentioned that there were more than seven hundred species in Belize and that that he knew the names of only half of them. Andy finally said, "Well, it is more important that I know how to buy food and ask directions in Spanish than it is to know the name of every tree."

Andy often quoted the Bible to Gabe, who had been raised as a Catholic but who was relatively ignorant of the scriptures. He once told Andy, "I haven't gone to Mass or confessed in years. I worked so much in those back-country camps that I got out of the habit. God wouldn't want me." But Andy reassured him, saying,

"All you need is faith in Christ Jesus. That's the way, the *only* way, to heaven. Believe in Him and repent. It's just that simple." Laine regularly encouraged Mora to read his Bible. He also prayed daily that Gabe and Darci would come back into fellowship.

On one of their longer hunting excursions, Gabe showed Andy his secret stash of gasoline, buried in the side of a small ridge at his uncle's wooded property, three miles west of Sarawiwa. Mora described his fuel storage technique to Laine. When he was working as a back-country logger, he had discovered that gasoline stored in thirty-three-gallon plastic drums with the bungs sealed tight was still usable for up to four years, even without the addition of a stabilizer. Stored the same way, diesel would last much longer if it was treated with an antimicrobial.

The food-grade blue drums that Gabe used for his gasoline had white gaskets in the bungs that swelled slightly but did not deteriorate. These blue plastic drums were stored inside fifty-five-gallon steel drums and shaded from direct sunlight. A dark green tarp was draped over the pair of drums. Mora found that the plastic drums expanded and contracted with the fuel as the temperature changed. With no air venting, the problems of water condensation, evaporation, and other contaminants were solved. And, he surmised, in the event that the thirty-three-gallon drum ever burst unexpectedly, the fuel would be contained within the larger steel drum.

It was on that same trip that Mora bagged the first iguana that Andy had ever seen in the wild. Mora stopped the big lizard with just one shot to the back of its head from his Marlin .22 rifle. This iguana was more than three feet long. It had a fat tail, which Mora said was a sign of good health. Iguana, called "bamboo chicken" by the Mora family, was a favored delicacy. Gabe said that to get his daughter and son-in-law to come visit, all he had to do was tell them that he planned to serve iguana.

During his recovery, Andy continued with his weekly HF radio contacts. More than half of them were successful. It was those Morse code conversations with his brother and fiancée that kept his spirits up.

Gabe Mora had cut back drastically on his driving after the Crunch began. But he would often ride his bicycle to Sarawiwa or even as far away as Dangriga to buy groceries. He would carry his Taurus .22 revolver on those shopping trips. Gabe would frequently spot wild game near the road and bring home some bonus protein.

Bloomfield, New Mexico
April, the Second Year

Lars and Lisbeth Laine spent a lot of time in their "ham shack"—a corner of their bedroom—on more than just Tuesday nights. They became avid shortwave listeners, doing their best to keep track of current events by scanning through the international broadcast bands mainly in the high 9 MHz and high 11 MHz ranges, listening to radio stations such as the BBC, Radio Netherlands, Radio Havana Cuba, Channel Africa, HCJB in Ecuador, and NHK in Japan. They also tuned up to 17.795 MHz to hear Radio Australia. It was disconcerting to hear the litany of very bad economic news, refugee movements, terrorist attacks, and massive riots. It was even more disturbing to notice when some of these radio stations dropped off the air.

The Laines also picked up valuable news listening to amateur radio operators from all over the United States. They had the most success listening to hams in the Rocky Mountain region and just east of the Rockies. But they found that it was more difficult for them to hear hams in the Northeast. At first Lars assumed this was because of poor propagation or weak signal strength. But then he came to realize that the real reason so few hams were heard in the Northeast was because of the tremendous societal disruption and the lack of power. Most of the time Lars merely listened to the conversations of other ham radio operators and never used his own microphone. It was only when Kaylee asked him to contact her family near New Braunfels, Texas, that they actually keyed the mic and made contact with a couple of hams. From them they learned that Kaylee's family was safe and well. He also checked up on Lisbeth's family in eastern Colorado. They learned that her mother had died in a diabetic coma but that her father and brother were still alive and working at a grain mill. Lars was never successful at checking up on his relatives on his mother's side. The Bårdgård family lived in Minnesota, one of the places where the population die-off was severe. There, a combination of harsh winters and relatively high population density combined to produce a huge depopulation.

32

Social Work

Sarawiwa, Belize
February, the Third Year

To get ready for his upcoming departure, Andy started buying compact backpacking foods and extra batteries for his ham radio and SureFire flashlight in Sarawiwa and Dangriga. He also solicited letters of introduction from both Gabe Mora and the consul from the American embassy.

After Andy had declared himself fit to travel, Gabe said, "I can give you a ride as far as Orange Walk, but first I will make inquiries about horse breeders there. I know that there are several. I'll give you a letter of introduction that you can carry."

At dinner two days later, Gabe announced: "I found you a horse breeder. His name is Pedro Hierro, and his ranch is just north of Orange Walk, not far off the Northern Highway. I hear he has some of the best horses in the district."

Knowing that he was soon likely to depart, in the privacy of his bedroom Andy pulled out his Primus stove. Working with a screwdriver, he extracted two of the duct-tape-wrapped one-ounce gold coins and then he carefully reassembled the stove heat shield.

Andy felt bad that the checks that had been sent to Darci by the U.S. State Department were worthless. So he gave Gabe his set of bicycle tools and his big Maglite flashlight, explaining that he needed to cut down on weight for his upcoming journey. After some prayer, he also gave Darci a one-ounce American Eagle, one of his last few remaining gold coins. As he handed it to her, he said, "You have been such a blessing. You have always made me feel welcome here, and I have shared your food—with your delicious cooking—for many months. This is the least that I can do to thank you. I won't take no for an answer."

Their drive to Orange Walk was enjoyable. Gabe pointed out a number of sights and filled Andy in on some details about the history of the country. As they neared Orange Walk, Gabe started pointing out dozens of Mennonite-owned farms. He explained: "They started moving here in the 1950s. Good folks. When the power grid went down, the Old Order ones didn't even notice. They don't believe in electricity. But I'm worried about how they've done when the Guatemalan gangs have come through, because they don't believe in guns, either."

He dropped Laine off at the front gate of the horse ranch. A simple hand-painted sign read: "Pedro Hierro—Caballos Excelente." The ranch's pastures were enclosed in sturdy white-painted welded tubular steel fences that looked like they had taken many hours to construct. A small, stout cinder-block house overlooked the pastures and a hay field.

Gabe said, "I should just leave you here. This guy doesn't know me, so I think it's best that you just introduce yourself. He might be more nervous if two of us go up there."

Andy nodded. Seeing that the gate was locked, he climbed over it. Gabe lifted Andy's pack over the gate to him, and Andy shouldered it. They shook hands through the gate, and Mora said earnestly, "God will see you safely home."

Andy nodded and smiled. "And you, as well. *Con Dios*, Gabe." He turned to walk up the hill. He saw that there were more than a dozen mares and nearly as many foals in the pasture to his right. Just below the house was a smaller one-horse stallion corral. The horse in it was a fine-looking dark chesnut stallion with a long mane and a gleaming coat. Andy heard Mora's car driving away.

An elderly man stepped out on the porch and eyed Laine as he approached. A woman about the same age looked on from the open doorway. The man casually cradled a double-barreled shotgun in his arms.

Andy waved and shouted, "*¡Saludos!* I want to buy a horse." The man thoroughly read both of Andy's letters of introduction. Then, even before talking about his available horses, Pedro Hierro asked Andy how he planned to pay.

Andy answered, *"En monedas de oro. Yo tengo un Krugerrand.* It is a one-ounce coin—*una onza de oro."*

Hierro's eyes brightened and he urged, "Come, come and see my horses."

The horses that Pedro Hierro had available for sale were in his back pasture. He whistled them in and shook a partially full bucket of grain. The *remuda* of nearly twenty horses came at them at a gallop. After they were all in the corral, Hierro deftly closed the gate behind them. Laine was impressed how quickly he moved, for an old man.

Andy rested his forearms on the corral's top rail and began to look them over. One of them looked a bit lame—perhaps a hoof problem—but all of the others looked like good, sound horses. There were a few mares, but most of them were geldings.

"Do you have any saddle-broken horses that are extra quiet? *¿Bien callado, tranquilo?*"

The old man pointed to a large chesnut gelding that was standing slightly separated from the herd, "*Sí, este caballo que está castrado.*"

To Andy, the big gelding looked like it had some strong bloodlines, perhaps Andalusian. There wasn't a spot of white on him, which he liked. The gelding appeared to be sixteen hands or better.

Andy asked its name: "*¿Cómo se llama?*"

"*Prieto.*" After a pause the horse breeder added: "*Prieto es muy tranquilo.* He is the most quiet of all my horses. No *resopla*—no big snorts from this one. Also, no *relinchos.*"

Andy cocked his head and asked, "*¿Qué? ¿Qué es 'relinchos'?*"

The old man explained: "A *relincho* you calls a 'whinny.'"

"Oh. *Muy bueno.* He is well broken for riding?"

"*Sí, sí, señor.* He is four years old."

Andy climbed into the corral and approached the horse. He looked the horse in the eye. He brushed the side of the gelding's neck and made a soft, cooing noise. Then he chanted the horse's name: "Prieto, Prieto." The horse swung his head around and put his nose below Andy's chin. Laine took a few minutes to scratch the horse on his poll, between his ears, and beneath his forelock. The gelding's mouth made a chewing motion in response. Andy examined the horse closely.

Andy pointed out some scars and some proud flesh on the horse's right rear flank and gaskin.

Hierro explained, "Those scars are where he was bitten by another horse when he was young. If not for those scars, I think he would have sold before now."

"Can I give him a test drive?"

The old man laughed, and nodded. "*Por supuesto.*"

Andy's "test drive" lasted more than an hour, with Pedro Hierro riding alongside on his favorite saddle mare. They rode to-ward the New River. Negotiating the upper banks gave Andy the chance to see that Prieto was confident on steep terrain. Crossing the river twice made it clear that he wasn't afraid of water.

The saddle that Andy borrowed was a good fit, although Andy would have preferred a thicker saddle pad. After working out some tack fitting issues (with one stop early on, to adjust stirrup height) and learning the horse's preferred gait, the ride went well. Andy and Prieto quickly developed a bond. The horse was obviously well trained and had good ground manners. Prieto didn't balk at being ridden over steep ground and rocky spots. He was also just as quiet as the old man had advertised.

They returned to Hierro's house at a trot. After they had un-saddled the horses, Andy looked the old man in the eye and said: "I like this *caballo*. He will do. Here is my offer: I trade you my one-ounce Krugerrand for your horse Prieto, along with this sad-dle, this bit and bridle, a pair of hobbles, a lead rope, and also a pair of large saddlebags."

Pedro Hierro nodded slowly and gave a thin smile. "Show me this gold."

When he left Pedro Hierro's rancho the next morning, Andy had all that he had asked for, plus a collapsing canvas bucket, a groom-ing brush, and a hoof pick. The saddle was soon modified with a leather punch and nylon straps, allowing Andy's backpack to be strapped on behind the saddle deck. An extra-large saddle pad protected the horse from the weight of the backpack. The pack's position made it awkward for Andy to mount and dismount the horse, but it obviated the need to use a separate packhorse. Andy's goal was to make a small signature when traveling.

It was thirty-five miles from the rancho to the Mexican border. He planned to cross at Santa Elena, just west of the large city of Chetumal, on the Rio Hondo. By evening he was camped in the jungle near the village of Chan Chen, just four miles short of the border. He gave the horse more than an hour to graze in a meadow while he ate his own dinner: chili, straight from the can. Then he led Prieto off into the jungle.

Andy hobbled the horse and camped on a small knoll. It was an anxious night for him. He was saddle sore and he felt cranked up. He desperately wanted to talk with Kaylee, but it was two days until his next scheduled contact. After a fitful night in his bivy bag, worrying about both the horse and the upcoming border crossing, he awoke at dawn. He had a breakfast of day-old johnny-cakes and some iguana tail jerky. He was already missing Señora Mora's cooking.

Before departing, he repacked his backpack, secreting the pistol and its accessories inside a large bundle of clothes that was secured by string. That went in the bottom of his backpack in the hope that it would be the last thing that would be searched by the customs officers.

Crossing the border was easier than he had anticipated. The Santa Elena border station was a simple structure. The sight of his horse passing through was only a little unusual.

Leaving Belize, tourists were supposed to incur a twenty-dollar exit fee, but this was waived for Andy after a glance at the consul's letter. When he stepped across the line to the Mexican side of the station, his passport check was perfunctory. The Mexican customs agent looked bored as he stamped Andy's new American passport. He just waved Andy through.

He had prepared himself by placing a bill of sale and a veterinary health certificate form letter from Hierro as well as his letters of introduction in the top of his saddlebag. He even had a half-ounce American Eagle gold coin in his pants pocket, ready to palm as a bribe if necessary. He was greatly relieved when it wasn't needed.

Just a few miles past the border, Andy led Prieto into some scrub brush out of sight from the road, and retrieved his pistol. He positioned the holster in its usual spot on his belt above his right buttock. He felt more at ease, knowing that the SIG was safely cradled there, ready for quick action. It was concealed by his leather vest, which he habitually wore unbuttoned. He kept his horse off the road, following what looked like a motorcycle trail that closely paralleled the highway.

The road west toward Ramonal was almost deserted. No buses were running, and just a few local ranchers' trucks went by. West of Lago Milagros, Andy could see that he was entering big rancho country. The soil was noticeably more sandy. In places the sand was snow-white. Barbed-wire fences now bordered both sides of the road. Still, the country seemed more like Belize than Mexico. The brush and trees were still the same. Only the truck license plates were different. Some of the fences sagged and looked comical, and Laine wondered how well they held cattle.

Andy wanted to turn north, but he knew that he first had to travel west for more than a week to skirt around the bottom of the Gulf of Mexico. Every day he rode toward the sunset, hoping and waiting for the turn northward. That wouldn't come until he reached Villahermosa, three hundred miles to the southwest. Andy hoped to make thirty-five miles per day, assuming he could find plentiful food and water for his horse. Theoretically, he could be home in New Mexico, 1,750 miles away, in just two months, but that was "as the crow flies." More realistically, he knew that it would probably take at least twice that long. There were deserts and mountain ranges ahead, and many unknown perils.

Traveling entirely at night would in some ways be safer, but he was afraid that he'd stumble into an ambush, and the mosquitos swarmed by the thousands. It took a heavy application of bug juice to discourage them. Taking pity on Prieto, Laine daubed a bit of insect repellent around the horse's eyes before sleeping each night. He dreaded leaving the mosquito-netted bivy bag each morning.

Laine close-hobbled Prieto every night and was pleased to see that the horse rarely wandered more than ten yards away from the bivouac bag. Some nights he hardly moved at all. The sound of the horse's breathing and the regular swishing of his tail were comforting. Andy hoped that he might give him some warning if a man or jaguar approached the camp. Andy even became accustomed to the horse's daily pattern of urination, defecation, and flatulence. Prieto often showed signs of anxiety for the first hour after Andy settled into the bivy bag each night. Then the horse would let loose a ripping fart, let out a loud breath through its nostrils, and finally stand still, often for the full night. This routine made Andy laugh the first few times that he heard it.

He got into the routine of grooming the horse twice a day, including picking his hooves. The most time-consuming part was searching for and removing ticks. He'd often find a tick on Prieto's belly or in one of his ears. If the horse shook his head in the middle of the day, Andy would stop, dismount, and check his ears for ticks. This was usually the cause.

Andy's first attempt at a radio contact from Mexico was two days later, on a Tuesday night. The propagation was so poor that he couldn't even receive Lars's previously strong signal. He gave up in disgust.

Prieto tried to linger with his hooves in the water after watering breaks. Andy would have liked to indulge the horse's preference, but he considered it a security risk. After all, creek and river crossings were high-risk ambush areas.

He also worried about his horse eating noxious weeds and made a point of only stopping and letting Prieto graze in grasses that he recognized. Sometimes the horse would get into a particularly tasty bunch of grass and be reluctant to move on. When that happened, Andy would have to tug quite hard on Prieto's reins, or if he was dismounted at the time, he'd ball up his fist with his thumb extended and dig his thumb into Prieto's chest while ordering him backward with the words, *"¡Hacia atrás!"*

Despite Prieto's few quirky habits, Andy was impressed with his intelligence and instincts. The horse had particularly good sense about snakes. Several times, Andy would be riding alongside the road at a trot and suddenly Prieto would come to a dead stop and lay back his ears. Each time there was a snake just a few paces ahead. If the snake was a fer-de-lance (called a "Tommy Goff" in Belize) or an unidentified snake species, Andy would simply guide the horse in a large circle around to avoid it. But if it was a large rattlesnake, Andy would dismount and tie up Prieto at a safe distance. Then he'd pin the snake's head down with a branch and decapitate it with his pocketknife. Rattlesnakes were good eating. But Prieto was so frightened of snakes that he'd start to prance in place. Andy learned that the only way that he could get close to Prieto when holding a dead snake was if he first hid it in a sack.

Because of the space constraints of his backpack, Andy could only carry four or five days' worth of food. By the time he reached the town of Escarcega, he was down to his last few bits of food. He saw a sign on a small masonry building with heavily barred windows: "Monedas Numismático."

A sign hanging inside the front window read "Abierto," showing that the store was open. As Laine dismounted, a boy wearing a large sombrero approached and asked, *"¿Le cuido su caballo?"* Andy nodded affirmatively. Andy handed the boy Prieto's reins. Expecting the wait to be twenty minutes, he told the boy, *"Aproximadamente veinte minutos."*

Just as at the coin shop in Germany, Andy had to be buzzed in.

The door closed behind him with a loud click. Just inside the door was another door. To his left was a small window where an armed guard sat. The guard glanced through the window at the boy and the horse.

Andy asked, "Can that boy be trusted?"

The guard grunted: *"Sí, mi chico es de confiar."*

Andy saw a sign above that warned that weapons had to be checked: "Registrar Todas Las Armas Aquí. ¡Sin Excepciónes!" He let out a sigh, and muttered: "Okay, your house, your rules." Under the watchful eye of the man, who was armed with an odd three-barreled antique shotgun, Andy made a show of slowly unholstering his SIG, ejecting its magazine, and clearing its chamber, locking the slide to the rear. He passed the pistol butt-first through the window and stuffed the magazine and loose cartridge into his front pocket. Then he handed the man both his CRKT tanto folding pocketknife and his Leatherman tool from his other pocket.

A second buzzer sounded, and Laine entered the main portion of the coin shop. He was surprised to see the shop was owned by a bald, wrinkled man in a wheelchair. The guard with the shotgun pivoted his stool and closely watched all that transpired.

The store was mainly lit by daylight from the windows, supplemented by some strings of white LED lights—the kind that he had previously seen used on Christmas trees. Andy surmised that the lights and door lock were solar-powered. Clever.

He asked the man in the wheelchair, "Do you speak English?"

"Yes, I do. Can I be of help to you?"

"I'd like to trade this Krugerrand for silver coins. I want to trade for whatever you think would be best for me to barter for food in my travel. Do you have some silver pesos, or maybe *Onza de Plata* coins? The condition is unimportant to me. My only concern is their silver content." He handed the storekeeper the Krugerrand.

It made Andy smile when he saw the coin dealer repeat the same steps to verify the authenticity of the coin that he had seen demonstrated in Germany. Some tools of the trade, he realized, were universal.

The man looked up with a smile and declared: "I can give you forty-eight silver five-peso coins of before 1958 minting, in trade for this coin. I'm sure that you know, the five-peso coins from this time is 72 percent silver and has .6431 of the troy ounce of silver."

Andy worked the math in his head. "Hmmm . . . how about fifty-five of those? That would be a more fair ratio."

"The best I can do in the trade is fifty-two."

Andy nodded and said: "That is acceptable to me, but only if you substitute ten one-peso silver coins instead of two of those five-peso coins."

"Yes, I can include some of the smaller coins, but they will all be the 1957 silver one-peso Juarez. These are a very common minting but not much wear on them."

"That is fine. We have a deal." They shook hands.

The coin dealer counted out the coins in piles of five on a blue felt-covered tray. Andy confirmed the count. The coin dealer placed them in a small canvas sack that was printed: "First Community National Bank, Brownsville, Texas." Seeing that sack made Andy grin. He was now feeling closer to the United States, and feeling anxious.

Andy wished the dealer well as he set aside a handful of one- and five-peso coins from the sack. This handful went loose into his pants pocket while the rest, in the canvas sack, went into his cargo pocket. After retrieving his knives and pistol, Andy reloaded and holstered the SIG. The guard gave Andy a friendly nod.

He was buzzed out the front door and found the boy standing there dutifully, still holding Prieto's reins. Laine dug in his pocket and pulled out a silver one-peso coin. He handed it to the boy, and said, *"Una moneda de plata, para ti. Gracias por su trabajito."*

The boy grinned, shouted *"¡Muchas gracias, señor!"* and ran off, singing.

There was a *pulpería* just two blocks farther west. The grocery store was half open-air, with seven rough-hewn tables beneath latticework for shade. Two bored-looking teenage guards with ancient Mexican Mauser carbines stood watch. The grocery had a surprisingly good selection. Andy bought two large bags of beef jerky (*carne seca*), a dozen apples, five large carrots, eight cans of chili con carne, a dozen sun-dried Spanish mackerel, six cans of chicken noodle soup, eight Big Hunk candy bars, and a sack of hard tack that was the size of two loaves of bread. After a bit of dickering, a price of one and a half silver pesos was agreed. His change was a peso coin that had been cold-chiseled in half. After seeing the prices asked at the *pulpería*, it was now no wonder that the boy had been so excited to get the silver peso.

It took a while to pack all the groceries into the backpack and saddlebags. As he did, Andy fed Prieto a carrot that he chomped with gusto. He nosed at Andy, hoping for another, but Andy was saving those for the coming days.

His progress through the states of Quintana Roo and Campeche was slow. He did his best to avoid large towns, but he actually did veer toward some small villages. In each he would always ask, "*¿Saben si mas adelante hay bandidos en el camino?*" ("Do you know if bandits await on the road ahead?")

At the village of La Pita, he got an affirmative response. There, a potbellied man warned Andy that a bandit gang controlled the village of Mamantel, just a few miles beyond. He drew Laine a map, showing him a road that skirted around the west side of the village. Andy thanked the man for the warnings and handed him two silver pesos with the words "*Gracias por su advertencia.*"

Andy waited until after dark to make his circuitous route around Mamantel. The ride was nerve-wracking but uneventful except for a couple of barking dogs.

His journey northward through Mexico soon got into a rhythm. After twenty to twenty-five miles of riding, Andy would look for some woods or dense brush that would offer a secluded campground. He would scan in all directions, first with his eyes and then with his binoculars, to see if he was observed. If anyone was present, he'd let Prieto graze or he'd pick the horse's hooves until the strangers had passed well out of his line of sight. He would then quietly lead Prieto into the woods, usually at least two hundred yards, or even farther when the woods weren't dense. Camping alone caused Andy lots of anxiety. He was often afraid that he might be observed and followed.

Andy's next shopping excursion was in the small city of Macuspana, in the state of Tabasco. The town was in a broad basin that was mostly agricultural, and he found a profusion of fresh produce at great prices. The thatched-roof Centro Mercado had plenty of flies, but the fruit and vegetables all looked fresh. The best bargain was a large sack of dried fish—enough to last Andy for more than a week. The sack was so large that Andy simply tied it to his saddle horn. Prieto snorted at it at first, but with some gentle correction from Andy, the horse left it alone.

Andy decided that it was best to work his way up the Gulf Coast, sticking to small roads. He had considered traveling a more westerly (and direct) route to New Mexico. But that would mean that water and the opportunities to buy food would be iffy, the terrain more rugged, and the grazing for his horse more uncertain. Traveling cautiously, he averaged only twenty miles per day. He skirted around the larger population centers like Minatitlán and Veracruz. He wanted to stay as far away from Mexico City as possible, since the city of 8.4 million residents was reportedly chaotic. Andy surmised that many of those problems must have been overflowing into its suburbs, and beyond.

On a Tuesday evening, Andy had a successful HF contact with Lars. He was thrilled to be able to use the call sign "4A/K5CLA"—with the "4A" prefix designating that he was transmitting from Mexico. The significance of the prefix was immediately apparent to Lars, but it had to be explained to Beth and Kaylee. As usual for his contacts, Andy gave Kaylee a weekly travelogue, letting her know the sights he had seen, how he was feeling, and, in this instance, a bit about Prieto's eccentricities.

That same night Andy was awakened by a strange commotion. He soon realized that it was Prieto stomping a pygmy rattlesnake to death just a few feet from Andy's head. Andy didn't even bother crawling out of his bivy bag. He just ordered Prieto to back off with, *"¡Hacia! Hacia atrás!"* Then he unzipped the bivy bag, picked up the well-trodden snake carcass behind its head, and heaved it as far as he could out of the campground. He zipped the bag back up and said "Good night, Superhorse."

As Andy passed north of Orizaba, the population density increased noticeably. There was more traffic on the roads, with a surprising number of motorcycles and mopeds. Some of the men looked unsavory. Andy had to be much more selective about where he camped. He was increasingly afraid that someone might see where he had ducked into the forest and attack him.

He often heard bursts of gunfire in the distance. These shots were too rapid to be just hunters. Obviously there was a big crime problem in the area, and it was being stamped out ballistically.

Near Zempoala, Andy had an amazing conversation with a local teenage boy who spoke good English. The boy was armed with a pump-action .22 rifle slung on his back with a length of white clothesline cord. Andy commented to him about how peaceful things seemed on the coast. The teenager explained, "That's because it's open season on *los caníbales de la ciudad*. When anyone sees them, they just shoot them. Then we burn or bury the bodies, so their friends don't come and eat them. It's all like something from a zombie movie."

"You're kidding, right?"

"No joke, *señor*. There have been hundreds from Mexico City and even some from Xalapa that we've had to kill. If you are ever seeing strangers with knives or machetes, and they have the blood-stained clothes, and that *look* in their eyes, you don't ask questions. Do not hesitate. You just shoot them."

"What look in their eyes?" Laine asked.

"*That* look. The animal look. You know it when you see it. After the first time, you recognize it *inmediatamente*."

The boy's comments made Andy shudder. Laine was dubious about what he'd been told until he heard it corroborated by a policeman in the next town. This made him anxious to get as far away from Mexico City as he could, as quickly as possible.

33

Avtomat Kalashnikov

"Anything that is complex is not useful and anything that is useful is simple. This has been my whole life's motto."

—Mikhail Timofeyevitch Kalashnikov

Prieto seemed healthy, and his hooves stayed in good condition. Other than mosquito bites, sand flea bites, and sunburn, Andy was also healthy. After he had gained his saddle muscles, the long days on horseback became more bearable.

After skirting Veracruz, Laine hugged the coast. In a few stretches with hard sand, he rode Prieto right on the beach, finding it less stressful than constantly looking over his shoulder, as he did when riding on the shoulder of the road. Occasionally, when the surf was light, he'd let Prieto walk in the shallow waves as they lapped up the beach. The horse liked having his hooves in the water. The beautiful scenery was distracting and Andy had to try to keep focused at all times. He had to fight to keep himself in at least a "Condition Yellow" frame of mind. As he rode down the beach, he would sing to himself and to Prieto. He often sang Jimmy Driftwood's bluegrass song "Tennessee Stud" and snippets of Mexican folk songs that he'd picked up. And whenever Prieto broke into a gallop in the shallow surf, he shouted repeatedly, "I'm coming home, Kaylee, I'm coming home!"

The stretch of coast between the towns of Zempoala and Vega

de Alatorre had an "Old Mexico" feel to it, and the locals were friendly. Many of them seemed curious about Andy and his horse. There were fewer horses, mules, and donkeys in this region than he'd seen inland, so young children would often run toward Prieto gleefully, wanting to see and touch *"el caballo grande."* Prieto seemed to put up with it well. But once he snatched a straw sombrero off a boy's head and started chewing it before Laine could stop him. Andy apologized for *"mi caballo travieso"* and gave the boy a silver peso coin. The boys ran off, carrying the mangled hat and the coin, shouting and laughing. Andy was surprised to have the boy's mother return a few minutes later, with three quarters of the coin. One quarter of it had been neatly chiseled out, explaining, "You have paid of my son too much for his sombrero."

As he moved up the coast, Laine's diet shifted toward bananas, coconuts, and dried fish. There were so many coconuts available free for the taking that he cracked open several extra ones each day. After drinking their milk, he scraped out the insides with his pocketknife and gave the pulpy coconut meat to Prieto, who licked it up eagerly.

Not wanting to make a wide detour around some lakes, Andy opted to ride directly through the city of Tampico. Knowing that it would be a full day's ride to get through Tampico and the many small towns clustered to the north of it, Andy decided to camp earlier than usual. He let Prieto graze an extra long time in a meadow that was a comfortable four hundred yards from the highway. Later, as he set up his camp in the middle of a large grove of coconut trees, Andy remembered an old Stan Kenton big-band tune that he had heard as a child, played on one of his Grandmother Bårdgård's 78 rpm records. It was called "Tampico." He sang quietly to himself:

Ay, Tampico, Tampico, on the Gulf of Me-hico
Tampico, Tampico, down in Me-hico

You buy a beautiful shawl
A souvenir for Aunt Flo
Authentic Mexican yarn
Made in Idaho, Ohhh . . .

Hearing Laine singing, Prieto gave him a snort. Andy chided the horse to be quiet: *"Cállate, Prieto. No resopla."* Andy carried on, but just humming, since he couldn't recall the rest of the song's lyrics.

The ride through Tampico the next day was unnerving. By ten a.m. the temperature was already in the nineties. As near as Andy could tell, several gangs controlled the city and the surrounding towns. He saw, individually and in pairs, a few men armed with a diverse assortment of AKs, bolt-action rifles, HK G3s, M16s, M4s, and pump-action shotguns. A few of them had neck tattoos that reminded him of the Guatemalans who had robbed him. This made Andy very nervous. Fortunately, none of the men ever tried to intercept his horse.

Several times while he was riding through Tampico, boys on bicycles would ride up next to Andy and ask one-word color questions, like *"¿Rojo?" "¿Azul?" "¿Negro?"* At first, Andy didn't understand them, and shrugged in response. Then he came to realize that they were asking Andy about his gang affiliation. He decided to bluff them by shouting, *"El fortísimo. Váyanse, chiquillos!"* ("The strongest. Go away, kids!")

Andy didn't start to relax that day until he had ridden north of the town of Ricardo Flores Magon, late in the afternoon. He was happy to be away from the Tampico gangland. After passing through several coffee plantations, Laine camped that night in a dense grove of trees a hundred yards up from a river. The hillside was steeper than he liked, but all of the level ground in the area had long since been cleared of trees. The moon was starting to wane but was still nearly full. Andy drifted off to sleep, stuffed full of wild bananas.

He was awakened by a snort from Prieto. Laine sat halfway up in his bivy bag and listened. He could hear something moving through the undergrowth, twenty yards downhill from his camp. In the moonlight Andy could see Prieto standing just ten feet away, with his nose pointing downhill. The horse's ears were alternating between being perked up and laid back. He was obviously wary about something. Andy's first thought was that it might be a jaguar. Then Andy heard a cough—a human cough. Laine slowly unzipped his bivy bag's "no-see-um" netting and pointed his SIG pistol in the direction where he'd heard the noises. Only his head and forearms protruded from the bag. Realizing that making any sound could prove fatal, he decided not to move. He couldn't further extricate himself from the bag without making noise. Listening intently, he could identify the sounds of two people walking up the hill.

Soon Andy could see that two figures were climbing the hill, coming directly toward Prieto. As they climbed up closer, Andy began to see some details. Both were muscular young men. Both were shaved bald-headed. One of them was wearing a white tank top. The other was wearing a white T-shirt. Both of them carried AK-47s and small rucksacks. Andy was uncertain if they might be local ranchers or coffee growers. When they were just five yards away, he could see that they were both looking at his horse. They hadn't yet detected Andy, who was sitting in a spot that was shaded from the moonlight. As they stepped closer, one of them shouldered his rifle and thumbed down its safety lever with a loud clack. It was then that Andy could see that they both had tattoos covering most of their arms and ringed around their necks.

Andy lined up the glowing green sights of the SIG on the head of the man who had raised the AK and pulled the trigger through twice, rapidly. The bandit went down instantly. Then he quickly shifted his sights to the other man, who was turning to point his rifle toward Andy's muzzle flashes. Andy fired rapidly, five more times, at the chest of the second man. He, too, went down, shouting. Andy took careful aim and shot each of the men twice more in the head. The shooting startled Prieto, and he shifted backward, dragging his hobbled front hooves in an odd jump. The horse snorted anxiously. The two bandits continued to thrash on the ground, bleeding out. A dog barked, far in the distance, perhaps a half mile away.

Andy fumbled in his sleeping bag, searching for a spare magazine. Finding it, he ejected the one in his gun and slapped in the spare. He tapped the butt of the pistol twice with his free hand, ensuring that the magazine was correctly latched in place. He was gasping, and he fought to control his breathing. After a minute, the two bandits finally stopped moving. He quietly wormed his way out of the bivy bag. His ears were ringing, and his hands were shaking.

Were there others? If so, how far away? Should he sit tight or flee? He decided to wait and listen. He waited for a very anxious half hour, hearing only the quiet sounds of Prieto breathing and the occasional high whine of mosquitos. He prayed silently and then decided that it was time to go. He holstered his pistol and then, after rolling and stowing his bivy bag, groped around until he retrieved the partially expended pistol magazine. He made a mental note to refill it when he had daylight available.

Moving quietly but quickly, he saddled and tacked up Prieto, but he left the horse's hobbles on for fear of his running off. He rubbed the horse's neck consolingly and whispered in his ear: "*Bueno, Prieto, muy bueno. Muchas gracias.* You are Superhorse."

He stepped down the hill to examine the bodies of the bandits. Both of them looked like they were in their twenties. The moonlight was just bright enough to make out their tattoos by. He could see that one of them had some large numbers tattooed on his neck. Most of the rest of the markings were swirling and geometric patterns. These were obviously crude prison tats.

He stripped the men of their rucksacks. The small packs were surprisingly heavy. He looped them over his saddle horn. Then he picked up their guns. He flipped up the one safety lever that had been released. One was a folding-stock AK, but the other had a wooden stock. The wooden stock, he saw, had been split and cracked—pierced by two bullets from Andy's SIG. Neither of the guns had slings, so Andy pulled a hank of OD parachute cord from his left saddlebag and quickly cut off two four-foot lengths. He tied them on as makeshift slings. Andy slung both AKs across his back. Then he inserted Prieto's bit, saddled him, and removed the hobbles. He walked north for two hundred yards, leading the horse through the dense trees and up onto level ground. Based on the setting moon's position, he judged the time to be about three or four a.m.

He swung up into the saddle unsteadily, unaccustomed to the extra weight of the two AKs. He nudged his heels into Prieto's flanks, prodding him forward. The horse went immediately into a trot. "Let's go, Prieto. We gotta lot of ground to cover before daylight," Andy urged.

He didn't stop for either breakfast or lunch. He rode hard, halting briefly only to water his horse at creeks. By six p.m. his stomach was growling, and he was feeling saddle sore. Even with regular shifting of the guns from side to side, the thin parachute cord that he'd used for ersatz slings was digging into his lower neck, rubbing it raw. He had covered nearly eighty miles, paralleling Highway 180 and intentionally bypassing the town of Aldama. Now, just ten miles short of La Coma, he dismounted and walked Prieto for the last half mile to cool him down. He halted in a small grassy opening in a forest far from the nearest ranch house.

After reloading the partially expended SIG magazine and unsaddling and hobbling Prieto, Andy dug into his pack and wolfed down some *carne seca* and an apple. Then he groomed the horse thoroughly. He heaped praised on the horse as he did so. He said over and over, "You are Superhorse," "*Muy bueno, Prieto,*" and "Some of God's blessings come with four legs."

As he did the grooming, he thought about the two rifles that he'd taken from the dead men. He concluded that it would be wise to keep one of them. Both of them were selective-fire models, with a full-auto selector position. Ideally he would have kept the fixed-stock AK, since they are more accurate and more comfortable to shoot. He had never liked the feel of folding-stock AKs with underfolding stocks. Their skeletonized butt plates were uncomfortable on his shoulder, and his cheek wobbled on the thin rails.

Working in turn, he unloaded both guns, popped off their top covers, and pulled out their bolt assemblies. Looking closely at each, he could see that he should keep only the folding-stock gun. The wooden stock on the other AK looked beyond repair, and the gun was old and rusty. Looking down its bore with a bit of white paper tucked into the receiver ahead of the open bolt to act as a reflector, he could see that the wood-stocked AK had a dark, badly pitted bore. But the folder AK was nearly new and it had a very good bore. He also realized that for some of his upcoming travel, he'd have to keep the gun concealed. For that, the folding-stock AK would be the obvious choice.

Andy oiled and reassembled the folding-stock AK. Then he reloaded it. He decided to keep the magazine and the entire bolt assembly from the fixed-stock AK to use as spares but discard the rest of the gun. He just left it on the ground. He mused about who would eventually find it there, and when. Perhaps an archaeologist. He whispered to himself, "*Durobrabis.*"

Next, Laine searched through the bandits' rucksacks. One of them had three spare loaded AK magazines, and the other one had two more. One of these magazines was a black polymer Bulgarian waffle magazine. The rest of them were typical Russian steel magazines, mostly in good condition, although one of them had heavy pitting. There was just one magazine pouch that held three magazines. He decided that it would be the largest size that he could comfortably carry on his belt, positioned on his left hip, so that it wouldn't bump up against the back of his saddle.

The packs also contained a Chinese-made LED flashlight, a cheap pocketknife, a bag containing marijuana and cigarette rolling papers, two bottles of insect repellent, and three pairs of socks. There was also a large plastic bag containing two dozen tortillas in an old bread bag, a half pound of some foul-smelling chicken meat, some refried bean paste in a Ziploc bag, and some rice. This food was suspect, so he buried it along with the marijuana eighty yards outside his camp, so that it wouldn't attract scavengers and so that Prieto wouldn't get into it.

That evening Andy had difficulty getting to sleep, so he put on some insect repellent and spent an hour braiding a sling out of seventy-five feet of parachute cord, praying as he worked. The resulting sling looked presentable and functional. He made it extra-long so that it would be usable when the rifle was slung across his chest. Then he crawled back into his bivy bag and zipped the mosquito net closed. As he tried to get to sleep, the events of the night before kept replaying in his mind. He concluded that there was little that he could have done differently. If he had tried to warn them off, he probably would have been shot and killed. If he had tried to flee, he probably would have been shot and killed. And even if he had surrendered and handed over everything that he owned, he probably would have been shot and killed. Andy whispered out loud, resignedly, "Same, same." Then he prayed, "Forgive me, Lord, for taking those lives. You know your Elect. I doubt they were saved, but I pray that they were. And please grant me rest, O Lord."

Andy searched his memory. After a pause he quoted: "Forasmuch as it hath pleased Almighty God of his great mercy to take

unto himself the soul of our dear brother here departed, we therefore commit his body to the ground; earth to earth, ashes to ashes,
dust to dust; in sure and certain hope of the Resurrection to eternal life, through Our Lord Jesus Christ; who shall change our vile
body, that it may be like unto his glorious body, according to the
mighty working, whereby he is able to subdue all things to himself."

Then he asked himself, "Were they saved? I have no way of
knowing. You can sort 'em out, Lord."

The next morning he awoke feeling more sore than usual. He
tied the new sling to the folding-stock AK and oiled the gun thoroughly. He folded the stock closed, leaving the gun in its more
compact configuration. Once it was rolled inside his extra sweater
and raincoat, the AK was unrecognizable to the casual observer.
Andy felt better, knowing that the gun was there and could be
loaded fairly rapidly if he ever needed it. He decided to get into
the routine of loading, oiling, and inspecting the gun each evening
when he made camp in the woods. But he decided the risk of ar-
rest was too great if he carried it openly when riding. It would be
wrapped up strapped atop his pack each day.

The additional gear made getting on and off Prieto even more
difficult than before. Raising his right leg over the pack was an
almost gymnastic feat. From a standstill, it was in fact often easier
to dismount in reverse, by twisting his left foot in the stirrup while
lifting his right foot over the saddle horn instead of over the back
of the saddle and pack.

While riding in the open country between Las Norias and San
Fernando, Andy started looking at the trash by the side of the
road. He was searching for a scrap of cardboard or a large flat
cardboard box. After half a mile he found an eighteen-inch-square
cardboard box that was just four inches deep. He dismounted and
picked it up, saying, "This'll do nicely." Walking and leading Prieto, he took a one-mile detour from the road.

Laine hobbled his horse and pulled a pen from his saddlebag. He drew a one-inch dot in the middle of the bottom of the box. He switched to the magazine with the pitting, henceforth designated his "target and hunting only" magazine. Laine left Prieto grazing and walked a hundred yards ahead. He set up the target box and stepped back twenty-five paces to zero the AK. After digging out the earplug case that he had brought from Afghanistan, he got down prone and deliberately fired a three-shot group. He found that the AK's sights were correct in the left-right axis, but the rifle shot high. He cranked up the front sight with his Leatherman tool until the rifle shot dead-on at twenty-five paces. Then he stepped back to seventy-five paces and fired again. In the entire process, he fired just seven rounds. Satisfied, he rewrapped and stowed the AK.

Still saddle sore, he rode only another ten miles before leaving the road to make camp northwest of San Fernando. He had to camp farther off the road than before to be out of sight, because the clumps of trees were becoming thinner and more infrequent.

Andy spent considerable time cleaning the bore and chamber of the AK. He wasn't sure if the ammo he'd taken from the dead bandits—all with Cyrillic markings—was corrosively or noncorrosively primed, so he wasn't taking any chances.

In his Ordnance Corps officer basic course at Fort Lee, Virginia, Laine had been taught that the rule was to clean a gun's bore, chamber, and bolt face for three successive days after shooting any suspected corrosive ammo. This was the only way to be sure that the corrosive priming salts were completely removed. Laine also took the time to unload all of the magazines and inspect each of them and every cartridge. He sorted the cartridges on his spread-out raincoat. Any cartridges that were dented or had loose bullets or corrosion were segregated and loaded into the "target and hunting only" magazine.

The grazing was becoming sparse, so Andy hobbled Prieto more loosely. But the next morning he found the horse standing just fifteen feet away.

Andy's breakfast was dried fish and two oranges. Prieto ate the orange peels. Just an hour later Andy reached a long-awaited goal: the fork in the road near the tiny town of Ampi La Loma. If he continued ahead to the northeast, Highway 101 would take him to Brownsville, Texas. But if he turned northwest, Highway 97 would take him to Reynosa, which was less populous. He veered his horse to the left at the fork (skipping the paved cloverleaf loop) and let out a whoop. He brought Prieto's pace up to a canter. Texas was so close that he could taste it.

A hard day of riding brought Andy nearly to the city of Reynosa. Before looking for a place to camp, he made inquiries with some local women who were carrying bundles of firewood on their backs. They told him that the Pharr Bridge across the Rio Grande at Reynosa had been roadblocked and the border station had been shut down. A *narcotraficante* gang ruled the town, they warned. A sporadic crackle of gunfire in the distance confirmed their warning. But they also told Andy that twenty-five miles west, at Nuevo Progresso—just north of Camargo—and opposite Rio Grande City, the bridge was open, and that the border stations were unmanned.

After a quiet ride to Camargo, Andy spent the next twenty-four hours quizzing the locals and reconnoitering the border crossing. From the woods on the south bank of the river, he used his binoculars to size up the situation on the Starr-Camargo Bridge. All through the day he saw people walking back and forth, over the pair of concrete bridges. Many people pushed wheelbarrows and carts filled with trade goods. There were no signs of anyone being impeded. He couldn't get a clear view of the border-crossing complex on the far side of the river, but there were obviously people passing through. He only heard two gunshots during the day. Both of those were in the late morning, about twenty minutes apart, and the sound came from the American side of the river.

Andy spent that night in the woods, a mile upriver. Seeing Texas on the other side of the river made it seem tantalizingly close. There were just a few small individual lights that he could see in the distance. Presumably they were candles and lanterns. The town of Rio Grande City, with fourteen thousand inhabitants before the Crunch, and now slightly less, was quiet and dark. He didn't hear any vehicles or generators operating after sunset. The only noise came from a few barking dogs. He fretted and prayed through much of the night.

The next morning he awoke to the sound of a dove cooing in a nearby tree. He bathed with buckets of water carried up from the river, and he shaved using one of his precious remaining scraps of soap. He combed his hair and tried to beat the grime out of his trousers. Then he brushed his teeth. Laine wanted to look presentable, just in case he was stopped. He said another prayer and saddled up. As he inserted Prieto's bit, he said to the horse: "Well, fella, this is our big day. You only speak Spanish, so let *me* do the talking."

Andy was anxious as he crossed the upper bridge. With Prieto at a trot, he passed two pedestrians on the bridge, both pushing wheelbarrows full of corn on the cob. The brown-painted border crossing station building was deserted. It was eerie, seeing the inspection booths unmanned. Aside from one abandoned pickup (on blocks and minus its tires) and some new graffiti spray-painted on two of the booths, the station looked intact and unmolested. Andy kept Prieto at a trot. As he rode, Andy whistled the tune "God Bless America."

He soon rode into an open-air market that was set up in the border crossing parking lot. Most of the tables displayed seasonal produce. Some of it was simply spread out on tarps on the ground.

The vendors were mostly Mexican, and the customers were mostly American. A few came in pickups, but there were plenty of horses and mountain bikes. Both were kept close at hand by their nervous owners. Nearly everyone seemed to be armed—either with holstered pistols or slung long guns, or both. Horses caused a few comical moments as the naughty animals snatched produce from the stalls unless their reins were held tightly.

With a grin that never quit, Andy bought a large sack of oranges, a bag of carrots, two candy bars, a can of peanuts, and some horsemeat jerky. He paid in silver pesos. His change was in the form of U.S. silver dimes and two pie-slice-shaped silver bits that had been chiseled from a Morgan silver dollar. The prices at the market seemed greatly inflated, compared to what he'd experienced in Mexico. But at least his silver peso coins were readily accepted.

Before leaving, Andy patted Prieto and praised him for being *"un caballo caballeroso"* (a "gentlemanly horse") and fed him a carrot. Andy walked Prieto to the gate. Before climbing back up on the saddle, he unstrapped the inherited AK-47 from atop his pack, unwrapped it, and slung it over his shoulder. After swinging up into the saddle, Laine reached into his saddlebag and pulled out a full thirty-round magazine. He swung the AK around to his chest and inserted the curved magazine. He gave a sigh of relief and said, "Ahhh . . . back in the land of the free."

In the coming days, Laine would habitually carry the AK slung across his chest with the sling looped around his neck, ready for quick action. If a situation looked particularly dicey, Laine would halt his horse and rotate the AK's stock to its extended position so that he'd be able to shoot accurately.

34

Reconnaissance

"... vaults of the central banks and return to the pockets and purses of private individuals, for gold is the only really sound money with intrinsic value. The desire to return to gold is understandable, and we hope to see it realized some day, although the argument in favor of the gold standard is not always stated in a valid way. The distinctive function of gold money does not consist in its intrinsic value or in the constancy of that value, which fluctuates even in the absence of government intervention. The excellence of metallic money in free circulation consists in the fact that it renders impossible the abuse of power of the government to dispose of the possessions of its citizens by means of its monetary policy and thus serves as the solid foundation of economic liberty within each country and of free trade between one country and another."

—Faustino Ballve, *Essentials of Economics* (1963)

Local commerce gradually began to expand in the Four Corners. For the first few years after the Crunch began, most of the local businesses were closed, due to lack of inventory. Others suffered from what Beth dubbed "buggy-whip syndrome." In essence, their products or services didn't translate well into the new economic reality. There was no more Internet. There was no more coffee being imported. And there was little need for weight-loss centers when so many people were going hungry. The few businesses that prospered were ones that specialized in repair and refurbishment.

Just weeks after the Crunch began, an informal open-air flea market started to blossom at the San Juan County Fairgrounds, on Highway 64, between Farmington and Bloomfield. This was where people brought fresh produce, used clothing, toys, and assorted household goods to barter. A large hand-painted banner read: "Flee Market." At first Beth thought that this was a misspelling, but then she realized that it was intentional.

The fairgrounds worked well as a barter venue. There was plenty of room for vendors to camp, and the stable buildings were available for horses. As this was one of the few regions of the country with an intact power utility and an operating refinery, the local economy was surprisingly resilient, and crime was relatively low. There was merely a shortage of new goods to sell. Meanwhile, most other parts of the country barely had functioning economies. And wherever population densities were high, chaos reigned.

The county fairgrounds were also considered a particularly safe place to conduct business, since there was an adjoining sheriff's department substation. The vendors were largely self-policing, and they only rarely had to summon the sheriff's deputies—mostly because of public drunkenness.

When Lars Laine made his first trip to the barter fair, with Reuben Phelps, he was surprised to see one vendor that had two tables full of radio equipment. This included some CB, FRS, GMRS, and MURS-band radios. A large sign read: "Will trade for fresh co-ax wire!" The man behind the tables was a grizzled old retired engineer who lived in a single-wide trailer house out past Cortez. He was displaying some "J-pole" antennas that he had constructed with PVC pipe and scrap wire. He had them already tuned for various bands. Lars asked him about how to mount the antennas.

The man answered: "If you want to talk to everybody, then you mount them vertically. But if you want to have your own private little network, then you mount them horizontally. Most people don't think about that, but when you use a CB antenna with horizontal polarization, it can attenuate signals transmitted by a vertical antenna by 20 decibels. Every 3 decibels of attenuation cuts the signal by one half, so that would be one sixty-fourth or slightly less signal power! That means very low probability of intercept by anyone outside of your private group that uses a horizontal antenna network."

Lars was impressed with the old man's knowledge. He nodded and said, "That's brilliant. Where do you get all this gear?"

"Oh, I go around to the little towns and ranches that are outside of the utility power grid. Out there, most folks got no juice, so they think of all these old radios as junk. I trade them gasoline, or corn, or charged car batteries for a lot of this."

With "ballistic wampum"—two hundred rounds of .22 Long Rifle ammo—Lars bought a pair of the J-pole antennas trimmed for the citizens band. Later that same day he and Reuben mounted them on the house—one vertically and one horizontally—so that with an antenna co-ax switch he could select them, at will.

Prescott, Arizona
September, the Third Year

News came to Prescott via the Arizona CB radio relay network that the La Fuerza looter army was about to attack Wickenburg. Ian Doyle volunteered to recon the situation, flying his Star Streak. Just as with several other recon flights in the past few years, assembling, fueling, and preflight checking the plane took less than an hour. They rolled the Laron out to the street, and Blanca gave Ian a hug. Despite the gasoline's age, the engine started easily. Ian taxied over to the street where he had first landed nearly four years before. It felt good to be back in the air. After several months of being ground-bound, it gave Doyle a rush to feel the sensation of speed and flight.

Flying to Wickenburg took only twenty-five minutes, which made the looters seem uncomfortably close to Prescott. Doyle first made a low pass over the Wickenburg Airport, just west of town. It appeared abandoned. There were four semi truck trailers parked perpendicular across the main runway at wide intervals. That looked very odd to Ian.

Still at low altitude, he approached the town from the west. Ian could see La Fuerza swarming through the town of Wickenburg en masse. He had heard on the CB that he would be seeing many houses that were already abandoned by their owners, who fled after hearing that the looters were coming.

Ian circled the town watching the calamitous events unfold beneath him. Several houses were on fire. The looters moved from house to house, taking anything of value. Ian held the stick with one hand and a pair of binoculars with the other. He did his best to tally and categorize the looters' vehicles. He was sickened to see women and girls dragged out of houses, kicking and thrashing, only to be beaten, stripped naked, and raped. He felt powerless to stop what he saw.

As he turned northwest on his third low orbit of the town, he was startled to see several tracer bullets flash up past his left wing. Suddenly he no longer felt like just a detached observer. Recognizing his peril, he stomped on the plane's right rudder pedal, throttled up, and climbed to higher altitude. He departed westward, intentionally choosing a long, circuitous route back to Prescott, to conceal his point of origin.

When he landed at Conley Ranches, his neighbors came running. He gave them a quick summary of what he'd seen and then a dire warning: "We need to get ready, folks. There's a world of hurt coming our way!"

Ian was thankful that they found no bullet holes in the Laron when they disassembled it.

35

Cut to Size, File to Fit, and Paint to Match

*"I fully understand the primary function of guns in the human con-
dition: to protect oneself against the aggression of others. If other
people are going to use them for the purpose of aggression, why,
that's all the more reason for me to own one (or in my case, considerably more than one)."*

—Kim du Toit

Many years before the Crunch, Ian Doyle was a college senior,
majoring in business at the University of Chicago. He was enrolled
in the Air Force ROTC program. One day at the cafeteria, as he
ate lunch with his friend Todd Gray, Doyle was introduced to Dan
Fong, a freshman who was majoring in industrial engineering.
Gray mentioned that Ian and Dan shared a common interest in
guns. So it wasn't long before Ian and Dan became shooting buddies. They took frequent trips to local gun ranges, both indoors
and outdoors.

Although he did a surprising amount of surreptitious gun-
smithing in the Industrial Arts Building's metal shop, Fong lacked
a workshop where he could work on guns with any expectation of
privacy. It was 215 miles from Doyle's home in Plymouth, Michigan, to Chicago, so other than on some occasional weekends spent
at home, Doyle was also without a private workshop.

Their need for workshop space was solved by Todd Gray. Todd's father had owned three hardware stores. Just a year after Phil Gray retired, he died of a heart attack. This was when Todd was a college sophomore. Phil Gray left behind a wonderfully equipped home carpentry and machine shop in a detached garage that sat behind the Grays' house. Most of the equipment was later willed to Phil's brother (Todd's uncle Pete). But while Todd was in college the shop sat idle and available for Todd to use. His father had amassed a large assortment of shop equipment, including a Unimat lathe, a small Bridgeport milling machine, a band saw, a radial arm saw, a power jigsaw, and a huge assortment of hand tools.

One evening Ian was invited to a pizza feed at Dan Fong's dorm room. Also there were Todd Gray, and his roommate Tom "T.K." Kennedy. After hearing about the shop, Doyle asked, "Have you got a welding rig?"

"Actually, I've got three: A basic oxyacetylene with small tanks, a 220-volt arc welder, and a wire-feed." He took a bite of pizza and added, "But I'm not very good with them."

"Well, *I'm* a welder!" Dan declared. "When I was in high school I spent half my time in the metal shop, faaab-ricating! Mostly it was various Rube Goldberg contraptions and even some metal sculptures. I'm pretty good with a torch. So if you don't mind, we'd like to come over for a Saturday or two—"

Doyle interrupted: "Or maybe three or four."

Fong continued: "—and do a couple of welding projects that the BAT-Fags wouldn't approve of, like . . ."

Todd grinned, but T.K. clamped his palms over his own ears, and half shouted in his Sergeant Schultz voice, "I know *noth*-think. I hear *noth*-think!" After a pause, in which he gave the others a stern look, T.K. said, "Look, what you choose to do is up to you guys. But I don't want to *know* what you are doing, understand? It's better that way. You guys can go and play 'Mad Scientist Takes Up Welding,' but count me out."

Ian soon rented a private mailbox at a Ship-It store on the west side of Chicago, using the name of Ian's cousin, who had died of a congenital heart defect at just two months of age. When he was seventeen years old, Ian had stumbled upon the dead boy's birth certificate, after having been asked to shred some of his mother's old papers. Since the deceased cousin was born three years earlier than Ian, Doyle's plan had been to have a fake ID so that he could buy beer before he turned twenty-one. But eventually it was just used for buying machine gun parts sub rosa.

The owner of the Ship-It shop was a shady character. In exchange for an extra thirty-dollar "processing fee," he didn't ask for anything more than the birth certificate and a dance club photo ID as proof of the identity of "Randall Stallings."

Their first project was a World War II–vintage Sten Mk II submachinegun. These 9mm SMGs had a very simple design using a tubular steel receiver. Parts sets for the guns (sans receiver) were cheap and plentiful. Finding several ads in the *Shotgun News*, Ian bought a "hand select" parts set for $220. From another vendor, he bought a 4130 steel receiver tube blank that already had a cutting template glued on. The magazines came from a third vendor who sold used but serviceable (and very greasy) thirty-two-round magazines for just $9 each. Doyle also bought just one scarce forty-round magazine, which cost $40 just by itself. All of these mail orders were paid for with U.S. Postal Service money orders that Doyle paid for with cash.

When the greasy parts set arrived, Fong was a bit disappointed by its condition. Several of the parts had rust pitting, and Fong pointed out that the stock extension was slightly dented, so it wouldn't fit on the receiver tube blank. Ian laughed and said, "Don't sweat it, Dan! We'll just cut to size, file to fit, and paint to match. It'll be easy!" Assembly did indeed turn out to be fairly simple. Aside from a touch-up weld and final finish, the Sten was built in just one weekend.

Their next project was more ambitious: an Ingram M10 sub-machinegun. Like the Sten, its parts set came from an ad found in the *Shotgun News*. The frame came to them in three pieces, to get around a recent BATFE ruling. The two side pieces of the frame came from one vendor, while the middle piece came from another dealer who advertised this as "The Missing Link!" After they spent an hour building a jig block to ensure that the pieces would be held at precise 90-degree angles, welding the three pieces together took just a few minutes.

Welding together the frame and assembling the M10 took the trio just one day. The time-consuming part was making the parts for the sound suppressor that attached to the M10's factory-cut muzzle threads. The suppressor was a clone of the famed Sionics brand, which was codeveloped with the Ingram SMG in the 1960s. The suppressor project took several weekends.

Dan and Ian started with a set of Sionics machining diagrams that they found advertised in *Gun List*. Ian was able to buy seamless aluminum tubing stock from a local vendor. The same company provided some aluminum bar stock that would be drilled and lathe-turned for the internal spirals. Fong botched cutting the threads on the first two tubes, but the later ones turned out nicely. Luckily, they had plenty of extra tubing stock, so they didn't need to make a second purchase.

The final touches in the welding and painting of the two guns were done in Michigan. This was because Todd's mother objected to the smell when her kitchen oven was used to cure the Alvin high-temperature engine paint that was used on many of the gun parts. Over a three-day weekend, Todd, Ian, and "the Fongman" took a road trip to Plymouth, Michigan, and worked in the garage at the home of Doyle's parents, who at the time were away on vacation. When he had been invited to join them, Tom Kennedy declined, declaring: "I don't know what your fascination with full-auto is! I can squeeze my trigger finger pretty fast, and *that's* not a felony."

The last-minute welding work in Michigan included attaching the front strap hanger for the Ingram and touching up the trigger-guard welds on the Sten, which Fong had declared "imperfect." For this they used Gray's portable oxyacetylene torch, which they brought along on the Michigan trip. This was the first time that Todd ever helped Ian and Dan do any of the welding. The paint curing was done in the oven of the Doyles' "summer kitchen" fruit-canning range, which sat in the screened back porch. The welding and painting weekend in Michigan turned into an extended pizza and root beer party for the trio.

Later that school year, Dan and Ian drove to the Upper Peninsula of Michigan to test their two new toys. They did so at Porcupine Mountains Wilderness State Park on a rainy weekend. Hiking deep into the forest for two hours on deserted trails across patchy snow assured them privacy for test-firing the guns. First they fired the M10 using special subsonic-velocity ammo. With suppressor attached, each shot sounded like little more than a hand clap. They fired just sixty rounds through it, mostly with the SMG's selector switch turned to the semiautomatic position.

After stowing the Ingram and its magazines in Ian's backpack, they got out the Sten gun. Because the Sten was not suppressed, they fired just twenty rounds through it. The first eighteen rounds were loaded into magazines with just one cartridge per magazine, to test to see if they were stripped out of the magazine properly when the bolt slammed forward. Like the Ingram, the M10 fed flawlessly. Finally they reloaded two magazines with three rounds each. These Dan shot in two quick bursts. The gun functioned as expected. They then pulled the stock off the Sten and re-stowed it in Dan's backpack. They didn't stop grinning for hours.

Originally the completed Sten was going to belong to Fong, while the M10 would be owned by Doyle. But after their test, Fong got cold feet and claimed that he didn't have a secure place to store an unregistered Class 3 gun. He asked Ian to buy him out of the Sten project. Doyle, who had a more cavalier attitude about legalities, was happy to do so. He hid the guns and their accessories in a wall cache in his parents' basement.

Eventually, Ian bought a spare barrel for the Sten that had a threaded muzzle. He and Fong then spent another two Saturdays in the Grays' shop, completing a 9mm suppressor that was almost identical to the "can" that they had built for the Ingram.

The two guns and their accessories were stored for most of the next fifteen years in the wall cache, sitting well oiled in plastic bags, each of which also contained a large packet of silica gel desiccant. All this time, Ian's parents were oblivious to their presence.

Three years before the Crunch, Ian had a permanent change of station (PCS) back to Luke AFB. Just after that move, he took Blanca and their daughter, Linda, on a two-week driving trip to visit relatives in Wisconsin and Michigan. While in Plymouth, he retrieved the submachineguns, bringing them home in tape-sealed boxes marked "Books." Once back in Arizona, he more extensively test-fired the guns out on a section of BLM land north of the old copper-mining town of Ajo. He put nearly three hundred rounds through the guns, with just one jam on the Sten, which he traced to a dented magazine feed lip. Not wanting to risk another jam, he buried that magazine at his impromptu shooting range. He spent the next day at home, cleaning and lubricating the guns and suppressors, and painting all of the magazines to match the guns. He stowed them in a pair of military surplus 20mm ammo cans and buried them under the crawl space of the rental house.

36

Emboscada

"If you're not shootin', you should be loadin'. If you're not loadin', you should be movin'. If you're not movin', someone's gonna cut your head off and put it on a stick."
—Clint Smith, director of the Thunder Ranch shooting school

Marathon, Texas
September, the Third Year

Andy's journey through Texas and New Mexico went by in a blur. He often pushed Prieto fifty miles in a day. His stops were predicated upon increasingly infrequent sources of feed and water as he progressed into desert country. When riding in open country near Marathon, Texas, Andy saw a group of five men who were standing around two pickup trucks parked on the shoulder of the highway. Since there were no houses nearby, it seemed an odd place for them to be stopped. He didn't like the feel of the situation. It smelled like an ambush. At a distance of eighty yards, he yanked the reins to the left and reinforced his intent by leaning leftward and applying pressure from his knee to urge Prieto into a tight turn, yelling, *"¡Ándale!"* His horse responded by breaking into a full gallop. Glancing over his shoulder, Andy could see one of the men raise a handgun, and two others shouldered M4 carbines.

The situation didn't look good. There were just a few undulations in the ground—very little to provide good cover. Andy jabbed with his boot heels and alternated jerks on the reins, putting Prieto into some rapid serpentine turns. He could see a small rise about sixty yards ahead. It was no more than three or four feet high. There was no other cover in any direction. Andy grunted to himself, "This'll have to do!"

He heard the crack of a rifle, followed by the distinctive snap of a bullet going past his ear. As he topped the rise, there was a tug at his sleeve as a bullet passed through. Andy reined Prieto to a halt at the base of the hill, which was thirty yards wide. He did his best to pommel off the saddle, even before Prieto came to a full halt in a cloud of dust. As he hit the ground, the AK jabbed painfully into his chest. There were several more rapid shots.

As he had practiced several times before, Laine ordered the horse down with a shout of *"¡Bájate!"* and a firm tug downward on the reins. Prieto obediently knelt and rolled to the ground. Andy was startled to see one of the reins hanging loose in his hand; it had been shot in half. He dropped to the ground, holding the remaining rein, and tugged Prieto's nose to the ground. The horse obligingly stayed on its side. The horse was still breathing hard and its nostrils were flaring. Andy lost sight of the men on the other side of the rise, but could still hear shots and bullets flying overhead. He extended the stock of the AK and flipped down its safety to the middle position. He crept slowly forward, low-crawling up the reverse slope of the rise. Once he could just see the tops of the men's heads and the roofs of the pickup trucks, he lay prone and shouldered the rifle. He could hear Prieto's heavy breaths behind him and hoped that the horse had the sense to remain prone. Laine took careful aim at a man armed with a rifle. He estimated the range was about 220 yards. He fought to control his breathing, paused, and slowly squeezed the trigger. The AK's wire stock bucked against his shoulder. The man that he had aimed at went down hard. Seconds later the others also dropped to the ground, out of sight. Andy cradled the AK in his arms and slithered backward down the hillock. He crawled over to Prieto and whispered reassuring words. He took a moment to wrap the remaining rein twice around a large flat rock that was size of a bread loaf. Rubbing the horse's chin consolingly, he said, "Stay down—*quédate abajo, Prieto.*"

He high-crawled five yards to his left and again crawled forward to near the crest of the hillock. He could see the pickups but could not see his attackers, who were concealed by some low scrub brush. Andy fired six times, aiming at the side and rear windows of the pickup trucks, doing his best to put the fear of God into the bandits. The windows disintegrated in showers of tempered glass chunks. Andy again backed off the hillock and swapped magazines, inserting a full one. Then he crawled behind Prieto ten yards to his right before gradually working his way back to near the crest of the hillock. He again found that he couldn't see any of the bandits. There was no more shooting coming from them. He scanned intently. Then he spotted one of the men, armed with a pistol, crawling toward one of the pickups. Taking a deliberate aim, he shot the man twice through the chest.

He could indistinct shouts from the men in the distance. Then, more clearly, he heard, "*¡Ahora o nunca!*" Andy echoed in a whisper, "That's right, it's now or never, and it's you or me. This, boys and girls, is where we divide the quick from the dead." Andy heard one of the pickup doors slam—on the far side. He caught a glimpse of someone dashing toward the other truck and fired three rounds rapidly before the man disappeared behind the pickup. He heard another truck door slam but couldn't be sure which one. He could hear the engines being started. Andy began firing in a rapid tempo, concentrating on the driver's-side doors of the pickups. The two pickup trucks lurched forward, kicking up dust, and they drove away quickly. He fired six more shots in rapid fire at the back windows of the pickups. He stopped shooting when they were four hundred yards away. In his excitement, he shouted, "Concealment is *not* cover, you dumb mothers!"

Andy crept back down the hill to assess his situation. He again switched the AK's magazine, then checked himself and the horse for injuries. All that he found was a hole in the right sleeve of his shirt and the severed rein. He muttered, "Thank you, Lord."

Andy again reassured the horse, patting his neck and repeating, "Superhorse. *Excelente caballo.* Superhorse." He decided it was best to wait, just in case the bandits hadn't all gotten away or the one that he'd shot had not yet bled out. After twenty minutes he pulled his binoculars out of his saddlebags, crept to the top of the hill once more, and spent a half hour with the binoculars, scanning the area where the trucks had been parked. He could see two bodies, one faceup and one facedown. Andy rose to a crouch and walked back to Prieto. He unwrapped the rein from around the rock. Without any urging, the horse stood up and shook off some dust. He led the horse fifty yards farther away to a substantial mesquite bush and tied on the rein.

Laine turned and walked in a wide semicircle, stopping frequently to look through the binoculars. He paused at seventy-five yards, knelt, and shot the two men once more each, both in the head. He then cautiously approached the bodies. He found that they were both black-haired Mexicans in their twenties. One of them wore a fancy black silk shirt and black jeans. The other was in faded blue jeans and a plaid shirt. A Browning Hi-Power pistol lay on the ground next to the hand of the one in the black shirt. There was no gun near the other body, but there were at least eight pieces of fired 5.56mm brass. It was obvious that one of his partners had taken the fallen man's M4.

Andy carefully examined where the trucks had been parked. There was a lot of blood on the ground, and chunks of broken grass. Then he walked back and more closely examined the two bodies, rolling them over and patting them down. All that he found in their pockets were a loaded thirty-round M16 magazine, two loaded Hi-Power magazines, and a Chinese pocketknife with a broken tip.

Andy pocketed the magazines and then picked up the Hi-Power pistol. He found that there were only three cartridges left in the magazine. He reloaded the gun with one of the full magazines and thumbed up its safety lever. Returning to the horse, he put his binoculars, the captured pistol, and the extra magazines in his saddlebag. He took a minute to redistribute the ammunition and magazines, putting a full magazine in the AK and three full magazines back into his belt pouch.

Before he left, he searched the ground behind the hillock and found the three-foot length of horse rein that had been shot off. He tied it on, rejoining the break with a square knot. "I'll have to stitch that," he said to himself. His throat felt parched, and he took a long draw of water from his canteen, taking down nearly half a quart. Finally, he eased himself up into the saddle.

He turned to ride south on the pavement for a half mile, then cut northeast across the desert. His plan was to take a wide roundabout, just in case the bandits were waiting in ambush farther north on the highway. This wide detour cost Andy a full day of riding.

After the excitement near Marathon, the rest of Andy's ride seemed mundane. Many of the locals were wary. They talked a lot about recent Mexican gang attacks and desperate looters from El Paso. "Watch out for the *narcotraficantes*," they warned. Only a few people were willing to trade silver for food. One man even wanted to charge Andy just for letting his horse use his watering trough. Clearly, West Texas was not the land of plenty. But near Valentine, Texas, Andy was able to trade the captured full M16 magazine for nearly a week's worth of food that included some ground cornmeal fried into bread balls, called dodgers. It was the first time that he'd ever seen or eaten them, but he had heard Kaylee talk about them.

before their journey. As he saddled the horse, he promised: "Just a few hours, and you'll be in alfalfa hay up to your eyeballs, buddy."

Too anxious to eat much breakfast, he munched on an apple and some Indian fry bread as he rode. For the first time in many months, he was self-conscious about dripping on his shirt. Andy declared, "Lord, let this be my last day traveling. Please, Lord, if you so will!"

The guards at the roadblock south of Farmington were satisfied when Andy showed them his surname stamped on his dog tags, and explained that he was the brother of Lars Laine. They seemed impressed to hear that he had ridden his horse all the way from Belize. Andy was surprised to see that the guards at the roadblock had three swivel-mounted muzzle-loading cannons. "Yeah, those are our 'engine block' guns. They shoot standard two-and-three-eighths-inch-diameter pistons. They'll go clean through a car. There are thousands of them that are available used around here, from the natural gas fields. Before the Crunch, you could buy them at just scrap steel prices. They're made out of 4140 stainless steel."

As he approached Bloomfield, Andy realized that it was Sunday morning, and that his brother, Beth, and Kaylee would likely be at church by the time he reached the Refinery Road. So he pressed on to town, turned right at Blanco Road, and urged Prieto from a trot to a canter.

Lars, and Beth, Grace, Kaylee, and Shadrach were at church, while Reuben and Matthew were at home, guarding the ranch. As Andy rode his horse up to Berea Baptist, he could hear the congregation singing. He tied up his horse, unstrapped his pack from his saddle, and set it inside the church foyer. With his AK slung muzzle down, he slipped into the sanctuary. His hands were shaking with excitement.

The congregation was singing "Eternal Father, Strong to Save." Demonstrating his flair for drama, Andy slipped in on Lars's blind side unnoticed and stood behind him. Lars and Shadrach were in the second-to-last row of pews. Beth and Kaylee were one row farther forward. They were standing beside Grace and two other eight-year-old girls, holding hymnals for them as they usually did. Just after the hymn ended, Andy tapped his brother on the shoulder and said: "Sorry that I was a little late." Lars gasped and grabbed Andy around his neck. Reaching into his shirt pocket and pulling out a plastic bag, Andy said, "Oh, I got those gas lamp mantles that you asked me to pick up for you on the way home."

Kaylee nearly fainted. The church erupted into a huge commotion, with lots of hugs and back slapping. Shouts of "Praise God!' spread like a wave across the church sanctuary. Even the two ladies in the nursery came out to give Andy a hug. Grace ran up to hug Andy around the waist, exclaiming, "Uncle Andy, we really missed you! You got so brown!"

The sermon, to mark Veterans Day, was in praise of military service and its biblical context. Andy and Kaylee sat holding hands all through it, intently gazing at each other, not paying much attention to the pastor's words. After the closing hymn and benediction, Andy stood up and announced, "I've never been one to waste any time, so I'd like to ask everyone to stay for a brief ceremony." Kaylee put on a huge smile and gave him a hug. Twenty minutes later they were married.

Moreland, Kentucky
December, the Third Year

In parts of the territory controlled by the Provisional Government, the supply of gasoline preceded the restoration of grid power. This was the case in most of western Tennessee and western Kentucky. In what was later seen as a brilliant move, Greg Jarvis, the owner of Apogee Solar, in Moreland, Kentucky, ran an AC power line over rooftops two doors down to the gas station that was owned by his second cousin, Alan Archer. The station was open six hours a day, six days a week, and did a booming business. Before the advent of the ProvGov currency, regular gas was twenty cents a gallon, and both diesel and premium gas were twenty-five cents a gallon. These prices were in silver coin.

A prominent sign hand-painted on a four-by-eight sheet of plywood warned, "Silver coin or ammo only! No paper dollars, checks, debit cards, or credit cards accepted." Archer and Jarvis worked out a credit arrangement with the Catlettsburg refinery. Under the terms of the agreement, they got gas and diesel in bulk at a 25 percent discount, and got their first two tank truck deliveries on credit. After that, they were able to pay in silver, from the proceeds of sales.

Within a few months, Jarvis and Archer launched several other enterprises. The first of these was a store selling packaged petroleum products—nothing larger than five-gallon cans, including kerosene, motor oil, and two-cycle fuel-mixing oil. By agreement, they charged the same prices as offered at the Catlettsburg refinery, but their profit came from buying in bulk at a discount. This store was located in one of the buildings that had "the big dang extension cord" draped over it—between Apogee Solar and the gas station.

The new Jarvis Lubricants store had previously housed a hardware store, but it had been stripped clean because the former owner had imprudently continued to accept payments in greenbacks. In the end he was left with a pile of worthless paper. He sold Jarvis the empty building and the remaining shelving for just two hundred dollars in silver coin. The new store was lit by a pair of 60-watt compact fluorescent lightbulbs. Nobody complained about the dim lighting.

Just as the crash began, Greg Jarvis had used a small-business loan to purchase 212 large REC brand photovoltaic panels at a closeout price. This served as his primary barter stock, through much of the Crunch. After the Crunch set in, he bought up as many deep-cycle batteries as he could find. Most of these came from a forklift company in Frankfort and from the golf cart fleets of two local golf courses. The shipment from Frankfort came by truck, COD, payable in silver. The batteries from the golf course owners were both barter transactions, paid for with compact solar power systems. One of these systems was installed on a golf cart, making the cart into a mobile, self-charging system.

Apogee also harnessed the excess power from their PV array that was not needed for their storefront by charging car and tractor batteries for a fee in their attached shop. This was a profitable business until the grid power was restored.

37

Assets

Andrew Laine was thrilled to be at the ranch with his new bride. After the hardships of the trail, putting in four-hour guard shifts five days per week seemed trivial. After dinner for several nights in succession, Andy described to Lars, Lisbeth, Grace, Kaylee, and the Phelps boys all of his experiences. He started with his time in Afghanistan and then Germany, France, England, sailing on *Durobrabis*, Belize, and his horseback ride through Mexico to Texas and New Mexico. They were captivated and asked him dozens of questions. Andy felt comfortable in answering most of them except for the details about his gunfights. Regarding those, he clammed up and gave them only sketchy descriptions.

During the quiet winter months he made a living by braiding custom rifle slings, belts, and bridles. Once supplies of parachute cord got scarce, he switched to braiding with horsehair. The coarse hair from horses' tails was more time-consuming to work with, but it was attractive, so he found that he could demand more for the finished product. In addition to the regular ranch chores, Andy also made a living the same way that the Phelps boys did: by hiring himself out during hay harvesting time.

Five months after his return, Andy and Kaylee bought a used Ford pickup truck. It was one of the almost countless white pickups that were seen in great numbers, driven by technicians who serviced natural-gas wellhead compressors. These trucks were typically equipped with tall "safety flags" that looked much like those used on dune buggies. The flags came into use in the 1960s, following a couple of spectacular head-on collisions, as pickups topped the rolling hills of the region on narrow, gravel roads. The field reps were notorious for driving fast, and gravel roads are unforgiving. Hundreds of these ubiquitous white pickup trucks sat idle after the Crunch set in. They were one of the key assets still held by the field service and field engineering companies. Only a small percentage of the field reps were still at work, so this left the majority of the trucks essentially surplus.

Andy thought that a field service truck would be the best choice for reliable transportation, since spare parts and tires were abundant. He realized that as the Crunch continued, gas and oil would be sporadically available, but that unless or until tire factories went back into production, tires would eventually become the key commodity. As he put it, "Just wait another four or five years. By then a like-new set of tires will be worth as much as an entire vehicle. Mark my words." He practiced what he preached and soon bought eight spare tires—already on rims and balanced—which he stored in a dark back corner of the barn. He eventually bartered for another complete pickup with a blown engine that was the same model year as their own, just for use as a parts rig. From this they could cannibalize parts and of course five more tires on rims.

Their pickup cost twenty dollars face value in pre-1965 silver coins. Ironically, the flat-tan paint that they needed for camouflaging the truck cost almost as much at the truck itself. Trucks were common, but good camouflaging paint was scarce.

Other than the tan paint, the only significant change that Andy made to the pickup was having it retrofitted with a traditional ignition system and carburetor. These came off a 1977 pickup that used the same Ford engine block. His father had once mentioned his survivalist friends doing this to vehicles for EMP protection, but an added benefit was that once thus equipped, a gasoline engine could run on drip oil, the condensate waste by-product of natural-gas wells. (The light oil or hydrocarbon liquids condensed in a natural gas piping system when the gas is cooled. This was sometimes called natural gasoline, condensation gasoline, or simply "drip.") A mixture of gasoline and drip oil can be burned in most engines. For an engine to run better on pure drip oil, they learned, it was best to retard the timing.

38

Threat Spirals

"Somewhere ahead I expect to see a worldwide panic-scramble for gold as it dawns on the world population that they have been hood-winked by the central banks' creation of so-called paper wealth. No central bank has ever produced a single element of true, sustainable wealth. In their heart of hearts, men know this. Which is why, in experiment after experiment with fiat money, gold has always turned out to be the last man standing."

—Richard Russell

Bradfordsville, Kentucky
December, the Third Year

Sheila Randall was not happy with the advent of the new federal currency. It was produced in such great quantities that inflation set in very rapidly. Her solution was simple: She would continue to take pre-1965 silver coinage in payment, and she still marked all of her prices in silver coin. But on her whiteboard she posted a conversion table for calculating payments in "Fort Knox Dollars." Initially, the multiplier was 10 to 1, but less than a year later it grew to 19 to 1. Everyone knew that that they were being robbed by the currency inflation, but there was nothing that they could do about it.

The old Federal Reserve notes were completely repudiated, but for the sake of convenience, pre-Crunch coinage was accepted at face value to serve as change for the new bills. (It was explained that minting and issuing new coinage would be a logistical nightmare for the fledgling government.) Thus, anyone who held large quantities of the old coinage had cause to celebrate. To "strengthen" the new Fort Knox dollars, the Hutchings government ordered the confiscation of all gold coins, all gold bullion, and any silver bullion bars 10 ounces or larger.

The bullion ban was largely ignored or circumvented, despite a death penalty for disobedience. Countless 100-ounce Engelhard and Johnson Matthey silver bars were band saw cut into ten pieces to get around the 10 ounce limit. Meanwhile, the total ban on private gold holdings helped contribute to the market value of silver rising in relation to gold, to the point where it took just 12 ounces of silver to buy 1 ounce of gold.

Much of the privately held gold bullion in the country was cast into rings. These were not intended to be worn, and in fact they were too soft to be worn regularly, since they were 24-karat. These rings were simply a means of avoiding prosecution under the bullion gold ban. Some of these rings were even stamped or engraved with their exact weight. Another substantial quantity of gold bullion was acquired by dentists, who took advantage of an exemption for "dental gold." Much of this gold was traded for dentistry services.

The conversations that Sheila Randall had with her customers, and those that she overheard, began to take on an ominous tone. People began talking about the corruption, nepotism, and uneven justice dispensed by the Provisional Government. They soon spoke of putting up some sort of resistance to Maynard Hutchings and his cronies. Often they couldn't articulate exactly how they might resist the government, but their voices became more and more strident as time went on. Gradually, it became clear that the Hutchings government would never restore the freedom and prosperity that they had been accustomed to before the Crunch. Sheila wondered: If people were being this vocal and this strident in public, then what must they be saying in the privacy of their homes? In a conversation with Deputy Dustin Hodges, Sheila asked, "What do you think will happen?"

"Well, I think there's a civil *war* coming," he answered gravely.

After a long pause, he added: "It's pretty clear there's no way that Hutchings and his camp followers are going to somehow magically reform themselves into an honest and law-abiding government all by themselves. They're gonna need at least a push of some sort, and I have a feeling it'll be a stout *shove*. And as for the 'peacekeeping troops' from the UN, there's just more and more of them every day, right? I don't see any solution except kicking them out of the country, because they're going to continue to throw their weight around and make our lives miserable. They're not here to restore order or to hand out charity. They're just here to take and take and *take*."

"So what are we going to do?" Sheila asked.

Hodges sighed. After another long pause, he answered, "We just keep our heads down and we pick our fights. If we come out slugging too soon, or fight them on their terms, then we're going to get creamed. But if we pick the time and the place, then we can do some considerable damage and they won't know what hit them."

39

Whirlwind

"You are as much serving God in looking after your own children, training them up in God's fear, minding the house, and making your household a church for God as you would be if you had been called to lead an army to battle for the Lord of hosts."

—Charles Spurgeon

The hundreds of thousands of Americans who were abroad when the Crunch began found themselves in a very difficult position. Those who were missionaries and tourists were largely forced to hunker down wherever they happened to be. With most airline and ship traffic halted, only a resourceful few, like Andrew Laine, were able to return to the U.S., in the first few years. Most of those who were stranded in non-English-speaking nations were quickly impoverished, and many died. American servicemen deployed overseas didn't fare much better. Hot spots like Afghanistan and Bosnia (where there was renewed fighting between Christians and Muslims after the Crunch) became untenable death traps for U.S. troops. Cut off from logistical support, they fought on bravely, but eventually their casualties mounted to the point where the units lost integrity.

A few soldiers were able to extract themselves with escape and evasion tactics, but most died from starvation, exposure, illness, wounds, or execution after being captured. Half of the entire U.S.

Marine Corps—heavily deployed in Afghanistan—was written off in this manner. The Maynard Hutchings government gave lip service to repatriating its stranded soldiers, sailors, and airmen, but in actuality it mostly did nothing.

There were a few notable exceptions. A contingent of U.S. Air Force technicians working at the solid-state phased-array radar system (SSPARS) at Clear Air Force Station, Alaska, survived two winters of isolation, eating mostly moose and bear meat. After a spring breakup, they loaded up in a mixture of military and civilian vehicles and convoyed to Fairbanks, Alaska. There they found that there was virtually no fuel available and the local populace was starving. With no other alternative, and joined by 372 residents of the Tanana Valley, they marched more than 1,500 miles to Lynden, Washington. What they dubbed "Colonel Haskins' Hike for Health" took seven months.

Humboldt, Arizona
May, the Fourth Year

La Fuerza ripped into Humboldt, Arizona, like a can opener. They had been in the looting business for so long that they were experts. They knew just how to approach various sorts of houses and businesses. Over time they had learned when to push hard, and when to wait, and how to expertly threaten and intimidate. The size of their force and their warnings via vehicle-mounted bullhorns made most residents panic and flee. They had also gained enough experience through hard knocks to know that when there was a certain threshold of resistance, it was best just to torch a place and consider it a loss. But they never just bypassed a house when there was heavy resistance. That would be a sign of weakness.

The contiguous towns of Humboldt and Dewey were easy targets. The houses were so spread out that they could be taken piecemeal. There was no planned resistance, so individual houses could be taken down sequentially, with little fear of being sniped at from behind. The loot was decent, but in recent months it was getting more and more difficult to find fuel. There were rumors that there was fresh gasoline and diesel being made in the Four Corners. Ignacio Garcia planned to move his force in that direction. His plan was to just pick away at the periphery to get fresh fuel, but not take on the owners of the refinery yet. There would be plenty of time for that.

40

Movement to Contact

"Of every One Hundred men, Ten shouldn't even be there, Eighty are nothing but targets, Nine are real fighters . . . We are lucky to have them . . . They make the battle, Ah, but the One, One of them is a Warrior . . . and He will bring the others back."

—Heraclitus (circa 500 B.C.)

A low rumbling sound came to Beth's ears. She looked up from her washboard. It was wash day, and as usual she was doing her laundry scrubbing on the front porch. That way she could dump the gray water directly on her flower beds. The sound was coming from the west. A moment later she identified it: a motorcycle engine. It sounded out of place on Road 4990, which for the past two years mainly had horse traffic. Even though the refinery was just a few miles down the road, gasoline was so precious that it was used very sparingly.

Beth was surprised to see the motorcycle slow down and come to a stop at their front gate. She jumped up and grabbed her M2 Carbine, which was leaning against the door frame behind her. She held the gun at low ready, the way Lars had taught her. The butt-plate was tucked into the pocket of her shoulder—a pocket that hadn't existed just a few months before. Beth had lost nearly 20 pounds since the Crunch began. The austere diet and vigorous outdoor work had quickly brought her weight down to 125 pounds.

With a shout, Beth summoned Lars. He accompanied her to the gate. They approached the county road cautiously. Lars carried his Valmet M62 and Beth had her carbine, both at low ready.

When they were twenty yards from the gate, the man shouted: "Mr. Martin would like to see you, sir, as soon as possible. He said it's important."

Lars answered: "Understood."

The man revved the bike's engine, turned in a tight circle, and drove back toward the refinery. Lisbeth and Lars gave each other curious looks.

Lars arrived at Martin's refinery just twenty minutes later. He was impressed to see that their security had not slackened in the three years since the Crunch began.

Seated in his office, L. Roy said, "Thanks for coming, Lars."

Martin paused, looking a bit anxious, and said, "You once mentioned that you're Finnish, but your given name is Lars. That's Norwegian, right?"

"Well, my dad was full-blooded Finnish, and my mom was mostly Swedish: her maiden name was Bårdgård. So that's why I ended up with a Swedish given name and a Finnish surname.

Martin replied, "Oh, I see. I've heard that the Finnish language is something unique, isn't that right?"

"Yeah. The Finns are sorta the black sheep of Scandinavia. The language is completely different from Swedish, Norwegian, Icelandic, or Danish. It's what is called a 'Finno-Ugric' language. The languages closest to it are Estonian and Hungarian. That's because—though they don't like to admit it—the Finns are actually the descendants of the Mongol Hordes. So it's no wonder that the rest of Scandinavia doesn't know how to relate to the Finns. It's like you're living in the suburbs, and then the Genghis Khan family moves in next door. That was about nine centuries back."

Laine paused, and then added: "Your man said you had something important to discuss."

Martin nodded. "Yes. I had a conversation on the forty-meter ham band with a gent in Prescott, Arizona. He said he had a crucial security concern to discuss. Then he made a very unusual request. He asked if we had anyone here that spoke Navajo. I said yes, and just a few minutes later I put one of my Navajo employees on the radio. Then his man and my man started yammering back and forth—you know, like the code talkers that were used back in World War Two."

Laine nodded.

"Okay, so after the translation was done, here was their message in a nutshell: They said that the big La Fuerza looter gang we've been hearing all those rumors about is headed toward Prescott. It's supposedly now more than two hundred men strong, and they have somewhere around fifty vehicles."

Laine let out a whistle.

L. Roy continued: "The folks in Prescott asked us to send help—to assist in whittling them down. There are some combat veterans from Tuba City and from Gallup—mostly Navajos—who already agreed to help, and they'll be heading to Prescott in a couple of days. They asked us to send at least six men. It's a bit risky, but I can see the wisdom of confronting La Fuerza now, before they are in our backyard. To my mind, this is sorta like Bush's War on Terror strategy: 'Go beat them up somewhere else so that we don't have to face them on our own soil.' I'm sure I don't have to tell you, La Fuerza is a bunch of *very* bad dudes. Lower than whale scum."

Lars again nodded and said, "Yeah, I've heard about their track record: brutal, unrestrained, unrepentant."

Martin leaned forward. "I think that it is wise to go out there, and do some attrition, and most importantly to try to take out their armored vehicles. Without those, La Fuerza will lose a lot of their combat effectiveness." He sighed and then continued, "So, through my code talker, I immediately promised to send eight men, three hundred gallons of gasoline, and at least one hundred and fifty Molotov cocktails."

Lars nodded and Martin said, "I need a man to be the team leader for the team representing Bloomfield and Farmington. I estimate that it'll be just a ten-day trip at most. You get in there, you kick some tail, and you get out. You'd need to get the team on the road within three days."

Before Lars Laine could comment, L. Roy continued, "Here's the deal: If you take this job, I'll pay you ten ounces of gold and a transferable, non-expiring credit for five thousand gallons of any fuel we produce here—even kerosene. You'll get five ounces of gold up front and five upon completion, plus the fuel credit. Each of the other men I pick will get about two-thirds of what I'm offering you."

Lars cocked his head and said, "That's a lot of risk for that sort of pay."

"You've got to recognize that it is your own best interest just as much as mine to see this threat removed or reduced. I have no doubt that Bloomfield is pretty high up on their target list. As we've discussed before, my refinery is an obvious plum, an obvious target. You know their modus operandi: if they come here, everyone living inside a thirty-mile radius will be at risk. Maybe even much farther than that. And since we've got gas and oil wells, we face an even bigger risk, which is that they'll come and want to *stay* and make this their home base."

Laine tipped his head and answered, "I concur. But even if we do this and we're successful, there will be a lot of lead flying in both directions. So I'll stand a good chance of assuming room temperature. That would leave my wife a widow, with no means of support."

Martin nodded and offered, "So then let me add this: you have my word of honor that if you or any of our men don't come home from this, or if you're disabled, then I'll quadruple your compensation. You'll have that in writing."

Lars let out a breath and said seriously, "Okay, but just one more thing: if I can help pick the team and *if* I can have the veto on anyone that doesn't seem trustworthy, *then* I'm in."

41

The Team

"Believe in your cause. The stronger your belief, the stronger your motivation and perseverance will be. You must know it in your heart that it is a worthwhile cause and that you are fighting the good fight. Whether it is the need to contribute or the belief in a greater good, for your buddy, for the team or for your country, find a reason that keeps your fire burning. You will need this fire when the times get tough. It will help you through when you are physically exhausted and mentally broken and you can only see far enough to take the next step."

—Master Sergeant Paul R. Howe, U.S. Army (Retired), *Leadership and Training for the Fight: A Few Thoughts on Leadership and Training from a Former Special Operations Soldier*

The next few days were hectic as Lars gathered his team and logistics. First on the list was borrowing a pair of crew cab pickup trucks, both with fifth-wheel-type trailer hitches, a horse trailer for one of them, and a flatbed trailer for the other. The owners gladly loaned them, knowing that they'd be helping to keep a looter army from invading their region. For impromptu camouflage, the trucks and the trailers were all hastily painted flat tan, with a few large irregular blotches in flat brown. This was done at the Garza Auto Collision shop in Aztec. Lars told Honoré Garza to rush the job and specifically not to worry about overspray: "We don't want any sharp lines or any distinct contrast: these have to blend in." Garza took that literally, so there was paint on the edges of the windows, and even the tire sidewalls and license plates were painted tan.

Laine picked seven members, all military veterans, and most of them experienced horse riders. Six of them were ex-Army—including a medic—and one was a former Marine. All had served at least one combat tour in Iraq or Afghanistan and had combat arms specialties.

Four of them—Brian Baugh, Pat Redmond, Chad Stenerson, and Dave Escobar—were refinery employees. The other three were Bob Potts (a friend of the Laines from church), Johanna Visser (a South African–born former Army nurse who had more recently worked as an EMT), and Hector Ruiz (a friend of L. Roy Martin who he'd met through the local Rotary Club). With the exception of Laine, everyone on the team was single or divorced, and most had been E-4s or E-5s when they left the military. Hector Ruiz had been a tank commander and had left the army as an E-7. Ruiz was about Laine's age. Lars had briefly toyed with the idea of including Shadrach Phelps in the team, but given his lack of combat experience he decided against it. He also rejected the idea of his brother Andy going on the mission. In the event that Lars didn't return, someone would have to see after the ranch.

Two of the men had their own horses, and two had loaners. All were geldings or mares picked for good temperaments and dark markings. As Lars put it, "Paint horses need not apply." Lars would ride Reuben's horse, Scrappy, a milk-chocolate-brown gelding that was particularly calm around the sound of gunfire. Aside from a small white blaze between his eyes, Scrappy blended in almost as well as a deer.

Lars would have preferred complete uniformity of equipment, but the exigency of the situation didn't allow them enough time to become familiar with new weapons. Lars and Pat Redmond (also a horseman) both had carbines chambered for 7.62x39mm (the

AK-47 cartridge), while most of the others had .308 rifles—three M1As, a PTR HK91 clone, a DSA FAL clone, and a Saiga .308. The logistical mismatch was Johanna Visser, who carried a Galil 5.56. She had bought it because it was similar to the R4 rifle she had been issued by the SADF before she went to college.

In a perfect world, Lars would have had the squad members all carry rifles with fully interchangeable ammunition and magazines. Instead he put Hector Ruiz and the other two men with M1As together in the "infantry" team along with Bob Potts, who had the Saiga. At least three of them would have the chance to share magazines, and of course Potts could at least use loose .308 ammunition stripped from M1A magazines. It took a bit of begging and bribing, but each man on the team soon had at least eight spare loaded magazines. For his own fighting load, Laine decided to carry eleven spare magazines.

The medic, Johanna, was part of Laine's cavalry team. They called themselves cavalry, but in actuality they'd operate as dragoons, fighting dismounted. Although Scrappy was accustomed to the sound of gunfire, they didn't have time to train the other horses. In essence, the horses were planned as little more than quick getaway vehicles. There was no way to predict how the horses would react to the sight of Molotovs exploding and fusillades of gunfire.

All of the men wore ACU desert digital pattern camouflage fatigues. The ACU pattern was generally disliked, since it looked like a gray blob from a distance. This was the main reason that they had been replaced by the U.S. Army with the multicam OCP uniform. But ACUs did blend in fairly well in sagebrush country, which predominated where they were heading. Also, by all wearing the same uniforms, they'd have the advantage of being able to quickly recognize each other from a distance.

They day after the team was selected, they began training. They started with patrolling formations, carrying unloaded rifles.

At the same time the horsemen practiced moving both mounted and on foot. By the afternoon the squad's movement and hand signals began to look professional, but not as smooth as Laine would have liked. They next practiced ambushes and immediate action drills, such as reacting to an ambush, reacting to ground and aerial flares, and breaking contact.

Their trigger time began the next day at Laine's ranch. Each rifle was meticulously zeroed for its owner. There was also time spent familiarizing each other with the peculiarities of handling all of the weapons, in the event someone had to pick up and use someone else's rifle. Next, Lars passed on a few practical tips about night fighting. One of the most important of these was: "You may not be able to see your sights well. So, if in doubt, *hold low*, since the natural tendency is to shoot high, at night."

Late in the afternoon, they were scheduled to drive to the refinery, to get a briefing and demonstration of the Molotov cocktails Little Ricky had been cooking up. Just after the team arrived, Lopez had them form a semicircle and explained, "If I had a few more days, I could have probably worked up some thermite grenades, but the clock is ticking, so *these* will have to do." He pulled out a mason jar filled with a honeylike substance.

Ricardo Lopez had perfected a flameless design that was much safer to use than traditional "lit-rag" Molotov cocktails. It was based on a design that had been described to him by his great-uncle, who had served as an adviser in Angola in the 1970s. Working in an open area for safety, wearing a respirator and static-grounded boots, Lopez first created a large batch of thickened gasoline. All through this process, an assistant with several fire extinguishers was standing by. Lopez did his thickening in an open-top fifty-five-gallon drum that was half filled with gasoline. This gas had been decanted from the top of a larger drum that had been allowed to settle. The goal was to get pure gasoline with no water.

Lopez and his assistants threw large quantities of foam pellets and scrap Styrofoam from shipping boxes into the drum and then stirred it with a length of broomstick. A surprisingly large quantity of Styrofoam was needed before the gas began to thicken. The stirring continued as more and more Styrofoam was added and quickly dissolved. Gradually the mixture thickened to the desired consistency, about that of molasses. Their end result was about thirty gallons of thickened fuel, which Ricardo dubbed "the Poor Man's Napalm."

Lopez then brought several stacked cases of one-quart mason home-canning jars to his open lab. Wearing gloves and a clear plastic face shield, he opened a carboy of automobile battery acid. He carefully decanted one half cup of the concentrated sulfuric acid into each mason jar and then filled the rest of each with thickened gasoline. They were then sealed with standard mason jar lids and ring. In case any of the acid might have dripped onto the exterior of the jars, they were each rinsed thoroughly, twice, using one of the refinery's portable emergency eye-wash fountains. After they had dried, two large rubber bands were slid onto the middle of each jar.

Back at Building 3, wearing a fresh pair of rubber gloves, Lopez made a saturated solution of potassium chlorate and put it in a broiler pan. He then soaked eleven-inch sheets of printer paper that had been cut into four-inch-wide strips. Then he laid out the strips on the pavement outside of the building, to allow them to completely dry. These were then stored in Ziploc bags. He noted that for safety it was very important to store the chlorated paper and the bottles separately, only attaching them just before use.

After successfully testing a couple of the Molotovs at the Bloomfield plant's "back forty," Ricardo put on a demonstration. "When you are ready for ignition," he explained, "slip a sheet of the chlorate paper under the rubber band. Then you just shake it to mix the sulfuric acid into the gasoline. Since these are dissimilar liquids, the acid won't stay in suspension too long—sorta like your oil-and-vinegar salad dressing. But it just takes *un poquito* droplet of the H_2SO_4 to touch the paper, and you get a flame." Hefting one of the paper-wrapped jars he said, "Like so. . . ." He shook a jar briefly and then lobbed it sixty feet, smashing it on the ground, where it immediately burst into a huge ball of flame and sent a black mushroom cloud skyward. There were shouts, hoots, and applause. Next, using his Vector V-93 clone, Lopez demonstrated how one of the Molotovs could easily be set off at a distance. He missed with his first shot, but the second one resulted in another gratifying ball of flame.

Each of the men on Laine's team was given three dummy Molotovs filled with water and one live one for practice. All of them did well except for Bob Potts, who was below-average height and had a weak throwing arm. He laughed at his inadequate throws and said: "Well, then I'll just have to get up close and personal, won't I?"

Laine's plan was straightforward: "Okay, we'll plan on two Molotovs for each car or truck, and say five or six for each armored vehicle." For commo gear, they used short-range tactical MURS handhelds. They were short on night-vision equipment, but there was no way to round up any more on short notice. Starlight scopes were more precious than gold in the new economy.

They carried 340 gallons of gasoline in five-gallon Scepter cans. The cases of Molotovs were strapped down on the flatbed trailer and covered with a brown canvas tarp. Another eight Scepter cans full of gasoline went into the bed of each pickup.

As a prearranged signal, the out-of-town teams from New Mexico and northeastern Arizona had blue rags hung on their radio antennas and front bumpers, for identification as "friendlies."

The drive west to Prescott was tense but relatively uneventful. It was eerie seeing long stretches of road that were completely deserted. Passing through each town was particularly stressful. There were roadblocks in Shiprock and another at the Tuba City junction, but in both instances clearance had been arranged in advance via HF radio. They were waved through these roadblocks with shouts of "Good luck!" and "Get some!"

42

A Prodigy

"The necessity of procuring good intelligence is apparent and need not be further urged."

—**General George Washington, while commanding the Continental Army, July 26, 1777**

The local volunteers mostly came from Prescott. Alex was disappointed that there were only two men that came from the town of Prescott Valley, which lay north of the highway between Humboldt and Prescott. Everyone met at the Conley Ranches clubhouse.

Cliff Conley did the initial organizing and rabble-rousing, but he soon handed the project off to Doctor K. Cliff opened the meeting, and after some introductions Doctor K. gave the "threat briefing." In just a few minutes, he outlined what they had learned about La Fuerza, their ruthless history, their current location, and their likely next moves. Then he transitioned by saying, "I'd like to turn the next part of the briefing over to a young man who has earned my respect in the past few days. Please meet Jamie Alstoba of the Navajo Nation." Doctor K. gestured with sweep of his arm to the back of the room.

There were loud murmurs in the crowd as a broad-faced boy, just thirteen years old and standing less than five feet tall, strode to the front of the meeting room. He wore scruffy stained blue jeans and a Pendleton shirt. Up until then he had hardly been noticed.

The boy spoke nervously in a high, early-adolescent voice, "Hey. My family, we live in Dewey, on East Antelope Way. The La Fuerza gang locked down the town 24/7, but they are fools and let kids my age and younger walk and ride our bicycles around, without hardly even noticing us. So I got to see exactly what houses they were in, and where they had their pea cups and armored cars parked. My dad sent me on my bike up here to get your help. I was sent to Mr. Conley, and he promised to help, and he sent me back to Dewey and Humboldt, to draw maps, the last two days. We transferred the Humboldt map onto this. . . ."

Doctor K. and Ian Doyle then carried in a large whiteboard from another room and set it on a pair of the meeting room chairs. It was marked "HUMBOLDT—As of 1400, Wednesday." The boy pulled a laser pointer from the back pocket of his jeans, and continued:

"Okay, so here is what I saw: about two-thirds of their gang is in Dewey, and about one-third in Humboldt. I counted four of the bank-type armored cars in Humboldt, and one of the Army-tank-looking ones, except on wheels."

Ian Doyle corrected, "Wheeled APC."

Jamie nodded and, using the laser pointer, said, "Right, APCs. I marked their positions, here, here, here, and a pair of them, here. As you can see, most of those are on East Prescott Street. I'm pretty sure of those positions, but of course they could have moved them since I left. I marked the houses with the gang members in them, in red. There were two houses on fire when I left. I marked those, and the ones that had already burnt down, in solid black. The ones that are just outlines I think are still either cleaned out by the gang, nobody home, or somebody at home but just waiting to see if the gang kicks them out. I marked some hills that you can use for cover to sneak up on the houses and the vehicles: it is what Doctor K. says is called a 'defilade approach.'"

There were murmurs of approval. Lars Laine, sitting in the

middle of the crowd shouted: "We need to get him an appoint-ment to West Point!"

Jamie Alstoba went on, still quite nervous, "Well, sir, before you 'gratulate me, let me tell you about Dewey."

Ian Doyle and Doctor K. carried out a second whiteboard, marked "DEWEY—As of 1400, Wednesday," placing it on an-other pair of chairs to the right of the first whiteboard.

The Navajo boy continued, "I don't have as many exact de-tails for you about Dewey, since the town is so much more spread out than Humboldt. Okay, so I counted seven of the boxy bank armored cars, mostly at the east end of town, parked on the road called Apache Knolls Trail, and three APCs, and those were on Apache Knolls Trail and South Tomahawk Trail, which is, uh, *parallel* to it, just to the west. They also had twenty, maybe thirty pea cups, kinda scattered along Apache Knolls Trail and South Tomahawk Trail, Sugar Leaf Lane, and east Tanya Boulevard. I think they picked that part of town because it has whatcha-call 'commanding high ground.' There's also some nice big houses there where they can party and crash. There are some hills with juniper trees on them behind them, which I think make the La Fuerza guys feel secure, but I think that is the best way to hit them: you sneak in on foot, coming down from those hills. And I noticed that their sentries spend all their time with their binoculars look-ing north and east, toward the highways, not looking behind them at the hills."

Using the laser pointer, Jamie said, "They have machine guns on tripods set up in this house here, and this one *here*. For some reason they don't park the armored cars and APCs in driveways. They keep them in a zigzaggy pattern all along both sides of each road. Doctor K. says that's for 'mutual supporting fire.' And I've got to warn you, they sleep in some of their rigs. Some of their pea cups are in driveways and some along the roads. I didn't see any of their rigs parked in garages or barns or shop buildings, but

I could be wrong. Bottom line is, there is a *boatload* of pea cups, armored cars, and APCs. So what you have in Dewey . . . is what Mr. Doyle calls a 'target-rich environment.'" The room erupted with laughter.

Jamie Alstoba waited for the laughter to die down, and then asked, "Any questions?

"Now, since then they may have looted a few more houses, but mostly for the last three days they seemed fat and happy. It's just party-hearty time. They were pretty deep into *Bizhéé' hólóní*— beer and booze drinkin'—even in the daytime. So if we attack them drunks in the middle of the night, we might catch them in a deep sleep."

In all, fifty-eight men and three women would be going to Dewey and Humboldt for the raid, and a hundred more were involved in gathering the requisite gear and ammunition and upgrading defenses in Prescott.

Lars Laine was asked to explain the plan to set fire to La Fuerza's vehicles. He rose and said, "If we get enough thickened gas burning in, on, or under most vehicles, it'll do the job. We can speed things along by puncturing fuel tanks with rifle fire. Assuming we have to destroy fifty vehicles, we anticipate needing about two hundred Molotovs. And that's the number we brought."

Ian Doyle observed that they had brought a motley assortment of rifles and shotguns. They included everything from World War I–relic Mausers and Springfield 1903s to high-grade bolt-action deer rifles. He was glad to see that nearly half of the volunteers had semiauto battle rifles, including M1As, FALs, HK91s, L1A1s, AK-47 clones, and AR-15s in various configurations. Other than his own Ingram M10, he learned that they had only a few full-auto guns. These included a registered Stenling submachine gun (a Sterling SMG, built on a Sten receiver tube), an unregistered M2 carbine, and two unregistered AR-15 selective-fire conversions. Ian considered handing out a couple of his M16s but then thought better of it, realizing that in untrained hands semiauto rifles would actually be more effective in the assault.

Based on their intelligence, six ten-member squads would attack Dewey and two ten-member squads would attack Humboldt. The attacks would be coordinated to begin at 3:10 a.m., just before moonset. They wanted the skies to be as dark as possible to facilitate their escape following the raid.

Laine realized that many of the people involved had no combat experience. So, for fear of ruining the element of surprise with a negligent discharge, everyone except for the two men with sentry removal responsibilities were instructed to travel with their gun chambers empty until 3:09 a.m.

Ian's sentry removal counterpart in Dewey would be Doug Parker, an Iraq war vet who owned an HK .45 ACP SOCOM pistol with a registered Gemtech suppressor. Parker seemed a bit boisterous, bragging that he'd make "one-shot stops to the ocular window." That worried Ian, especially when Parker admitted that he had no formal handgun training. Parker's small-arms training in the Army had all been with M16s, M4s, and M240Bs. In Iraq he had been on a 4.2-inch mortar crew.

It was decided that the two team leaders for the coordinated attack would be Lars Laine (for Dewey) and Alex Doyle (for Humboldt.)

They used a 60-power spotting scope. To reduce the risk of the sun glinting off the front lens of the scope, they made a foot-long extension tube from scrap cardboard and attached it with strips of olive drab duct tape. Their first vantage point was a long east–west ridge that lay between Humboldt and a mountain called The Anthill. Then they surreptitiously hiked to the military crest of a small hill on Eagle Drive, overlooking the sprawling ranchette developments of Dewey.

Prone in the brush, they had a great view of the closest houses that were occupied by La Fuerza. Lars thought that the full-length fur coats worn by their women looked comical. He noted that both the men and women carried rifles, carbines, or submachine-guns at all times.

The scouting team's observations confirmed what Jamie Alstoba had described. He was also apparently correct about the times that guard shifts changed: six a.m., noon, six p.m., and midnight. Lars mentioned that it was good that they were six-hour shifts: "We want them to be exhausted and not very alert when we hit."

They ran through several rehearsals. The most important one, he stressed, was the "Break Contact Under Fire" drill. He told them, "You'll need to do this and do it *right*, so pay attention."

There were five eleven-member squads, plus two platoon leaders and Blanca, who was designated as the vehicle guard. The Molotovs and ignition papers were distributed evenly among the assault team members. Nearly everyone except the medics carried four Molotov jars each. The jars were carried in backpacks and satchels with sheets of bubble wrap for padding.

Each team member carried enough food and water for two days. "The goal is for you to be able to escape E&E—to get out of La Fuerza's way and safely home. This is a one-shot deal, so use your own best judgment about how and when you get home," Lars explained.

Doctor K. helped Lars conduct the inspections. They made sure that each team member carried a full canteen or hydration pack of water, and that each team had their rifles with loaded magazines but empty chambers. To check for noisy gear, they had each team member jump up and down in place.

Three squads were assigned to hit Dewey and the other two to hit Humboldt. Their approach was slow, circuitous, and cautious. The vehicles had all of their side and taillights covered with duct tape. Their headlights were covered similarly, leaving just half-inch slits exposed. This provided such poor road visibility that they drove toward Dewey at just over a walking pace. The infantry teams parked their vehicles almost a mile north of Dewey. Since they were quieter, the dragoons' horses were tied up only a half mile away east of Dewey, in a brushy draw.

As per their instructions, the team members didn't wrap the special ignition paper around their Molotovs until after they had dismounted from their vehicles and horses.

The two platoons split up just before midnight. They spent more than two hours approaching Humboldt and Dewey at a very slow pace. They sat spread out on line. The platoon leaders walked between their respective squads, pointing out particular vehicles to torch and whispering final instructions. At 2:45 a.m. both Ian Doyle and Doug Parker started their approaches to the two towns.

Parker was able to spot the sentries easily, since they were both smoking cigarettes. Approaching the first sentry from behind, he shot the man in the head from a distance of ten feet. The bullet went through both sides of the guard's cranium and he dropped immediately, hardly making any noise other than the sounds of his arms and legs thrashing and a low gurgling. The pistol had made a sound that was much like a hardback book being dropped on a floor. Parker approached the downed sentry, who was still twitching. Wondering if he should use his knife to slit the man's throat, he instead simply stood on his throat until he lay still.

Parker then walked toward the center of Dewey, to where he knew a second sentry was seated in the passenger seat of an open-top Jeep. The sentry turned toward him and asked, "*Cómo?*" Parker was seven yards away. He raised his HK pistol and pulled the trigger. The bullet grazed the side of the man's head. Wounded, the sentry tumbled out of the Jeep and ran, stumbling. Parker fired twice more but missed. The sentry ran into the nearest house, and the door banged shut.

Because Parker did not have a radio, word of his botched shots did not reach Doctor K. for three minutes. Even though they had lost the element of surprise, he decided to go ahead with the attack as scheduled just two minutes later.

Meanwhile, in Dewey, Ian Doyle had approached the nearest sentry at a normal walking pace. He thought it was best to appear nonchalant. Ian said quietly, *"¡Hola!"* At a distance of less than three paces, the guard realized that he didn't recognize Doyle. But by then it was too late. Ian raised the M10, which was loaded with subsonic ammo. The gun's selector was set to semiautomatic. It coughed twice and bullets hit the sentry in the cheek and forehead. The man's head snapped backward and he dropped into a twitching heap. With the large Sionics suppressor attached, the Ingram didn't make much more noise than a loud hand clap. It didn't even alarm nearby dogs. Ian soon repeated the process with the other two sentry positions that they'd scouted out before. The first was sitting on a Chinese nylon folding camp chair in front of a bank armored car. He never made it out of his chair. The other one was standing on a driveway with his back to Doyle, sipping from a wine bottle. Only this last sentry made any significant noise, when his wine bottle and Romanian AK clattered as they fell on the concrete slab driveway.

Ian glanced at his watch. It was 3:10 a.m. He was pleased that La Fuerza was still oblivious to their presence. He knelt and twisted the M10's cocking handle 90 degrees, putting it in a safe position. Then he replaced the partially expended magazine with a full one from his satchel. Realizing that things would soon get very noisy, he flipped the gun's selector switch to the full-auto position.

The three Humboldt squads crept forward, keeping roughly online. Lars raised a clenched fist, and the signal was passed down the line, signaling a halt. He checked his watch. It was 3:11 a.m. Ian Doyle trotted up to Laine, and whispered, "I got all three guards. I think the gang is still asleep and clueless."

They shook hands and Lars said, "Good job, Ian. You can get back to your squad." Lars waited, watching the nearby houses and frequently glancing down at his wristwatch. At precisely 3:15 a.m. he shouted, "Now!" They all started throwing their Molotovs at the parked vehicles. The firebombs burst into flames, making surprisingly little noise but lots of light. But then the shooting started, and it soon rose in an ear-shattering crescendo. A few of the Molotov jars failed to break, but most of these were soon deliberately broken by rifle fire. Any vehicle that wasn't immediately set ablaze became the recipient of some of the remaining firebombs. There were so many Molotovs exploding that the street was lit up almost like daylight.

After the firebombs were expended, most of the raiders dropped down prone and continued shooting. Lars fired half a magazine from his Valmet M62, aiming carefully at muzzle flashes or movement inside the house windows. The volume of rifle fire from the houses soon surpassed that coming from the raiders. Laine could hear bullets snapping by and felt one bullet catch the brim of his boonie hat, nearly tugging it off his head.

Laine saw a man to his right go down hard. He was kicking and clutching his chest. Lars ran to him and saw that he had been hit twice in the upper abdomen and was gushing blood. The worst of the two wounds was next to his sternum. Laine had seen a wound like that—a "heart hit"—once before, when he was in Iraq. He saw that the man was a member of the infantry team. Two tracer bullets whizzed by, uncomfortably close. Realizing that the man would be dead in moments, Lars dashed away to get out of the line of fire.

After running behind some brush, Lars stopped and knelt down. He leaned his Valmet up against a rock and pulled out a pop flare cylinder that he had earlier removed from its shipping tube. He fumbled with his prosthetic hand, slipping the flare's cap onto its base. He slammed it on the ground. After a bang and a whoosh, a red star cluster flare burst two hundred feet above him. That was the planned signal to withdraw.

Laine snatched up his Valmet and bellowed above the gunfire: "Alphas, cover! Bravos, move!" He deliberately fired the rest of the magazine wherever he saw movement or muzzle flashes in the houses occupied by La Fuerza. A stream of tracer bullets from one of La Fuerza's machine guns went over his head. As he reached the bottom of his magazine, Pat Redmond ran by with his M1A at the high port position, shouting, "Let's get the flock out of here!"

Now Lars shouted, "Bravos, cover! Alphas, move!" He jumped up and trotted to the rear, reloading his rifle as he ran. His rubber hand made reloading cumbersome. He dropped the empty magazine into the dump pouch on his belt, just as he had done in Iraq and Afghanistan.

After traversing fifty feet, he stopped and turned to kneel and aim his rifle. He shouted, "Alphas, cover! Bravos, move!" He fired an entire magazine, shooting roughly once per second at any likely targets. Then he shouted, "Bravos, cover! Alphas, move!" He ran again, reloading as he ran.

In this leapfrogging manner, Laine's dragoon team got over the hill in relative safety. Lars noticed that Hector Ruiz had his rifle slung while all the others had theirs held at high port. They quickly counted off and formed a Ranger file. They jogged two hundred yards over a second hill to their horses. With so much running while carrying a heavy load, Lars was winded by the time he reached Scrappy. The horse was prancing in place, obviously nonplussed by the gunfire and explosions. To his right, he saw that Johanna was looping the sling of her Galil over her saddle horn. Just as he was about to put a foot in the stirrup, Hector Ruiz ran up with his rifle still slung and clutching his left arm to his chest. He grunted, "I gotta little problem here, Johanna."

Hector pulled back the sodden sleeve of his ACU shirt to display a nasty grazing wound that ran up the back of his forearm.

The deep gash was eight inches long and spurting blood at the upper end. Pat Redmond held a red-lens penlight to provide Johanna enough light to see what she was doing as she positioned a Combat Application Tourniquet on Hector's biceps. Then she strapped a large bandage over the wound.

As she worked, Johanna told Ruiz, "Let's ride a couple of miles and then we can stop and I'll staple this up. If we somehow get separated, loosen this CAT tourniquet after twenty minutes. If it starts bleeding a lot, then retighten it as needed. But don't leave it on for more than thirty minutes at a time." She seemed concerned that the bullet had chipped a bone in Hector's elbow.

"We'd better get moving," Laine urged. "I don't want to be here when those bad attitudes come over the hill. That may be in just a couple of minutes."

"Yeah, we better go. I'll be okay," Hector agreed.

Johanna nodded. "I'll keep my horse right behind you, Hector."

Laine's team quickly mounted their horses and rode north. As they rode, they could see the majority of the infantry teams streaming over hills, heading east. Lars felt good, knowing they'd be back at their vehicles and out of the area before daylight.

The two squads that attacked Humboldt didn't fare nearly as well as the Dewey teams. When they threw their Molotovs and started shooting, they were answered with withering return fire. The extent of their casualties did not become apparent until they returned to Prescott.

43

Escape and Evasion

"The moment the idea is admitted into society that property is not as sacred as the law of God, and that there is not a force of law and public justice to protect it, anarchy and tyranny commence. If 'Thou shalt not covet' and 'Thou shalt not steal' were not commandments from Heaven, they must be made inviolable precepts in every society before it can be civilized or made free."

—John Adams, *A Defence of the Constitution of the United States Against the Attacks of M. Turgot* **(1787)**

Blanca's instructions were simple: "Stay with the vehicles. If our trucks get spotted by anyone from La Fuerza before the scheduled kick-off time for the raid, then radio the team leaders and let them know immediately."

She waited, listened, and prayed, clutching her Mini-14 GB. Then she heard shooting and explosions in the distance, right on time. An hour later she heard the teams start to return, crashing through the brush. Ian was with them but Alex was not. In accordance with their plans, all the vehicles departed at 5:30 a.m. Everyone had been warned that if they didn't make it to the parking area by then, they'd be on their own to E&E their way back to Prescott.

Back at the Conley Ranches clubhouse, they had an anxious day of waiting. Stragglers came in, only two of them wounded. At just after five p.m., Ian greeted a man in his fifties who had just arrived. He was carrying two rifles, an M1 Garand in his hands and a Ruger Mini-14 slung across his back. Ian recognized a distinctive camouflage sling on the Mini-14: this rifle belonged to his brother Alex. He asked the man: "Where's Alex?"

Looking glum, the man shook his head slowly from side to side in response. "He got shot bad, through a lung. We couldn't stop the bleeding.

"Did he say anything, before . . . before he died?"

"No, sorry. He was just coughing, and then he died."

Ian's eyes welled up. "Well, thanks for letting me know. You can keep that Ruger," he said.

The man shook Ian's hand and thanked him, and then he turned to go check in formally with Doctor K.

That evening the Four Families began frantically packing up their gear, their clothing, and their meager supply of remaining stored food. Two of the families decided to move to a fairly heavily defended compound in Prescott Valley. They'd take a circuitous route, looping around to avoid La Fuerza's suspected avenue of advance. The other two families, led by Doctor K., had decided to leave the region entirely. They would travel in two RVs and four SUVs. One of the SUVs was Alex's Ford Excursion. This vehicle, along with nearly all of Alex's gear, had been given to Doctor K. by Ian. Ian explained that even if he had wanted it, the cramped space and weight limitations of the two Larons were unforgiving. All that Ian kept from Alex's room was some 5.56mm NATO ammunition and nine Mini-14 magazines. Previously, Alex had explained to Blanca to beware of using anything except original Ruger factory-made magazines in her rifle. "All of the other brands of magazines—the aftermarket ones—are jammamatic junk," he warned.

Doctor K. offered to have Ian and Blanca come with him in his Fleetwood diesel-pusher RV. But without trailers there would be no way to take the Larons. Ian answered him quickly, "Thanks for the offer, but I'd rather stick with what we know best, and that's flying. Let's just wish each other God's speed."

Ian Doyle had already toyed with the idea of paralleling the route that they had planned to take the RVs, leapfrogging from airport to airport. But he concluded that his best chance of finding a truly safe refuge before either running out of fuel or running out of luck was to head to Todd Gray's retreat in north-central Idaho.

Lars had an anxious morning, waiting for his infantry team to arrive. He penned an after-action report and asked to have it delivered to Doctor K. Bob Potts was the last one back, arriving at eleven a.m. He was dripping with sweat. By the time he arrived, the horses were already loaded in trailers and the rest of the team was packed up and ready to go. After some handshakes and a long pull on a canteen, Potts and the others climbed aboard the pickups. There was no ceremony. There was no celebration. They had done what needed to be done, and they were just happy to be heading home. Lars was anxious to be well away from La Fuerza before they had the chance to regroup. Hector's arm was decorated with a new row of thirty-seven surgical staples. He said the arm was painful, but regular doses of pain meds from Johanna Visser made it manageable. Other than Hector's wound, Lars's team got away unscathed.

They drove beyond Flagstaff to Winona the first night and camped just off Twin Arrows Road, east of town. They were all edgy and had difficulty sleeping. Shortly after they left the next morning, they were surprised to see a small herd of elk on a hillside just above the road. They braked to a halt and Chad Stenerson rested his scoped M1A across the hood of the lead pickup. He dropped a cow and a bull in rapid succession. This took six shots. The other elk fled into the nearby timber. In less than an hour the elk that had been shot were gutted and dragged down to the pickups. With all eight members of the team working together, dragging the elk down to the trucks was relatively easy. But it took considerable effort to get them up on the fuel trailer. After that, the rest of the trip home was speedy and trouble-free.

With two of the gold coins that he had earned from the Humboldt raid, Lars bought two 9mm pistols, a Glock 17 and a Glock 19. These used magazines that were largely interchangeable, although the short magazines from the Model 19 would not work in the longer-gripped Model 17. Together, the two pistols came with just five magazines and one holster. He badly wanted some more magazines, but they were a scarce commodity. Few people were willing to part with any extra magazines. As one Navajo vendor explained it to Beth, "In bad times, when people are shootin' at you, what exactly is a *spare* magazine? There's no such thing. You can never have too many. Same thing for ammo."

The only magazines that the Laines often saw regularly offered for sale at the flea market were military-surplus M16 alloy thirty-round magazines, which had been produced in huge numbers. But even those now had ridiculously high asking prices. Seeing the depleted shelves and such high prices on a visit to Zia Sporting Goods in Farmington, Beth commented, "We really should've invested in magazines and ammunition. It would have been a better investment than silver. Lars sighed and replied, "Yeah, you're right. Ammo is practically *worth its weight* in silver, these days, and magazines are a you-name-your-price kind of item."

Lars would have actually preferred to have bought a couple of SIG P226 or P228 pistols to be compatible with Andy's first pistol, but those were much more scarce than Glocks. In the new Age of Deep Schumer, beggars couldn't be choosers. He also realized that his chances of eventually finding spare Glock magazines was much better than finding spare SIG magazines, since Glocks were made in much larger numbers.

44

Ignis

"Vengeance has no foresight."
—Napoleon Bonaparte

Ignacio was furious. He spent the hours before sunrise running from house to house, assessing the damage. He radioed his cousin Simon in Humboldt. Adding Simon's tally, he concluded that every one of La Fuerza's armored vehicles had been destroyed by fire. So were more than half of the pickups and vans. Further, more than half of the gang's loot, ammo, and fuel were gone, destroyed in the fire and explosions. Some twenty-six of his men and three women had been killed. Another fifteen men had been wounded, and of those, three were not likely to live.

Only one of the men who had attacked them had been captured. He lived under torture only long enough to tell them that the raiders had originated from Prescott. Ignacio was whipped up into a genuine frenzy. He ran from truck to truck, screaming *"¡Bastardos! ¡Venganza, venganza! ¡Matenlos a todos!"* ("Bastards! Vengeance, vengeance! Slaughter them all!")

They spent the next day and a half salvaging what they could from the wrecked vehicles, and requisitioning more pickups and vans from all over Humboldt and Dewey. They ended up with an odd assortment. Several were bright colors, but that didn't matter.

They just needed enough to get all of his men to Prescott. He was going there soon, and going for blood.

Two days after the raid, they had stolen enough trucks and vans to have room for everyone to ride. Simon and Tony met with Ignacio Garcia over lunch. Simon asked, "What is the plan of operations?"

Garcia grunted: "We drive to Prescott and we burn it down."

"That's the plan? The entire plan?"

"Here is the entire plan: We go there, and we burn the city to the ground, and we kill everyone. I mean *everyone*, and their children, and their dogs and their chickens and their goats."

Simon nodded gravely. He knew that Ignacio was still extremely angry and that he wouldn't take any advice. So he merely echoed, "Okay, we go to Prescott tomorrow, and we kill them all."

After a pause, Simon added: "I'll have everyone go look for more road flares."

45

Bug-out

"It is an uphill struggle, but I wish that we could distinguish more carefully between freedom and liberty. These conditions are not the same, though they are certainly related. Freedom is the absence of restraint—a physical circumstance. Liberty, on the other hand, is a political situation denoting the lawful capability of the citizen to defend himself and his near and dear without interference from the state. Note that the Declaration of Independence forcibly and particularly establishes the blessings of liberty upon ourselves and our posterity. I like to carry a pocket copy of the Declaration, plus the Constitution, in my travels. It is a good thing to have in hand when discussions arise."

—The late Colonel Jeff Cooper

By Doctor K.'s count only thirty-one members of the raiding party had returned to Prescott by the next evening. And of those, only three had been slightly wounded. He said bluntly, "There's no in-between with high-velocity rifle bullets. Its usually either something minor or you bleed out, deader than disco."

La Fuerza didn't arrive the next day or even the day after.

The towns of Prescott Valley and Prescott were in a state of alarm following the raid. Even though the raid was deemed a success, they had clearly stirred up a hornet's nest. Then they heard on the CB that Prescott Valley had been bypassed and that La Fuerza was heading directly toward Prescott.

Blanca paced the bedroom. She asked Ian: "What do you think will happen? I mean, you burned up most of their vehicles, but you say that you maybe killed just a few of La Fuerza."

"They're going to be out for blood, that's for sure. They have to know that we came from somewhere close by. Worst case is they captured one of our missing in action and they made them talk. That would mean that they'd head straight for Conley Ranches. It will be a total freakin' bloodbath."

Blanca half shouted: "Then we've got to go! At least be 100 percent ready to go, *muy pronto*."

Ian and Blanca soon assembled and fueled their planes. They packed everything aboard that they could, leaving very little room. They waited for an indication that the looter army was heading toward Prescott.

"Maybe we can get up to Idaho. Two of my old college buddies, Dan Fong and Todd Gray, are up there. They're survivalists. You remember me talking about them, right? Dan is a total gun nut. He must have two dozen guns. Todd set up a real survival retreat up there; it's stocked with *years'* worth of stored food, gardening seeds, fuel tanks, the whole works. The Fongman is part of that retreat group. If anybody is still alive and kickin' after the Crunch, it's gotta be them. With our skills, they'll probably take us in."

"*Probably? Maybe?* That isn't a lot to go on."

"Our only other option is about to be overrun. Todd's place in Idaho is the only place I can think of that'll be safe."

As they climbed, they could see below that almost half the buildings in downtown Prescott were ablaze.

Blanca keyed her microphone and said simply: "*Ay, ay, ay.*"

Following a sectional aviation chart, Blanca navigated the pair of Larons to Cedar City, Utah.

The airport was on the northwest side of town, just west of I-15. Upon landing there, they were surprised to find 100LL avgas was being offered for sale at the airport. The FBO operator told Ian that he'd recently taken the gas out of hiding, because word had come that they'd soon get a fresh supply coming from Oklahoma. "I might as well sell off the last 110 gallons of my old gas, since the new stuff is coming in from the Provisional Government," he said.

"What Provisional Government?" Ian asked.

"Fort Knox. Haven't you heard?" the airport manager answered.

"Nothing solid, just some rumors. So that's for real?"

"Sure it is. We're going to have some kinda UN regional administrator. But they've promised us local autonomy."

Ian cocked his head and asked, "What's *that* supposed to mean?"

"We don't know yet, but hey, any government is better than no government."

Ian gave his wife a glance and then commented, "Well, in *my* book, there is only one rightful form of government—a constitutional republic—or I'd rather have *no* government. One of my college professors was a heavy-duty Libertarian. He wore a lapel button that said, 'There's No Government Like *No* Government.'"

Blanca chimed in, "I second that motion!"

In the end, Ian traded an Olin 12-gauge flare gun kit, one hundred rounds of 9mm ball ammunition, and twenty dollars' worth of junk silver for forty-three gallons of gasoline.

The FBO manager let them sleep in a mostly empty hangar, next to their planes.

The next day, grossly overweight, they took an extra long roll and took off. They followed I-15 and occasional GPS fixes to the long paved strip north of Brigham City, Utah. Aside from some bumpy air, the flight was uneventful.

They carried with them a brief letter of introduction from the FBO manager in Cedar City. This was handed to his cousin, who ran the airport at Brigham City.

Their reception there was friendly, but it was obvious that food was in short supply. One of the men at the airport confided that Mormons from all over the country had descended on Utah just as the Crunch set in. "They all had relatives here, so it seemed safe. The problem is that Utah consumes more food than it produces locally. So even though a fair number of families had stocked up, in accordance with the church guidelines, all that stored food is gone by now. People are gardening like crazy, but a lot of places have very limited water. So unless those big Albertson's and Safeway grocery trucks start rolling again soon, there's gonna be starvation here, plain and simple. That's why everyone's so anxious to see the Provisional Government."

Ian and Blanca spent two days in Brigham City. In three separate transactions they bought forty-one gallons of gas. This cost Ian eleven dollars in junk silver, two hundred rounds of 9mm hollow point ammo, a hammer, a pair of snap ring pliers, and a Fluke brand volt-ohm meter. Ian was troubled by the quality of some of the gasoline, which had not been stabilized. There were paraffin streamers visible in it. So he laboriously took all the gasoline and filtered it though a chamois car polishing cloth into a large drum. He then added a bottle of Gold Eagle brand "104+" octane booster and part of a bottle of alcohol. The alcohol, as he explained to Blanca, would absorb any water in the gasoline. They let the gasoline settle overnight. The morning before they departed, Ian pumped it out of the barrel—again through a filter—and filled their various tanks, bladders, and bottles. They left the last two gallons of the gas behind in the bottom of the drum just in case it was water-contaminated.

The next day of flying brought them to Grangeville, Idaho. Seeing the patchwork of fields on the Camas Prairie reassured Ian.

He toggled his mic switch and said: "*Ay, mira, conchita.* This is big time agricultural country. I don't think anybody is starving up there."

The airport sat at the north edge of town. After several inquiries, they were able to barter for just twenty-three gallons of gas. For this, Ian spent their last ten dollars in junk silver and traded another 120 of their 9mm ball cartridges. Again they spent the night in a hangar. Blanca mentioned that their breakfast brought their food supply down to just a couple of days. "You know, Ian, at the rate we are burning through our silver and ammo, we are cutting this little venture pretty close," she warned.

"I know, I know. We just have to pray hard and trust that The Fongman and Todd are still there."

The next day there was foggy weather, but the fog looked thin. They climbed into brilliant sunlight and continued north over the Camas Prairie and then over the Clearwater River Valley to Bovill, Idaho, on the eastern fringe of the Palouse Hills.

Approaching Bovill, they saw that the terrain was rolling and mostly wooded. Low on fuel, their planes were now considerably lighter. There was no airport at Bovill, but they were able to land on Highway 8 just west of town. The hamlet was so small that they just taxied up to the junction of Highway 3. Landing so close to town got everyone's attention. A swarm of children and teenagers ran up to the planes, just after they shut down their engines. In answer to the Doyles' queries a local woman said that she knew Todd and Mary Gray, said that they were safe and well, and explained how to find their ranch house. A few minutes later she brought the Doyles a road map and a Clearwater National Forest map. On the latter she pinpointed the ranch.

The flight to the ranch took only three minutes. Blanca spotted the Quonset-style barn that was opposite the Grays' property. As they circled, they could see a woman armed with a rifle in a large fenced garden behind the house.

Ian thumbed the mic switch for his Icom transceiver and said delightedly, "There it is, Blanca! That's *definitely* Todd's house. It's just the way the Fongman described it."

Eyeing the trees below, Ian judged that the breeze was light. They circled and sequentially touched down on the gravel county road, with Blanca taking one extra orbit. They taxied until Ian's Laron was opposite the Grays' lane and mailbox. As they shut down their engines, Blanca radioed, "I sure hope we'll be welcome here."

Ian touched his mic switch and responded, "I trust that we'll be. We just have to live by faith."

Acknowledgments

Above all else, it takes faith and friends to survive. I've been blessed with a lot of friends, and they have helped to strengthen my faith in Almighty God.

This novel is dedicated to the not-so-fictional Group: Conor, Dave, Hugh, Jeff, Ken, Linda "The Memsahib" (RIP), Mary, Meg, P.K., Roland, and Scott. Keep your powder dry!

My special thanks to my new bride, Avalanche Lily, for her inspiration, encouragement, and diligent editing.

Also, my sincere thanks to the other folks who encouraged me, who contributed technical details, who were used for character sketches, and who helped me substantively in the editing process: Antonio, Azreel, Ben and Angela, Brent F., Chris F., Cope, Daniel C., "The Other Mr. Delta," the staff of FEUS, Grizzly Guy, Ignacio L., Jerry J. in Afghanistan, Johannes K., Keith K., Dr. Mark L., CW3 J.S., Dave M., Michael H., Dean R., "SNO," and Terrie.

Thanks to my editor Emily Bestler at Atria Books for her patience and for her eagle eye.

Also my thanks to J.I.R. for his articulate summary on "haves and have-nots," and to D.S. in Montana, for his valuable input on TBIs.

This novel is about calamitous times. We are reminded:

> Because I have called, and ye refused; I have stretched
> out my hand, and no man regarded; But ye have set

at nought all my counsel, and would none of my reproof: I also will laugh at your calamity; I will mock when your fear cometh; When your fear cometh as desolation, and your destruction cometh as a whirlwind; when distress and anguish cometh upon you. Then shall they call upon me, but I will not answer; they shall seek me early, but they shall not find me: For that they hated knowledge, and did not choose the fear of the LORD: They would none of my counsel: they despised all my reproof. Therefore shall they eat of the fruit of their own way, and be filled with their own devices. For the turning away of the simple shall slay them, and the prosperity of fools shall destroy them. But whoso hearkeneth unto me shall dwell safely, and shall be quiet from fear of evil.

—PROVERBS 1:24–33 (KING JAMES VERSION)

I implore you: Get right with God, and get your Beans, Bullets, and Band-Aids together! Our only certain hope is in Christ Jesus.

James Wesley, Rawles

The Rawles Ranch
July 2011

Glossary

?: Ham radio shorthand for "I'm going to repeat what I just said."

10/22: A semiautomatic .22 rimfire rifle made by Ruger.

1911: See M1911.

73: Ham radio shorthand for "Best regards." Always used singularly. (Not "73s.")

88: Ham radio shorthand for "Hugs and kisses."

9/11: The terrorist attacks of September 11, 2001, which took three thousand American lives.

AAA: American Automobile Association.

ABT: Ham radio shorthand for "about."

ACP: Automatic Colt pistol.

ACU: Army combat uniform. The U.S. Army's "digital" pattern camouflage uniform that replaced the BDU.

AK: Avtomat Kalashnikov. The gas-operated weapons family invented by Mikhail Timofeyevitch Kalashnikov, a Red Army sergeant. AKs are known for their robustness and were made in huge numbers, so that they are ubiquitous in much of Asia and the Third World. The best of the Kalashnikov variants are the Valmets, which were made in Finland; the Galils, which were made in Israel; and the R4s, which are made in South Africa.

AK-47: The early-generation AK carbine with a milled receiver that shoots the intermediate 7.62 x 39mm cartridge. See also: **AKM.**

AK-74: The later-generation AK carbine that shoots the 5.45 x 39mm cartridge.

AKM: "Avtomat Kalashnikova Modernizirovanniy," the later-generation 7.62 x 39 AK with a stamped receiver.

AM: Amplitude modulation.

AO: Area of operations.

AP: Armor-piercing.

APC: Armored personnel carrier.

AR: Automatic rifle. This is the generic term for semiauto variants of the Armalite family of rifles designed by Eugene Stoner (AR-10, AR-15, AR-180, etc.).

AR-7: The .22 LR semiautomatic survival rifle designed by Eugene Stoner. It weighs just two pounds.

AR-10: The 7.62mm NATO predecessor of the M16 rifle, designed by Eugene Stoner. Early AR-10s (mainly Portuguese-, Sudanese-, and Cuban-contract, from the late 1950s and early 1960s) are not to be confused with the present-day semiauto only AR-10 rifles that are more closely interchangeable with parts from the smaller caliber AR-15.

AR-15: The semiauto civilian variants of the U.S. Army M16 rifle.

ASAP: As soon as possible.

ATF: See **BATFE**.

AUG: See **Steyr AUG**.

B&E: Breaking and entering.

Ballistic wampum: Ammunition stored for barter purposes. (Term coined by Colonel Jeff Cooper.)

BATFE: Bureau of Alcohol, Tobacco, Firearms, and Explosives, a U.S. federal government taxing agency.

BBC: British Broadcasting Corporation.

BDU: Battle dress uniform. Also called "camouflage utilities" by the U.S. Marine Corps.

BK: Ham radio shorthand for "Break," this means "Back to you," with no need to use call signs.

Black rifle/black gun: Generic terms for a modern battle rifle, typically equipped with a black plastic stock and fore-end, giving these guns an "all-black" appearance. Functionally, however, they are little different from earlier semiauto designs.

BLM: Bureau of Land Management, a U.S. federal government agency that administers public lands.

BMG: Browning machine gun. Usually refers to .50 BMG, the U.S. military's standard heavy machine-gun cartridge since the early twentieth century. This cartridge is now often used for long-range precision counter-sniper rifles.

BOQ: Bachelor officers quarters.

BP: Blood pressure.

BX: Base exchange.

C-4: Composition 4, a plastic explosive.

CAR-15: See **M4.**

CAS: Close air support.

CAT: Combat application tourniquet.

CB: Citizens band radio, a VHF broadcasting band. There is no license required for operation in the United States. Some desirable CB transceivers are capable of SSB operation. Originally twenty-three channels, the citizens band was later expanded to forty channels during the golden age of CB, in the 1970s.

CHU: Containerized housing unit. A CONEX retrofitted with a door, window, top vent, power cabling, and air-conditioning unit, as used by servicemen in Iraq. Spoken "Chew."

CLP: Cleaner, lubricant, protectant. A mil-spec lubricant, sold under the trade name "Break Free CLP."

CO_2: Carbon dioxide.

COD: Collect on delivery; cash on delivery.

CONEX: Continental express, the ubiquitous twenty-, thirty-, and forty-foot-long steel cargo containers used in multiple transportation modes.

COPS: Committee of Public Safety.

CP: Command post.

CPY: Ham radio shorthand for "Copy."

CRKT: Columbia River Knife & Tool.

CU: Ham radio shorthand for "See you (later)."

CUCV: Commercial utility cargo vehicle. The 1980s-vintage U.S. Army versions of diesel Chevy Blazers and pickups, sold off as surplus in the early 2000s.

DE: Ham radio shorthand for "from." This is used between call signs.

DF: Direction finding.

DMV: Department of Motor Vehicles.

Drip oil: The light oil or hydrocarbon liquids condensed in a natural gas piping system when the gas is cooled. Also called natural gasoline, condensation gasoline, or simply "drip." A mixture of gasoline and drip oil can be burned in most gasoline engines without modification. Pure drip oil can be burned in some gasoline engines if the timing is retarded.

E&E: Escape and evasion.

ES: Ham radio shorthand for "and."

FAA: Federal Aviation Administration.

FAL: See **FN/FAL.**

FB: Ham radio shorthand for "Fine business." Usually means "That's great" or "That's wonderful."

FBO: Fixed base operator. Typically a small private airport's refueling facility.

FEMA: Federal Emergency Management Agency, a U.S. federal government agency. The acronym is also jokingly defined as "Foolishly Expecting Meaningful Aid."

FER: Ham radio shorthand for "for."

FEUS: Farmington Electric Utility System.

FFL: Federal firearms license.

FLOPS: Flight operations.

FN/FAL: A 7.62mm NATO battle rifle originally made by the Belgian Company Fabrique Nationale (FN), issued to more than fifty countries in the 1960s and 1970s. Now made as semiauto-only "clones" by a variety of makers. See also **L1A1.**

FOB: Forward operating base.

Fobbit: Derogatory nickname for soldiers who rarely go outside the defensive perimeter of a forward operating base (FOB).

FORSCOM: U.S. Army Forces Command.

Frag: Fragmentation.

FRS: Family Radio Service.

Galil: See **AK.**

GCA: The Gun Control Act of 1968. The law that first created FFLs and banned interstate transfers of post-1898 firearms except "to or through" FFL holders.

Glock: The popular polymer-framed pistol design by Gaston Glock of Austria. Glocks are a favorite of gun writer Boston T. Party.

GMRS: General Mobile Radio Service, a licensed UHF-FM two-way radio service. See also **FRS** and **MURS.**

GMT: Greenwich Mean Time.

Gold Cup: The target version of Colt's M1911 pistol. It has fully adjustable target sights, a tapered barrel, and a tighter barrel bushing than a standard M1911.

GOOD: Get out of Dodge.

GPS: Global positioning system.

Ham: Slang for amateur radio operator.

HF: High frequency. A radio band used by amateur radio operators.

HI: Ham radio shorthand for "laugh."

HK or H&K: Heckler und Koch, the German gun maker.

HK91: Heckler und Koch Model 91, the civilian (semiautomatic-only) variant of the 7.62mm NATO G3 rifle.

HOA: Homeowners' association.

HR: Ham radio shorthand for "here."

Humvee: High-mobility multipurpose wheeled vehicle, spoken "Humvee."

HW: Ham radio shorthand for "how."

IBA: Interceptor body armor.

ID: Identification.

IFV: Infantry fighting vehicle.

IPI: Indigenous populations and institutions.

IV: Intravenous.

K: Ham radio shorthand for "Go ahead."

Kevlar: The material used in most body army and ballistic helmets. "Kevlar" is also the nickname for the standard U.S. Army helmet.

KJV: King James Version of the Bible.

KL: Ham radio nickname of Kaylee Schmidt.

KN: Ham radio shorthand for "Go ahead" (but *only* the station that a ham is already conversing with).

L1A1: The British Army version of the FN/FAL, made to inch measurements.

LAW: Light anti-tank weapon.

LC-1: Load-carrying, Type 1 (U.S. Army load-bearing equipment, circa 1970s to 1990s).

LDS: Latter-day Saints, commonly called the Mormons. (Flawed doctrine, great preparedness.)

LF: The aircraft designation for aircraft from Luke Air Force Base, Arizona.

LP: Liquid propane.

LP/OP: Listening post/observation post.

LRRP: Long-range reconnaissance patrol.

M1A: The civilian (semiauto only) equivalent of the M14 rifle.

M1 Abrams: The United States' current main battle tank, with a 120mm cannon ("main gun").

M1 Carbine: The U.S. Army semiauto carbine issued during World War II. Mainly issued to officers and second-echelon troops such as artillerymen for self-defense. Uses ".30 U.S. Carbine," an intermediate (pistol-class) .30 caliber cartridge. More than six million were manufactured. See also **M2 Carbine.**

M1 Garand: The U.S. Army's primary battle rifle of World War II and the Korean conflict. It is semiautomatic, chambered in .30-06, and uses a top-loading, eight-round en bloc clip that ejects after the last round is fired. This rifle is commonly called the Garand, after its inventor. Not to be confused with the U.S. M1 Carbine, another semiauto of the same era, which shoots a much less powerful pistol-class cartridge.

M1A: The civilian (semiauto only) version of the U.S. Army M14 7.62mm NATO rifle.

M1911: The Model 1911 Colt semiauto pistol (and clones thereof), usually chambered in .45 ACP.

M2 Carbine: The selective-fire (fully automatic) version of the U.S. Army semiauto carbine issued during World War II and the Korean conflict.

M4: The U.S. Army–issue 5.56mm NATO selective-fire carbine (a shorter version of the M16, with a 14.5-inch barrel and collapsing stock). Earlier-issue M16 carbine variants had designations such as XM177E2 and CAR-15. Civilian semiauto-only variants often have these same designations or are called "M4geries."

M4gery: A civilian semiauto-only version of an M4 Carbine with a 16-inch barrel instead of a 14.5-inch barrel.

M9: The U.S. Army–issue version of the Beretta M92 semiauto 9mm pistol.

M14: The U.S. Army–issue 7.62mm NATO selective-fire battle rifle. These rifles are still issued in small numbers, primarily to designated marksmen. The civilian semiauto-only equivalent of the M14 is called the M1A.

M16: The U.S. Army–issue 5.56mm NATO selective-fire battle rifle. The current standard variant is the M16A2, which has improved sight and three-shot burst control. See also **M4.**

M60: The semi-obsolete U.S. Army–issue 7.62mm NATO belt-fed light machine gun that utilized some design elements of the German MG-42.

MAC: Depending on context, Military airlift command or Military Armament Corporation.

Maglite: A popular American brand of sturdy flashlights with an aluminum casing.

MICH: Modular/integrated communications helmet.

Mini-14: A 5.56mm NATO semiauto carbine made by Ruger.

MNI: Ham radio shorthand for "many."

MOLLE: Modular lightweight load-carrying equipment.

Molotov cocktail: A hand-thrown firebomb made from a glass container filled with gasoline or thickened gasoline (napalm).

MRE: Meal, ready to eat.

MSG: Mission support group (U.S. Air Force).

MSS: Modular sleep system.

MURS: Multi-use radio service. A VHF two-way radio service that does not require a license. See also **FRS** and **GMRS.**

MVPA: Military Vehicle Preservation Association.

MXG: Maintenance group (U.S. Air Force).

Napalm: Thickened gasoline, used in some flame weapons.

NAPI: Navajo Agricultural Products Industry.

NATO: North Atlantic Treaty Organization.

NBC: Nuclear, biological, and chemical.

NCO: Noncommissioned officer.

NFA: The National Firearms Act of 1934. The law that first imposed a transfer tax on machine guns, suppressors (commonly called "silencers"), and short-barreled rifles and shotguns.

NiCd: Nickel cadmium (rechargeable battery).

NiMH: Nickel metal hydride (rechargeable battery) improvement of NiCad.

NM: Ham radio shorthand for "Name."

NWO: New World Order.

OCP: Operation Enduring Freedom camouflage pattern, commonly called "MutiCam."

OG: Operational group (U.S. Air Force).

OM: Ham radio shorthand for "old man." All men are OMs in the ham world.

OP: Observation post. See also **LP/OP.**

PBO: Property book officer.

PCS: Permanent change of station.

PERSCOM: U.S. Army Personnel Command.

Pre-1899: Guns made before 1899—not classified as "firearms" under federal law.

Pre-1965: U.S. silver coins with 1964 or earlier mint dates with little or no numismatic value that are sold for the bullion content. These coins have 90 percent silver content. Well-worn pre-1965 coins are sometimes derisively called "junk" silver by rare coin dealers.

ProvGov: Provisional Government.

PSE: Ham radio shorthand for "please."

PT: Physical training.

PV: Photovoltaic (solar power conversion array). Used to convert solar power to DC electricity, typically for battery charging.

PVC: Polyvinyl chloride (white plastic water pipe).

QRF: Quick-reaction force.

QRM: Ham radio shorthand for "interference from another station."

QRN: Ham radio shorthand for "static."

QRP: Ham radio shorthand for "low-power (less than 5-watt) transmitters."

QRZ: Ham radio shorthand for "Who is calling me?" If used at the end of the contact, if QRZ is sent instead of SK, it means "I'm listening for more calls."

QSB: Ham radio shorthand for a "fading signal."

QSO: Ham radio shorthand for a "contact (conversation)."

QSY: Ham radio shorthand for "Change frequency."

QTH: Ham radio shorthand for "location."

R: Ham radio shorthand for "I heard everything you said and don't need you to repeat anything."

ROTC: Reserve Officers' Training Corps.

RPG: Rocket-propelled grenade.

SADF: South African Defense Force.

SBI: Special background investigation.

SCI: Sensitive compartmented information.

SIG: Schweizerische Industrie Gesellschaft. The Swiss gun maker.

SK: Ham radio shorthand for "silent key."

SOCOM: Special Operations Command.

SOP: Standard operating procedure(s).

SSB: Single sideband (an operating mode for CB and amateur radio gear).

SSPARS: Solid-state phased-array radar system.

Steyr AUG: The Austrian army's 5.56-mm "bullpup" infantry carbine. Also issued by the Australian Army as their replacement for the L1A1.

S&W: Smith and Wesson.

SWAT: Special weapons and tactics. (SWAT originally stood for "special weapons assault team" until that was deemed politically incorrect.)

TA-1 and TA-312: U.S. military hardwire field telephones.

TAD: Temporary assigned duty.

TARPS: Tactical aerial reconnaissance pod system.

TDY: Temporary duty.

Thermite: A mixture of aluminum powder and iron rust powder that, when ignited, causes a vigorous exothermic reaction. Used primarily for welding. Also used by military units as an incendiary for destroying equipment.

TK: Tom Kennedy.

TNX: Ham radio shorthand for "Thanks."

TS: Top secret.

TU: Ham radio shorthand for "Thank You."

UAV: Unmanned aerial vehicle.

UR: Ham radio shorthand for "your" or "you're," depending on context.

USAEUR: U.S. Army, Europe. Spoken "Use-ah-Urr."

USAFE: U.S. Air Force, Europe. Spoken "You-Safe-ee."

VAC: Volts, alternating current.

Valmet: The Finnish conglomerate that formerly made several types of firearms.

VDC: Volts, direct current.

Viper: The popular nickname for the F-16 fighter. (Its official moniker is the "Fighting Falcon," which most F-16 pilots detest.)

VW: Volkswagen.

VY: Ham radio shorthand for "very."

WD-1: U.S. military-issue two-conductor insulated field telephone wire.

YL: Ham radio shorthand for "young lady." All females regardless of age are designated YLs in the ham world.